FLOWERS IN YOUR HAIR

AN IVY RIDGE NOVEL

ALICE DANIELS

Flowers in Your Hair

ALICE DANIELS

*To everyone who has supported me and my books.
I'll never be able to thank you enough.*

CONTENTS

PLAYLIST

Animal- Noah Kahan
About Damn Time- Lizzo
Butterflies-Kacey Musgraves
Electric Love- BØRNS
Everything Has Changed (Taylor's Version) - Taylor Swift
& Ed Sheeran
Everywhere, Everything- Noah Kahan
Feeling Whitney-Post Malone
Flowers in Your Hair- The Lumineers
Hallucinogenics- Matt Maeson
ivy-Taylor Swift
I Will Remember You-Ed Sheeran
Labyrinth- Taylor Swift
Late Night Talking- Harry Styles
Sparks Fly(Taylor's Version)- Taylor Swift
Stubborn Love- The Lumineers
Sugar, We're Goin Down- Fall Out Boy
Sunflower, Vol. 6- Harry Styles
Virginia (Wind In The Night) - The Head And The Heart
warm glow- Hippo Campus
Would That I- Hozier
You're Gonna Go Far- Noah Kahan
XO- Beyonce

https://open.spotify.com/playlist/
oJDc3FbB6mTiStnusJmtPd?si=a547592c8c324428

CONTENT WARNING

Dear Reader,

Flowers in Your Hair contains subjects that may be triggering to some, including on page scenes depicting fat phobia from ex-boyfriend and former best friend, discussion of trafficking and drug circles in the context of a police investigation, and scenes with a grandparent in the hospital in a coma after brain surgery.

Take care of yourself. Your mental health matters more than a book.

JOSIE

The familiar *snip* of the scissors through the sage green stems of the roses sends a shiver of excitement through my body. The deep burgundy petals fall to the table and I watch them with rapt attention. Sure, it might be because it's freaking freezing in my small, dimly lit garage in early April, but I'd like to think it's due to excitement.

Tomorrow is my first wedding as a professional florist. I opened my business six months ago, and have done well for myself making bouquets for funerals, anniversaries, and other moderately sized events. But this is the first wedding I'll be doing on my own as the owner of my business. I used to work with an older gal who lived up north for years until she retired. She asked me if I wanted to take over her company, and while the offer was good, I wanted to make a name for myself. Pave my own path and all that.

My ex, Zack, loved to patronize me about how being a florist would never pay the bills, or get me very far in life. At first, I thought it was tough love, his way of making sure I knew I would have to work for it, but when I mentioned moving somewhere new and starting my own business, his patronizing and unkind words toward me got worse. So, I dumped him. I don't need that sort of negativity in my life.

I set off on my new adventure, getting all the necessary things lined up. My best friend since forever, Tessa, is still bummed that I moved. We used to do everything together, and even lived together. We talk on the phone as much as possible, but living about an hour from each other and both working full time can be tough to make time for each other.

Much to my mother's dismay, I moved further away from her, to a small town called Ivy Ridge. I'm not a stranger to Ivy Ridge, having visited a few times in high school, and when I worked with the other florist, setting up some venues. I fell in love with the small town back then, and continue to love it every day I reside here.

It's not like I don't love my family. I wanted room to spread my wings, make it on my own. Moving away from my parents and hometown was bittersweet, but if I'd stayed, my parents would have tried to micromanage me. They have good intentions, but I want to be known as more than Josie, Kevin Carter's daughter. Dad is the sheriff, and I know it sounds stupid, but I feel like people would only buy from me because of that, not because they think I'm talented.

I worked hard the first few months I lived here, getting all my licenses and business essentials set up, while also working at a restaurant to keep making money. When I bought this house a few months ago, the first thing I did was set up a little area in my garage to use as what I call "flower central."

By posting the arrangements I've made and sharing fun behind the scenes stuff, I've been able to gain a small following on social media. I've also taken to leaving my business cards in random places. Bulletin board at the grocery store? Check. Dropping a card as I walk through Target? Check. Leaving one on the table when I'm done eating at a restaurant? You know it.

A girl's gotta do what a girl's gotta do.

When my cell phone rang a few weeks ago, I picked it up, fully expecting it to be a spam call. But when the sounds of a frantic voice screeched inside my ear, I nearly dropped my phone from shock and excitement. A desperate bride, Megan, had just found out that her original florist was going out of business and could no longer do her wedding. I guess one of her friends had found one of my business cards a few days prior, looked me up on social media, and when Megan called her in a panic, she immediately suggested me.

I set up a meeting with Megan and her husband-to-be, where we went over what she wanted, what I could do, and agreed on a contract that very day. Of course, I gave her full disclosure that this would be my first solo wedding, and she had every right to look for someone else, but she just said, "We all start somewhere, right?"

Megan's wedding flowers have been my number one work priority ever since. Today, the day before the wedding, is when all my planning will come to fruition. I picked up the flowers this morning, and have been working on them since. The vases are boxed up and in the back of my car, along with my extra buckets and supplies I might need. Five of the six bouquets I need are ready to go, delicately set in a bucket with a few inches of water, and placed in the cooling fridge I specifically bought for business needs like this.

I'm currently working on the bridal bouquet, which is a beautiful mix of burgundy and dust pink roses, leatherleaf, and stems of baby's breath. The differing colors compliment each other so perfectly, and when I hold it out to look at it, my eyes well up with tears. Not from the beauty of the arrangement—*though it is incredible, if I do say so myself*—but from the realization that this bouquet could be a life-changing bouquet. This event could mean big things for me, could move me up in the ranks in the wedding world, which is what I've always wanted.

I've dreamed of the day where I might see my name on wedding websites, tagged on social media when couples reminisce about their big day, my schedule fully booked without an inch of breathing room. I want to help people have the wedding of their dreams. Don't get me wrong, I love making arrangements for someone's loved one, whether it be celebratory, or in remembrance, but there is just something that I've always loved about the magic of weddings.

Finishing up Megan's bouquet, I get started on the seven boutonnieres for the groomsmen. I label the container with the groom's boutonniere with a large scribbled 'I' for Isaac, then get to work on the extra corsages and boutonnieres for the family members.

Though I'm somewhat aware of hours passing, the next time I look at the clock, I see that it's nearing three am. Shit, I really need to get some sleep if I'm going to be presentable. Luckily, everything is done, for now. At least until I get to the venue and can get the vases set up. I quickly pack up the corsages and boutonnieres, stowing them away in the fridge for the night. I flick the lights in the garage off, and walk up the few steps into my house.

The house is dark, but my cat, Velma, greets me at the door. She stretches, sticking her butt up into the air, purring loudly as she does. "Hi sweetie," I murmur, bending down to give her a little scratch. She leans into my touch, her purrs growing louder as she starts weaving her way between my legs. I straighten up, letting her do her thing, listening to her meow and purr as if I'd abandoned her for days. To be fair, I was in the garage for quite a while. Maybe that feels like a long time to a cat.

I walk through my home, stifling a yawn. The room is bathed in warm light, and I open a cupboard, blindly reaching around for a granola bar. When I finally get it in my hands, I open it, taking a huge bite out of it. It's stale, the granola and chocolate chips crumbling onto the counter in pieces, but right now, it's hitting the spot. My rumbling stomach is appeased for now, and hopefully will be until morning, when I can grab a breakfast sandwich and coffee somewhere on the way to the venue.

The venue isn't far from my place. I plan to leave by about nine so I have enough time to get there, set up the ceremony area, pass out bouquets and corsages, then head to the reception area to set up. I mentally review the day I've carefully scheduled as I finish my granola bar and wash my face.

I shrug out of my clothes, slipping on my favorite sweats and hoodie and setting my alarm before practically collapsing into bed from exhaustion.

This wedding could be my make or break. As my eyes fall shut, I recenter myself, and again, go over the plan for tomorrow. I need to make sure everything is perfect.

2

ANDREW

"**S**hots!" my best friend, Isaac, shouts from the end of the bar.

"Dude, I think it might be time to slow down. You don't want to be hungover for your own wedding, do you?" I ask, resting a hand on his shoulder.

He shakes his head, his eyes falling shut slightly in his drunken haze. "Good point." He boops me on the nose. "Pretty sure Megan would kill me if I came to our wedding smelling like tequila."

"You've got that right, my friend." I make a slicing across my neck motion to the bartender, and luckily, he doesn't question it, giving me a thumbs up. I nod gratefully, wrapping my arm around the shoulders of my childhood best friend. I could give two shits about the rest of the guys; Isaac is my main priority tonight. There's seven groomsmen total, and combined with the ushers, random cousins, family members, and college friends, the group have all but taken over the bar tonight. It's still early, just before midnight, and Isaac is in his happy drunk phase.

"Let's get you to your room, Turbo," I tease. He snorts at

my nickname for him, but comes willingly. I stop when I see Nick, one of the other groomsmen, flirting with one of the bridesmaids. "Hey, he's going to bed." I point at Isaac.

"Sounds good man. See you in the morning," he replies.

I tip my chin to him, then guide Isaac through the halls of the hotel connected to the vineyard, Meadow Grove Winery. For this weekend it's the wedding venue, but it's also his family's business. I know my way around pretty well, having spent a lot of time here as a kid with Isaac. Once we're outside the room we are sharing tonight, I use the keycard to open the door. He stumbles across the threshold, falling face first onto the plush queen sized bed with a groan.

"Andyyyy," he slurs. He knows I hate it when people call me Andy. "Megan's my best girl, but you're my best friend." *Oh dear, here we go.* "I know how much you want to get married, but you just gotta go with the flow. It's gonna happen when it happens my man."

I pat him on the back, feeling the sweat through his dress shirt. I yank my hand back in disgust, wiping it on my black pants. "Thanks, Isaac. You're right. You got lucky and met the girl of your dreams when you were what, fifteen? Sixteen?" I struggle to remember exactly what year Isaac met Megan. At this point it seems like they've just always been together.

"Fifteen," he slurs. "I love that girl and have wanted to marry her ever since I can remember, but we were kids. Just kids!" He takes a deep breath then continues his drunken ramble. "Of course she had to finish med school, then residency. And according to her, 'no one wants to plan a wedding in the middle of their residency'," he mimics her voice, then giggles at the end. "Oh well, I get to marry her now. She's worth the wait."

"You guys are definitely meant to be." I roll Isaac over, taking off his shoes. "Get up, you're gonna be pissed at me if you sleep in your clothes."

He nods, slowly sitting up on the edge of the bed. He takes off his dress shirt, and slides out of his slacks, leaving him in only his boxer briefs, undershirt, and socks. He burrows himself under the blankets, and is snoring within a minute.

I chuckle to myself. I pull his phone out of his dress pants pocket, and set it on his nightstand, plugging it in. I fill a paper hotel cup of water from the bathroom tap and set it on his nightstand. Then I dig my own phone out of my pocket, and text Megan, Isaac's bride to be.

ME

Hey Megs, he's passed out cold, but I made sure he didn't drink too much. Just happy drunk.

MEGAN

Thank you so much, Andrew. We owe you.

ME

Nope, just promise to do the same thing for me when I get married.

MEGAN

You got it. It'll happen sooner than you think, I just know it.

ME

Ironically, Isaac just said the same thing.

MEGAN

Hmm, sounds like we both know best.

I plug my own phone in, and head into the bathroom. I really am excited about tomorrow, in more ways than I can help, but I confided in Isaac a few weeks ago that I was jealous. Not of him being with Megan, hell no. She's like a sister to me. No, I'm jealous of their relationship, and how settled and secure they are. I want that. I'm sick and tired of the meaningless dates that never lead anywhere.

But, like they both said, I have to be patient. Although, it's getting more and more difficult. At the age of twenty-nine, I have no potential prospects. My mom keeps telling me I have to stop searching for it, that when it's meant to be, it will just happen, and the right woman will appear. She and my dad are high school sweethearts, so they didn't have to search or even wait. Part of me wants to believe my mom, but the other part is set on finding *her*, finding my future.

My brothers all like to give me crap about how desperate I am to settle down, but what do they know? My oldest brother Jason, is lonely, but is more focused on caring for his toddler. Thomas cares more about his work as a police officer than anything, and Beau? Well...Beau is hung up on his best friend Marley, yet won't do a thing about it.

With a sigh, I shrug out of my dress shirt, hang it on the hanger, and slide off my dress pants. We have an early morning, not nearly as early as the ladies, but we all have tasks we are assigned to. Isaac has to direct the family members to their various tasks, the other groomsmen are setting up the chairs for the ceremony, and I have to meet the florist and help her get everything unloaded. To be honest, I have no idea why I'm the one working with the florist. I know virtually nothing about flowers, except that roses are typically red. I'm definitely not qualified for a job like this, but I'm also willing to help in any way I can.

I send off a message to the guys, letting them know not to be out too late, because we have jobs to do in the morning. I try not to sound like a dick in my message, and I'm relieved when they all send a 'thanks' or a thumbs up in reply. I don't know these guys as well as I do Isaac, as he met most of them when he was in the Twin Cities for college. Meanwhile, I was here in Ivy Ridge, learning everything I could about the family woodworking business. Cunningham Bespoke Woodcrafts, started by my great-grandpa, carried down by my Gramps, and now, me. I've never regretted it though. Not for a minute. Spending all that time with Gramps is not something I will ever resent. I always knew that when I grew up this was where I was meant to be. I love the life I've made for myself, I'm just missing a partner to stand by my side.

The groomsmen are good guys, but most of the time we've spent together, they've all been drunk, or well on their way to drunk, so I don't really know their actual personalities. I'm pretty sure most of them are still stuck in their frat boy party age, and Isaac has made a few passing comments that he believes the same.

Sure, I drink socially and go out every now and then, but it's not my whole personality. Especially at our age. Hangovers aren't as easy to recover from now as they were at twenty-two.

I leave the bathroom, heading over to the empty bed, listening to Isaac's aggressive snores. He sounds like a fucking fighter jet plane. He stops breathing for a moment, before snorting loudly, and rolling to his other side.

How the fuck does Megan sleep with that every night? He never used to snore this bad. Does the man have sleep apnea? I climb into my bed, and scroll my phone for a bit, googling sleep apnea symptoms. I decide he definitely has it and make a mental note to tell Megan about it once the wedding is over, before reading a few articles about some recent trade of a hockey player to our team. Soon my eyelids grow heavy and I start to drift off.

3

JOSIE

Springtime has always been my favorite season. It's such a beautiful time of year. All the trees are growing back their leaves in vibrant shades of green, flowers are blooming, and we get to see the sun for longer and longer each day.

The smell of the flowers in my car adds to my excitement as I pull into the gorgeous winery, following the directions from Megan about where she told me to park so I can unload everything. She told me I would have someone to help me unload and help with a few other things, but she never told me a name, and I'm not about to text her now and ask who I should be looking for. It's her wedding day, she has plenty of other things to think about.

It's after ten, so thankfully, I have plenty of time. I'm practically tingling with anticipation, and I can't help but smile as I slide my car into park. My phone bings with a new text message, and I automatically smile when Tessa's name is on the screen.

TESSA

Good luck today! You're going to kill it, and everyone will love what you do!

ME

Thank you! I'm anxious, but excited. I'll update you later!

TESSA

Perfect, I need to give you some news anyway!

ME

Can't wait!

I slide my phone into my pocket, putting it on silent. I vaguely wonder what her news might be, but I have other things to think about today.

There are people walking around everywhere. Guys dressed in shirts and shorts are setting up chairs over on the concrete slab, and there's a beautiful arch set up with shimmering dusty pink fabric draped on the sides.

I can only imagine how gorgeous things will be once everything is set up and ready. The background boasts picturesque woods, with evergreen trees and wildflowers growing in the distance. To my left, there are rows and rows of grapevines. I let out a wistful sigh, just imagining how beautifully my arrangements and design plans will look at this venue. It's really everything I'd hoped for.

A man crosses the front of my car, pulling me out of my daydream. I'm stunned by how charmingly handsome he is. Brown hair, shaved close on the sides, with natural waves and mussed curls on top, as if he's run his hand through his hair a few times this morning. A single curl hangs over his forehead into his eyes, and I immediately want to push it back. The thought shocks me, it's not something I would normally do, but yet my fingers itch to touch the soft curl.

His cheeks are flushed, as if he's been exerting himself, and I can't help but stare at him. Muscular, but not overtly so. It makes me wonder what he does for a living. I get the feeling he works with his hands.

He rounds the front of my vehicle, and when he sees me in the driver seat, he gives me a bright smile. The look of exertion previously on him fades as he waves at me. The man looks almost giddy to see me, though I've never met him.

I roll down the window, and he leans down, resting his arms on the car. His smile stays on his face as he speaks. "Let me guess, Josie?"

I nod, my tongue twisted and dry, rendering me unable to speak for a moment. I swallow the lump down. "Um, yeah. I'm the florist," I finally croak. "Am I in the right spot?"

"Yep," he says, offering me his hand. His hands are rough and dry. "I'm Andrew. The Best Man. I'll be helping you out this morning. You tell me what to do. I'm your lackey." The warmth of his hand reverberates through my body, all the way from my head to my toes. I have never had this sort of reaction toward a man before, and I don't quite know what to think of it. I banish the reaction and chalk it up to nerves from doing my first wedding.

I chuckle awkwardly, taking my hand back as he releases it. I turn my car off, and he steps back from the open window as I climb out. "Right, okay. First, can you show me where I can get the bouquets and boutonnieres set up?"

"You got it." He gestures to my car. "Should we grab the stuff, so we don't have to take as many trips?"

"Right, yes. That's a good idea." I head to the back, opening the hatchback, and start handing things to Andrew. He takes the box of bouquets in one hand, an empty bucket in the other. I grab the box of boutonnieres and the bucket with my scissors and other supplies. Andrew tips his chin in the direction we need to go, and I follow as he leads me into the winery. My eyes adjust to the warm light inside, and I suck in a surprised gasp. Though I had looked up photos of the venue, there's something about seeing it all setup with tables, decor, and twinkly lights for a wedding. All that's missing is the flowers.

"Wow," I mutter. "This place is incredible."

Andrew turns, his chocolate brown eyes gazing at me. A smile ticks at the corner of his lips. "Yeah, it is. I always forget that people aren't as used to its beauty as I am, especially if they've never been here."

My gaze wanders, taking in the dark cherry wood ceilings, and the large wooden beams that cross it. The room would be too dark, but a twinkling chandelier and huge windows exposing the beautiful view fill the space with a golden light. The walls are lined with wooden barrels, adding to the all over charm of the winery.

"Do you work here?"

Andrew shakes his head, a smile tugging on his lips. "Nope. Isaac's family owns it, and he's my best friend. We spent a lot of time here growing up."

I nod, still dumbstruck by the regal beauty of this place. It's the perfect mix of classy and elegant, while also not being too formal. It's incredible. "Wow," I repeat.

Andrew chuckles. "Come on, I'll show you where you can set up."

He guides me down a hall to a large room that appears to be some sort of conference room, and sets down the box on the table. I do the same, setting my things next to where he placed his box on the table. "I have a few more things I need for here, then if you have time, I'd love help with unloading the outside stuff."

"I'm yours for the next hour," Andrew says. "I am to be of assistance in any way possible—bride's orders." He cracks that giddy smile again.

"Great. I really just need help unloading, and then you're free," I reply. Andrew shrugs, and leads me out to where my vehicle is.

Together, we get the last of the reception stuff, and then he helps me unload the rest and walk it to where the ceremony will be held. He enlists the help of a few other groomsmen, whose names I didn't catch, and within five minutes, everything is unloaded and ready for me to get to work.

I organize all the pieces, setting the flower bundles I'd made last night aside, getting the ribbon ready to tie to the chairs. I let myself slide into the zone, trying to ignore the distracting attraction I felt toward Andrew. I don't even notice him behind me until he speaks.

"Where do you need me, boss?"

"Hmm?" I ask, a little startled. I wave him off. "I'm good, like I said, I just needed help unloading. I can handle it from here. You go do your thing."

"Now, Josie..." he drawls, tsking and wagging a finger at me. "I was given a job to do. So tell me. What can I do for you?"

I scoff, my stomach fluttering with butterflies at his insistence. "Fine. You can take the bundles of flowers, and tie them to the chairs. The bows are already done, so you just need to use the little metal ties to anchor them to the chair. Got it?"

"You got it, boss." He winks, then gets to work right away, picking up one of the completed bundles and works on attaching it to the white chair. I inspect his first one to make sure it looks okay, before nodding my approval. He grins triumphantly, before starting on the next. I turn away and take a second to ground myself and focus on the job at hand. There's no use in getting all flustered over a man I'm sure I'll never see again. I continue my own work, tying the bows and making sure everything is perfect. When I'm done, I help Andrew finish attaching the pieces to the chairs.

After, I move to the next step of getting flowers up onto the beautiful wooden arch. I look around my stuff, searching for my step ladder. *Oh no.* "Hey, Andrew?" I call, spinning around. "Did you see a step stool anywhere?"

He glances around my things, shaking his head. "Not that I can remember. I don't think I even saw one in your car."

"Crap," I murmur. "Okay, I need your help then." I wave him over, and grab a chair from the front row. I kick off my shoes, leaving me in just my socks. I set the chair up in front of the arch, and turn. Andrew is right behind me.

"You're going to hold these while I climb up." I set the flowers gently into his waiting hands, and make sure I have my wire cutters, and extra wire in my pockets. "Then, you're going to spot me."

"Should I go get you a ladder?" Andrew asks, raising his brow. "This doesn't exactly seem safe..."

I wave him off. "It's fine. We're running short on time anyway. You need to get ready for photos, and I need to get the bouquets ready."

I climb up onto the chair and get myself in the right spot. Once steady, I turn, holding out my hands for the flowers. He doesn't notice right away that I'm waiting, but I watch him take a big sniff of one of the bigger roses, then lift his head, quirking his brow as if he didn't expect it to smell good. I smirk, giving him a moment. He's adorable.

When he realizes I'm ready, he carefully transfers it to me, and I get to work. Only, I'm shocked when a pair of warm hands settle on my waist. "Uh, whatcha doin there?" I ask. My arms raise with goosebumps at the casual touch, and it's like his hands send a shock to my core, increasing my heart rate and blood flow.

"Spotting you," Andrew replies. I can't really turn and look at him to see his expression, so I keep working.

"I didn't mean that you have to hold me, just... you know, be there in case I fall," I say with a shrug, thankful that he can't see my face, which is sure to be burning up right now. It's been a long time since a man has touched me, and though Andrew does it so casually, it manages to light a fire in me. My ex never lit a fire within me, that's for sure.

"Well, if it's all the same, I'd like to keep a hold on you. Can't have the florist take a tumble on my watch." I can hear the grin in his voice, but the message behind his words is surprisingly sincere. I can tell that he actually doesn't want me to eat shit.

"Alright," I answer. I give myself one more second before turning my attention back to the flowers.

After a few minutes—though it feels like an hour with his hands on my hips—I'm done with the arrangement. "I'm coming down." I drop the wire cutters and extra wire to the ground before I bend, expecting Andrew to drop his hold from my hips, but he doesn't. His hands move with me, and when my shirt rises, his fingertips brush the skin on my back and hips, jolting me with awareness at his proximity.

Shocked, I stumble the last bit, falling backward into his

chest. "Oh no," I screech, my arms flailing, trying to grasp onto something, anything.

"I've got you," Andrew murmurs into my ear, the hands that were on my waist now wrapped around my body. He holds me close to his chest, and I breathe heavily. "See, that's why I wanted to keep a hold on you."

"Makes sense." My heart thumps, a giddy feeling rising in my chest. This man has me all sorts of flustered. I feel my feet hit solid ground, and I start to pull away from him. I need to get away from his touch before I do something stupid, like fall onto his lips. "Sorry about that. Maybe I should have let you get a step ladder."

He's hesitant to let go of me, probably afraid I'll trip or something, but after a long moment, he does. He shakes his head when I turn to face him. "I guess next time you'll know to listen to me." His brown eyes crinkle at the edges as he winks. This man is turning me to putty with every wink, every glance in my direction.

I nod, trying to hide the smile on my face. I put the chair back in its spot, then take a few steps back to admire my work. I snap a few photos of the arch and the chairs for my social media, before gathering the rest of my supplies and buckets, bringing them back to my car. Andrew is behind me, carrying a few things as well.

"Thanks for all your help," I say as I close my trunk. I don't think I could have done it without you." And I really mean it. There's no way I could have gotten everything done so efficiently this morning without him. I make a mental note to look at my business budget and calculate the cost of hiring an assistant if I'm going to continue into the wedding industry.

"Not a problem, I enjoyed it."

I raise my brow, not believing him for a second. "Sure," I

tease. "I bet you would have much rather spent the morning with the guys having drinks and talking football."

Andrew shrugs. "I was happy to help, Josie. Hug it out? I'm a hugger."

"Umm," I pause, a little unsure. "Sure?" Before I can even open my arms to accept his hug, he has his thick arms wrapped around my shoulders, squeezing me tight into his chest. His arms aren't the hard rocks of muscle I'd anticipated. He's muscular, don't get me wrong, but his chest is warm and inviting with soft edges. I'm unable to reciprocate, as my arms are pinned to my sides. It's hard to breathe when he's squeezing me so tight, but somehow, I manage to get a whiff of his cologne; a crisp scent that reminds me of a rainy day.

The hug lasts for longer than I would have anticipated, and his warm personality is so inviting that I lose myself for a long moment, dreaming about what it might be like to be with a man like him, compared to the cold and aloof Zack. He moves his arms slightly so I'm able to wrap my own arms around him, squeezing him tightly in return. I don't miss the slight rumbling of appreciation in his chest.

If he keeps hugging me for any longer, this is going to be bordering on more than just a friendly hug. Do I want that? I have to shut down the little voice in the back of my head that is screaming, *"Yes! Let the sexy man hug you for as long as he wants!"* But the rational voice is screaming, *"there's no way he's single!"*

As quickly as he initiates the embrace, he lets me go, and my arms drop to my side. I'm suddenly anxious to get away from him, out of fear of making a fool of myself.

"Well, thanks again." I wave as I walk inside the building, heading down the hall to the room we set the bouquets in.

I can't help but admit that I find Andrew very attractive. I mean, who wouldn't? The dark curly hair, adorable smile, kind eyes. There is no way a guy like him is single, and the most attractive thing about him isn't even his looks. No, it was his wit, and his warm, caring personality. Some guys - *cough, cough, Zack-* would have complained about having to help the florist or found a way to get out of it, but not him.

I feel an unsavory amount of jealousy for the woman that he's with. I mean, she's got a good one, and I've known him for all of an hour.

4

———

ANDREW

I yank the white tulle disaster up my chest, sliding my arms through the sleeves. When Megan suggested this a few months ago, I hesitated for all of two seconds. Isaac is totally going to lose his shit, but fuck is it going to be worth it. Pretty much everyone knows that we are doing this, except Isaac.

There's a knock on the door, and my brother Beau's best friend, Marley, who is also the photographer, steps in. "Oh hell yes," she snickers. Her long brown hair is twisted up on her head, bangs hanging over her forehead, and she's wearing a soft dusty pink blouse that matches the flowers Josie was setting up. The sleeves of her blouse cut off just above her elbows, showing off the arrangement of tattoos on her arms. She's wearing a pair of black slacks, black flats, and her signature shiny gold nose ring.

I, on the other hand, am wearing a wedding dress.

I hold my arms out, spinning in a circle for her to see the look. The full, fluffy skirt billows around me, and for a moment I totally get why young kids like to spin in their dresses and skirts. This shit is fun.

I stop twirling, the dress resting against my legs again. I still have my dress pants and undershirt on, but my dress shirt, tie, and suit coat are hanging on the back of the door Marley just walked through.

"Good, right?" I ask Marley, lifting my arms again.

"So fucking good," she says. Before I can realize what she's doing, she whips her phone from her pocket, and I hear the click of the camera.

"Don't you fucking dare, Marley." I stride across the room toward her, my dress swishing at my ankles with each step. She's going to send the picture to my brothers, I know it.

"Too late!" she shrieks.

I pinch my nose. "You're a pain in my ass."

"I'm the sister you never had."

"You could say that again," I mutter. I tuck her under my arm as she opens the door.

"Ready?" she prompts, holding the door open.

"I suppose," I grumble, but really, I'm fucking excited as hell.

Marley leads us outside, and I spot Isaac standing at the tree line, his back to me. Marley whispers directions in my ear, pointing at the second photographer who will be taking pictures from a different angle.

I listen intently, stopping in the spot she tells me to. Out of the corner of my eye, I see Josie, the florist, adjusting a few of the guys' boutonniere. She's so fucking cute, I swear when she pulled up, my heart stuttered in my chest.

Gorgeous strawberry red hair, with freckles spattering across her nose and cheeks. She's got ample curves with thick thighs, and a full set of tits.

Yeah, I noticed her tits. Sue me.

It was hard not to ask a million questions about herself,

but I knew that once I started talking to her, I wouldn't want to stop. I knew she needed to focus on her job today, so I shut my mouth. If anything, I didn't talk enough. I felt like I was making things a little awkward.

Shrugging off the thought, I settle my eyes on her again for a short moment, ignoring the flare of jealousy I feel as she helps the guys. I'm totally going to play dumb so she has to help me with my boutonniere. Anything to get close to her again. She smells like the flowers she brought, a sweet, rosy scent. She's in a pair of black leggings that make her ass look fucking phenomenal, black flats, and a blue short sleeved blouse.

"Okay, *Megan*," Marley says, pulling my attention back to her. She looks at me with wide, irritated eyes, and mouths, "*pay attention, dickhead.*"

I shrug, ready for the next step.

"Alright," Marley says. "Isaac, Megan is going to step up behind you, and tap you on the shoulder three times, and then you can turn around. Okay?"

He nods. His arms are folded in front of him, and I can tell he's nervous. You can visibly see the tension in his shoulders. He's totally freaking the fuck out, and he needs this moment from me to help him chill out. I've known him since we were three. He needs to get out of his head. And a joke like this is exactly what will do the trick.

I'm grinning as I take a few steps forward, holding the hem of the dress up so I don't trip. With one last glance to my right, I spy Josie's eyes on me. Her eyes are filled with humor, and there's a soft smile gracing me. God, she's so fucking adorable. My smile widens.

I turn back to Isaac, tapping his right shoulder three times. When he turns, his face goes through a wide range of emotions in a matter of seconds.

First, his head is down and he sees the white tulle of the dress, and his eyes light up. Then, his eyes trail upward, and I see the confusion at the ugly as fuck dress. The only one at the thrift store we found that would fit a five foot eleven grown man. Then, when his eyes meet my chin, he gets momentarily pissed, and last, when he realizes what we've tricked him with, his eyes fill with humor. "You fucker," he says, shoving my chest, sending me stumbling a few steps.

We both break out into boisterous laughter, the click of the camera in my ear. Isaac throws his arms around me, tugging me into a long hug. "Isn't it beautiful?" I murmur in a high pitched voice. "I had it made just for our special day."

I gesture to the dress, then step back and spin for him, like I did earlier for Marley. Isaac snickers, his hand reaching up to cover his mouth.

"Yes, you look stunning, honey," he teases back, running his hand down the tulle cupcake dress.

"Bet you can't wait to see it on the floor later," I flirtily say, booping his nose like he did to me last night.

"You asshole," Isaac laughs.

We take a few more pictures of me in the dress, some nice, some cheesy like you would at prom. He even wraps his arms around my waist and I throw my arms up *Titanic* style, complete with the *"I'm flying, Jack!"* quote. By the time we finish the round of photos, the tension has left Isaac's shoulders and there's a broad smile across his face.

I'm grateful when I walk back into the winery to one of the dressing rooms, and am able to change back into my suit.

I head back outside a few minutes later, still adjusting my tie, to see the actual first look. Of course, Isaac cries, and so does Megan. She truly does look stunning. Her blonde hair is loose down her back, and she's wearing a simple satin gown, with a deep cut in the back. Now, I'm not one to ogle my best friend's soon-to-be wife, but as someone who's known her forever, I can truly say how gorgeous she looks today, and not only with what she's wearing. Pure happiness is radiating from her.

I head toward the rest of the crew, grabbing the last boutonniere out of the box, and spot Josie helping Austin, a groomsman, pin his to the pocket of his shirt. When she's done, I wave her over.

"Josie, I can't seem to get this. Can you help?" I ask, giving her my best smile. I even do that thing where I tilt my head to make me look all innocent.

She furrows her brows at me. "I just watched you pick it up from the box, Andrew. Did you even try?" She tries to make her voice sound irritated, but I can tell she's just teasing.

I don't say anything, since she's already walking over to me. She grabs the flower before taking the pin out, and arranging it on my lapel. A thought pops into my head, and I only have mere moments to see it through.

"Ouch!" I say quietly, not wanting to draw the attention of everyone.

"Oh god." Josie steps back, dropping the flower to the ground. "Did I stick you?"

I dramatically rub at my chest. "Yeah, you stabbed me," I state. "I think you drew blood."

"Oh god," she repeats, fingers fluttering at my jacket. "I am *so* sorry, I've never done that before, oh god. I feel so bad." A light sheen of sweat breaks out on her brow, and I decide maybe I've let it go on long enough.

"Josie," I say, trying to get her attention as her hands continue to feel all over my chest for an invisible injury. "Josie," I repeat. This time, she stops, her blue eyes lifting up to meet mine. Her eyes are glassy, and tears are about to spill over. "I was teasing you. You didn't stick me, I prom-ise." I bend over, picking up the discarded flower.

"I'm *so* sorry, Josie. I didn't think it would scare you that bad," I whisper, handing her the flower. Her jaw drops to the mossy ground, and her cheeks turn bright red.

"You were joking?" her voice wobbles.

I cringe. "Yeah. Not my best work I guess."

"You jerk!" she whispers, smacking me against my chest. "I thought I seriously hurt you! These things are a pain in the ass to put on, and I've stuck my own finger like fifteen times already today."

"Shit."

"Yeah, shit."

"I really am sorry?" I say as a question, opening my arms for another hug. The hug from earlier nearly gave me a hard on, and to be honest, I'll do anything to get my arms around her again.

"I suppose I can forgive you." She's already back to work, though, ignoring my open arms, shoving the pin through the lapel as she secures the flower. She mumbles words that I don't quite catch, all the while her hands are on my chest again. I watch her intently, watching her focus, not even caring that she totally has a reason to *actually* stab me with the tiny little needle now.

"There," she says, adjusting the flower until it sits just right. She removes her hands from my chest, and I instantly miss her touch. "Now, don't mess with it again."

"Pinky promise." I offer her my right pinky, and she takes it. I don't miss the way her face pinkens again, high-lighting her freckles, or the warmth of her finger. After she drops her hand, she goes back to the box of flowers, and I can't help but let my gaze track her. I try to multitask, and make sure none of the other guys are staring at her ass in those tight black leggings that hug her every curve as she bends down to pick up her stuff, but of course they are. And I, of course, can't say anything, because for one, she's not my girl, and two, I don't want to make a scene by punching them out.

Instead, I grit my teeth, watching as she straightens her back and walks toward the main building.

We follow Marley around for the next forty minutes or so, taking pictures in every combination imaginable. When cars start to pull into the parking lot, Megan is led back to the building to hide out until all the guests arrive and she can make her grand entrance. Isaac walks around, greeting the guests, getting lots of hugs and back slaps from friends, extended family, the whole works. The rest of the girls head in with Megan until we are set to go down the aisle.

I'm walking with the Maid of Honor, Fallon, Megan's best friend from college. She's super nice, and has a daughter named Presley, who is the flower girl. She looks cute as can be in her white tulle dress and mini bouquet. Last night at the rehearsal, I could tell she was nervous, so I offered to walk down the aisle with her, and toss a few flowers.

I could tell she wasn't sure what to say, until she turned around and saw her mom holding up a thumbs up for her. She's a pretty cool kid. I think she's maybe five or six, though I've always been terrible at guessing ages, so she could be twelve for all I know.

I follow everyone inside, using my spare time to take a leak. Marley is standing guard outside the doors to the girls dressing room, which is right across the hall from the men's bathroom.

"Hey, I've been meaning to ask you something." Marley stops me with a hand on my forearm.

"What's up?" I answer.

She drops my arm, stepping back into her post. "I've been tossing around the idea of doing something called a blind date photoshoot."

"What the fuck is that?" I ask, my brows raising, and an immediate concern for her safety sputters out my mouth. "You better not be meeting up with dudes from dating apps or some shit to photograph them, Mar."

Marley scoffs. "No, you goon. Let me finish."

I wave my hand in a "*go on*" motion.

"It's essentially a blind date. You fill out a few forms, and I set you up with someone based on compatibility. From there, we set up a date where the two of you can meet, and we do a cute photoshoot. I've seen ones ranging from a cute engagement like photoshoot, to a couples boudoir shoot."

"*Boowhat?*" I pause, taking in her words again. "Hey, why do you keep saying '*you*'?" I ask, shoving my hands in the pocket of my slacks.

"Boudoir," she reiterates. "Look it up. I'm not explaining that to you. I keep saying *you*," she pokes her finger into my chest, "because I was going to see if you could be my first victim."

Ummm, what? I cough out a laugh. "Funny."

"Not joking."

"Why do you even want to do this?"

"I've seen it going around on social media, and it looks really fun. The pictures always turn out incredible, and the chemistry between the two subjects is so fun to see develop through the pictures. It would be a really fun addition to my portfolio. And," she adds on slyly. "I've also seen that a lot of the time, the couples set up for the blind date sometimes end up together. I even saw one couple that got married."

Okay, I admit it. Now, she might have my interest. What can I say? I want to settle down, find a partner. I'm a lonely motherfucker.

"Fine. I'll fill out the forms. But this better not be some kind of prank that Beau set you up to do."

"I swear on my grandma's grave, this is all my idea. Beau doesn't even know." Marley waves her hands in surrender.

I let out a shudder. "You really had to swear on your dead grandma? Now I'm thinking about her funeral, Marley."

"You're the one that chose to get up close and personal with her casket," Marley accuses. She giggles at me, wiping a hair from her eyes.

"I was seven years old, Marley. I thought your dad was handing out butterscotch candies to everyone. He kept shaking everyone's hands, and I know how much your grandma loved that candy, so I put two and two together."

Now, she's fully laughing, tears streaming down her flushed cheeks at the shared memory. "God, Andrew, I still can't believe you looked in her casket for candy."

"*I didn't know she would actually be in there!* I was short back then, okay?"

"Alright, fine, fine." Marley stops laughing and holds out her hand. "I promise you, this shoot is with the best of intentions. I want you to meet someone."

I shake her hand firmly. "What about Beau? You gonna set him up with someone too?"

Her hand limply drops from mine. "Nope."

I nod. Probably best not to egg her on. She and Beau have been best friends since we were kids. She grew up in the same cul-de-sac as us, and they were inseparable from day one. My other brothers, Thomas and Jason, became friends with her brothers, Kenny and Prescott, which left me as the tagalong. As the youngest, that's to be expected though.

I feel protective of Marley, like she's my little sister, even though she's older than me by two years. I also have a very strong reason to believe she's in love with my brother, Beau, but she'll never say anything about it. I've been trying to pound it into Beau's head for the last couple of years that he should give it a shot with her, but he always shuts me down. *"I don't want to ruin our friendship."* and *"There's no way she has feelings for me."*

So yeah, the mutual pining and mutual bullshit is pretty fucking annoying, but I'm sure they will find their way to each other eventually.

"I gotta take a leak before the ceremony. You need anything?" I ask, putting on my big brother hat for a moment.

"Nope. Keep an eye out for an email with the forms though, okay?" She stares me down, letting me know how serious she is.

"You got it, lil sis."

"Not your sister," she grumbles as I let the door to the bathroom fall shut behind me.

"You will be someday," I say under my breath.

On the way out of the bathroom, I stop by the reception hall. Josie is practically skipping around the room, setting full vases on each and every table. The head table where we will sit has a beautiful arrangement of flowers lining the front of the table, and some draped over the shimmering white tablecloth.

Her hair is a bit of a haphazard mess. It looks like she tried to put it up in one of those alligator clips, or what do they call them? Crocodile clips? Whatever, I can't remember. But half of her red hair falls out around her face, the other sticking straight up like the feathers of a turkey. Or maybe a peacock. They're more majestic.

I watch her for a moment as she sets another vase on a table, then fiddles with a few flowers until they are in the perfect spot. She's in the right profession. She has an impeccable eye for detail, and it's clear she's been doing this for a long time. If she's stressed, she doesn't show it. The only reason I would guess she's under any pressure is due to her peacock hair. But that could be from her moving around so much.

I stride over to her, shoving my hands in my pockets. "Hey, you," I say, catching her attention.

She looks up, eyes widening when she sees me. "Is the ceremony already over? There's no way?" She starts muttering to herself, digging around for her phone in the pockets of her leggings.

"No." I reach out my hand to stop her, resting it on her forearm. The instant tension that rolls through my body almost makes me choke on my words. "I was just checking in. We still have about fifteen minutes before it starts. You're good."

"Thank god."

"So, are things going okay? Need anything?" *Please need my help.*

Josie shakes her head, already shifting her attention back to the bouquet. "Nope, things are actually going really well." *Dammit.* She puts her hands on her hips as she moves her eyes across the room, taking in her handiwork.

"You say that as if you're surprised," I state.

"Well, it is my first solo wedding, so yeah, I am a little surprised." Josie shrugs.

"Wait, this is your *first* wedding?" I ask, completely flabbergasted.

"Not ever. I was an assistant for a while so I've done quite a few weddings, but never on my own. You couldn't tell? I feel like I'm a disaster."

"Not in the slightest. I could have sworn you've been doing this for years."

"Nope." She shakes her head. "I opened my business about six months ago, and I've never done an event, only special occasion bouquets, or a funeral here and there."

"Wow…" I breathe. "You're incredible."

Josie clams up, her jaw tightening. "Thanks."

"I mean it, you really are amazing, Josie. You have real talent."

"Thanks, that's kind of you," she says, her cheeks flushing slightly at my compliment. I can see the subtle signs that she's trying to get back to work.

"I'll leave you to it, but if you need something, *anything*," I reiterate, "grab one of the managers, they are all super nice, and willing to help."

She nods again, and I grit my teeth as I turn away from her. I can't catch a vibe with her. I don't want to flirt and make her uncomfortable, but I also don't want her to get away. There's this increasing tension I feel toward her every moment I spend with her, and I don't want to lose it. I consider turning around and asking for her number, maybe asking her out, but I stop myself. The more I think about it, the more I realize she probably has a boyfriend. There's no way she doesn't. I mean, seriously, she's incredible. Utterly gorgeous, sweet as can be, and owns her own business? Yeah, her boyfriend is a lucky man.

It couldn't hurt to ask though. Maybe there is a chance that she's magically single.

Crap, maybe I shouldn't do that photoshoot Marley brought up, especially if I want to ask Josie out.

I'll have Marley ask Jason, or Thomas. They've been griping about being lonely lately. Then, I'll somehow come up with a way to ask Josie if she's single after the ceremony. I'm ready to bring out the big guns and get my flirt on.

Decision made.

5

———

JOSIE

I'm packing up the last of my supplies in my vehicle when my name is called. The ceremony has just ended, and the guests are making their way to the reception area, while the bridal party hopped on a party bus to go for a quick spin out to take some sunset photos with the photographer's second shooter.

I turn my attention to the voice calling my name, and I'm met with a face I'm not familiar with.

"Josie, right?" The girl huffs, clutching her camera to her chest.

"That's me," I say with a shrug, offering her my hand. She shakes it firmly, grinning at me. She is absolutely gorgeous, her long brown hair with bangs bringing out her eyes. The tattoos scattered on her arms give her a whimsical vibe that I love. "What can I do for you? Is something wrong with the flowers?" My heart thumps hard in my chest as the momentary self-doubt rushes through me.

"No, the flowers are absolutely stunning. Megan is obsessed."

I heave a sigh of relief, shaking out my hands. "Oh good."

"Heck, I should probably introduce myself," she says. "I'm Marley. I'm the photographer, and I'd love to get a business card from you. When I have meetings with potential clients, sometimes they ask for advice on other aspects about their big day. I'd love to recommend your business."

"Oh my god, seriously? That would be amazing," I gush, my hand coming up to my mouth in my shock.

Marley smiles. "Seriously. Here, I'll give you my info too." She takes a card out of her back pocket, a shiny gold logo with her business name, *Chrysalis Photography*, and other information on it.

"Wow, thank you," I say sincerely. tuck her card into my pocket, then rummage through the boxes in the back of my trunk, finding a card for her after a moment.

"Are you new in town?" Marley asks, looking at my card before tucking it into her own pocket.

"Yeah," I say. I run a hand through my disheveled hair wondering where the heck my claw clip ended up at. "I moved here about... Six, no... seven months ago I think?"

"Welcome to Ivy Ridge, we're lucky to have you. We've seriously been needing someone like you. Do you have a storefront?"

I shake my head. "Not yet. I took a look at a few on main street, but it's currently out of my budget, so I'm working out of my garage for the time being."

Marley nods. "I bet your partner loves that you're taking up all the garage space."

"I don't have one," I laugh, feeling slightly uncomfortable."That's why I was able to move here. I broke up with my boyfriend because he wasn't very supportive of my career goals. So I dumped him, changed towns, and bought a house. Now I have no strings holding me back." I bite my tongue, worried I'm oversharing.

Marley's brows raise as I speak. "Good to know."

"What?" I ask, raising my own brow.

"Nothing, nothing." She waves off my concern. "Speaking of strings. Wanna get a drink or something sometime? I need more girlfriends. I pretty much have one friend, and he's my childhood best friend. He's a piece of work, and sometimes it's nice to bitch about things that he will never understand."

I can't help but laugh, grateful that she's sharing with me so openly in return. "Yeah, I get that. I'd love to," I say. I've been meaning to put myself out there more and find some friends, but making friends as an adult is hard. It's not like when you were a kid and you got seated next to someone in your class, and instantly became best friends. Or asking the girl next to you on the swings if she wanted to play *Ring Around The Rosie* with you.

"Great! Can I text you?"

"Yep, my number is on my card. Text me anytime."

"Oh, yay! Ugh, I can't wait. I need girl time."

"Same," I chuckle. I miss Tessa and having her so close by, but I need to spread my wings here, or I'll turn into a hermit.

"Hey, I saw you got to meet Andrew?" Marley states like it's a question, surprising me. Is she with him? An odd feeling of jealousy pangs at my heart, and I try my best not to show it on my face. I mean, it would totally make sense for them to be together. They're both gorgeous, and in the short amount of time I've known both of them, I feel like their personalities would mesh well.

"Yeah, I did. He seems like a nice guy," I answer guardedly.

"He's awesome. Like a brother to me. I noticed him helping you this morning, so I thought I'd see what you thought of him. He's kinda goofy, but in a good way."

A sigh of relief that they aren't together threatens to escape my lungs, but I hold it in, grateful I don't embarrass myself any further. However, I think Marley picks up on my relief. Her eyebrows shift subtly and her mouth quirks into a smirk. Before I can challenge her, or tell her I'm not interested in Andrew- *even though I really could be*- she speaks again.

"I should get going. I need to take some more pictures of the reception area before people make a mess of things. It was so good to meet you, Josie. I'll be in touch!"

I say goodbye, waving to her as she heads into the reception hall.

I get into my car and allow myself a small, satisfied smile. *I think I just made a new friend.*

After driving home and unloading all my things, I head into the house, giving Velma a pat on the head before heading straight to the shower. She follows me in as I start the water, and watches me as I climb in. She curls up into a little ball next to the vent blowing warm air, and promptly falls asleep.

Sometimes, I'd love to be a cat. No worries in the world, except where you're going to take your next nap.

When I've rid myself of all the sweat and stink from the day, I get out of the shower, dry off, and get dressed in my coziest sweats and hoodie. I shuffle out to my living room and promptly flop onto my couch, my hair still twisted up in the towel.

Velma follows, of course, and sits herself right into my lap. I turn on an old episode of *Friends*, and settle in. I swipe through the photos I took today, and choose which ones I want to post to my social media. I aimlessly scroll for a bit while petting Velma. The pictures I post get a few likes, including one from my mom, and one from a spam account.

Why is social media so freaking exhausting? I spent hours on a graphic and logo for my business a few weeks ago, and though I shared it on both my personal and business socials, it got barely any traction. The marketing component of owning my own business drives me nuts.

Velma purrs her contentment in my lap, and I remember the card Marley gave me earlier. Instead of shoving Velma off my lap to fish it out of the pocket of my leggings, I try to look Marley's account up from memory. Thankfully, I find her page fairly quickly.

I scroll through her photos, completely entranced by her work. She has an amazing talent, and I'm almost jealous. Not only are the photos, and her subjects gorgeous, but so is the editing. The way she makes the pictures almost glow, or have a soft, muted feel, is incredible. I hit the follow button, then something catches my eye in her bio.

> Now accepting applications for stranger sessions!

Below is a link to a form. I hesitate for a moment, then click it. I mean, what's the harm in looking, right? It's not like I have anyone in my life. I've seen some of the shoots people do for these stranger sessions, and they are *so hot.* The tension between the two people by the end of the shoot is so intense you can practically feel it through the screen.

Without second guessing it anymore, I read through all the questions. I fill out my answers truthfully, and making it as realistic as I can. I'm even honest when it asks about bad habits.

    Forgets to switch laundry over to the dryer, and has to rewash multiple times before remembering.

    Listens to sad Taylor Swift songs when I'm depressed, therefore making myself more sad.

The next section is for accomplishments, or things you want to brag about.

I list starting my own business, owning my house, and a few other things I'm proud of.

I fill out the form quickly, listing off my favorite music, TV shows, pet peeves, where I want to be in five years, until I reach the last question. It's not really a question though, more so an acknowledgement of Marley's terms and conditions, and how she is not liable for any sort of heartache that could come from the process. Not a bad idea to put that in there. People will try and sue for anything nowadays, so it's best to cover your bases.

After I click the button acknowledging that I've seen it, I submit the form. To be honest, I'm not entirely sure why I did it. I'm content with how things are right now, and I don't need a boyfriend.

Though, I have to admit it would be nice to have someone to cuddle up with. Zack, my ex, was never much of a cuddler, even after sex. Not that I'm a super clingy person, but sometimes you need a good cuddle. My thoughts stray to Andrew and the way his chest felt under my fingers earlier today. How it might feel to rest my head on it. I can't believe he scared me like that. I've pinned so many boutonnieres that it's almost second nature. But when he jumped and said *"ouch"* I was ready to dig my own grave. I'd been so embarrassed and scared that I'd done some real damage.

He seems to be the type to goof around though. I mean, the man wore a literal wedding dress that he more than likely found at a thrift shop to surprise his best friend. I will admit though that he was nice. But he *was* the best man, and it was his literal job to be helpful today.

I can't get his easy smile out of my mind though. The way his bright white teeth practically glinted in the sunlight, or the little flecks of auburn in his curly brown hair.

Ugh, maybe I need to get laid, if I'm thinking this much about a guy I met once. And as I decided earlier, there's no way a guy like him is single. Not possible.

My phone lights up with Tessa's name. She's totally going to flip when I tell her about today. The wedding, meeting Andrew, and signing up for the photoshoot, which is unlike me.

"Hey!" I answer.

"Hey, Josie," Tessa replies. "How did today go?"

"Oh my god," I say. "It went so amazing. The venue was gorgeous, and the sweetest groomsman helped me get things set up. And I think I made a new friend? Her name is Marley and she was the photographer. I just signed up to do a stranger photoshoot with her, and I've never done anything like that before, but I am so. Excited." I sigh heavily when I finish my outburst of excitement over my day.

"Wow... Uh, I'm glad you had a great day, Josie." Her voice is soft, almost hesitant, and I think I hear whispers in the background. "Listen, Josie, I have news."

"Right," I say, remembering her text from earlier. "What's up?"

"Shortly after you left, Zack texted me."

My brows pinch at the mention of my ex. "What did he say?"

There's a pause. "He asked me out on a date."

"He what?"

"Yeah, he asked me out, and I agreed."

I give myself a moment before I reply. Tessa knew how Zack and my relationship ended, and how he didn't always treat me the best. "So your news is that you went on a date with him? Why did you wait six months to tell me?"

"It wasn't just one date." She breathes heavily. "We've actually been together now for five months. I'm moving in with him, so I figured now is the time to tell you."

Shock is my first emotion. I bite my tongue of all the expletives I want to hurl her way, but I know that wouldn't be smart. "I... I don't really know what to say, Tessa. I'm not going to lie and say I'm not hurt by this. He didn't treat me well. You were there when he pointed out how much weight I'd gained after starting that new birth control."

"He's changed, Josie. He's a completely different person. He's supportive, and kind, and I love him so much. And to be fair, you had gained a lot of weight."

"That's not the point!" *Do I really need to explain this to her?* "The point is that he didn't treat me with respect, and now you are with him, and just expect me to be all hunky dory with this?" I stop myself before I say more. "I need some time to sit on this, to be okay with it. This hurts, Tessa."

"Josie, I'm sorry, but I love him. He's not who he was with you, and I want you to be supportive of this relationship. I think he might be the one."

"I might have been more supportive if you hadn't lied to me for months, Tessa. I need some space, please. I'll let you know when I'm ready to talk."

The line is silent, and then there's a click and a beep, letting me know that she ended the call.

Velma has curled up in my lap, seemingly sensing my discomfort, so I soak up all the love and warmth that she's providing me. Maybe I'm being overdramatic, but the way Tessa went about this hurts. I don't know how to reconcile the fact that the man who shot down my hopes and dreams and body shamed me more than once is dating the person who is supposed to be my best friend.

6

———————

ANDREW

I hop off the bus, gravel crunching under my feet with each step I take toward the reception. I was distracted the entire ride, not feeling as present on Isaac's day as I would like to. I just couldn't wait to get back and see Josie, see if she's single, then hopefully ask her out on a date. If she's single of course. If not, I'll just walk away with my tail between my legs.

The ride was a bit hectic, with the wedding party doing shots, and the guys taking turns dancing on the built in stripper pole. Which, I mean, I did go a round on. Can you really blame a guy? I've already put on a wedding dress today, so it's not like I can get any more embarrassed. Plus, it was fun.

Marley is off to our side, snapping pictures of us stumbling off the bus. Everyone is well past tipsy, and on their way to buzzed. I can feel the heaviness of alcohol in my head, but I'm determined to slow down and stay even keeled.

"Mar," I call, moving off to stand behind her. "Have you seen Josie?" I'm careful not to disturb her too much, making

44

sure she gets the shots of everyone having fun, and the bride and groom kissing as they step down the stairs of the party bus.

Megan has her bouquet in one hand, and a seltzer in the other. Isaac has an arm around her waist, tugging her in for a long, and *messy* kiss as soon as they are on solid ground.

Marley multitasks well. "Yeah, she left about twenty minutes ago after she got everything set up. Why?" It's hard to tell, but I think I can see the remnants of a smirk behind her camera.

"Fuck," I curse under my breath. "I was going to talk to her. Figure out if she's single." With the bride and groom stepping around the side of the building for a moment alone, I now have Marley's full attention.

"Oooh, Andrew, do you have a crush?" Marley taunts.

I stutter over my words, trying to come up with a reason as to why I don't have a crush, but then I remember that I'm no longer in high school, and Marley could be of assistance in these circumstances.

"Yes."

"Well, I do know this..." She draws the words out. "She told me she's single. We were talking a bit earlier."

Hope blooms inside my chest, my heart pounding harder with each second that passes. "Marley, you're amazing." I step to the left about to head toward where Isaac and Megan are, but Marley stops me, resting her hand on my arm.

"What do you think you're doing?"

"Gonna ask Megan for her number." I jerk my thumb in their direction.

"Oh, no you don't." Marley grips my forearm in her tiny hands. "They are currently canoodling behind that wall, and then I'm going to steal them away to take their sunset portraits. I promise I'll talk to Megan about it, but you will not press her about this, nor will you ask her until later tomorrow. It's her wedding day, she doesn't need to be worrying about giving you her florist's number."

I pause, knowing she's right. "Ugh, fine. You're right. It's their day. I'll talk to her about it later this week."

"Good. Now, get your ass inside, and take that gloomy look off your face, it's not attractive."

"Marley, did you say I'm attractive?" I throw a hand up to my chest, gasping in mock surprise.

"You are going to drive me batty, Andrew."

I walk backwards, pointing to her as I do. "Yeah, but you love me. I can't do your photoshoot anymore. I want to see what happens with Josie."

Marley waves me off, not saying anything further before I turn and head into the building.

I shake off my last bit of disappointment that she's no longer here, and head toward the bar, getting myself a can of beer. It's going to be a good night, and I'm going to be present and bring the energy for Isaac and Megan. Tomorrow I can start making a game plan on how I'm going to find, and get to know Josie.

7

ANDREW

It's been almost two weeks since the wedding, and I'm no closer to finding Josie than I was that night. Megan won't give me her phone number, claiming something about a confidentiality clause, but I almost don't believe her. She's never been a good liar.

The only thing I have to remember her by is the alligator clip —*or whatever it's called*— of hers. The day after the wedding when we were all cleaning up, I found it in the room where we put her stuff when I helped her unload. She must have taken it out of her hair at some point and forgotten it there. Call me a romantic, call me a weirdo, but I have the clip sitting on my dresser, waiting for the moment I can give it back to her.

In between commission drop offs, client meetings, and actual work, I've been walking around town, looking at bulletin boards, scouring the paper for ads, trying to find her floral company. I've asked around, trying to find someone, *anyone*, who might know anything about the new florist in town. I don't remember her saying the name of her business.

Shows how much I pay attention. I assume it has her name in it, and I'm having no luck at all finding anything.

Marley has been practically begging me to do her stranger shoot, as she calls it, but I'm still hesitant. I really want to find Josie, but with each day that passes, I'm losing hope.

I was cocky at first. Thinking to myself, *we live in a tiny ass town, how hard can it be?* Well, apparently a lot harder than I would have thought. I even logged back in to my Instagram account that I haven't used in years, trying to find her. I searched like forty different versions of her name, with the words flower, florist, florals, after it, and nothing.

It did, however, remind me that maybe I should be better about posting my own work on social media. Gramps hates all things technology, but I want my- *our-* work to get out there for everyone to see. I just have no idea how to do it.

My phone buzzes in my back pocket as I continue sanding the dining table I'm currently working on for a family out of town. The client is an older lady, but apparently has a huge family with like six or seven kids, who are all starting to have their own children. She was super sweet, telling me all their names and their jobs, and how only two of her kids are biologically hers. When I asked if she adopted, she laughed, saying that just because they weren't her kids, legally or biologically, they were still hers, still family. I thought that was pretty sweet.

I finish the round of sanding before pulling my phone from my pocket. Marley's name is the first thing I see when I slide open the screen.

MARLEY

Hey. I know you really don't want to, but can you at least fill out the forms for the photo shoot? I got an application from a girl I think you would hit it off with.

ME

I'll think about it.

MARLEY

You've been thinking about it for two weeks. Are you really so hung up on a girl that you spent an hour with? Is this some sort of Cinderella situation? Are you going to carry your boutonniere around and ask every person you meet if they know who created it?

ME

No, but that's not a half bad idea. Maybe I should. Could go along with the hair clip of hers I found.

MARLEY

That was a joke.

ME

But it gave me an idea.

MARLEY

Did you keep the boutonniere? Pretty sure most guys just chuck them. And wait. You have her hair clip?

ME

Would it be weird for me to say that I kept the flower?

MARLEY

Yes? But also no? It's kinda sweet.

ME

And the clip? Yeah. I found it during take down. I'm keeping it until I can give it back to her. It was probably expensive.

MARLEY

Andrew, those things are not expensive.

We're getting off track. Can you please please please fill out the forms? I think this could be good for you.

ME

Fine. But I'm not making any promises of doing a photoshoot.

MARLEY

That's what you think.

Thanks. I think this could be really awesome for both of us.

ME

You know I could never say no to you.

MARLEY

I didn't even have to give you puppy dog eyes, or bribe you with candy this time. You're getting soft on me, Andrew Cunningham.

ME

Oh no, I expect a full bag of Easter Egg Reese's candy for my efforts. It's only fair, Marley Bell.

MARLEY

Ugh. Fine. But only because those are the superior kind of Reese's.

I'VE JUST FINISHED DROPPING off the finished table a few days later for the gal with a million kids, and I'm heading back toward home when my phone rings. Of course, it's Marley. Ever since I filled the form out, she's been bugging me for more information.

For a minute, I thought about filling out the forms with lies, and bullshit stupid answers, but then I felt bad and didn't want to upset Marley, so I went through and changed my answers.

"Yes?" I answer, knowing exactly what this conversation is going to be about.

"Hey, are you free tomorrow?"

I think through my mental calendar, then decide I really should buy an actual calendar, and use it. "Umm I think so, besides Sunday Brunch at Mom and Dad's, but you already know that."

"Yes, sorry, I meant after."

Since we were kids, Marley and her family have always come over for Sunday brunch after church. We've all grown up now, but it's a tradition that has somehow stayed, even though none of us go to church anymore.

"I don't think anything, probably watch the baseball game."

"Okay, wear something nice tomorrow please. Like a pair of dark jeans, and maybe a button up shirt."

"Why?" I ask, we haven't dressed up for brunch in years, unless it's a holiday or something to celebrate.

"Just, do it please. I want to try and take some photos of the families. And I think Jason said Lennie's getting taller, so I figure it's a great time to do some updated family photos."

At the mention of my three year old niece, I soften slightly. "Alright fine, but only for Lennie." His ex-fiancee skipped out on Jason and Lennie when Lennie was a few months old. Didn't even come to her first birthday party. Drugs took over her life.

Jason has full custody now, and hasn't seen his ex, Talia, since.

"Ugh, thank you," Marley sighs, the tension leaving her voice.

"Were you really that worked up over me potentially not wanting to dress up?"

"No," she quickly replies. "Just trying to make a plan and make sure everyone is on the same page. That's all. You know how your brothers can be."

"I guess that's true," I say. "Let me know if anything changes and I can wear a t-shirt, okay?"

"Don't count on it." Marley says a quick goodbye and hanging up the phone.

I pull into my driveway, and shut off the truck. I climb out, heading into the house. My golden retriever, Travis, is sprawled out on the couch. He's sleeping like a log, snoring and all. My mom hates his name, but I think naming an animal such a distinctly human name is hilarious.

Travis is a great dog. He loves to come with me for runs, or swimming in the lakes. He also loves to hang out with me in the shop. I click my tongue, and he wakes up immediately, his tail wagging furiously against the couch.

"You know, you have a perfectly good bed over there," I say, pointing to his sixty dollar memory foam bed. I'm pretty sure he rolls his eyes at me, because a moment later, he's stretching down off the couch, grumbling as he does. "For being three years old, you sure act like an old man." I head toward the kitchen, grabbing a snack and my water bottle from the counter.

Once I have a snack, I head to the sliding door that leads

to the backyard and my shop. I bought this house from my grandparents a few years ago, and while I've had to do a lot of updates on it, it's a good house. I sort of didn't have a choice when it came to buying it, because of the shop out back. Gramps has been working out of it since he was a kid, and I followed in his footsteps.

Travis slinks through the door as soon as I open it, running down the porch steps to pee on every possible bush and tree in sight. I got him fixed when he was young, but he still feels the need to mark his territory on literally everything.

I whistle sharply, and he runs back to me, following in my steps as I walk toward the shop. I don't have any work to do tonight, so I should enjoy the night off, but for some reason, I need the peace the shop brings. I feel restless, unsettled.

Opening the creaking door, I'm surprised to see the lights on. That's weird. I could have sworn I turned them off after loading that table into the truck.

My gaze lifts to the figure in the back corner, sitting in the recliner, fast asleep. Gramps.

Travis zooms through the shop, kicking up sawdust in his haste, and jumping straight into his lap. He startles, chuckling when he realizes it's just the dog. "Travis, you can't do that, you'll give me a heart attack," his deep weathered voice teases.

"Maybe you shouldn't be breaking into people's shops and you wouldn't get so scared," I tease back.

Gramps sits up in his chair, his white hair sticking out in different directions from his nap. Travis hops down after licking his face a few times, then starts to do his usual rounds.

"I think I have the right to come to my own shop every once in a while," he says.

"You know I don't care. I'm just giving you shit." I stride over to him, sitting down in the other recliner next to him. "How'd you get here?" I ask. "I didn't see your car out front."

"Your dad dropped me off after we had a late lunch. I told him I wanted to see some projects you've been doing, and figured you could run me home after."

I nod, knowing I'd do anything for this man. I've always been close with Gramps, partially due to the fact that he taught me everything I know about woodcraft, and partially because he gets me. We have the same personality, always have.

I was always the one set to take over the business. My dad had an affinity for it, but he never loved it the way Gramps or I did. My brothers have all spent time with us out here in the shop, but they had different career goals. I think Gramps thought the family business would die with him, until I came along. As a kid, I would spend hours and hours out here, watching him work, making my own treasures, too. My first real project was a jewelry box for my mom when I was ten, and I continued on from there. By the time I was in high school, I was working right alongside him.

I love that I can build something that can potentially outlive a person, just from a block of wood. The larger projects, like the dining room table I just did, never cease to amaze me. I also love the more intricate work. I do my fair share of whittling and carving, and I especially love to carve designs into bookshelves, or tables. Gramps taught me the ins and outs of the business itself after I graduated high school, rather than just wood working. I learned how to do the books, set prices, taxes, you name it. When he officially retired a few years ago, I was ready to take over. Granted, he should have retired years before he actually did, but he always said he wanted to give me the best foundation he could.

And he did. I have a steady clientele, as well as leads to events and other ways to grow our business.

I understand more than words can say why Gramps needed to come to the shop. He knows he's always welcome, and I will often find him out here, looking at my work. Never to judge, but to observe the work, and to find the solace that being here brings.

"Yeah, I'll bring you whenever you're ready," I say to Gramps. "Did you hear we are doing family pictures tomorrow at Sunday brunch with the Bells?"

Gramps gives me an odd look. "No, who told you that?"

"Marley called me on the way home, and told me to dress nice."

"That girl," he grumbles. "She's lucky she's good at what she does, or I'd have to give her more crap about makin' me dress up like a hooligan for a few pictures."

"She's the granddaughter you never had," I tease.

He raises his eyebrows. "If your brother would get his head outta his ass and ask her out on a date, then maybe she'd be my actual granddaughter," he mutters.

"You're telling me," I chuckle. "I tried to talk her into it a few weeks ago, but of course she denied me every step of the way."

"It seems that everyone knows they're supposed to be together but themselves." He shakes his head.

"You got that right."

"Speaking of love," he starts. "Anyone you've got your eye on lately?"

It's like he knows. He's always been able to hear the

words I don't say. I shrug, running a hand through my hair. "Not really."

"Something's got you all twisted though," he says.

I nod. "Yeah. I met a girl at Isaac's wedding a few weeks ago. She was the florist, and god, Gramps. She was gorgeous. I swear, I was about ready to ask if we could do a double wedding."

"You're really caught up on her. Why don't you seem happy then?"

"I can't find her," I murmur.

"Son, you know my hearing aids don't work for crap. You need to speak up."

"I can't find her," I say, louder, frustrated with myself.

"Ahhh, a little Cinderella situation, huh?" Gramps smirks.

"That's what Marley said too. She left before I could talk to her again. *Woo* her."

"You'll find her," he says, patting his rough hand on my knee. "If it's meant to be, it will be."

"Says the man who met his wife at nineteen at the diner she worked at, and was married to her within two months," I joke, shoving him lightly.

Gramp's eyes light up as he thinks about his late wife, Grandma Irene. "She was a good one, I had to snatch her up before anyone else could." I know talking about Grandma causes him pain, but he also loves to talk about her, to remember her.

I nod, thinking about the little moments of love that I frequently witnessed between Grandma and Gramps. Sure, my parents also showed me how to love a partner well, but I want the old time love that Grandma and Gramps had. The seemingly effortless, carefree love.

"It's a small town, you'll find her," he repeats, ever so confident. "Now, let's go inside. I need a sandwich."

"Didn't you just go for lunch with dad?" I ask.

"Yeah, but he's on a health kick, and he ordered me a salad." Gramps stands up from the recliner, groaning as he does. He stretches out his back slightly, reaching for his cane.

He starts heading toward my house, Travis following behind closely. I can always count on Gramps for sage advice, that's for sure.

I get Gramps settled in at the dining table with a turkey sandwich, when Travis starts barking like crazy. I stride over to where he is at the front door, spotting my brother Beau heading up the driveway.

He doesn't knock, just opens the door, walking in like he owns the place. He's dressed casually, his long hair tied back on top of his head. "What are you doing here?" I ask.

Beau shrugs. "Bored, figured I'd see what you were up to. Thomas is on duty, and Jason is with Lennie at a birthday party."

I scoff, then joke. "So what you're saying is that I'm your last resort?"

He doesn't deny it.

"Wow..." I joke, but really, I'm not mad. "I take it Marley is busy too?"

He doesn't say anything for a moment. "Don't know. Wedding season is starting, so yeah, I'm sure she's busy."

"Got it. Gramps is here." I jerk my thumb toward the kitchen.

Beau tilts his head over, looking past me into the kitchen. Gramps sits at the table eating, idly patting Travis's head now that he's realized it's only Beau. Beau toes off his tennis shoes, walking through my house. "Gramps," he greets, patting him on the back. He heads to the fridge, digging around for something appetizing to him. I stride into the kitchen area, sitting at the table across from Gramps.

"Beau," Gramps says. "Marley busy today?"

Beau pauses, staring into the fridge. "I'm sure." He chooses not to elaborate, and Gramps gives me a subtle smirk.

"Andrew here has found himself a princess," Gramps says, changing the subject back to me. I widen my eyes, hoping Gramps will shut up.

Beau closes the fridge, coming away with an apple, and a bottle of water. "Tell me more." His lips quirk in a quick, but unmissable smile.

"She slipped away like Cinderella, and he's all torn up about it." Gramps takes a bite of his sandwich.

Beau glances at me, raising a brow. "Cinderella, huh?"

I pinch my nose. "I met her at Isaac's wedding. She was the florist, and she left before I could get her information. Megan won't send me her phone number, or even her email beause of some confidentiality clause."

Beau nods. "Fair. How're you going to find her?"

I shake my head. "Don't know. Just hope our paths cross? I couldn't find any information about a new florist in town on social media."

"Damn. I'm sure it'll work out." He takes a bite of his apple, then changes the subject. "Thomas is off at seven, wanna go out to Blue Ox tonight? Jason said he'll be there too, since Lennie wanted a sleepover with Mom and Dad."

A night out with my brothers at Jason's brewery does sound like a good time, and it's been a while since we all were together, just us four. "Count me in." I lift a finger to point at him. "Don't bring up my Cinderella, though."

"Why not?" There's a hint of mischief in my brother's eye, and I don't know what to think of it.

"I need to figure it out myself. I don't need Jason's insightful words, or Thomas's ridiculous suggestions." Thomas has always been a little over the top, especially when it comes to romance. He's a hopeless romantic, but would never admit to it.

"You got it," Beau agrees.

8

JOSIE

My hands shake as I comb my fingers through my tousled hair. I can't believe I'm actually doing this.

I never thought I would actually, willingly sign myself up for not only a blind date, but for someone to photograph said blind date.

When Marley texted me last week, telling me she had found a potential match for me, I was shocked. I mean, firstly that it happened so fast, and second, that it even happened at all.

I almost backed out fifteen times, but I'm making myself go. I'm still a little hurt over Tessa and Zack getting together, and it's been hard to reconcile it. But it's coming up on a year that I've been single, and I'm ready to get out there again. Even if nothing comes from it, it will be a good experience. Something to get me out of my comfort zone.

My red hair is curled into loose waves to frame my face, and I put on a small amount of makeup, which is exponentially more than my usual mascara and eyebrow pencil. A light layer of foundation, some shimmer to my eyelids, and I even made sure to curl my lashes. I apply a soft pink lipstick to accent everything. I only wish I could find my favorite claw clip to bring along. I misplaced it a few weeks ago, and haven't seen it since. I love having the option to throw my hair up if need be.

I have on my favorite dress, a dark pink sundress with cute floral designs all over it. I absolutely love this dress, and wish I could buy one in every color.

Velma hops onto the bathroom counter as I check my hair one last time, fluffing it up and tucking a strand behind my ear.

"Hi sweet girl," I murmur, running my hand down the length of her back. She purrs, pushing herself into my hand, taking all the good pets I'm giving her. She's a pretty low maintenance cat who loves her snuggles, but also knows when she wants to be left alone. She'll curl up in the guest bedroom in the corner of the bed, and sleep for hours if she wants to be left alone. She's like me in that sense. Fine with people, but also needs plenty of time on her own to recharge.

As I pet her, I can't help but wonder who Marley has picked out for me, or what the qualifications were to match him with me. Before I agreed, she asked me what my boundaries were, and what type of shoot I wanted to do. Apparently a couples boudoir shoot was an option, if we were interested in that.

I respectfully declined, mainly because a boudoir shoot is something I want to do on my own first, then *maybe* someday with someone I know and am fully comfortable with. However, she mentioned that she more than likely would prompt us to kiss, or have him hold me at times, much like an engagement or couples shoot.

I told her I'd be okay with that. And I will, I just... need to work myself up to it. She also told me that he is extremely attractive, and that he's about 5'11" so I'm free to wear heels. I almost laughed when she said that. I am definitely not a heels gal. Sure, every once in a while I can be, but most of the time, I prefer sandals, or my Hey Dudes. I asked her if she could give me any more information on him, but she said no, that she didn't want to give away any more identifying information. That it was better for the chemistry of the shoot if it was a total surprise.

Once Velma has had enough pets, she hops off the counter, rubbing her back against my legs, before darting off into the second bedroom. "Bye, Velma," I call out, as if she cares that I'm leaving. I grab my bag from the hook next to the garage door, and lock up behind me as I leave.

My only instructions were to go to the city park at two, and when I got there, to text her and stay in my car.

I drive through town, rolling down the window to let some of the fresh air in the car, my heart pounding the closer I get to the park. To be frank, I'm totally petrified. What the hell was I thinking, doing something like this?

I almost pull out my phone to call my mom, but figure that would do more harm than good. She'd probably convince me I was about to get kidnapped, and call the local police for good measure.

No, I can do this.

I shake out my clammy hands, gripping the steering wheel as I turn down the drive toward the park. There's a few cars parked in the lot, including a small Camry and a large work truck with a *Cunningham Bespoke Woodcrafts* logo stickered to the side doors. A few rows down is a mini van, with a mom helping her kids out of it, one at a time, before finally pulling a carseat with an infant out.

Once she gives them the okay, the kids dart toward the nearby playground, squealing and screaming in delight as they do. I park next to the van before rubbing my clammy palms up and down my thighs, trying to get rid of the sweat. I pull out my phone, texting Marley that I'm here, and she responds that she'll be here in a minute. I close my eyes and lean my head back against the headrest, trying to give myself a minute to breathe.

9

ANDREW

"I cannot believe you tricked me into this," I grumble, my field of vision completely black thanks to the bandana Marley tied over my eyes.

"Hey, you'll thank me for it later," Marley says, her voice high pitched and excited.

"How are you so sure?"

"Because, I know you." She spins my body so I'm facing a new direction. "Stay here while I go get her."

"Do I even get to know her name?" I call, unsure of how fast she's walking away.

"Nope," calls Marley, her voice already fading into the distance.

Great, I think to myself. I shove my hands into the front pocket of my jeans. If anyone walks by me right now, I have no doubt that they would call the cops on me. I mean really, who wouldn't? You've got a blindfolded man, with a camera set on the ground next to me. Seems a little sketch if you ask me.

With my luck, my brother Thomas would be the one to take the 911 call. He'd get here, see me like this, and tease me for the rest of time.

I still cannot believe she tricked me into this. Initially, I was shocked and a little pissed that *family portraits* turned out to be an ambush. When I showed up to brunch as the only one dressed up, I instantly knew something was up. It wasn't until Marley insisted she and I drive separately from the rest of the family to the park for pictures that I really gathered the extent of her conniving. When I pulled into the park and saw none of the other family members here, I was ready to get into my car and drive away.

Marley claimed she would tackle me if I tried, and to be honest, I believed her. She was always the feisty one as kids, and I have no doubt she would do whatever it took to make me stay. But I can't stay too upset with her. Especially since she's just trying to keep me from becoming a cranky bachelor for the rest of my life.

She also produced a massive bag of *Reese's* Easter Eggs from the backseat of her car, so that helped.

I scratch at the blindfold where it's tied at the back of my head, wondering what the next hour of my life will be. Will it be life changing? Sub-par? I mean, I know we're going to kiss, Marley told me as much. You can tell a lot from a kiss. Sometimes, it's just that, a kiss. Other times, an explosion of tension, heat, and lust.

I haven't really experienced the latter more than a few times, but who knows, maybe that will change today.

I can hear Marley's voice as she leads the girl toward me, her voice soothing and directing.

"Alright, perfect, you stand here," she directs. She taps me on the shoulder, letting me know she's going to talk to me now. "If you reach down with your right hand, you can clasp her hand in yours." I nod, taking my hands out of my pockets, letting my right hand search for my mystery girl's hand.

When our hands connect, I notice instantly that her hands are freezing, and not only that, clammy. She must be as nervous as I am. A small shiver zings through my body at the feeling of her touching me, and I wonder what that's all about.

"Okay, now, both of you, take a step back so your backs are touching." We do as she says, and our backs touch. She's warm, and shorter than me. I can feel her shoulder blades rest just under mine, and her head rests in between my own shoulder blades.

"Perfect, okay," Marley murmurs. "I'm just going to adjust your positioning a little bit, so just let me move your bodies a bit." I nod, and feel Marley adjusting the angle of my head, and hips, even the angle of my feet.

I hear her shuffling through her bag, and stepping back in the grass. "Okay, when I say so, I want you two to take off your blindfolds, and turn around. I'm going to take a few pictures first, so it will be a minute."

I hear the click of the camera as Marley takes picture after picture. My heart rate climbs in anticipation, and I start to bounce on the balls of my feet, unable to keep the movement under control.

"Stop bouncing," Marley coaches.

"Can't," I murmur. I hear mystery girl gasp at the sound of my voice, but I'm unable to discern anything more from her.

Marley chuckles, snapping a few more pictures. "Alright, on the count of three, turn around and take off your blindfolds."

"One..."

"Two..."

I find myself counting out loud with her, all the tension leading up to this one moment.

"Three," Marley counts.

I turn around, carelessly yanking the blindfold from my eyes, and dropping it to the ground. It takes a moment for my eyes to adjust to the bright sun of the spring day after being submerged in darkness for so long, but when they do, I'm met with the blue eyes that I've been thinking about non-stop for the last two weeks.

My Cinderella.

"Three," I say along with Marley, turning around and whipping my blindfold off, not even caring one bit what it's doing to my hair.

My eyes adjust after a moment, and I gaze up at the man who I've been wondering about for the last few hours. I take in the furrow of his brow, the way his chocolate brown eyes are wide with... knowing? His brown hair is curly at the top, and he's wearing a light blue dress shirt that is tight across his chest and arms, the sleeves rolled up to show off his impressive forearms.

I'm stunned silent for a moment. When the man says my name, recognition hits me like a freight train.

"Andrew?" I question at the same time as a panty dropping smile breaks out onto his gorgeous face.

"Holy smokes." He takes both my hands in his, then drops them to pull me into a tight hug. "Josie, I've been trying to find you for weeks."

"You have?" I ask, completely dumbfounded. Why would Marley set me up with Andrew? There's no way he's single.

Right?

"What are you doing here?" I'm completely lost.

In the background, the camera clicks and snaps pictures every second of our whole interaction.

As he pulls away from our embrace, he looks down at me, wonder in his eyes. "Marley made me do it," he says, looking over at her. "She's been trying to convince me to do this for weeks, and now I know why. I've been talking about you non-stop ever since the wedding."

My mind is spinning with all this information, but I can't get one thing out of my mind. "Wait, don't you have a girlfriend?" I ask. Andrew's gaze sharpens, and his hands clasp mine again.

"No, I don't. Did someone tell you I did?"

I shake my head, lost in his eyes. One of his hands lifts, taking mine with it as he pushes away one of the curls that went haywire from the blindfold. "No-uh," I stammer, unsure of how to say this. "I guess I just assumed you did."

"I don't," he murmurs, staring into my eyes. "I definitely don't." The hand that pushed the hair behind my ear now rests on my face, cupping my cheek as he stares at me in awe. "*Holy shit, I have your crocodile clip.*"

I'm so thrown off by the randomness of his words that they don't even register for a long moment. "My... what?"

"Your alligator clip," he reiterates, dropping his hand from my cheek, and gesturing wildly as if pulling his hair up in the back of his head.

"My claw clip?" I chuckle.

"Is that what they're called?" Andrew rubs a hand over his face, eyes wandering before looking down at me again. "Who cares, I have your claw clip. Is this really happening? Am I dreaming?"

Marley lets out a cackling laugh. "Andrew, stop being so fucking dramatic."

"Hey, you're the one that's been lying to me for literal weeks! You just drop my dream girl in my lap and expect me to be all hunky dory in point five seconds? I think not."

Did he just call me his dream girl? Hold the phone. *What?*

"I need to reboot or something," Andrew continues. He takes my cheeks in his hands again, those fucking brown eyes looking at me like I just saved his puppy from a burning building.

"You are real."

"Uh, yes?"

"Holy shit. Okay. You're single? Like really single? No boyfriend hiding behind the bushes that's going to jump out and yell 'punk'd' or something?"

I stutter out a laugh. "No. I'm really really single. Is there a girlfriend hiding in the woods ready to jump out and yell at me?" I ask in return.

Andrew's shaking his head, totally incredulous. "Fuck no."

I shake my head right back. "Then I guess we're good."

"I still can't believe Marley planned this. She knew at the wedding that I wanted to find you, and here we fucking are."

"Here we fucking are," I repeat, smiling up at him.

"You're cute when you swear." He traces my bottom lip with the tip of his thumb, dragging it slowly.

Did someone light my panties on fire?

His thumb keeps caressing my lip, when a voice interrupts the heated moment. "Okay, can I bug you two to try a few different poses now?" Marley's voice is a bucket of cold water dumped over my overheated body.

I clear my throat, taking a step back from Andrew. He does the same, but there's still the heated tension between us, crackling like a live wire. I know he can feel it too, just like I did that first night.

"Right, yes," I murmur, turning my attention back to Marley. Andrew takes a step closer to me again, taking my hand in his. Marley notices, and smiles at me, while also subtly winking at me.

I shake my head slightly, not bothering to hide my returning smile though.

"Now that we have the initial introduction photos out of the way, let's go for a little walk. I'll follow behind you two, and stop you every so often for posing. Got it?" Marley lifts her finger, swirling it around, motioning for us to turn and start walking. My hand is still enveloped in Andrew's and I note the callouses and roughness of his hands.

"What do you—"

"Where did you—" Both Andrew and I start speaking at the same time, then proceed to burst into laughter. Andrew regains his composure first as we walk, toward nowhere in particular. "Where did you grow up?" he asks.

"I grew up not far from St. Cloud, a small town called Brooks Hill, about the size of Ivy Ridge." Andrew swings our entwined hands between us. "My mom and dad still live in my childhood home. It's only about an hour from here."

Andrew nods thoughtfully. "Why Ivy Ridge?"

I shrug. "Why not?" Probably best not to do a deep dive into all my insecurities and past within the first five minutes of a date.

He smiles down at me, a dimple on his left cheek making itself known. "Well, I for one, am glad you picked us."

"Me too," I answer, trying my best to hide the flush I feel staining my cheeks. I tilt my head downward, clearing my throat as I do. "What do you do for work?"

Andrew rolls his shoulders back, and I can tell by the way his eyes immediately light up that he does something he genuinely enjoys. "I'm a carpenter. Well, woodworker is probably the proper terminology. I took over my grandpa's business a few years back. I make tables, bookshelves, chairs, you name it."

That explains the roughness of his hands. Not that I mind. I find it sexy that he works with his hands. "Wow, I'd love to see some of your work," I say.

"I'd love to show you my shop," he replies, and I don't miss the dimple making its appearance again.

"Ooo, sounds fancy."

Andrew chuckles, giving my hand a gentle squeeze. We continue slowly walking, surrounded by trees and bushes. It feels like it's just him and me, but I know that's not true, as I can hear the frequent click of Marley's camera, and her footsteps crunching behind us. She stops us a few times, having us pose in various ways, before sending us on our merry way again. Andrew easily picks up the conversation where it left off.

"It's really not fancy. Though it does have a couple recliners and a couch tucked in the back," he concedes.

"Sounds way fancier than my 'workshop'." I make air quotes with my free hand.

"Nah, I bet yours is awesome."

"No," I laugh. "You'll have to come see. I'm lucky enough to have a fridge and a piece of plywood."

Andrew's brow furrows for a short moment. "Hmm," is all he says in response.

We reach the edge of a small pond, equipped with a

wooden dock that appears aged, and is no longer in its best condition. It's probably been forgotten for years, left to sit through the winter cold and snow. "Oh, this is perfect!" Marley calls, stepping up behind me.

"Uh, what?" Andrew questions. His eyes are wide in disbelief. "Mar... this doesn't look too safe."

"Andrew, are you kidding me? It's fine, you know how sturdy these things are." To prove her point, she skirts around us, stepping onto the dock straight to the middle, and jumping up and down a few times. The dock doesn't budge, and Andrew seems to be appeased.

"Alright, fine. Josie, is this okay?" I appreciate him asking, rather than just deciding for the both of us.

I shrug, not really all that concerned. I'm pretty sure I've been on worse docks. My high school boyfriend and I would do whatever we could to get out of our parents' respective houses, and I distinctly remember one late summer night where we went to a pretty sketchy spot. It was a small pond, much like this one, and there were no houses in sight, but there was this old rickety dock. For a high school boyfriend, he was actually pretty sweet. He laid out a blanket for us, and together, we watched the stars for what felt like hours. With us being the horny teenagers that we were, there was also a lot of other stuff happening while we were watching the stars... if you know what I mean. For a seventeen year old, he sure was good with his tongue. That dock was in about ten times worse shape than this one.

"Come on, it will be fine." I drag Andrew onto the dock by our clasped hands. He groans, but I get the feeling he's just being dramatic.

Marley squeals happily, then from the grass, starts directing us. "Okay, Andrew, I want you to angle your body a little bit more to the right. Great, now Josie, face him, but make sure you're still turned toward me. Perfect! Ugh, you guys are so perfect for this." Andrew has his arms looped around my hips, while I'm on my tiptoes, my arms wrapped around his shoulders. The camera starts clicking, and in this position, I get an even closer look into his eyes. There are beautiful flecks of gold around his pupil, reminiscent of gold leaves.

I'm about to say as much, when Andrew beats me to it. "You know, you have more gray in your eyes than blue. I didn't notice that before." He stares intently at me, and in this moment, I completely forget about Marley, and the fact that we are being photographed.

"Oh, uh, yeah." I take my hand from his shoulder to tuck my hair behind my ear. An anxious habit. "That's what my sister always says, but my mom says it's impossible to have gray eyes."

"Well, I strongly disagree with your mom."

I laugh softly, not wanting to break this tension between us. My heart thumps loudly in my chest, and I'm sure if Andrew listened hard enough, he could hear its rapid beat.

"Andrew, can you rest your forehead on hers?" Marley calls, her voice seems so far away, almost muffled from the heavy pounding in my ears.

Andrew nods, then follows her instruction. His forehead touches mine, and our noses touch. If it is even possible, my heart beats even faster. Instead of fists around his neck, my hands turn to putty, one sliding up into his hair, the other resting between his shoulder blades.

"Has anyone ever told you you have an adorably small nose?" Andrew whispers. A laugh bursts from my lips, and my head drops from his forehead to his chest. I can't stop giggling, because, no, no one has ever told me that before.

"Umm, no," I continue to laugh. His right hand strays from my hip, up my body to my chin.

With a delicate touch, he lifts my chin so I'm looking at him again. "Well, it is."

I get back into the correct pose, just as Marley calls out from the grass. "Think you two are ready for a kiss?"

"What do you think, petals?" Heat courses through my veins at the sweet nickname. *Shit, I'm going to fall in love with this man, aren't I?*

I nod, my eyes widening with every second that passes.

"I need a yes or no, petals."

"Yes," I croak, and just as fast as the word leaves my lips, his mouth is on mine. His kiss isn't harsh, no, it's soft, meaningful, unhurried. He's kissing me like he has all the time in the world to do only that. It's meticulous in the best way.

One of my hands slides up into his curls, and I tangle my fingers at the root. The other does its best to pull him even closer to me so my breasts are pressed against his chest.

I'm hit with the scent of his cologne, the same cologne he had on the night of the wedding. It's subtle, but enough for me to know it's there.

I let my lips tangle with his, losing myself even further into this kiss. I swear to god, I've never been kissed like this before. He has no endgame, no ulterior motives. He's just kissing me to kiss me, because it feels good. *Right.*

My heart thumps loudly in my ear, my stomach trying hard to contain the butterflies as I shift my feet, settling down onto my heels, so I'm no longer on tiptoes. Andrew adjusts, one hand at the small of my back, the other sliding up to cup the base of my neck, keeping me close to him. We pull apart for only a moment, breathing heavily as we do.

It's not even a second later when Andrew is pressing kisses along my jawline, up to the base of my ear. He inhales sharply, then says, "Josie, you really know how to make a guy weak in the knees."

And just like that, my own knees go weak. I slide further into his arms, and thankfully, he has a good hold on me. "I think the same could be said for you," I tease weakly.

"Oh my god you guys, that was *incredible*," Marley gushes, and I feel myself steady as I remember her presence.

Andrew chuckles, the low rumble vibrating against my chest. "Glad we could be of service. Now, are we done? I'd kinda like to see if Josie wants to go on an actual date."

"As much as I want to say yes, I still have a few more ideas in mind." Marley sounds apologetic, but I take a step back, waving her off.

"No worries, I've got time." I turn my gaze back to Andrew. "Right?"

He lets out a dramatic sigh, tucking my hair behind my ears again. "I suppose, but I'm going to complain the whole time," he teases.

"I would expect nothing less," Marley jokes. She snaps a few more pictures while we are still on the end of the dock. "Before we move to the next setting though, think I can get one more kiss out of you? You have no idea how great these photos are going to turn out."

"Sure," I say. Andrew agrees as well.

"Okay, for this one, Josie, I want you to jump up into his arms, and wrap your legs around his waist, okay?"

I flick my gaze to her, widening my eyes. I try to subtly shake my head. Sure, he's got muscles for days, but I also have rolls for days. I'm not necessarily what some would call thin. My grandma used to say I was big boned. It took me a while to realize that wasn't necessarily a compliment. I don't think this man can carry me like that for a long time.

Zack told me once that I was too heavy for him to carry for more than a second.

Marley widens her eyes in return, and we have a silent conversation with our eyes.

Andrew clears his throat. "Listen, I- uh- I don't exactly know what's happening with the crazy eyes, but we don't have to do that pose if you aren't comfortable, Josie."

"She's fine," Marley says, and I squeak at her, trying my hardest to relay my worries.

"No," I interject. "Andrew—"

"If you're about to say what I think you're about to say, you should probably not say it," Andrew interrupts, stepping closer to me. He bends down slightly, wrapping his arms around me.

"Oh, and what was I about to say?" I'm feeling a *little* sassy at the moment.

"I think you were about to assume that I couldn't lift you."

"I—" I stop. "Fine. You're right. You are very strong I'm sure, but I'm not lit— Ahh!" I squeal as I'm suddenly lifted. Andrew's hands are on my ass, thankfully covered by my dress and the pair of shape-wear I thoughtfully put on today. My arms fly to wrap around his neck, my legs around his waist. My hold tightens around him, and I look down at Andrew, my vantage point totally different now that I'm in his arms.

"You were saying, petals?" he cheekily states.

"You're going to pay for that," I tease, knowing full well I'm not going to do anything about it.

"Can I take my punishment in the form of kisses?"

"Hmm," I playfully respond, using a hand to tap on the tip of my chin as if I'm deep in thought. "I guess we have to see how well you can kiss."

"Challenge accepted." His lips take mine again, and just like before, I'm immediately lost to the kiss. God, has kissing ever felt this good before? I truly can't remember.

There's suddenly a loud cracking noise, and Andrew grunts, his body jerking.

I briefly register the ground disappearing from under us and the sensation of falling, and I only have a moment to react; pulling my head back and screeching, before Andrew's arms are wrapping around me tightly as we fall into the waist deep, freezing cold water.

I thankfully remembered to hold my breath, but Andrew doesn't let go of me, standing almost as soon as his legs hit the pond's murky ground. My eyes open when we're above water, and the first thing I see is Marley bent in half, laughing hysterically while trying to hold her camera up to capture what's happening. "Are you—guys—okay?!" she croaks between cackles.

I try to pry myself from Andrew, but he doesn't let me budge. No, he just yells to his friend. "What the hell, Marley! I told you the dock was going to break!"

"Andrew let me down," I murmur. "You can't carry me soaking wet."

"I can, and I will. Besides, we need to stay close, maintain warmth." He seems unharmed if he's still flirtatiously joking. He doesn't make a move to let me down, just starts striding to shore as if he doesn't notice my weight.

When we reach shore, he thankfully lets me down, and I make quick work of adjusting my now soaking wet dress. It clings to my body in probably a very unflattering way, so I do my best to squeeze out excess water, and fluff it out.

Marley snaps a few more pictures, saying, "Alright fine, I guess that ends today's session. But, I do want to take a few more sometime, when you two aren't waterlogged. Would you be up for it?"

Andrew glares down at Marley, not in a mean way though. More of an older brother, *I told you so*, way. "Only if Josie's okay with it."

I nod. "Yeah, I'm fine with it."

"Yay," Marley squeals, clapping her hands together twice. "Okay, let's head back to the cars, Josie, I have some extra clothes you can borrow."

I start to follow Marley, looking back to Andrew. He's staring at me, a smile taking over his face. "What?" I ask him, curious as to why he's looking at me like that.

"Nothing, just... most girls would freak out if they got dunked into freezing cold water on a date."

"I mean, it's not like you did it on purpose, right?"

He shakes his head, waving his arms in front of him, water droplets flying everywhere. "No, fuck no," he stammers. "Hell, I didn't even want to go on the dock in the first place. I think you're really great, Josie."

"I think you're really great too, Andrew."

He nods, kicking a rock at his feet, and I could swear there is a hint of a blush creeping up his neck. "If I asked you on a real date, you might say yes?"

I gasp, feigning shock while clutching my chest. "Wait, this isn't a real date?"

"No, yes, wait!" Andrew panics. "It is, it is, I just mean like a date where we don't have my brother's best friend following us around the whole time. Yeah?"

I laugh. "Yeah. I'd love to go on a real date with you, Andrew."

He sighs in relief. "Okay good. Maybe I can take you out for dinner?"

"That sounds perfect."

"Is it too eager to say tonight?"

I shake my head. "Not too eager at all. Though I would like to get some dry clothes on, and maybe a shower first?"

"Oh, totally. I vote we throw Marley in the water next time she takes pictures of us."

"Deal," I say.

Andrew takes my hands again, and though both our fingers are cold, they warm quickly with the shared body heat.

11

ANDREW

Walking toward the cars with Josie's hand in mine has me feeling on top of the world. Despite being soaking wet, my body is thrumming with energy and heat. The water was freaking cold, but feeling Josie clutching to me like I was her lifeline was something I never want to forget.

She however, probably wants to forget every moment of it.

Josie's cheeks are still slightly flushed, and I'm not sure if it's from the chill, or what I perceived as embarrassment while she tried to wring out her dress.

To be totally honest, I'm still in a state of shock. When I took that blindfold off and Josie was standing in front of me, I think I blacked out for a minute. I'd been hyping up our reunion for the last few weeks in my head, and honestly, this was better than I could have imagined.

My feet are squelching with every step, my sopping wet socks trying to eliminate the water from them with each movement. Once we get to our vehicles, I reluctantly drop Josie's hand.

"Can I get your phone number?" I ask, feeling slightly nervous she might decline.

"Oh, sure," she hurriedly says. "I left my phone in my car, otherwise, I'd be in a tough spot right now." She must have given Marley her keys earlier, because Marley tosses them to her. Josie unlocks her car, digging her phone out from her glovebox. Marley hands me my own phone from her back pocket.

I unlock the screen, seeing a voicemail from Gramps, as well as a few texts from my older brothers, Jason, Thomas, and Beau.

BEAU

So how's your surprise date, Andrew?

JASON

Yeah, Marley was talking it up before you got to brunch. Gramps thought it was hilarious.

THOMAS

Wait, I missed something. This is why I hate being on duty and missing Sunday Brunch. I always miss the drama.

JASON

Our brother here has been hung up on a girl for weeks now, and Marley set them up on a blind date today.

THOMAS

Oh hell yeah. That's awesome.

BEAU

Marley has been talking my ear off about it for weeks. I guess she really likes this girl, and wants to be friends with her. She keeps griping at me for monopolizing all her free time. Says she doesn't have enough girlfriends.

JASON

Are you sure you aren't subconsciously monopolizing her free time so she doesn't meet a guy who isn't you?

BEAU

Fuck off. I can't go there with her.

THOMAS

Can't? Or won't?

ME

First off, Marley is the best, any guy will be lucky to have her. Secondly, she just set me up with the most amazing girl. The date went amazing. Well, until Marley had us stand on the rickety old dock down at the pond, and we ended up in the freezing cold water.

JASON

Damn. Bet the water made your dick shrivel right up.

THOMAS

I cannot wait for these pictures.

JASON

Lennie wants to know if she finally gets an aunt.

ME

You told her I was going on a date?

JASON

Well, it was hard not to when that's all anyone was talking about after you and Marley left. She doesn't have any cousins man, she eavesdrops on adult conversations. Not my fault.

BEAU

Note to self. Make sure Lennie isn't in
hearing distance when talking about...
adult things.

ME

Tell Lennie I'm working on getting her an
aunt.

But seriously guys, I really like this girl.

THOMAS

I can tell.

I look up from my phone to Josie. "Sorry, my brothers
are blowing up my phone." I open up a new contact, and
hand my phone to her. "Last chance to back out."

She smiles, lowering her eyes to my phone, typing in her
contact information. She also opens a new text thread, and
sends herself a smiley emoji. "There," she states. "Now I've
got your number too."

I chuckle, sliding a hand through my wet hair. Water
drips down my arm and face, droplets flying everywhere. A
few drops land on Josie's arm, who giggles, and brushes
them off casually.

"Sorry," I mutter. "Do you still want to go out tonight?"

Josie smiles, her nose scrunching slightly. "Yes, I would
love to. What time are you thinking?"

"I can pick you up in a few hours? Maybe six
o'clock?"

She looks at her phone, checking the time. "Yeah, that
should work. I'll text you my address later."

I nod, excited to spend some time with her. "Great."

"Okay, you two are adorable. I owe you another session
since this one ended this way. Deal?" Marley says. I'd
completely forgotten she was here.

"Deal." I side step toward her, tugging her in for a tight hug.

"Ew, Andrew, you're all wet, stop!" she screeches, trying to yank herself free.

"And whose fault is that?" I tease, letting her go. She steps back, wiping her hands down her now wet shirt. I notice a tattoo on her arm that I've never seen before. "That new?" I point to the leaves twining around her left wrist delicately.

Marley nods. "Yeah, I got it last week."

"Cool," I say. Marley has been getting tattoos since the day she turned eighteen. She and Beau actually got one together on her eighteenth birthday. Something to symbolize their friendship. She has quite a few tattoos, and I'm sure I've never even seen all of them.

"Josie, still on for drinks next week?" Marley calls as she walks backward to her car.

"Yes!" Josie says, smiling brightly at her. "I can't wait."

"Same," Marley says. "I'll be in touch." She winks, then gets into her car, leaving Josie and I alone, *finally*.

"So," I mutter, taking both Josie's hands in mine. She looks up at me with a smile, her red hair that was once curled in beautiful waves, now hanging limply around her face. Not that it matters, she still looks incredible. "I'll pick you up in a few hours, alright?" God, I'm so reluctant to let her go, afraid that if I leave her alone, she'll disappear again for weeks.

Josie nods, then drops her hands from mine. She waves shyly. "I'll see you soon, kay?"

I nod, clearing away the lump in my throat that's telling me I am such a sucker for this girl. I head over to my truck as she gets into her vehicle, but I don't get in until she's driving away.

THE LAST FEW hours have been pure, unadulterated torture. I showered as soon as I got home, and now, I've been in the shop, putzing for the last hour, waiting for the moment I can get in the truck to drive to Josie's place. I've fielded calls from each of my brothers, as well as what seems like a hundred texts. Of course, Jason tricked me into answering his call, claiming Lennie wanted to talk to me. He knows I can't say no to her.

When I answered the phone, I put on my happy uncle's voice, only to be completely obliterated by my oldest brother. He had made his voice all high pitched to sound like Lennie, and only when his voice cracked within the first three seconds did I realize that it wasn't Len.

Of course, he then told me that Lennie was napping. I should have known. He needed to know all the details, and I willingly gave them to him. He laughed his ass off when I told him we ended up in the pond, then praised me for asking her on an official date tonight.

I slide my palms over a gorgeous piece of sanded cherry wood that I plan to use for a new jewelry box for my mom. Travis is at my feet, following my every move. For a moment I consider doing a bit of work to pass the time, but decide not to since I already changed into my nice jeans and shirt, and I don't want to dirty them.

As if by thinking about her I summoned her, my phone buzzes with a text next to me on the shop bench.

JOSIE

Hey, my address is 1407 Ridgewood Dr.
I'm ready when you are. But no rush if you
aren't ready till later!

ME

I'm ready. Just have to get in the truck. Be
there in ten. Can't wait. ;)

JOSIE

Same. See you soon!

I send off a message with a thumbs up, shoving my phone into my back pocket. "Travis, let's go," I call to him, striding toward the shop door. He follows close behind, keeping pace with my almost jog. The sun is shining, afternoon heading into early evening.

I open the sliding door, and Travis flies into the house. He runs straight toward his food bowl, and I give him a little snack, figuring it will tide him over since I'm not sure what time I'll get home.

I'm probably the worst date planner ever, because I have absolutely nothing planned for tonight. I hope she doesn't think I have some extravagant itinerary, because in reality, I just want to spend time with her. Doesn't matter what we do.

I say goodbye to Travis, heading out the garage door to climb in my truck. Minutes later, I'm pulling onto Ridgewood Drive, scanning the house numbers for hers. When I spot 1407, I swing my truck into the driveway.

It's a cute house. A small, gray, rambler style with a large front window, where I can see a cat perched on the back of the couch, scanning the outside world. There's a long flower box below the four pane window, filled with blooming, colorful flowers. Not that I would expect anything less from a florist.

I shift the truck into park, and turn the key. After I hop out, I smooth my shirt a bit, not wanting to appear a rumpled mess. Quickly running a hand through my curly hair, I try to make sure it stays out of my eyes. I should really get a cut, but every time I go, they always cut it too short, or the curls lay wrong for a month afterwards.

Striding up to her front door, I shove one hand into my pocket, the other, ready to knock on the front door. I knock a few times, and see the cat scurry off the back of the couch into another room.

Chuckling under my breath, I can't help but imagine what Travis would think of a cat. He hasn't really been around one before, so that might be interesting if they were to meet.

Jeez, am I really that confident about her that I'm thinking about the potential of introducing our pets to each other? A year ago, a thought like that would've sent me into a tailspin of erratic thoughts, but now? I'm ready for something steady. A feeling of contentment washes over me.

"Andrew," Josie's soft voice calls from somewhere beside me. I turn my head to the left, to see her peeking out the garage door. "That door is broken, come here." She waves me over, so I step down the few steps, my feet crunching over the rock pathway. Like earlier, she has light makeup on that highlights the blue of her eyes.

Her strawberry hair is twisted on the sides, flowing into a low bun at the base of her neck. Soft spiral tendrils of hair frame her face, and her lips are painted a light pink hue. She looks so natural, effortless. She's wearing a different outfit than earlier, no doubt the other one is in the wash. She has on a pair of light denim jeans, a black shirt tucked into the high waisted pants, with a soft cream colored cardigan over it. It's simple, yet she looks amazing. The way her jeans settle right at the curve of her hips, flowing perfectly with her body.

"You look amazing, Josie," I say honestly, holding myself back from taking her lips in a bruising kiss.

Her freckled cheeks flush ever so slightly. "Thanks, it's not much, but I figured I would change if I needed to once I asked what we were doing."

"You're perfect."

The door opens wider, Josie taking a step back for me to step into the garage. An overwhelming floral smell hits my senses, but not in a bad way. It's soothing, refreshing. I realize then that my hands are empty. Fucking hell, why didn't I get her flowers or some fancy shit? God, I really am the worst date, no wonder I'm single.

"I just realized I should have brought you some flowers or chocolate or something," I murmur, reaching down to take her hand. "I'm sorry, that wasn't thoughtful of me."

She only smiles, her cheeks pinkening slightly. "Andrew, take a look around you, I have plenty of flowers. You being here is all I need."

I look around me, realizing that she is, in fact, right about the flowers. "Ha," I chuckle. "Good point." On a second glance around the room, I take in her setup. Her "workstation" if you could call it that, is two sawhorses with a piece of plywood laying on top. Various tools are scattered all over it, and my brow furrows.

"Is this where the magic happens?" I ask, trying my hardest to keep any sort of worry or concern from my voice at her workstation. She deserves something more than a piece of plywood. I smooth my hands over the rough surface, then look at her. She glances at me, her blue eyes wary.

"I know it's not much, but it's all I can afford at the

moment. Someday, I want to have a storefront so I don't have to work out of my garage."

I nod along, glancing at the piece of wood, trying to gauge the dimensions. "That would be amazing. Would you have the store downtown?"

Josie shrugs. "I think so. I feel like foot traffic would be best there. I just have to save enough money to afford the lease and the move."

"You'll get there," I say, reaching down to clasp her hand in mine. I give it a gentle squeeze, proud of her for what she's already accomplished in a short time. "Do you have more weddings coming up?"

"Not at the moment. I'm still waitressing at a diner in town, and this is the side gig at the moment. Although one of the funeral homes has been giving me a lot of clientele, so I might be cutting my hours soon. How morbid is that?" she chuckles softly. "The more people die, the more clients I might get."

I chuckle lightly. "Could be worse, you could be working at the funeral home, where your whole wellbeing is people dying."

She visibly shudders, her mouth quirking into a grin. "Yeah, that's... wow. I've never thought of it like that before."

I give her palm another gentle squeeze, and reluctantly let go of her hand.

"I really don't need to change? What do you have planned?" Josie asks.

"To be completely honest, I don't have anything planned. I got as far as getting here, and then I couldn't think past that."

"Hmmm," she murmurs, tapping her pointer finger to her pink shaded lips. What I'd give to kiss those lips again, maybe bite down on that plump bottom lip. "To be honest, I don't know much about this town. I should, since I've lived here for a while now, but I guess I don't get out much. Is there a place where you always go with friends?"

I raise one of my shoulders, and run my hand through my hair while I think. Sure, we could go to the small bar one of my high school buddies owns, but it usually get's pretty crowded and loud in there. I want to be able to hear her while we chat. A movie is out, because we wouldn't have any time to talk, and I'd spend the whole time trying not to make out with her like a teenager on his first date. And I'm definitely not going to be taking her to Jason's brewery. Even if he weren't working tonight, his staff would definitely be sure to pass along that I had taken a date there.

"Why don't we just get into the truck, and see where it takes us, yeah?" *Please don't think I'm corny.*

Josie smiles widely. "Sure, let me grab my bag and my phone." She steps aside, quickly running into her house, the wooden screen door slamming behind her as she does. A moment or two later, she emerges, locking the door behind her. She's got a small brown crossbody leather bag across her chest, her phone in her right hand.

"Ready?" she asks, smiling up at me.

"You bet," I say. "After you." I hold my arm out for her to lead the way. She leads me out her garage, flicking off the lights, basking us in darkness before opening the door to lead us out to the warm glow of the early evening.

I open the passenger side door for her, offering a hand to help her into the tall truck. She climbs in, and as soon as she's buckled, I gently shut the door, and head to my side of the truck. Once I myself am in and buckled, I reverse the truck, heading nowhere in particular.

"I still cannot believe Marley set us up today," Josie says from the passenger seat.

"To be honest, neither can I. I wasn't kidding when I said I'd been looking for you for a few weeks." A realization slams into my mind. "Oh shoot, I forgot your alligator clip."

Josie giggles, the sound sinking right into my chest, warming it like a hot cup of coffee. "You mean my claw clip?"

"Yeah, whatever they call those things."

"Don't worry about it, I'm sure I'll get it back from you eventually."

Eventually. My brain and heart stick on that ten letter word, because it means she sees this as more than tonight, right? She wouldn't say it if she didn't.

Perhaps I'm getting too far ahead of myself.

I nod, knowing that if I said something my voice would more than likely crack, and I'd look a fool.

"How long have you been friends with Marley?" Josie pulls me out of my little thought bubble.

"Long time," I say, turning my truck onto the main road that leads toward downtown. "Her family moved next door when we were in elementary school, and the rest is history. She's my brother Beau's age, but we've always been close. She has two older brothers, Kenny and Prescott, though we aren't as close to them. They live a few towns over."

Josie nods along thoughtfully. "So you two have never..."

"Dated? Hell no. That girl is my little sister, even though she's older than me." I spare a glance at Josie, watching her freckled cheeks pinken. "If I ever made a move on her, my brother would murder me. I think they're the only two who don't realize they're meant to be."

"Wait, really? They've never crossed the line?"

"Not that I know of. It's only a matter of time though. I mean, they're in their thirties. It's about time they realize it."

Josie shakes her head in disbelief. "Maybe they need someone to shove them in that direction."

"Nah, we've tried. It will happen when it happens."

"You've got me invested now," Josie teases. "I expect updates." She sucks in a gasp, startling me. "Ooooh, maybe we could come up with a code name or something for them, or 'Operation get Beau and Marley together at last'."

I snicker softly. "Yeah, petals, I'll keep you updated. Though I think we need a better name for it."

"Yeah you're right. It's a bit of a mouthful." She glances out the window, rubbing her hands up and down her thighs. "Did you decide on somewhere to go?"

I shake my head. "Not yet, just seeing where the evening takes us."

"Sounds like a plan. Will you get annoyed if I keep asking you questions?"

"Never," I answer. I reach out, resting my right hand on her thigh, squeezing gently. Her thick thighs might be the death of me. I can see it happening.

"How many siblings do you have?"

"Three. I'm the youngest. Three older brothers. Jason's the oldest, then Thomas, Beau, and me."

"Wow, that's a lot of testosterone." Josie grins. Her hand rests atop mine on her thigh, and her thumb caresses my skin gently.

"Yeah, I'm pretty sure the only reason my mom never lost it was because of Marley. She's her honorary daughter."

"That's so sweet. Are any of your brothers married?" She pauses. "Well besides Beau, I know he's not."

"Nope, we're actually all single. Jason has a daughter though, Lennie. She's three, now, I think? Cutest kid ever. I have no shame in admitting that I'm a sucker for her. I'll do whatever she wants."

"I bet you're an amazing uncle." Josie squeezes the top of my hand gently.

"She's a good kid. Her mom, Talia, ran out on them shortly after Lennie was born. Drugs and booze were more important to her I guess. She relinquished all parental rights too. We haven't seen her since." My heart aches at the thought. Talia could have been an amazing mother if she didn't let the drugs take over. I know it pains Jase anytime Lennie asks about her mom. Maybe someday he'll find someone to love them both the way they deserve.

"And she's your only niece or nephew?" Josie asks, bringing me back into the present.

"Yep. Tommy is more concerned about his work, and well, Beau, as you know, has a stick up his ass," I chuckle.

"What does Thomas do?"

"He's a police officer," I answer. "Scares the shit out of me the stuff he does and sees, but he loves to serve and take care of the community. He even has one of those German Shepherds that can smell drugs and stuff like that. His name's Arson. He's an awesome dog."

"It sounds like it," Josie says, then pauses, her face growing serious. "I suppose I should tell you about my felonies then."

My heart literally drops into my asshole. Throat tightening, I try to take a breath to ask her what she could have possibly done to get a felony. *Multiple* felonies. There's no way this sweet, innocent, adorable human could have multiple felonies. She has to be teasing me, right?

I clear my throat. "Um, what do you mean, felonies?"

Josie waves a hand in front of her face, completely nonchalant. "Oh it's no big deal. Just one charge of grand theft auto, one charge of burglary."

A squeak escapes my throat as I grip the steering wheel tighter. My free hand is still on her thigh, as I try to think of how this girl could possibly have done these things. Don't get me wrong, I'm all about the reformation programs in prison, and helping people that deserve it. I just never would have guessed that Josie would be the type of person to steal a car and burglarize something.

"Andrew," Josie squeaks out, her lips pursed, like she's trying to hold back laughter. "I'm joking. I don't have any felonies."

A gust of air escapes my lungs in relief. "Oh god, really?"

"Yes, I was kidding," she giggles. Her peals of laughter alleviate the weight that had settled in my stomach, and soon, I'm laughing right along with her.

"You know, I totally get that people have a history, but I never would have pegged you for a felon." My heart is still thumping loudly.

"If I ever stole something, it was totally unintentional." Josie lifts my hand, entwining our fingers together. "I think it's really cool that your brother is in law enforcement though. My dad is the sheriff in my hometown. Has been for I think nine years now?" she ponders.

"Great, so when I meet him, should I expect him to be sitting on the front porch with his gun?" I ask, chuckling at the thought.

Josie giggles. "Nah, he's a softie for me, though he might pull you aside and try to scare you. My mom will probably force feed you her homemade pumpkin bread though."

"Fuck yeah." I roll to a stop in front of a stoplight, and

give the air a fist bump. "I love pumpkin anything. Pumpkin Spice Latte? You bet your ass I'm driving thirty plus minutes to the nearest Starbucks as soon as they're in season."

The light turns green, and my foot eases off the brake to accelerate slowly. "Your turn," I say. "Do you have any siblings?

"One. I have an older sister, Jess. We aren't super close, but we don't have a bad relationship by any means. She lives in Missouri with her husband on an Army base. I think we'd talk more if she lived here still, but she's happy, and that's all that matters. Her husband, Brandon, is a nice guy too."

Making a split second decision, I pull into the old rundown bowling alley. "Well hopefully you're able to catch up with her soon."

"Yeah," Josie drawls. "I take it you decided what we're doing?" She eyes the flickering lights of the bowling alley.

"I promise it's not as bad as it looks." I squeeze her thigh, shutting off the truck and climbing out. I round over to her side, opening her door. Josie is still staring up at the sign, and I watch as her smile grows.

"This is so cool, Andrew," she gushes. "I haven't been bowling since I was a kid."

"Really?"

"Yeah, we didn't have a bowling alley around us, so we never went."

"Well, get ready, cause you're about to get clobbered," I tease.

"Aren't you supposed to play it cool on the first date? Let me win and all that?" She climbs out the truck, placing her hands on her curvy waist, jutting her right hip out.

I shrug, stepping in close to wrap my arms around her

waist. She giggles as I nuzzle my head into her neck, tickling her soft skin. "Don't worry, I'll teach you."

"I know how to bowl," she says, exasperatedly, though she's putty in my arms, her body melting into mine. "Though perhaps I need a few pointers."

12

———

JOSIE

ndrew leads me into the bowling alley, taking my hand in his. The carpet is exactly what you'd imagine a bowling alley to have. Dark with spots of neon swirls and patterns. *We Can't Stop,* by Miley Cyrus booms through the speakers, and the song throws me back in time to a smelly high school dance in the gym.

There's one other group here, a bunch of teens that seem more interested in the pizza on their table than bowling. Of course, they hoot and holler when one of their friends gets a strike, then they go right back to their food. Though I can't say I blame them, the pizza smells incredible.

Hand in hand, we head toward the counter, where an older gentleman who looks asleep sits. His head is resting in his open palm, elbow bent and resting on the counter to hold him up. His jaw is covered with a prickly, unkempt beard, his entire being just... dirty. Andrew gently clears his throat, and the man wakes with a jolt. He grunts, shifting so he's sitting up straight.

"Sorry 'bout that," he grumbles, rubbing his hand over

98

his face to wipe away the exhaustion. "Two?" he looks back and forth between us. His gaze lingers on me, dragging his eyes up and down my body, landing on my chest.

"Two," Andrew confirms. Seemingly without thought, Andrew drops my hand, shifting himself so he's in front of me. The worker, who's name tag reads Orlando, makes me slightly uncomfortable, so I'm grateful for the small gesture. "What's your shoe size?" Andrew asks me, still keeping me shielded.

I tell him, and he passes along the information, handing me the shoes before grabbing his own. I step back, and Andrew leads me by the small of my back to the farthest lane, opposite of the group of teens. "Sorry," Andrew murmurs. He sets down his shoes on one of the benches, then pulls me into his chest. My chin rests against him as I look up into his eyes. "That dude gave me weird vibes. He probably didn't mean anything by it, but I didn't want him looking at you like that."

I nod against his chest. "It's okay. I appreciate you looking out for me. I didn't really like him either. He was off. I can't think of a better way to describe it. Let's forget about it, and have some fun, yeah?"

Andrew seems wary still, but when I look around my shoulder to where Orlando sits, he's already passed out again. "You're right," Andrew agrees. He looks down at me, tucking a hair behind my ear, kissing me gently on the cheek. "I don't think you're ready for the greatness you're about to witness, petals."

"You're on," I tease. With that, I pull myself out of his arms, and sit down on the creaky bench, kicking off my shoes. Thank goodness I didn't put on a pair of sandals, so I have socks on. I slide the clunky bowling shoes on my feet, tightening the laces, then stand, and walk over to the rack of balls. Andrew is finishing up lacing his own shoes, so I grab myself a purple shimmering ball. My internal thoughts war with each other as I hold back a dirty joke about balls.

Andrew rises, meeting me in two steps. I stand still, holding the ball in my open palms. Andrew reaches behind me, grabbing a red ball. His fingers slide into the holes, and he gets a devilish grin on his face, waggling his eyebrows. He's practically daring me to make the joke, but I hold back. I will not show this man how much of a weirdo I am on the first date. Nope. No siree. Not me.

Before I realize it, Andrew is reaching around me, grabbing another ball. With a bowling ball resting in each palm, he eyes me straight on and deadpans, "Like my balls?"

It's all so absurd and childish that I burst out laughing, clutching my stomach. We laugh hard enough that the teens on the opposite side of the alley stop looking at their phones to glare at us. Apparently, our laughter is too much for them.

When our laughter dies down, Andrew puts the other ball back onto the rack. "Ah, that's a classic. I couldn't help it."

"I think we have the same type of humor, because I was holding back no less than three different ball jokes."

"See, this is why I know we're a good fit." Andrew's eyes burn as he looks at me, and suddenly, I want to jump him like the horn dog I am.

Andrew gets the console set up, typing both our names so they appear on the screen. "Ladies first," he says, winking with his right eye. He holds out his arm, gesturing for me to go ahead.

I smile, and step up onto the sleek wooden platform. I wasn't lying when I told him it had been a long time since I bowled. My sister, Jess, had a bowling party for her fifteenth birthday. I would have been twelve, so, yeah, that was the most recent time. But it can't be that hard, right? It's gotta be like riding a bike.

I step forward, taking a deep breath, hoping that I don't make too much of a fool of myself. With that, I aim down the middle, and drop my arm back before swinging forward to release the shimmery ball down the aisle. Instead of the strike that I was manifesting, the ball slides right into the gutter about ten feet after it hits the ground with a loud thud. I cringe, watching as the ball disappears.

I turn around, and try to play it cool. Andrew is standing by the ball thingy, hands in the pocket of his jeans. He rocks back and forth on his heels, his eyes alight with humor as he tries not to laugh at me.

"In my defense, it's been a long time," I argue preemptively.

He holds his hands up, palms facing me. "Hey, I think you did great." He gestures at the board. "And you've even got one more shot. Shake out the cobwebs."

The purple ball shoots out of the machine. With a scowl, I grab it, heading back onto the platform. I get myself into position, taking another deep breath. When I send the ball down the aisle this time, it doesn't immediately hit the gutter. Though it does slow to nearly a crawl as it heads toward the pins. With giddy anticipation, I watch as it rolls toward the far left edge pins.

It hits two pins, knocking them down. Throwing my hands in the air, I let out a little whoop of victory. "Ha, I did it!" I jeer, heading toward Andrew. He's standing in the same spot as before, his smile no longer humorous, but proud? "Your turn." I poke my finger into his chest.

Andrew steps back, and grabs his ball from the machine. He pulls me in for a quick side hug, and presses a gentle kiss to the top of my head. "Petals, I hope you don't hate me, but I physically cannot be bad at bowling, so this is not intentional."

With that, he steps onto the platform, and stands tall as the pins reset. I get the feeling I'm about to look like a fool, but honestly, I could care less. I'm just happy to be here, having fun with him.

Andrew lobs the ball down the aisle at an impressive speed, knocking down all but two pins in the process. My jaw drops to my chest, and when he turns around, he appears slightly sheepish. "It's not intentional, I promise." He eyes me down, and I laugh at how bummed he seems.

"Holy shit, what are you, a prodigy? Is this your way of telling me you're in a bowling league or something?"

"No," Andrew laughs. "In case you didn't notice, there isn't much to do in this town, so we've always had birthday parties, or any other celebration here. Or if it was just a boring Saturday night, my brothers and I would all come out and compete. Eventually, we started picking up some skills." He shrugs, grabbing his ball again.

"Well, I'm impressed. I expect lessons now," I say, tilting my head.

"Hmm, I think I can manage that." Andrew steps backwards toward the alley, spinning around. He takes a moment to get his bearings, then the ball is hurtling toward the two pins standing. Of course, he hits them, and they fly backwards.

He turns around again, smiling as he watches the screen above my head sing his praises for his spare.

"ALRIGHT, now you're just getting cocky," I say to Andrew. After a few games, he's racked up an impressive five strikes, and an additional spare. Meanwhile, I think I've knocked down a total of six pins. Andrew has offered to help, and has given me plenty of tips, but I think I'm just not quite strong enough to get the ball moving as fast as he can.

"I promise, I'm not. I can start trying to suck?" Andrew questions, shrugging his shoulders. "I don't mind losing."

Laughing, I grab my ball again. "No, don't! I like seeing you win, I just think it's funny how comically bad I am."

The place has cleared out now since the group of teens left. Our friend at the counter, Orlando, has left, replaced by a young girl with jet black dyed hair and eyeliner covering both her eyes. She's gorgeous, but my only thought is how long it must take her to get it all off every night. I barely wear makeup, and it's a hassle to get off.

Andrew ordered a pizza not too long ago, and the girl brings it out, setting it on our table. I set my ball back down, crossing over to the table. The pepperoni and sausage pizza is steaming, clearly just having come out of the oven. "Thanks, Sasha!" Andrew calls as she heads back toward the desk.

"You know her?" I ask, sliding a piece onto the paper plates she brought with.

"Yeah, she's a good kid. One of my buddies from high school's little sister. Though, everyone knows everyone here."

I shrug, blowing on the pizza in an attempt to cool it. "If everyone knows everyone, how come it took you two weeks to find me?" I laugh as Andrew's smile droops, and he groans.

"I tried, petals. You're a tough girl to find," he says. He

flops down into the chair across from me, grabbing a slice. "I asked everyone I saw if they knew of the new florist in town, and one of them knew you, but couldn't remember your business name. I swear, I tried."

"Andrew, it's fine," I laugh. "You act as though I was missing for five years, not a missed connection of two weeks."

"It felt like five years," Andrew grumbles under his breath. "While we are on the topic, what is the name of your business?"

I take a bite of pizza right as he asks, so I try to chew the flaming hot food, while trying not to appear as if my mouth is burning from the inside out. Any other day, I would have spit it out right away, but that probably wouldn't be a great impression on the first date.

"You alright?" he asks. "This shit is super hot."

I nod, taking a long drink of my pop. "I'm good. Just wasn't expecting it," I croak. Clearing my throat, I tell him about my business. "It's called Ivy Ridge Floral. I probably could have come up with a better, more creative name, but I was in a bit of a hurry to get my LLC up and running. Any other ideas I had were way too cheesy."

"Wow, you were really right under my nose this whole time," Andrew scoffs good naturedly. "Personally, I love it. I don't think you have to have a super creative name for something to work. A lot of it has to do with your work ethic and skills."

He pauses, taking a big bite of pizza. "I agree," I state. Without thinking, my next words bubble to the surface before I can stop them. "My ex thought all the names I came up with were stupid. He said I needed to have something super out there, so people would be more intrigued."

Andrew chews quickly. "Well, he's a idiot, for a multitude of reasons. The first being that he let you go. Second, sure, a creative name can help, but like I said, it's about the craft itself."

"I agree." *Totally just going to drift by the remark about my ex letting me go.*

"I mean look at me," he continues. "Cunningham Bespoke Woodcraft." He gestures at the sky. "My great-grandpa came up with that, and we're still here. We aren't here because of the name, we're here because of the quality work we do."

"I guess I've never thought of it like that," I say, pondering that. I knew Zack was an idiot, but my parents and best friend Tessa even mentioned that they thought Ivy Ridge Floral was too bland. Andrew's encouragement helps more than he realizes. "Thanks, I needed that."

"Needed what?"

"The pep talk. I didn't exactly have an abundance of support when I moved out here, so I've been doing it all on my own." I look away, not wanting to see the inevitable pity on his face.

"Lucky for you, I'm hard to get rid of. I'm like a leech. Stuck to you. Though, I won't suck all your blood. I'm not some weird sparkly vampire."

"Did you just compare yourself to Edward Cullen?"

He shrugs. "Just saying, it's gonna be hard for you to get rid of me. Can I ask you why you say you didn't have support?"

I nod. I knew this would be coming, especially since I brought Zack up. It stings a little more with Tessa's recent confession. "I worked with an older woman in my town for about seven years. She owned the only floral company in town, and she put an ad out asking for help with set up for events, and that sort of thing. I applied and got the job right away. She taught me everything I know about flowers, and events. When she was ready to retire, she asked if I wanted to take over her shop. In retrospect, maybe that would have been a better, easier idea, but I wanted to do it on my own. I didn't want an entire client list handed to me."

Andrew nods thoughtfully, showing me he's listening. "I'd been tossing around the idea of opening my own business for a while, but Ramona retiring really gave me the push I needed. My boyfriend at the time, Zack, told me time and time again that he thought it was a stupid idea, turning down her offer."

His face reddens, and I can tell the thought of me with someone else is what's causing it. "Why did he think it was stupid?"

I take another bite, trying to think of the words. "Zack was pushy about our future. He wanted to have an exact timeline of things and where we were heading, but I couldn't give him that."

Andrew's grip around his cup tightens.

"He didn't understand why I wanted to wait until things settled down. I knew deep down that I wanted to make a name on my own, and anytime I brought it up, he would tell me how stupid it was, because I was being grandfathered into an already thriving company. I also knew, deep down, that he wasn't the man for me. I stayed with him for comfort. We'd been together for a while, so we had a routine, a way of living. Walking away from that was scary, but I'm glad I did."

Andrew nods in agreement. "I can get that. It's kind of the opposite for me. The girls I'd been with wanted to get out and live anywhere but here, but I've always felt like this was where I needed to be. I love the work that I do, the legacy I get to carry on. But I also understand why you wanted to make your own."

"Thank you," I murmur. "I told my parents that I declined her offer, and my mom got upset. She told me that I was running from my future. A lot of the things people close to me were saying had truth to them, but I know that this is what I was supposed to do. I was supposed to get out on my own two feet and start from scratch."

"Hey, you won't hear any complaints from me. I'm all about following the path you find best for you. My brothers all had the option to take over Gramps shop, but they had other paths, my dad included. This is my path. It sounds like starting out on your own was yours."

"I think so, moving here especially. Everything feels so right here. Even though I'm still getting on my feet, and everything is so new, it hits differently. I don't feel like I'm just going through the motions, day by day."

"I hate to ask, but I'm curious." Andrew hesitates. When I nod, letting him continue, he does. "Why did you and your boyfriend break up then?"

"He wasn't supportive. I told him my plans, and how I was going to move, so I could start without my parents breathing down my neck. I told him he could come with me."

I chuckle at Andrew's pursed lips, his brows furrowed in discontent. "Obviously, he didn't come with me. He told me I was making a mistake, said some other cruel things about me, and I pretty much broke up with him on the spot."

"Damn," Andrew mutters. "Sounds like he's a stand up guy."

"Oh yeah, a real winner. My best friend called me a few

weeks ago. Apparently she's dating him now, and they're in love."

Andrew cringes.

I laugh. "Yeah, don't get me wrong, I'm happy for her. Besides the fact that she'd been with him for five months, and didn't tell me." Finishing my last bite of pizza, I wipe my greasy hands on my napkin.

"Are you serious?" Andrew asks incredulously.

"Yeah. I've been trying to process it and be happy for her, but I'm still hurt. If she'd told me right away, maybe things would be different, but he really wasn't a great guy to me."

"Have you talked with her since?"

I shake my head. "No. She's texted me a few times, but I've told her I need some time to think things through."

"That's fair, and to be honest, I think you have every right to be upset."

"Thanks," I say. "I think my mom is still having a hard time with the move and breakup, not that she was fond of Zack," I continue, feeling like I'm overtaking the whole conversation. "I think she's just ready to be a grandma. She retired earlier this year."

"Ah, yeah. My mom went stir crazy after she retired. She would make meals for us and drive around town, dropping them off at work for us every day. We had to sit down and tell her we didn't need lunch every day. It got better once Jason's little girl was born. She's really an awesome grandma, and Lennie loves spending every day with her."

"Your mom watches her everyday?"

"Sure does. They go to the library and all sorts of other events in town. It helps them both get the socialization they need." Andrew smiles.

"That's adorable," I say. "Sorry, I kinda spilled my life

story on you there. You probably don't want to hear about my ex boyfriend on our first date."

"I disagree," Andrew murmurs. "I love listening to you talk. No matter what it's about. Although, not that my opinion really matters, but it sounds like you're better off without him."

"I couldn't agree more," I say, offering up my plastic cup of pop. He clinks our glasses together.

We finish eating, and once things are cleaned up, I decide it's time to egg Andrew on a bit. "Ready for another game? I think I can beat you this time." I move to grab my ball from the machine where it sits when Andrew's arms wrap around my waist from behind.

His low, rumbling voice tickles as his lips caress the outside of my ear. "Hmmm, we'll have to see about that, won't we, Josie?"

I nod, words failing me. He's so soft, yet strong against my soft body, that I don't know how to react. Zack had muscles, sure, but he also was an accountant who worked a desk job. He lost a lot of the muscle he had, whereas Andrew works with his hands everyday.

Good god, I'm so fucking screwed when it comes to this man. A lock of his curly brown hair hits my forehead as his head tilts lower for his lips to meet the flushed skin of my neck.

My body betrays me when heat moves downward, my panties growing wetter with every second that passes. I'm sure he can totally tell how aroused I am, especially since his hand is now moving from my hip, up my soft stomach. I don't even have time to cringe at the thought of him touching my belly rolls when his pointer finger slides between my breasts, his palm splaying above my heart. He holds me close, as close as physically possible.

"You ready?"

I nod in response, my throat dry. If I spoke right now, I'm sure it would sound like the croak of a frog.

Andrew abruptly releases me, stepping backward. With his hands no longer on me, the fog around my thoughts clears. "You were just trying to throw me off my game, weren't you?" I point an accusatory finger at him as I turn around. His eyes go round with mock horror. "That's plain mean."

"I would never," Andrew gasps. "But you better get moving, Josie-girl."

I scowl, strutting up onto the wooden platform. After taking yet another minute to breathe and calm my racing heart, I lob the ball down the alley with every ounce of strength I have. It's not much, but the ball flies down the shiny wood, hitting the center pin forcefully.

The pins fall to the wood with a clatter, and Andrew starts to cheer behind me. I just got a strike.

Holy shit, I did it! I spin around, thrusting myself into Andrew's waiting arms. He catches me easily, and my legs wrap around his hips tightly.

'That was amazing, Josie!" Andrew croons into my neck, but I'm too busy inhaling his intoxicating scent to process his words. Why does he smell so good? My fingers tangle in his hair, and I do the only thing that I can think of. I kiss him.

I kiss him, feeling the passion burning through my body. The hands he has gripping my ass squeeze tighter, and my legs tighten around him in response.

His tongue parts my lips, and I'm grateful I didn't put more lipstick on. Though, I'm sure it would be hot to see him with my lipstick smeared all over his face. A low rumbling works its way up his chest, vibrating as our mouths battle for dominance. The moan escapes his lips, and I nearly combust. Tension amps up in my body, trying to relieve the ever growing ache between my thighs.

His hair is surely becoming a mess from my fingers, but kissing him is the only thing I can do. It's as though my brain refuses to think of anything but Andrew.

I think I can feel the subtle hardness growing between his legs, pressing up against my jean-covered pussy. He pulls our lips apart, and we catch our breath, resting our foreheads together.

The position we are in mirrors the one Marley put us in earlier, though this time, we don't end up face first in a freezing cold pond. No, this time, when I open my eyes and look around, I'm met with the eyes of an uncomfortable teenager.

Sasha clears her throat, pushing some of her dark hair away from her face. "Andrew," she murmurs, her voice soft. "Um, we're closing. It's after nine."

I can't help it, a laugh slips out of me, and I release my tight grip of Andrew's hair, and waist. I slide down his body, but he doesn't let me step away. No, he turns us so that I'm standing in front of him, my back to his chest. Something thick and hard presses against my ass, and he wraps his arms around my waist again like he did before.

"Sorry about that Sasha, didn't realize what time it was. We will get out of your hair." Despite the fact that he has a raging hard on, his voice is calm and collected. When Sasha is out of earshot, I spin around, hiding my face in his chest.

"I cannot believe she witnessed that. We were practically humping each other!" I whisper into his chest.

"Nah, we weren't bad." Andrew pulls back, stepping toward the bench. "Though, we should really pack it up. I'm not done yet, though."

"We can come back another time," I murmur, kicking off my bowling shoes to slide on my comfy hey dudes.

"That's not what I meant."

"Hmm?" I lift my head to meet his gaze. I'm still in a little bit of a fog, the world slightly hazy after that incredible kiss.

"I meant that I'm not done kissing you."

—————

13

ANDREW

"I meant that I'm not done kissing you." I watch as Josie's already bright pink cheeks flame red, her freckles more pronounced. "So we better hurry up."

Josie nods, already slipping into her shoes. I do the same, then grab both our shoes in one hand, taking her hand in my other. "Let's pay and get outta here."

Five minutes later, the bill is paid, and Sasha keeps avoiding my eyes as though she's embarrassed about what she saw. It's probably a good thing she stopped us before we got carried away. I seem to lose all rational thought when it comes to Josie.

I help Josie into the truck, and when she's buckled, I repeat the steps from earlier. Close her door, then round the hood of the truck to climb into my own seat. Once I'm buckled and pulling onto the street, I reach out, taking her hand again. My thumb rubs patterns across her skin. "Now what?" The sun has set, and the town is bathed in darkness besides the street lights, and the lights from a few businesses that are still open.

Josie, a little breathless, says, "You pick."

"How can I pick when all I want to do is taste you again?"

"I won't stop you." Her words come out breathy and seductive, and I glance over, catching a glimpse of her in the glow of the street lamps.

"Fuck," I curse, my throbbing cock growing even harder.

"Now you're getting it," she says.

"Hold that thought," I state through gritted teeth. Of course, Josie's not listening. She does her best to lean over the center console, and then her lips are at my ear for just a moment.

"I think I want to see your shop," she murmurs, rubbing her hand on my inner thigh. "What do you think?" Before I can react, or try and grab her to keep her close to me, she's back in her seat, squeezing my hand tightly.

Normally, I'm not the guy to have sex on the first date, but something about Josie is sending me into a spiral. Gone is the shy, submissive girl from before. She is totally different than I would have guessed. She's brazen, in control, telling me what she wants. And right now, what she wants is me. Who am I to deny that, when all I want is her?

I do my best to keep my focus on the road, thankful my place is not far. When the yellow house comes into view, I'm thanking all the gods above for small victories. Josie has sat silent next to me the entire five minute drive after her request to see my shop, but I didn't miss every single time she glanced over to me, biting that plump bottom lip.

I swing into the driveway, shifting into park. I fly out, meeting Josie on the other side, helping her out of the truck. I rest my hands on her hips, letting her slide down to the ground. My fingers slide under her shirt accidentally, but I feel the goosebumps that erupt on her skin. When she's on solid ground, I move my hands from her waist to clasp her soft hand. I tug her away from the truck toward my door.

She follows quickly as I lead her through the darkness up the front steps. The house is still dark, but Travis lets out a few barks to let me know that he is, in fact, still here.

The heavy wooden door flings open, revealing Travis waiting by the door, his whole body wiggling in excitement.

"Aww, is this your dog? What's his name?" Josie drops my hand, crouching down to receive lots of slobber filled kisses from Travis. I close the door behind me, and flick on the light.

"Travis," I tell her, taking every ounce of self control I have not to pull her up off the ground. Josie on her knees is doing something to me.

"You named your dog Travis?" she asks, chuckling as she pets him.

"Hey, it's a strong name for a strong dog," I say. "And, you can't tell me it's not the funniest thing having a dog with a very human name."

She shrugs. "I suppose that's true." Josie croons at Travis, and the sucker he is, eats up every ounce of the attention. He starts talking to her. Literally talking to her. Well, in a way that only a golden retriever can.

Josie embraces him, having a full on conversation with my dog while I stand watching, my boner standing strong.

"Andrew, this dog is so cute, I can't stand it. Oh yes you are," she says in a baby voice.

"Yeah, yeah, he's cute," I murmur. I bend down making sure to get really close to her ear as I whisper. "Do you remember that we had plans?"

I feel her entire body shiver as she nods. "Mhmm, plans. Yes. Plans."

"I'd like to see those through. What do you think?"

She nods again, and I slide my hand under her armpit to pull her to her feet. I shoo Travis down the hall to the guest bedroom, closing the door with him behind it, then head back toward Josie. Without another word, our lips crash together again, and I swear, if I died right now, I'd die a happy man. I hold her to me, pulling her over to my couch. I had plans to get to my bed tonight, though I'm not so sure we will make it that far.

My hands tangle in her hair, gripping the strands at the base of her neck, pulling it free from the tie keeping the bun in place. Her shiny red curls tumble out, framing her face.

The backs of my legs hit the couch, and I sink down, taking her with me. Josie straddles my legs, taking total control of every movement. She grinds her warm heat against my hardness, our jeans adding a friction to her movements.

In between kisses, she gasps, "I'm— I'm not looking for a hookup."

I kiss down her neck, answering, "I'm not either."

"This feels different, right?" she asks. She tilts her head back, giving me complete access to her neck. I kiss down her neck and chest, leaving little marks in my wake.

"It's different," I mutter against her skin. "So different."

"Good," she gasps, and her fingers tighten at the nape of my neck. One of my hands stays wrapped around the curve of her waist, the other snaking up to slide her cardigan off her shoulder. She throws it off her body as if it's burning her, and pushes me back so she can take her turn kissing my neck.

"You smell so fucking good," she murmurs. I don't know if she realizes she said it out loud, but either way, I'll take the compliment.

With her cardigan off, I use my free hand to wrap

around her neck gently. I don't squeeze, just guide her head where I want it, and right now, I want her lips on mine, not my neck. She groans with delight at the touch, and starts moving her hips against mine again, grinding down with each rocking motion.

"Are you trying to end this before it has a chance to start?" I grunt, already feeling pressure at the base of my spine.

"No," she breathlessly murmurs. "Just trying to show you the end goal."

"Jesus woman," I groan. I take her hair in my palm, twisting it around my wrist to tilt her head. "Remind me to give you your clip," I say.

Josie laughs, "You and that fucking clip."

"It's my glass slipper," I say, kissing her softly.

"Your what?" Her hips buck as I reach the top of her jeans, tracing the edge with my fingertip.

"My glass slipper. You left it behind, much like Cinderella left behind her glass slipper."

"You were going to use my claw clip to try and find me?" she asks, emotion thick in her voice. "That's so sweet."

"I can't take all the credit, Marley gave me the idea, but essentially, yeah. The clip, or the boutonniere." I nip at her bottom lip, soaking up the soft moan that she gives me in response. My finger toys with the button of her jeans, and she leans back, giving me permission to open them.

Instead of delving further, I slide my hand up and underneath her black shirt, feeling the softness of her stomach, and the warmth there. Josie shivers, her fingers tightening in my hair.

Cupping her full breast, I squeeze gently and slide the cup down, feeling the swell of it. Her nipple hardens under my fingertips, and I give it a little tug. She sighs heavily at the touch, arching her chest further into me. I'm about to ask to take off her top so I can pay attention to her other breast with my mouth when without warning, she slides off my lap and onto her knees. The cup of her bra slides back into place, and I inwardly groan. She darts her fingers to the button of my own jeans, her eyes flicking up to mine, asking me silently.

Unable to wait even a moment longer, I open the button, lifting my ass up slightly to slide my jeans down. I'm left in my gray boxers, my cock straining against the fabric. I swear, I've never been this hard in my life, and Josie, sitting on her knees in front of me is like a vision straight out of heaven.

"Can I?" she tentatively asks, sliding her warm hands up my thighs. I'm nodding before I even have a second to process her words, and then her fingers are up my thighs, gently squeezing my cock through my weathered boxer briefs. I can't help the jolt that surges through my body at her touch, and I can only hope and pray that I don't blow my load too soon.

With the way she's touching me though, I'm not holding out hope. What can I say? It's been a while.

Josie slips her hand under the waistband, and pulls. I lift my hips again so the briefs come down easily. My dick springs free, and Josie nearly pounces on it. Her lithe fingers wrap around the shaft, slowly pumping it up and down. Her hands on me are painfully good, although I realize I'm not touching her, and that in itself is a crime.

"Hold on," I mutter, sitting forward. I reach behind my neck, grasping my shirt and yanking it over my head. Josie's eyes widen as she takes in my naked body. The way she's eye fucking me right now is doing things to my ego, that's for sure. I gesture to her shirt. "Can you take it off?"

Josie nods, eyes still on me, as she reaches down to the hem of her shirt, pulling it up and over, tossing it onto the floor in a heap next to mine. Her tits are practically spilling out of the pale pink bra she has on. I groan at the sight, because holy fuck. Her breasts are so full and I cannot wait to rip off her bra and get my mouth, my hands, *anything* on them.

A vision of me painting my cum all over them makes me groan, lower and longer than I had before, and I lean farther forward to take her mouth again. I try to pull her back up my lap, but she shakes her head against the kiss.

"No, I— Can I do this, please?" she nearly whimpers. I don't think I've ever met a girl so interested in giving head, but... I don't want to complain. I nod, surely looking like a bobble head with the aggression of it. Josie's tongue darts out, licking that lower lip I love so much. She scoots forward, letting me look up and down her gorgeous body.

Any guy that says they don't like curves on their girl is a fucking liar. Because right now, Josie is kneeling in front of me, and there is not a single sharp edge on her body. Every edge is soft, rounded, full, and she's so goddamn beautiful, I can't think of anything but her. Nor do I want to.

She takes my cock in her hands, and gives me an innocent doe-eyed look before she purses her lips, and let's spit roll off her tongue onto the head of my cock. "Fuuuck," I groan, one of my hands running down my face, but only for a second because I cannot miss a moment of this.

Josie licks up the spit, sliding her tongue up my long shaft. Her lips part, taking my cock into her mouth. "Holy-" I grunt, but that's all I get out before Josie is sucking the life out of me. She works her tongue on the underside of my cock, her hand gripping the base, collecting her spit and using it as a lubricant to move it up and down.

My legs quiver with anticipation of her next move, and I really think this woman is my soulmate. Never in my life have I been so close to coming in such a short period of time. Josie takes her time, giving me the best goddamn blow job of my life.

When her little hand reaches down and starts playing with my balls, I'm done. "Josie, you gotta stop," I grit out between clenched teeth, desperately trying to keep my cool.. "I don't wanna co-"

She pops off my cock, licking her lips, and leaning back onto her heels. "You really don't want to come?" She pouts.

"Not yet," I choke. "God, where did you learn to do that?" I wave my hands in front of me before she speaks. "Nope, nevermind, I don't want to know that."

Josie chuckles, reaching her hand out to take my cock again. I bat her hand away. "Woman, unless you want me to come in two point five seconds, you will drop that beautiful, magical hand of yours."

I point an accusatory finger in her direction, and she only laughs. "It's your turn," I say. I pull her to her feet, and then take my place on the ground, kneeling in front of her. When I look up to meet her eyes, a devilish glint appears. "May I, my lady?" I goof, in an elaborate British accent.

"You may," she responds, giggling slightly.

I slide her jeans down her legs, and the creamy paleness of her thighs instantly makes me want to take a bite out of them. Don't ask me why, but for some reason, it's what I want. Her blue cotton undies have a literal wet spot on them, and I can't help but lean forward, and lick her through them. The fabric dampens from my tongue, and I stand up, too eager to wait a moment longer. I slide the panties down, and turn Josie so her back faces the couch.

"Sit," I order.

For just a moment, she appears sheepish, glancing down at my fabric couch.

"It's— I'm gonna get it messy," she whispers, as if it's some sort of secret that I'm about to eat—no, *devour*— her pussy.

"Good, then I'll always be reminded of this moment," I state matter of factly. I gently push her down to sit on the couch, and take my place on my knees, mirroring the position we were in earlier, but opposite.

Her cunt is glistening, wetness covering her folds. "Mmm," I groan. "I think this might be my new favorite meal."

"But you haven't even tasted it yet," Josie cheekily responds, and I don't give her another second to make a snarky remark. I practically dive head first into her soaked pussy, sliding my tongue through, tasting her, savoring every moment of this magic.

"Oh my god," Josie squeals, her hips jerking.

"Hold still, petals," I moan against her, reaching up to rest my palm against her stomach, sliding it to grip her hip, holding her down. She relaxes into the moment, her head lolling back to rest on the back of the couch. My tongue finds her clit, and I get to work on making her feel good. I watch her responses, listening to her body to find what exactly she likes.

"More," she groans.

"You need more?" I taunt. "How about my fingers, you want them?"

"God, yes please," she nearly cries. I slide one finger to her dripping entrance, gathering slickness before I slide in. She sucks in a loud gasp, her mouth opening in a silent cry.

I pump my finger in and out, feeling her tight walls clench around my finger. My tongue gets back to work. I glance up and see one of her hands slide up to play with her tits, taking them out of the bra, pinching and squeezing the nipples, I groan into her cunt, losing my mind watching her.

She's so different than I thought. So secure, she knows exactly what she wants, what she needs, and she isn't afraid to ask. "Andrew, oh god," she groans, her hips grinding into my face.

Her other hand reaches down, tangling my hair between her fingers, holding my head hostage in her delectable pussy. I take that as a cue to add another finger, so I do, curling and pumping two fingers inside her.

"I'm so close," she cries, rocking her body into mine. "Fuck, Andrew!"

I let my tongue do the hard work, not changing my rhythm, and feel her pussy clench tightly around me. *Fuck*, I can't imagine how it would feel to have her do that on my cock.

Her thighs shake, holding my head still between her legs, and I am happy to stay where I am. I carry her through the aftershocks of her orgasm, until she shoves my head away, closing her legs to me. "Holy fuck," she breathes heavily.

"Same, Josie-girl," I state, smirking at her. Her hair is a disheveled mess, but honestly, I'm proud to have been the one to mess it up. I stand, ready to go for another round, but Josie's flying off the couch, taking my cock in her mouth again before I can even say a word.

"Shit—" I curse. Her hand cups my balls again, rolling them in her fingers, while her mouth works me to an impressively fast climax. I barely even have time to register that I'm about to come, to warn her, when I feel my balls tighten. The release is nearly instantaneous.

"Josie," I grunt, holding back the thrusts of my hips. My

hand grips the nape of her neck, watching as she takes every drop of the cum.

When she slides her mouth off my cock this time, a drop of cum and spit slides out the corner, and her tongue darts out to lick it free.

"So, is it time for you to show me your shop?" Josie asks, standing up and grabbing her discarded shirt.

Holy hell, this girl.

14

JOSIE

I have no idea who the hell that girl was just now, but I am not mad about it. I've never been so sexually confident in my entire life. Sure, I haven't slept with a hundred men, but still. I was with Zack for years, and never once did I tell him I needed more during oral.

Andrew makes me confident. I didn't even worry about the stomach rolls, stretch marks or the fact that one of my tits is a cup size bigger than the other. I don't even think he noticed. Zack used to point it out all the time, but Andrew... God, have I really been missing out on good sex for so long? Did I just accept that it would always be sub par for me?

I slide my shirt over my head, finding my underwear discarded on the floor. Putting jeans on is the last thing I want to do right now, but I'm not exactly in a spot to ask him for clothes. I start putting my jeans on, pulling them up and buttoning them, cursing their existence.

"I'll be right back," Andrew says, turning and running down the hall. He's still naked as he was the day he was born, and I chuckle inwardly at his pasty white butt, compared to the rest of him. Thumping footsteps fly down the hall, revealing Travis's golden fur as he barrels toward me. I sit down on the couch, and he nestles himself between my legs, wiggling his butt and trying to be a seventy pound lap dog. I crow at him, giving him all the pets and snuggles, not even caring that I'll be covered in dog hair.

I've wanted to get a dog of my own for a long time, but when you work the random hours I do, between the diner, and potential floral events, I didn't want them to be alone for whole days. So, I've held off.

Andrew bounds down the hall in a pair of loose jogger sweats and a worn *Minnesota Blue Herons* hockey tee. He has a few different items in his hands, and I glance at them in confusion.

"Here." He holds out the items. "I brought you something else to wear. To be honest, jeans sound like the last thing I want to put on, and I figured you felt the same." I take the items from him, finding a pair of black sweats, and a shirt that will probably fit me like a dress.

"Are you sure? I don't want to overstep."

Andrew shakes his head. "Even if I drop you off in twenty minutes, or if you stay, I want you to be comfortable. They're just clothes, you can keep them, or bring them back to me next time."

I try to hold back the giddy laugh that's threatening to escape over the thought of *next time*. Really though, I'm grateful. These jeans are making me want to crawl out of my own skin. I take the clothes, and Andrew shows me to the bathroom. Travis follows close behind, and I swear he pouts as I shut the door with him behind it.

After I change and clean up, trying to fix the rats nest that is my hair, I head out of the bathroom and toward the front door where my shoes sit. I fold my discarded jeans and set them on the ground next to my bag, checking my phone in the process. There's an unanswered text from Marley, and one from my mom, inviting me for brunch in a few weeks.

MARLEY

How was your date? This is me trying not to pry, but also super curious.

ME

It's… good. Still going actually.

MARLEY

Ooooh. Okay, I'll leave you be, but please please call me if you need anything!

ME

Will do! Thanks for setting this up, btw.

MARLEY

No problem! I had a feeling when I met you that you two might be a good fit.

ME

Thanks again!

I tuck my phone into the pocket of the cozy sweatpants, and rub my hand down the front of the shirt Andrew gave me to wear. I can hear Andrew rustling around the kitchen, Travis's paws clicking on the linoleum floor. I follow the noise, and Andrew greets me with a wide smile.

"What's that for?" I ask, unable to stop my own smile. His smiles are contagious.

"I like seeing you in my clothes."

"Ah, so this was all a trick to get me into your clothes?" I cheekily remark. I step over to the counter, nudging him with my hip. He drops a bag of pretzels onto the counter, sliding his arms around my waist to pull me into him.

"Is that such a bad thing?" he murmurs, tilting his head

down to kiss me deeply. With reluctance, he breaks us apart. "We should get out to the shop before I lose myself in you."

I copy his remark. "Is that such a bad thing?"

Andrew squeezes my ass gently before leading me out of the kitchen. He directs me to get my shoes, so I run to the front door, slipping them on before meeting him back at the sliding porch door. He takes my hand in his, and Travis bounds through the open sliding door before we even have a chance to take a step. He runs down the porch stairs, doing a quick lap around the back yard, stopping a few times to pee on various bushes and trees.

Andrew whistles sharply when he disappears from view into the dusk evening. Of course, he races back, circling our legs as we walk down the pebbled pathway to the shop. It's a large building, similar to a barn, but slightly smaller.

The red wood of the barn is faded, the dark grain of the wood peeking through. The trim of the doors and windows are a bright white, standing out against the deep red. A sign hangs above the door, reading "Cunningham Bespoke Woodcraft." The same logo that's on the side of his truck. We reach the heavy door, Andrew pushing it open easily. The instant smell of wood hits me, but it's not a bad smell. No, it smells eerily homey. Fresh.

Andrew flicks on the lights, illuminating the shop which is much larger than it seems from outside. The back wall has a line of gorgeous cherry wood cabinets lining it, with a work bench underneath. Various tools and wood pieces are scattered on it. To my right is a table saw, and another machine that I can't place the name of. It's been a long time since I've been in a wood shop, probably since my middle school industrial tech class. I distinctly remember making an owl shaped key holder. We wood burned our designs into it, and it still hangs proudly in my parents' entryway.

There are large vents and fans as well, presumably to clear out the fumes from lacquer and other finishing products. Another large work table is in the center of the room, pieces of wood clamped together on it for a project. There's a gorgeous bookshelf in the far corner next to a deep brown leather couch that looks comfy as hell, and a well-loved green recliner next to it. Andrew stands beside me, watching my reaction with intensity.

"I love it." I squeeze his hand, and his brown eyes light up. He's so proud of his shop, of his work, anyone can see that.

He pulls me further into the building, pointing out various items he's working on, and their future purposes. He goes into great detail about the dining room table he custom made, having dropped it off only yesterday. Seeing him so passionate about what he does is adorable, and endearing.

We reach the back of the shop, where the couch is, and Andrew pulls me down onto it. I sink into the deep couch, letting myself rest on his side. His arm wraps around me, and I feel his lips press against the top of my hair.

"I'm sure my hair is still a mess." I chuckle.

Andrew smirks, using his hand to try and tame it. "A bit, but knowing I'm the one that made a mess of it is making it that much sexier."

I shove his chest playfully. "You said your grandpa taught you everything you know, right?"

"Yep," Andrew starts. "I was probably five when I started spending full days here with him. Sure, I would hang out with him before, but there's a lot of shit in here for a kid to get into, and they didn't want me to get hurt. From then on, I was here every chance I could."

Travis climbs up onto the couch next to me, snuggling into my side. I mindlessly pet him, and soon enough, he's snoring softly.

Andrew continues, telling me how his brothers and dad never had the interest, or skill in continuing the family business, but he did. His grandma passed shortly after he graduated high school, and his grandpa started teaching him more of the ins and outs of the business, readying him to take over. His dad helps with the financials and logistics of it all, but otherwise, he's in charge. He inherited the house, as well as the shop. He told me about how his grandma passed. Gramps woke up one morning, and thought she was sleeping, but when he checked on her, she was already long gone. They later found out it was an aneurysm that had ruptured.

We talk for hours and hours on end. About his childhood, my childhood, likes, dislikes, you name it. The warm glow of the lamp is cozy, especially after Andrew turned off the overhead light. We've moved positions more than once, but now we're settled.

Andrew lies on his back lengthwise on the couch, while I lay partially atop him, the other half of my body slid between his side and the back of the couch. Travis is at our feet, sleeping soundly.

"We should probably go inside. I can bring you home," Andrew murmurs, his voice gravelly and low.

"Mhmm," I murmur my agreement, but make no effort to move. My head is pressed against his chest, his warmth sinking deep into my body. His heart thumps steadily in my ear, and my eyes drift closed to the feel of his arms around me.

15

JOSIE

A loud throat clearing startles me awake. I fly up into a sitting position, trying to get my bearings. "Wha—" I mumble, rubbing my hands over my eyes. Below me, Andrew jolts, sitting up, wrapping his arms around me protectively.

He groans as his eyes adjust. He pulls me closer into him, and my eyes flutter open to see an older gentleman standing in front of us. His white-gray hair is combed over to the side, and if I knew it wasn't a Sunday, I would have assumed he just came from church.

He's wearing a pair of black slacks, paired with a button up striped long sleeve. His arms are crossed on his chest, and he has a look of disappointment, and also, *satisfaction* on his face.

"I'm going to give this one guess," he says. His voice is low, gravely, and filled with mirth. "Cinderella?"

"Gramps, it is too early for this. What time is it anyway?" Andrew asks before I have a chance to react.

It makes perfect sense that this is his Grandpa, but I can't believe that he knows about me. I mean, we had our first date yesterday. Has he really been talking about me since the wedding?

"It's seven-thirty," Gramps answers. "You're usually up and at 'em at six, but I can see you had a distraction."

Andrew rubs his palm up and down his face. "Mhmm. Gramps, this is Josie, Josie, this is my grandpa, or Gramps, Earl Cunningham."

I rise from my spot on Andrew's lap. I offer him my right hand, and he shakes it, his hands rough and calloused, much like Andrew's. "Nice to meet you, Earl," I say, trying to hide the tremor in my voice. I'm not scared of him, no, I'm just utterly and completely embarrassed. I am, however, feeling very grateful that I'm wearing clothes. They're obviously Andrew's, but still. Better than my birthday suit.

"Likewise, Cindy," he says on a laugh, shaking my hand firmly.

Andrew stands, shifting himself to stand behind me, wrapping his arms around the curve of my waist. My cheeks heat at the easy show of affection in front of his family, but also, I feel pride in knowing he's not afraid to show it.

They talk for a few minutes while Travis sits at our feet, patiently waiting, his fluffy golden tail sliding across the floor while it wags.

"I'll leave you to it," Earl says, stepping back. "I just thought I'd stop by on my way to group this morning, see how that date went, but as I can see, it went very well."

My cheeks heat, and I worry that he thinks I'm some sort of hussy, but Earl catches my eye, giving me a sly wink. It eases my worries for the time being.

"Toodaloo, Cindy," Earl teases as he leaves the shop. Andrew holds me for another moment, listening to a car start in the driveway and pull away.

"That's one way to start the morning." Andrew laughs.

"Sorry about that. He comes and goes as he pleases, and usually it isn't a problem. I should have remembered that he always stops by on Monday mornings, though." Andrew hesitates, clearing his throat before continuing. "He goes to a grief group at the library on Monday mornings. He'll never admit it, but it's helped him a lot since we lost Grandma."

I turn in his arms, wrapping my arms around his waist. "It's gotta be hard. I can't imagine losing the love of your life, so unexpectedly."

Andrew nods, hugging me to him, his head in the crook of my neck.

"He had a really tough go for a while, but he's gotten much better." Andrew pulls back from our hug, looking at the clock on the wall behind me. "Shoot, do you need to be at work this morning?"

I shake my head. "No, I work at noon, a short shift today, so I have time."

"Wanna get breakfast?" he asks, voice hopeful.

"Yes please, but can we stop by my house first, so I can change?"

"What, you don't want to be seen in public wearing my clothes?"

I scoff. "Unfortunately, I have to say no. For now at least."

"So there's a chance?"

I shake my head. "Sure," I answer with an easy laugh.

CLANGING noises sound from the kitchen, music blaring, amidst loud voices talking back and forth. Andrew chose to drive us a town over for breakfast, claiming this diner has the best biscuits and sausage gravy. I'm not complaining though. The twenty minute drive just means I get to spend more time with him.

"Hey, kiddos," an older gal greets us at the hostess stand. She eyes our interlocked hands, a small smirk toying on her lips. "Just two?"

"Yep." Andrew squeezes my hand as he speaks.

The waitress, who's name tag reads Louise, directs us down the aisles of booths to the far corner, giving us some semblance of privacy. She motions for us to sit, then offers us two menus. "Coffee? Water? Bloody Mary?" she asks, whipping out her little writing pad.

"Coffee and water, please," I say, giving her a soft smile.

"Water, and a small apple juice, please," Andrew states.

Louise doesn't write down our order, simply turns and heads to the POS system at one end of the counter.

For a Monday morning, this place is hopping. Nearly every seat at the counter is filled, and every booth. The few scattered tables are all full too.

"This is a pretty busy place," I muse.

Andrew looks up from his menu. "Oh yeah, breakfast is their big meal. Come here at four o'clock and you won't see more than five people. The food is still great, but breakfast is their primary crowd."

I turn my attention back to the menu, scanning, looking at the abundance of options. Of course, I'll probably end up getting the biscuits and sausage gravy like Andrew suggested, but I still want to browse, see if there is anything else that might catch my eye.

We don't speak as we look, but it's thankfully not an awkward silence, the kind where you're avoiding conversation. I don't think I've experienced that with Andrew yet.

Louise drops down our drinks on the table, as well as a cup of individual creamers for me. "Ready to order?" she asks, a forced smile on her face. Her voice is gruff, and slightly impatient, but I don't think it has anything to do with us. Just the way her voice is, and her job.

"Yes," Andrew and I say at the same time.

We take our turns ordering, both of us getting the biscuits and sausage gravy and hash browns. Once Louise is away, I open a single creamer, and pour it into the black coffee, then add a sugar packet, stirring it with the spoon I unwrapped from the napkin.

"Not a coffee drinker?" I offer, starting up the conversation.

Andrew shakes his head. "Nah, I don't have much of a need for it. I have enough energy as it is. If I had any more, I would probably never sit down. You?"

I nod. "To be honest, I don't drink it often, but when I'm out for breakfast like this, I love to have something warm to drink. It's a weird comfort thing."

"Fair," Andrew chuckles. "My mom drinks a minimum of a pot a day. Though ,I'm pretty sure she drinks decaf. Can't imagine how she would be alive with all that caffeine in her system." I laugh along with him. "It's probably just a habit after all these years, though."

I nod. "My mom always says that too. Most of her coffee drinking is purely habitual."

Andrew takes a sip of his water, glancing around the diner. When he sets down the water, he dries the condensation off of his palm with the paper napkin, then offers his hand to me, laying it face up on the table. I rest my palm in his, and our hands naturally intertwine.

"Is it too soon to ask when I can see you again?" he asks. His voice is low, but hopeful. Brown eyes lift up to meet mine, those gold flecks making their appearance again as the sun drifts through the window onto our table.

A loose curl is hanging over his forehead, and my free hand itches to run my fingers through it, pushing it back off his face. "Not at all," I answer.

A boyish grin pops onto his face as his eyes gleam at my response. "Thank god," he says. "What does your schedule look like?"

I pull out my phone from my pocket, opening the calendar. I have a few floral arrangements to make this week, and I don't want to stretch myself too thin, between work, and floral stuff. I swipe open the screen, ignoring the notifications on the screen.

"Let's see," I murmur, swiping through my week. "Today I work till five thirty at the diner, and tomorrow I have two floral deliveries. So I'll start working on those tonight." I continue making my way through the week, rattling off my schedule, until I look at Friday through Sunday. "I'm off all weekend, including Friday."

Andrew thoughtfully nods, thinking to himself.

I interject, my heart pounding in my chest. insecurities rising. "Sorry, I'm not usually this busy, I just have been trying to take on more," I stammer.

"Hey," Andrew softly says, squeezing my hand. "It's good that you're busy. You're starting your own business. I expected that. I was only thinking through my week, and if I have anything going on this weekend."

I nod, my pounding heart starting to slow. Of course, Louise pops in at the perfect moment, dropping our plates in front of us.

The steaming food smells so good I want to inhale all of it in one bite. Andrew reluctantly frees my hand, and we both grab our forks to dig in. "What do you think about

Friday night?" Andrew questions. "I could pick you up after I'm finished at the shop."

I nod, shoveling the first bite of biscuit smothered in gravy into my open mouth. At the first explosion of flavor, I don't bother holding back the moan that I repressed before.

Andrew's eyes widen, his jaw dropping. I cut the moan off immediately, panicking that others might have heard it.

"Oh my god, I'm so embarrassed," I say, cringing. I drop my fork, pick up my napkin and wipe my mouth with it as I look around, desperately searching for anyone that may have heard it. When my gaze returns to Andrew, he still has that shell-shocked look on his face.

"Holy shit," Andrew says through gritted teeth, his jaw clenching tight. "That was the sexiest thing I think I've ever heard. I have half a hard on right now."

"Oh shut up," I laugh. "You're ridiculous."

"I'm serious," he groans, tilting his head back to hit the wall behind him. "You eating biscuits and gravy is my new fantasy." He runs both his hands through his hair, then down his face, before he sits straight.

He shakes his arms out. "Alright, I think I'm good now. No more moaning, or I can't be held accountable for my actions."

I laugh, taking another bite of the delectable breakfast. I nearly moan again, this time to purposefully tease him, but hold back.

"So, Friday?" I ask in between bites.

Andrew finishes chewing, nodding aggressively. "Yes, please."

"You're eager," I state, fully aware that I'm dying on the inside of having to wait until Friday to see him again. It hasn't even been a full twenty four hours since we met for the second time, and already, I'm attached to him. *Good lord, I'm in for a ride.*

"Sure am," Andrew agrees.

We finish our breakfast, talking in between bites. He pays the bill, even though I try to pay, reminding him that he paid for bowling last night. He insists, giving Louise a generous tip before leading me out of the still crowded restaurant.

On the drive home, I admire him again. I'm sure he can see me staring, but he doesn't say a word. He talks the whole time, telling me more stories about his childhood, and brothers. I listen, focused on learning about him, while I take in his facial features. The gentle slope of his nose, the small scar above his right eyebrow, the way he has a bit of stubble growing after not shaving this morning.

A warmth bubbles in my belly, and I don't try to stop it. How is it even possible to be this attracted to someone? To feel this connected to him after less than twenty four hours?

We pull into my driveway, and the warmth fizzles into a freezing block of ice. I don't want to say goodbye, but I need to.

I reluctantly climb out of the car, and Andrew does the same, walking me to the garage door.

"I'll see you Friday, okay," he states, rather than asking.

I nod, taking him into a hug. My chin rests on his chest, and I gaze up into his eyes. "We can make it four days," I say, more for myself.

"Right." He sounds utterly unconvinced.

Andrew tilts his head down to my lips, kissing me soft and slow. With each second that passes, the kiss grows more desperate, and I ache for more. I crave more. I want to feel him inside me, his lips all over my body again, but I tell myself that I need to stop. I can wait. Friday is only four days from now. I can make it.

16

ANDREW

I'm pretty sure this has been the longest week of my entire existence. Sure, Josie and I texted pretty much non-stop, talked on the phone every night, and I had my work to keep me busy, but it's like there has been this literal hole in my life now that I know she's out there.

An old country song plays on the stereo in the corner while I work in the shop. Travis is curled up in his bed in the corner, chewing on a bone. I'm sanding down my current project when the door flings open aggressively, two of my three brother's striding in. Thomas is in full uniform, his Ivy Ridge badge over his left collarbone. His gun is holstered on his right hip, and his German Shepherd K9, Arson, darts through the shop, tackling Travis. They wrestle, growling and chomping at each other as they play.

Beau follows behind Thomas, hands shoved into the pockets of his dress pants. In his light blue dress shirt, he looks the part of a small town realtor.

"Hey," I call, straightening my back, and dropping the sander to the counter beside me. "What are you guys doing here? Don't you have jobs?" I tease, gesturing to their clothes.

Beau chuckles, running a hand through his long chestnut brown hair. He has the same curls that I do, only he chooses to keep it long, long enough to hit his shoulders. He frequently puts it in a bun, or styles it so it looks professional. His shirt covers the majority of his tattoos, though you can see a few of the designs peeking from the sleeve at his wrist.

Thomas is the one that speaks up. His thumbs are hooked on his bulletproof vest in the middle of his chest, our last name stitched into the fabric. "Nah, we both had some free time, and I caught Beau speeding, so I told him I wouldn't give him a ticket if he came with me to berate you." Thomas has always had a bit of a wild side.

"Dude, I was not speeding," Beau grunts, shoving his shoulder into Thomas. "Maybe I should report you to the chief for pulling over unsuspecting citizens for no reason."

"I had reason," Thomas states. "I wanted you to come with me to Andrew's."

"Whatever," Beau grumbles. He's been in a mood lately, and it makes me wonder if he's finally feeling the effects of fifteen plus years of blue balls, thanks to the one and only Marley Bell. "So, what can you tell us about your new girl?"

Wiping my palms down the front of my work shirt, I ignore them for a moment, side stepping the wrestling dogs to take a pull of ice water from the stainless steel bottle I have on the opposite side of the counter.

"I don't know that there's much to tell yet," I say. I can already tell my poker face isn't strong, because Beau scoffs.

"Yeah, right."

"Seriously, man. I don't need to know everything, just some minor details, y'know?" Thomas inserts.

Lifting up the bottom of my shirt to wipe some of the dirt and sweat from my brow, I give in. "Fine, she's gorgeous. Red hair, blue-gray eyes, sweet as can be. She moved here from Brooks Hill, lives about five minutes away from me. She's a florist, while also working at the other diner in town. She has an older sister who lives in Missouri with her husband, and her parents still live up in Brooks Hill. Happy?"

Thomas smiles, the little gap between his teeth making an appearance. "Very pleased, thank you. When do we get to meet her?" he asks.

"When I feel like it," I curtly respond. "It's still new, you guys."

"Tell me why you look like you're about ready to propose then?" Thomas asks. He stalks over to the couch, pulling the dogs apart. Flopping down onto it, he throws his arms behind his head.

"I'm not ready to propose," I scoff.

"You know, Tommy might have a point," Beau ponders. He follows Thomas, sitting on the opposite side of the couch. "In the time that I've known you, which has been your entire life, I can't say I've ever seen you like this over a girl. If I didn't know any better, I'd say you're already planning your life together."

I don't say a word, because to be honest, he has a point. I'm not trying to propose anytime soon, but something feels different about this. I've never yearned to spend so much time with a person before. It feels right.

"Ooooh, Beau, I think you got him." Thomas chuckles. "Seriously, dude. You like her?"

I nod. "Yeah. We only went out once, and it was incredible. She spent the night."

Thomas tries to hide it, but his jaw drops. "You slept with her on the first date? You never do that."

"Not that it's any of your business, but we didn't sleep together. We did other things, but we didn't have sex. We fell asleep on the couch talking."

"Haha, I was waiting for you to confess," Thomas says, holding out a hand to Beau. "Pay up, sucker."

"Wait," I say, waving my hands in front of me. "What do you mean, confess?"

"Gramps and I went out for lunch yesterday, and he told me all about how he found you two out here that morning, and she was in your clothes," Thomas explains. "Of course, I had to tell everyone. Beau and I made a bet at how long it would take for you to tell us. I told him I could get it out of you today, but he didn't think so."

Beau slaps a twenty dollar bill into Thomas's waiting palm. "Thank you," Thomas practically sings. He stands from the couch, coming over to my side to slap me on the shoulder appreciatively. "For what it's worth, I am being serious when I say I can tell you like this girl. You seem different."

I nod, not really sure what else I can say to him. "Thanks."

His radio buzzes on his chest, a voice talking fast through the static. I have no idea how he can understand a word the dispatcher says, it all sounds like a garbled mess to me.

"Shit," he curses, clicking his tongue to get Arson's attention. "We've been working on this case for weeks now, and we might have the guy cornered. I gotta run. Arson, let's go." He whistles sharply for his dog. Arson darts to his side, running with Thomas out the shop door. His cruiser starts up immediately, and a moment later, sirens blare as he takes off toward the call.

I bite my tongue, withholding the words I want to say. None of us particularly like that Thomas is a police officer, and it's purely selfish reasons. Thomas has always been the one to dive head first into the action, even as a kid. He'd fight the bullies for the other kids in his class, always protecting the people he cares about.

We spend a lot of time worrying about him, because you never know if one day he might get injured, or worse. While I'm glad he isn't working in the Twin Cities, there is still crime and dangerous people here in our small town. Thomas has told me some of the shitty things he sees, and none of us want to tell him how much it scares us. He's doing what he loves, and that is making sure we all live in a safer place.

"I hate when that happens," Beau says, standing up as well. He strides over, standing next to me, where we both lean up against the countertop.

"You and me both," I murmur, giving my pounding heart a moment to relax. Thomas is a smart man. He knows how to keep himself safe.

"What are you up to tonight?" Beau asks, thankfully changing the subject. "I think Marley and I are going to Blue Ox, wanna come?"

I shake my head. "Nope. I'm taking Josie out."

Beau nods. "Ah. Well, the offer is there. I'm sure we'll be there for a while. Sounds like there's a band tonight, and you know how much Marley loves the bands. I think Jason wants her to get some pictures for his social media too."

"Lennie staying at Mom and Dad's?" I ask.

"Probably." Beau shrugs. "I think she usually does when there's a band, or event he needs to be there for."

"True," I say. "Maybe next time Josie and I will come say hi."

"Sounds good."

"Wanna talk about it?"

"Talk about what?" Beau asks, doing his best to hide his annoyance with me.

"You've been pouting since you walked through the door, and I don't think it has anything to do with losing the bet with Thomas," I say pointedly. I shove him in the shoulder.

"I have not been pouting."

"Sure," I drawl. "What did Marley do now? Did she get a new tattoo that makes her even hotter?"

Beau growls, turning on me immediately, pressing his hand to my chest. "You don't get to talk about her like that."

Time to poke the bear.

"Why not? It's not like she's your girlfriend."

"Andrew, I swear to god," he murmurs, dropping his hand from my chest to run it through his hair.

He looks like he's in physical pain, so I lighten up on him a bit. "Seriously, what's wrong, Beau?"

"Nothing," he says.

"You can ask her out, you know. What's the worst thing that could happen? I mean, it's Marley. She's your person."

"Yeah, she's my best friend. How many times do I have to tell you she's *just* my best friend. Nothing can ever happen between us. I can't lose her, Andrew." His eyes are pained, brows pinched together.

"You wouldn't lose her," I state. "But I'll drop it. If Josie wants to go to the brewery tonight, I'll text you, but I think we might just spend some one on one time together."

"Yeah, that's fair," Beau says, the earlier darkness fleeing. "Have fun tonight." He turns, heading for the door.

"Hey," I call. "I'm sorry."

"Nothing to be sorry about," he says, giving me a gentle wave as he leaves.

I feel bad for taunting him, but he and Marley need to get their shit together. Anyone that doesn't know them already thinks they are a couple.

I get back to work after a few minutes, working on the project that I can't wait to complete. I have a feeling it's going to be my favorite one yet.

JOSIE TEXTED me about fifteen minutes ago, letting me know she was home from the shift she picked up at the diner, and that I could come over whenever. I, of course, promptly stopped what I was doing, and ran inside to shower. I showered, shaved, and now I'm in the truck on the way to her place.

I pull into her driveway, spotting her cat, Velma, in the front window again. I climb out of the truck, shutting the door and shoving my hands into my pockets. The rickety garage door is shut, and I stride up to it, remembering what she said last week, that her front door doesn't work well. I can hear music playing from inside the garage, and the song sounds vaguely familiar. I knock a few times, but I don't think she will hear me, with how loud the music is. After a long moment with no response, I open the door slowly, giving her a moment to hopefully see the movement. Through the crack in the door, I spot her at her small workstation, swaying her sexy hips to the beat.

With the door open fully, I step through, shutting it

behind me. "Josie," I call, trying to get her attention without frightening her too badly.

She spins around, a hand dropping to her stomach. "Jeez, Andrew, you scared me!"

"Sorry." I cringe. Striding over to her, I bend my knees slightly to wrap my arms around her waist. "I didn't mean to scare you. I knocked a few times, but I think your music was a bit too loud."

Josie chuckles, leaning into my chest. "My bad. I can't help but listen to this song at full blast."

Unwrapping my arm from her waist, I use my free hand to tilt her head up, brushing a soft kiss to her lips. "Hmm," I moan. "What song?"

"Uh," she breathes, her eyelids fluttering as she tries to process her thoughts. She shakes her head slightly, opening her eyes to reveal her slightly glossed-over eyes. I feel a weird sense of pride, knowing I can affect her so much with such a small action. "It was *Animal*, by Noah Kahan."

"I knew I recognized it." I gently kiss her again. "He's great."

"I agree," she mumbles.

"I missed you this week." I don't care if I sound like a love struck teen when I tell her that. I *am* a love struck teen when it comes to her.

"We talked everyday, Andrew," she jokes. "But I missed you, too."

"I have something fun planned for us tonight." I squeeze her. She looks up at me, eyes wide.

"What might it be?" she questions.

I shrug playfully. "Guess you'll have to wait and see. Are you ready?" I glance down, noticing her outfit. In a cute pastel pink cardigan, tucked into a tan corduroy skirt, with sheer black tights and black boots on, she looks so fucking cute.

"Yeah, I'm ready."

"Well, don't you look adorable," I say. I take a step back to get a better look at her. Motioning my finger for her to give me a twirl, I watch as her face heats, and she smiles.

"Really, you want me to spin?" she giggles. "It's not all that great of an outfit, Andrew."

"I strongly disagree," I state, twirling my finger again. This time, she takes heed of my wordless instruction, spinning slowly for me to get a good look at her. Her red hair is straight tonight, hanging down to the middle of her back, and she has on minimal makeup, only using it to accentuate her already beautiful features. "Mhmm," I mutter. "God, you're perfect, petals."

Unable to keep my hands off her, I close the small distance between us, tugging her close to me again by her hips. She gazes up at me, her face flushed.

"You really like my outfit?" she asks, sounding unconvinced.

"I really, *really*, do." Showing her just how much, I cup her chin, kissing her. She tastes like a sweet cherry cocktail, and it is the perfect compliment to Josie herself.

"Alright, let's get outta here before we never do," I say when we break apart. I shift my hips backward to try and hide my growing dick, but I'm pretty positive she already knows, as there's a glint in her eye, and her brow raises.

"Let me grab my bag." She darts into the house, leaving me in her garage alone. I'm quite thankful for the moment alone, as it gives me a chance to get the blood from running any further south.

17

———

JOSIE

When I asked Andrew what I should wear or expect tonight, he didn't really give me much to go off. He simply told me to wear something I'm comfortable in. Nothing too fancy though. I figured I would meet in the middle, and wear something comfortable, that was also sort of nice. I got this skirt a few weeks ago online, and I've been itching to wear it. Tonight is the perfect time.

The look on Andrew's face when he saw what I was wearing was adorable. I know this is only our second date, but watching his reactions to me makes me feel more worthy, more beautiful, than I have in years. Zack never treated me horribly, but he also didn't make me feel beautiful.

Sitting in Andrew's work truck, I'm enjoying the feeling of his hand entwining with mine, thumb rubbing circles over my skin. I've tried to stop the goosebumps that have formed on my flesh multiple times with no luck. Every touch, kiss, and moment with him has my body feeling like I'm floating, not a care in the world, only wondering when I can get his hands on me again.

"Do I get a hint about where we're going?" I ask. His brown hair is styled tonight, the curls a bit more tame than I'd like them, to be totally honest. I like his rugged, disheveled curls. He's in a navy button up shirt, with a pair of nice pants, and shiny black shoes. Compared to him, I feel slightly underdressed, but when I mentioned it to him, he shrugged me off, saying, "Pretty sure no one is going to be looking at me when you're at my side."

I couldn't help but smile at that. He sure knows how to make me feel good.

"No hints, no clues," Andrew says, smiling at me. The golden hue of the sun setting behind us makes him look like a Disney Prince.

"Fine," I grumble, inserting a little whine into my tone, trying to get some sort of information from him.

Moments later, my question is semi-answered, when we pull into the parking lot of the craft store. The sign above the door reads *The Paper Kite*. There are a few cars around, and a sign on the door says, *"Paint 'N Sip, Every Friday at 6."*

My eyes widen, and a giddy excitement crashes over me. Is this really what we are doing? I can't believe a guy would willingly go to a Paint 'N Sip, let alone plan one as a date night. Then again, Andrew has proved me wrong more than once now.

Andrew shifts into park, letting go of my hand to do so. "So, how do you feel about painting?"

A silly laugh bursts out of me, and I look over at him, smiling. "Really? We're going to Paint 'N Sip?"

Andrew nods. "If you want to, yeah. My mom told me about it a few weeks ago, and I remembered it this after-noon. Thought it would be fun to try. Apparently the theme tonight is floral arrangements. I thought it was pretty fitting."

"Oh my god, yes I want to go," I squeal. Andrew gives me a toothy grin, clearly happy with my reaction.

He climbs out of the truck while I sit in my seat, still shocked at how good of a date idea this is. Before I can get out, he's at the door, opening it for me, and offering his hand to guide me down. He doesn't let go of my hand as he leads me to the glass door. I stop when I notice a *For Rent* sign in the window of a storefront a few businesses down.

"Everything okay?" Andrew asks, looking at me to see where my gaze has strayed to.

"Hm?" I ask, my attention back on him "Oh, yeah. I saw a for rent sign a few doors down, so I was looking at it, that's all."

Andrew glances at the store front. "My brother, Beau, is a realtor. I can text him if you want to do a showing? We could probably see it tonight if you wanted."

"What? No, no," I stumble over my words in my haste. "No, I was just dreaming. Really."

"Okay, well the option is there. He's probably got all the contacts you would need in a market this small."

"I'll keep it in mind, really. I'm not in the market to rent or buy right now."

"That's fair."

I turn my eyes away from the store front, back to the cute craft store in front of me. "Let's go in, I want to see what we're painting tonight."

Andrew opens the door for me, and chattering voices fill the room. We follow the voices down the aisle to where there is an open area with long tables set up, tiny easels with small canvases on each table.

There's a small group of women at the front of the

room, passing around glasses of wine. They turn when they hear us arrive, their eyes widening when they see us. My face flushes, and I glance down at my outfit, looking for stains, or a boob that has fallen out or something, based on their reaction.

One of the women even clutches a hand to her heart, gasping, "Andrew Cunningham, never in my life would I expect to see you here."

Andrew chuckles, shaking his head as he replies, "You make me sound like a hermit, Norma."

"You may as well be," she states. She waves her arms in front of her dramatically. "Never mind, never mind. Tell me who this beautiful girl is." Norma strides down the aisle of tables and chairs to stand in front of us. My hand grows clammy in Andrew's palm, and I subtly try to pull away. He gives my hand a reassuring squeeze.

"This is Josie, my date. Josie, this is Norma, my great-aunt."

Norma's smile widens, and the other women in the back all "aww". I offer my right hand to Norma, and she takes it, shaking my hand softly. Her hands are wrinkled and soft, and her strong floral perfume itches my nostrils so badly I have the urge to hold back a sneeze. All in all though, she reminds me of my own grandmother who passed away when I was a senior in high school. Her white gray hair is short, and curled in fluffy waves around her head. Her blouse is a cream color, with a matching cardigan over top. She has on a pair of brown slacks, with a set of pearls hanging around her neck. If I didn't know any better, I'd say she was dressed to go to a Sunday church service, rather than a Paint 'N Sip at the local craft store.

"Nice to meet you," I offer when she drops my hand.

"You too, dear. Are you new in town? I don't think I've met you before."

I nod. "Yeah, I moved here about half a year ago from Brooks Hill."

"Oh, yes, one of my granddaughters moved there after college, with her late fiancé. Such a cute town."

"It really is."

"What brought you here?" she asks.

"I was ready for something new. I started my own floral company, and I wanted somewhere that I could start from scratch," I answer, leaning into Andrew's arm. He squeezes my hand again.

"Oh, you're the new florist?" Her voice rises an octave, and she waves her friends over. "Gals, this is the new florist, she did the flowers that Ken got me for our anniversary last week. Oh honey, those flowers were just gorgeous, and they lasted so long!"

I do my best to show her how grateful I am. "Thank you so much, I'm so glad you loved them. I love hearing back from people, so thank you for the kind words." My chest warms at her remarks. I haven't gotten too much feedback yet from customers, good or bad, so to have her tell me this has me practically giddy.

"Say, since you're here, can I put in an order?" One of the other older ladies asks. "My granddaughter graduates high school soon, and I'd love to get her a bouquet."

"Absolutely," I say, an overwhelming excitement bubbling up. "I can give you my card. Call me later and we can discuss what I have available, or can order in." I reach into my bag, pulling out a few business cards that I have on me. They all take one, staring down at them in excitement.

"Yes, perfect!" She practically sings. "This is so wonderful. Our town hasn't had a florist since Doris retired."

Andrew chuckles. "While I love the enthusiasm for my girl, ladies, I'm going to steal her away now. I believe we are about to do some painting." He points to the front of the room where a woman who appears to be in her forties stands, a wide smile on her face. Andrew leads me over to a table in the third row, with only two seats at it, and two canvases, blank, and ready for paint.

Meanwhile, my mind is still stuck on the fact that he called me his girl. Is that what I am? I mean, I wouldn't be opposed to it, but isn't it a little soon to be making things official? I don't have time to question him though, as the woman in front begins to speak.

"Hello, everyone," she begins. "Looks like we have a lot of our regulars here this evening," she nods to the group of women with Norma, "and some newcomers." She waves at Andrew and me. "Welcome to Paint 'N Sip. My name is Lucy, and I'm the owner of The Paper Kite. We have a few more coming, but I figured we could start with some of the basics. First, I want everyone to know that just because there is alcohol here, it does not mean you have to drink it. We have non-alcoholic options available to you, as well as some snacks, over on the opposite wall." She points in the direction of the table filled with various food items.

"Next up, tonight's theme is florals. I have the example canvas up front." She points to the displayed canvas, which has a simple design on it. Two daisies, one pink, one red, with a gradient background. I've never been an artist, but I'm looking forward to having some fun with tonight's activity. Lucy finishes her introductory information, giving everyone a few minutes to grab some snacks, and a drink of their choosing.

Andrew squeezes my thigh gently. "I can go get us some drinks, what would you like?"

"Hmm," I ponder for a long moment. "I'm not huge on wine. Surprise me?"

"You got it, petals." He rises, heading off to the table of food and drinks. While he's gone, I let my gaze explore the store. Behind me, there are rows and rows of yarn in varying shades and types. In another aisle, there are canvases of all sizes, along with any other supplies you might need for painting or sketching. My attention is drawn to the main entrance at the sound of a bell chiming.

A woman dressed in a pair of black dress pants that hit the middle of her ankle, a burgundy top, and a black blazer enters the store. Her platinum blonde hair is slicked back into a ponytail, with not a hair out of place. She is the definition of professionalism and class. My eyes stray downward when I see a little girl clasping at her leg. She appears to be about five or six, and her long brown hair is in two braids on either shoulder.

She tugs on the hem of her mom's blazer, and she bends down to let her daughter whisper into her ear. She smiles, eyes glittering as she looks across the room. Straightening, she waves to whomever she was smiling at, and the child tucks her face into her mother's side.

I'm surprised when I turn my gaze, to find that it's Andrew she's waving at. Andrew strides over to our table, setting down a plate of snacks, and two cans. "Josie, come with me?" he asks. I like that he always gives me an option, never telling me what I should do. I nod, a little confused, and honestly? I'm a little jealous that this gorgeous woman is waving at him. I know I shouldn't, and have no reason to, but he's such a catch that I can't help it.

I stand from the wooden chair, fixing my skirt so I don't flash anyone, and take the hand Andrew is offering.

"Hey, Fallon," he says when we get closer. He leans over slightly, waving gently to the little girl. "Hey, Presley."

"Hi, Andrew," she murmurs, her voice sweet and soft.

"Are you going to paint with your mom tonight?" Andrew asks her. At the mention of the activity, she lights up, nodding aggressively. She smiles widely at Andrew, revealing her two front teeth to be gone.

"Yes, and I'm going to paint the prettiest flower, and then I can show it to my grandma when she comes to visit me this weekend," she says, her voice growing louder with each word.

"Holy buckets, that's going to be so fun!" Andrew cheers. He offers his hand for a high- five, and Presley smacks her palm to his in an impressive high-five. Andrew dramatically shakes out his hand, wincing in pain. "Ouch, kiddo, you've got a strong arm."

Presley's smile widens, and she looks up to her mom. "Mom, he said I'm strong, did you hear?"

Her mom rubs the top of her head. "I sure did, honey."

"How have you been, Andrew?" the woman asks. She gives me a graceful smile, and some of my jealousy melts away.

"Things have been good," he says. He lets go of my hand for a moment, wrapping his arm around my shoulder. "Fallon, this is Josie, my date."

"Nice to meet you," I say, offering her my hand. She takes it, giving my hand a gentle squeeze. Her eyes are the most beautiful shade of green, and a glance down at Presley reveals that she has the same eyes.

"Likewise," Fallon says. She drops my hand, then uses a pointer finger to tap on her chin. "I feel like I've seen you before. I recognize you."

Andrew interjects. "Oh, you have." I look up at him,

noting that he only has eyes for me right now. "She was the florist for Megan and Isaac's wedding."

"Oh my god, that's it!' Fallon proclaims. "God, you have such incredible talent. Presley kept the bouquet that you made her, and a few of the rose petals that she tossed down the aisle."

I turn my attention to Presley, who is now looking at me like I hung the moon. "I'm so glad you liked your flowers, Presley! Maybe someday I can make you another bouquet."

Presley aggressively nods, her toothless smile widening with each movement. "Yes, please!" she practically squeals.

"You got it," I say. I lift my eyes back to Fallon. "Now that Andrew mentions it, I totally recognize you, too. You looked stunning at the wedding."

"Thank you," Fallon says with a grateful smile. "It really was an incredible day."

She's about to say something more, but Lucy calls the group to attention. We wave goodbye, and Andrew leads me back to our table. Presley and Fallon sit closer to the front, in the row behind Norma and one of her friends.

Lucy gives the few newcomers a moment to get their things together. Andrew scoots his chair closer to me, pulling the small plate with him. "I got us a bunch of random snacks, and then, I got some drinks to try too." He hands me one of the cans, labeled Dry Pear Cider. At first glance, it isn't something I would pick for myself, but I'm willing to try it because it does sound like it could be good. I'm not familiar with the brand though. Blue Ox Brewery. Inspecting the label closer, I see that the company is local to Ivy Ridge.

"Oh, that's cool, it's a local place." I crack open the can, and take a sip. It's totally different than what I thought, the dryness of the cider also joined with the subtle sweetness of the pear flavor. "Wow, this is really good," I say, taking another drink. "Have you ever been to this brewery?" I ask. I hold out the can, offering him a sip.

Andrew's eyes light up with a hint of humor, but I can't quite place why. A curl falls over his forehead, and without thinking, I automatically push it away from his eyes. Andrew chuckles, taking my hand from his face, pressing a kiss to my fingertips before giving me my hand back. "Yeah, I guess you could say I've been there a few times."

"Maybe we can go sometime," I offer. "There are so many places I still need to try here."

"You bet," he murmurs, leaning over to kiss my temple. I take another sip of the cider, and Lucy starts the class.

18

ANDREW

"You know, I really don't understand how mine turned out so bad," I state. Our paintings are sitting in the backseat of my truck as I drive us toward her place. Hers is a beautifully painted replica of the example, only she went all out, changing the colors of her flowers, even going as far as adding more into the background. Mine, however, is the definition of color theory gone wrong. I tried to mix a few colors to make something fun and bright, but it only turned into a deep green that was oddly reminiscent of the color of Shrek's skin. "I followed every single step, by the book."

Josie's currently looking out the passenger window, desperately trying not to laugh. She curls her hand into a fist, resting it on her pursed lips. After a long moment, she speaks, and I can tell she's trying her best not to cackle as she does. "I think your painting is great, honey. You need practice, that's all."

Ignoring the flutter in my chest at her calling me "honey", I continue. "You're saying that because you like me. It's horrible. You can say it." At a stop sign, I reach over, hooking my thumb under her chin so she's looking at me. "Say it."

Josie purses her lips again. I start driving, only moments away from her house now. "I do like you, a lot. And I also think that your painting is fine," she whispers. Her eyes begin to water from the strain of holding back her laughter. It's fucking adorable.

"Petals..." I tease. I pull my truck into her driveway, shutting it off.

"I'm not gonna say it, Andrew."

"I'll get it out of you, one way or another. That's what relationships are all about, right? Honesty?"

Josie gasps slightly, hesitating a long moment before speaking. "Is that what this is? A relationship?"

I shrug. "I think it's headed in that direction, don't you?" I honestly hadn't really considered the alternative.

Josie nods. "I didn't want to assume, but yeah. I think so too."

I lean over, kissing her cheek. A beautiful sunset glows outside the window, haloing around Josie's head. The bright oranges, purples, and yellows mix with the blue of the sky, looking like a painting of its own. "I think we stay on this course then, don't you?"

"Yeah, I agree." Josie nods, her eyes hazy with lust as she looks into mine. "It's fast though, right?"

I shrug. "Fast doesn't mean bad. We move at the pace best for us. If you need to slow down, we slow down. Right now though? I'm good."

I swear, Josie is staring right into my soul. "Yeah. I'm good too."

"Good. Now, can I meet your cat? She's stared at me like I'm a demon both times she's seen me, so I'd very much like to prove to her that I'm not."

The laugh that falls from Josie's lips is twinkly and light. "Velma's a sweetheart. She would never stare at you like you're a demon."

"I beg to differ," I scoff. We both climb out of the truck, meeting at the hood. "I swear to you, when I picked you up earlier, she had it out for me. Looked like she was ready to break through that front window." I point to the window in question, spotting the tabby cat curled up into a little ball, weirdly resembling a cinnamon roll with her coloring.

"You're ridiculous," she murmurs through a laugh. She takes out her key, unlocking the garage door and leading us in. She walks up the two steps to the door that leads inside, unlocking that as well before stepping in, and to the side for me to enter her home.

When I walk in, all I can smell is her. That sweet, floral scent that follows her, but is never too strong, always light and just enough to make you crave a little more. The kitchen is painted a deep wine color, the cabinets a crisp white to offset it. It's not a color I would have picked for my kitchen, but it's perfect. It's so her.

In the corner of the countertop sits a turquoise blue stand mixer, just waiting to create something. Her stove and fridge are slightly outdated, but then again, I have shag carpet in my basement, so I'm not one to judge.

Josie kicks off her boots, leaving her flat footed in her tights. I follow suit, sliding off my shoes and leaving them against the wall next to hers. She shuts the door behind us, and strides purposefully through her kitchen. "Velma," she calls. The twinkling sound of a bell alerts me to her presence as I follow Josie through her house. It's small, but adorable. Much like her. In her living room there is a small entertainment center, fixed with picture frames and small decor items. I spy Josie in all of the photos, along with a couple I'm guessing are her parents. Other frames feature a woman who looks so like Josie that it has to be her sister, as well as a few with friends.

I stare at the photos for a moment until something tangles around my feet, distracting me. When I look down, Velma is twining herself around my legs, purring loudly. She's meowing like crazy, acting like I'm her long lost best friend. "Why hello, kitty," I say. I bend down, offering her my hand. She sniffs gently, then licks my fingertips with her scratchy sandpaper tongue.

"I told you," Josie says with a smile. She's sitting on her couch, her legs tucked underneath her.

"Yes, you did," I concede. I straighten, heading over to where she sits. I flop down next to her. "What are you doing the rest of the evening?" I'm not going to overstay my welcome, but fuck, I really don't want to leave.

"Um..." she whispers. "This." She gestures to her living room. "Are you staying? We can watch a movie or something."

"Do you want me to stay?" I ask. Because I need to know for sure. I acknowledge internally for a moment, how fast we really are moving. Maybe *I need to cool it,* I think, unwillingly.

"I want you to stay. Please," she quickly answers, taking my hands in hers. She slams her lips against mine in a harsh, yet controlled kiss. When she pulls away, her eyes widen. "Oh no, what about Travis? He can't be alone this long."

I shake my head. "He'll be okay for a little longer. It's not like I'm staying the night."

Josie nods. "I guess." She looks down at her hands, her shoulders slumped.

"Hey." I tilt her head with my finger. "What's the matter?"

She shakes her head. "Nothing, I feel bad for Travis. Maybe we should go to your house, so he's not alone."

"Petals, I promise you he's fine. If you really want to, I can let him out quickly and come back, but we don't have to hang out at my place just for him. He can be alone for more than a few hours at a time."

"Are you sure?"

I softly chuckle. "Yes, I'm sure. He's a good boy. Sometimes, I think he prefers it when I'm gone anyway."

Josie still seems unconvinced. Trying to think of a way to distract her, I pull her from her spot on the couch so she's straddling my hips, much like she did on our last date. Her shirt is bunched up, and I have to move my hands so I don't automatically squeeze her ass. She gasps in surprise, and I slide my hand around the nape of her neck underneath her hair. I tilt my head as I pull her down to connect our lips. She moans at the contact, and I feel my jeans grow a little tighter.

"Fuck," I groan into the kiss. She's so goddamn good at kissing. My tongue slides against hers, tasting the cider that she had earlier. Just a hint of sweetness. Our lips move together, and we break apart at the same time.

"You're good at distractions," Josie says. Her forehead drops to mine as she catches her breath.

"Yes, I am." As much as I want to take her, right here, right now, I also want to savor her. I slide her off my lap, trying to ignore her little whimper of displeasure.

"That's mean," she whines.

"Petals, I promise you, there is plenty more where that came from."

"Show me," she brazenly responds.

I shake my head, my dick throbbing angrily. "Not tonight. Tonight, I just want to be with you. We went zero to one hundred last week, and I want you to know that I'm not just chasing you for sex. I want this to be more." *Fuck it, I'm not cooling it. I'm showing my whole hand.*

Josie's eyes soften. "I want this to be more too."

"Doesn't mean I don't want to, though," I grumble, leaning over to whisper in her ear. "Just means that this time, I get to work you up, build up the tension, one kiss, one touch at a time."

Josie sucks in a breath. "Okay," she replies as she breathes out.

"Good," I answer. I kiss down her jawline to her lips, giving myself one more taste for tonight.

She snuggles into my side, using the remote to turn on the tv. I wrap my arms around her, throwing my legs up onto the ottoman. Velma hops up onto my lap, purring loudly again when I pet her.

On the arm of the couch, Josie's phone starts buzzing incessantly. She looks down at it, scoffing.

"What is it?" I ask. I'm not trying to pry, but also a little curious, based on her reaction.

"My ex, Zack. He called me yesterday too. I didn't answer, but he texted me today, telling me I need to forgive Tessa."

My gut churns, wanting so badly to punch the shit outta this guy for irritating her. "Anything I can do to help?" I ask.

"Nope, I'm ignoring them for now, I just need to figure out what to say to them eventually."

"Good for you, petals." I press a kiss to her temple.

Josie squeezes my midsection, then sits up on her knees. "Did I tell you I booked a few more weddings?" Her voice is elated, eyes shining.

"Holy shit, you did?" I lean back, my eyes widening, mirroring her excitement.

"I did!" She nods, her face turning a cute shade of pink. "One of them is in a month, though she has actually been on my books for a while, and another toward the end of summer. Both clients came from Marley. I owe her, big time."

"She won't see it that way," I say, scooting Velma off my lap so I can turn sideways to face her. "She is happy to help anyone. That's who she is."

"Well, she brought me you." She blushes again, her freckles standing out. "And she is helping me get my business off the ground, so I need to do something for her." Josie pushes back another loose curl from my forehead. "Maybe I can help her and Beau get together."

I chuckle. "Good luck. I've been trying for years."

"Maybe a new perspective could help," Josie says with a smile. She lifts her fingertip to tap the tip of my nose. "Perspective can change everything."

"Very good point," I reply, booping her nose as she did mine.

"I might need to look into hiring an assistant."

"How come?" I ask. "You seemed to have everything under control at Megan's wedding."

She nods. "Yeah, because I had you. I didn't realize how badly I needed a second set of hands until I had you helping. You helped more than you realize."

The solution is simple, really. "I'll be your assistant."

"No," she stammers over her words. "I couldn't ask you to do that. What if you have plans? You don't want to spend your whole Saturday being my assistant."

"It's a good thing you didn't ask, then. Josie, I *want* to help you. Anything I can do to spend time with you is something I want to do." I peer into her eyes, so she knows I'm being truthful. "How about we give it a test run at the wedding, and then if it doesn't work, you can hire someone."

She thinks for a moment before smiling widely. "Alright, you've got a deal. Maybe someday I can help in your shop too," she says.

"I'd love that." I lean forward, kissing her softly.

19

JOSIE

"I still can't believe Andrew had no idea what I was planning," Marley says, smiling at me over her steaming cup of coffee. Her bangs are hanging over her eyes, long brown hair curled in loose waves to frame her face. She looks cozy and cute in a pair of black leggings, and an oversized sage green sweater. I treated her and Megan to breakfast this morning as a thank you. My phone has been ringing off the hook the last week with calls for weddings a year in advance, events that don't even have a date set yet, and so much more. Word of mouth is a pretty crazy thing.

I smile, feeling my cheeks heat at the mention of his name. Megan snickers over her cup of tea. "Needless to say, we were both pretty surprised," I say.

"Marley, do you have any of their pictures ready yet?" Megan asks. Megan's blonde hair is pulled into a low bun at the nape of her neck. She's dressed for a day at the clinic in a flowy floral top and high waisted black dress pants. Her shiny black heels are the perfect tie in for her outfit. I feel a bit like a slob next to her, but when I mentioned it, she gushed about how jealous she was that I could wear whatever I wanted for work, which made me feel better.

She shakes her head. "Not quite." She glances up at me, cringing slightly. "Sorry, things have just been so crazy with wedding season picking up. I promise I'll get to them soon."

I wave her off. "Don't worry about it. It's been what, a month? No rush. Speaking of, how much do I owe you for the session?"

Marley gasps. "You think you're paying for that? Not a chance."

"But—"

She interrupts me. "No. This was my treat. I've been wanting to add this type of shoot to my portfolio, and when I met you and saw how you and Andrew acted around each other, I couldn't not have you two be my first subjects. No charge." She narrows her deep brown eyes, daring me to challenge her.

I sink back into the booth. "Alright, but if you change your mind—"

"I won't."

"But *if* you do, you know where to find me."

Megan is the one to speak up next. "Josie, did Marley show you pictures from my wedding? The pictures of the flowers turned out *incredible*."

"Crap, I totally forgot I was going to send you those! Ugh, I'm such a mess lately." Marley picks her phone off the table, typing frantically. A moment later, my phone lights up with a text from her, a link to the photo gallery. "Feel free to use those for promo, or whatever you want."

I scroll through the photos, my eyes welling with tears. It's probably stupid to be this emotional over pictures of flowers, but it's like seeing all of my dreams come to fruition. "Wow, Marley. Thank you."

"Thank *you*," Megan answers first. "I'm so thankful we found your information, and it worked out for you to take us on as clients. The day wouldn't have been nearly as beautiful without your help."

Marley pipes in. "And don't do that thing where you try to downplay your talent. You're incredible."

I simply nod. Words fail me. To have these two talented women give me such high regards is something so comforting. It gives me hope that this is something I will succeed at.

"Also, we're friends now." Megan simply states. "Marley and I decided that you're part of our group. We're small but mighty."

Laughter bubbles up my chest. "Thank you, I would love that. I don't have too many girl friends, like I was telling Marley at your wedding. My best friend and I... it's a long story, but I'm taking some space away from her."

"Yeah, you'll fit in. Marley's only other friend is Beau."

Marley swats Megan's arm. "Hey!"

"Am I wrong?" Megan taunts.

"No, but still."

Megan drapes her arm over Marley's shoulders, kissing her cheek with a loud smack. "You know I love you. Annnnd," Megan drags the word out.

Marley slaps a hand over her mouth before she can say anything else. "Don't you say a word about it."

Megan sits back, mimicking zipping her lips shut.

Marley nods. "Thank you."

I don't say anything, though I know exactly what is silently being talked about. I haven't even met Beau yet, but if anything Andrew says is true, I know that he needs to get his shit together when it comes to Marley.

My phone buzzes on the table next to us. Andrew. I can't help but smile at the sight of his name. I silence the ringer, I'm not going to answer when I'm out with my friends. Marley peers across the table, and when she sees his name, she grabs the phone.

"Hey!" I gasp, reaching across to swipe it back from her. She slides her finger across the screen, answering it for me. She doesn't say a word though, just holds the phone out for me to grab. I purse my lips in confusion, but take it from her outstretched hand. Andrew's voice carries through the line.

"Josie-girl?" his voice is worried.

"Hey, sorry," I answer. "My phone slipped."

"Oh gotcha."

"What's up?" I ask.

I can practically hear his shrug through the phone. "Missed you. Wanted to see what you were doing."

My cheeks heat. "I'm out for lunch with Megan and Marley right now, but I think I should be free after. I can stop over if you want?"

"Oh shoot, you're out for lunch? Petals, why did you answer? I don't want to interrupt your time."

I chuckle. "Marley's the one who answered. I was going to text you but she snatched my phone."

"Sounds like typical Marley." There's a shuffling from through the phone, and I pull it away from my ear for a moment. "But yeah, come over when you're done, I want to show you something. Tell the girls I say hi."

We exchange goodbyes, and hang up. I set my phone down, giving Marley a soft glare. "I was trying to be nice and not answer the phone while we are out to eat, but then you had to swipe the phone from me!"

Megan snorts. "You don't have to ignore him for us. In fact, we *want* you to answer the phone."

I raise my brow. "Um, why?"

Marley is the one to respond this time. "Because, we are

excited for you. We want you two to be together, and if answering the phone at lunch can help with that, then that's what we want."

I shake my head. "You guys are so weird." They both nod in agreement. "Next time, I'm not answering it. He can be patient."

"Since we are on the subject, can I ask how it's going?" Marley asks.

A wistful sigh falls from my lips before I can think twice about it.

The girls both burst out in "*awww's*". "Tell us everything!" Megan reaches across the table, clasping my hand in hers, squeezing tightly.

"There isn't much to tell. We've been out on a few dates, and are spending a lot of time together." I shrug. I shouldn't downplay it, because in reality I can feel myself falling head over heels for him.

Marley squeals, clapping her hands together. "I knew you two would be perfect together."

"Andrew would not shut up about you, I had to come up with some bullshit excuse about a confidentiality clause to get him off my back. It all worked out though, thanks to Marley."

I agree. "Yeah, that's for sure. I owe you big time, Mar."

She waves me off. "You can do my flowers when I get married."

I raise my brow. "Is that happening soon?"

Marley goes pale. "No no no. Just, um," she stutters. "Eventually. Not soon. Not like I'll marry anyone anyway. I'm going to die alone. All alone."

Megan pulls Marley into her side as she tries to hide the tears welling in the corner of her eyes. "Enough about me."

I clear my throat, sacrificing a little bit of my humanity

to take the attention off her. "I'm pretty sure he's trying to kill me."

That perks her right up. "I'm sorry, what?" Marley is ready to throw hands.

"No," I practically shout. "Not actually. I mean, he's on this kick of 'going slow'" I make air quotes with my fingers. "And I swear to god you guys, my vagina is a needy whore."

Their eyes widen, and they stare at me, completely silent. "He's withholding sex?" Megan whispers.

"Yes," I whisper back. "Not to be mean, though. The night of our first date, things got hot, like, *really hot*, really fast, and on our next date, he told me he wanted to take things slow. To prove that he wants something more. Not just sex. But I know that, I can tell, I feel the same way about him. And you guys. I think he's trying to kill me. He keeps giving me little teases, little touches and glances that make my panties melt, and fuck me sideways, I need him." I sag into the seat, all the air leaving my lungs in a puff.

Marley bursts into laughter. "Oh my god. That is such a fucking Andrew thing to do, with the gallantry and shit. It's sweet, don't get me wrong, but holy shit. A girl has *needs*."

"My vibrator has gotten a lot of action," I mutter under my breath.

Megan cackles.

"I'm not going to pressure him, obviously, but I feel like a ticking time bomb." I drop my head in my hands, pushing my hair back from my face.

"I think it's cute, but I totally get the ticking time bomb thing. It'll happen when it happens," Megan says, taking a sip of her tea.

Once the bill is paid, we walk to our vehicles together, and hug goodbye, with plans to meet up soon, next time at the brewery in town. I guess Marley loves when there's bands there, and sometimes they host karaoke nights.

Climbing into my car, I plug my phone in, peeking at my messages before I drive across town. I have two messages, one from my mom, and one from Tessa. With a huff of irritation, I open the message from Tessa.

TESSA

Josie, please, answer me. I really miss you, and I've said I'm sorry. We can move past this.

A crazed laugh falls from my mouth, and I swipe out of the message from her, opening the message from my mom.

MOM

I just saw Tessa at the grocery store, and she seemed a little out of it. Is everything okay with you two?

I drop my head to the steering wheel. I'm so irritated with this whole situation.

With the line ringing, I put it on speakerphone as I pull out of the restaurant. Mom answers after the second ring. "Hi, honey," she says.

"Hey Mom," I reply. "I figured it would be easier for me to call then try and explain what's going on over text."

"What's going on with Tessa?"

"She's dating Zack."

"What do you mean, she's dating Zack?"

"They are in a relationship, and moving in together. She told me over the phone about a month ago. I guess they've been together since shortly after I left. She just didn't tell me until the phone call."

Mom pauses, not saying anything for a moment. "Are you okay with them being together?"

"Yes? No? Ugh, I don't know, Mom. I'm hurt that she didn't tell me, and hurt because she saw first hand how Zack treated me, and she still decided to give him a chance anyway. Does she not understand the concept of girl code?"

"I'm sorry, honey. I know how hard that must be. But I'm sure it will work itself out. How are things going otherwise?"

"I'm happy here. I am getting clients, and making friends, and I— I met someone." I've been hesitant to tell my mom, not out of shame, or fear, but because she tends to get overly excited at potentials.

"You met someone?" Her voice slowly raises an octave.

"Yes, and it's still early, so don't freak out."

"I won't, I promise. Tell me everything."

"His name is Andrew, he runs his own woodcraft business, and he was born and raised here in Ivy Ridge." I keep it short and sweet. If I give her more detail, she'll start fantasizing about what our babies will look like.

"Well that's great, Josie. I can't wait to meet him."

I pull my car into Andrew's driveway, and Travis rushes toward my car from the backyard. He's got a dopey look on his face, tongue flying in the wind as he runs to me. "Mom, I have to go. I'll call you later, okay?"

"Okay dear, I love you."

"I love you, too." We hang up, and I take a second to collect my emotions, then open the door to greet Travis.

"Hey pretty boy," I coo, scratching the top of his head. "Where's your daddy, huh?" Getting out of my car, I wipe my eyes, feeling a little stupid for getting emotional.

I walk down the driveway to round the side of the house, heading straight for the shop. Andrew spends a majority of his time here, I'm learning. Classic rock is blaring through the open door, letting the early spring air into the shop.

Andrew is oblivious to my arrival, his back to me. He's bent over a project, singing along to the song as he works. His arm muscles flex as he uses the saw to cut, and I decide it would be smart to step out until he turns the machine off. I don't need him to cut a hand off by accident. I don't do well with blood.

When the saw shuts off, I step back in, knocking loudly on the frame of the door. He spins to face me, his face breaking out in a loose smile. "Hey Josie-girl," he says, purposefully walking over to me. His face is slick with sweat, white tee covered in sawdust and wood stain. He brushes his hands down the front of his jeans before he reaches out, cupping my face softly.

His lips brush against mine in a now familiar kiss, sending that heat blazing through my body yet again. When he pulls back, his eyes hold mine. "How was lunch?"

I smile. "It was good. Those two are so fun, I'm excited to spend more time with them."

"I'm excited, too," Andrew answers. "We need to get out with everyone to the brewery."

"That's what we were saying earlier when we left. I really want to go sometime."

"We will," he says. He pushes my hair back behind my ear. "You okay? You seem a little off."

I shrug. "Yes and no."

Andrew leans back against a workbench, crossing his arms in front of his chest. "What's going on?"

"Tessa and Zack keep trying to contact me. Mom saw Tessa at the store today, and so I had to tell my mom how we are kinda not talking right now."

Andrew raises his brow, silently urging me on. "I just wish she would give me the space I'm asking for. I'm sure I'll be fine, but right now…" I trail off, uncomfortable.

"Do you want me to talk to them?" Andrew lowers his voice, trying to have a menacing growl to it.

A snort escapes my nose, because as hot as it is to think about him standing up for me, I simply can't imagine him next to Zack. The two of them are so vastly different, it makes me wonder what I ever saw in Zack. I mean really, he didn't have many redeeming qualities.

"Oh, is that so funny?" Andrew asks, his voice still low and growly.

"No," I frantically say, rushing over to rest my hands on his warm arms. His skin is damp with sweat. "No, I only laughed because the thought of you standing next to him is comical. You are daylight compared to his storm cloud, that's all. You don't have to talk to him, or Tessa for that matter. I'll text her again and tell her I need a little more time, but I know I can't put it off forever."

"That sounds good to me," Andrew agrees, relaxing his arms to pull me into his chest. I let him hold me for a short moment, before pulling back.

"As much as I love your hugs, I don't quite like feeling your sweat on my cheek."

"Fair," he responds with a laugh.

I step further into the shop, heading to the back where the couch is. Travis has cuddled up on his bed, and is gnawing on his favorite bone. I sit down on the couch, crossing my legs underneath myself.

"I told my mom about you," I confidently say.

"Hmm, did you?" Andrew follows behind me, watching as I sit down. "And what did she have to say?"

"I didn't give her much of an opportunity to say

anything. I only told her I met someone, and your name." I shrug. I can feel my face heating, and my hands break out in a clammy sweat.

"Did you tell her I was your boyfriend?" His eyes are wide, bright and happy.

"Um. No. We haven't, uh, I guess I could have, but I wasn't, I didn't," I stumble over my words, because *fuck*, did I just assume the status of our relationship?

"Petals," he laughs. He comes to stand in front of me, then drops into a squat, taking my shaking palms off my thighs. "You can tell her I'm your boyfriend. If that's what you want. I know I want to be your boyfriend, but if you're not there, that is fine too."

I let his words simmer in my brain. Andrew, my boyfriend. "I think that's what I want. Yeah."

"Yeah?" His brow raises.

"Yeah. You're my boyfriend." I grin.

"Does this mean I can change my relationship status on Facebook to 'in a relationship'?" he giddily asks.

"When was the last time you even used Facebook?" I ask in return.

"I don't know, but I've always wanted to change my status to *in a relationship*, and never did with any of the other girls I dated." His smile is wide, like a child on Christmas morning.

"Yeah, you can change your relationship status," I tell him. "I'll change mine too."

20

JOSIE

The last few weeks have felt like a whirlwind in the best possible way. Andrew and I have spent most of our free time together, at either his house, or mine. He's helped me deliver arrangements, clip flower stems, and even seemed curious about putting together a bouquet. I let him create his own bouquet for his mom. Her birthday is this weekend, and he wanted to do something nice for her. We spent time in his shop while I watched him work on various projects, snuggling with Travis on the couch. His grandpa stopped by a few times while I was there as well, and we watched Andrew work while we talked. He told me all the embarrassing stories I could ever want about Andrew, all while watching his face turn a bright cherry red as he worked, trying to ignore my hushed laughs. Earl really is a sweet gentleman.

Tomorrow I have another wedding on the books. After a handful of meetings and phone calls with the bride, we settled on the arrangements and florals she wanted. She's extremely laid back, making this whole process easy on me.

I'm sure I'll have brides in the future that have me rethinking my career choices, but for now, I've been lucky.

Once the date was ironed out and official, I started placing orders and arranging my schedule to accommodate. While I tried to tell Andrew he didn't need to be my assistant, he insisted. He's currently making sure all my vases are accounted for and in the back of my car. I'm getting the bridesmaids bouquets finished up and in the fridge for the night when he walks back in, Travis following behind.

Travis has been coming over a lot too, and he and Velma tolerate each other surprisingly well. Travis runs to my side, sitting on his hind legs, giving me the cutest puppy dog eyes.

"Aww, do you want some pets?" I bend down, snuggling up to him. His tail wags furiously against the concrete floor of the garage, and Andrew chuckles.

"I'm pretty sure he likes you more than me, petals."

"Nah, I'm just someone new, that's all."

"You're not new, not anymore," his voice is tight with conviction.

I shrug, standing up and wiping my hands on the front of my jeans. I suppose it has been a couple months now. "I have to finish a few more things, and then I think I'm ready for tomorrow. You can head out if you need," I say, silently hoping he wants to stay. We haven't spent the night together since the night of our first date, when we fell asleep in his shop. He's proved his point of wanting me for more than sex, and the aching need for him grows every second I spend in his presence.

"I was thinking," he slowly responds, stepping up to press his front against my back, wrapping arms around me. The heat of his body is burning a fire of desire through my icy, pained, veins. "We could watch a movie?"

A shudder wracks through my body, hoping, wishing, *praying* that he means something more. "A movie is good," I squeak, keeping my face turned from him to hide the redness and my shaky hands. Andrew slides next to me, turning so he can rest his back against the fridge, hooking one leg across the other. His arms are crossed over his chest, the fabric of his black tee tight around his biceps.

Brown eyes filled with pure lust stare down at me. I turn my gaze away. *Breathe. Get it together, Josie.* "Okay, I need fifteen minutes to finish this."

"You got it, petals." Andrew shifts off the fridge, cleaning up the loose petals and leaves from my workstation, and sweeping the floor for me. The incessant heat fades momentarily while I continue to work, doing my best to ignore the flutters trying to claw their way up my throat.

When I'm finished, I slide the perfected bouquets into the fridge, and do a final count, making sure I have the correct amount of corsages, boutonnieres, and bouquets. After a third time counting, I'm content that I'm ready for tomorrow. Andrew is going to help with the heavy lifting, and anything else I might need.

Hands slide around my waist to the front, where thumbs hook onto the belt loops of my jeans. The heat climbs. Andrew's warm breath tickles my cheek as he squeezes me tightly. "Done?" he asks.

"Finally," I murmur, turning around into his chest. His hands stay at my waist, moving with me to rest on my ass. *Stop being such a horny bitch, Josie. Play it cool.* "What do you want to watch tonight?"

"Doesn't matter. I just wasn't ready to leave yet," his voice is husky, tickling my inner ear. He tugs me closer, allowing me to tilt my head to look into those golden brown eyes.

My hands shake with anticipation as I step back from him. Andrew lets his arms drop, his eyes growing heated as I walk backwards away from him. "Let's go inside," I breathlessly say, my voice betraying me.

Andrew nods, and I spin, heading up the stairs into my house. I try to walk slowly to hide the urgency I feel, but I can tell I'm practically sprinting. The heat between us is getting to be too much to bear. His heavy footfalls follow close behind. I fling the screen door open, running into the house, kicking my shoes off with each step. I hear the thud of Andrew's boots, and the tippy tap of Travis's paws.

With heavy breaths, I stop in the middle of the kitchen. Travis runs right past me, heading for the living room to find Velma. I'm pretty sure he likes her more than she likes him. Andrew stands in front of me, and I swallow hard, trying to eliminate the giant lump that's set up shop in my throat.

Andrew is the first to break the staring contest, striding over to me, reaching down to clasp my hand in his, dragging me into the living room. He turns the lamp in the corner on, casting a warm glow over the room. Travis is curled up on the couch, staring at us, waiting for the two of us to join him. "Travis, get down," Andrew commands, though his voice is soft. Travis gives us a sad look, his face the literal definition of *puppy dog eyes*. He flops to the ground, circling a few times before laying down, tucking himself into a little cinnamon roll.

"Come here," Andrew says, even though he still has a hold of my palm. He sits on the couch, pulling me down next to him. The large picture window faces the street, my couch settled in front of it, the blinds open. Anyone that passes by can see in my house, and I've never cursed the window as much as I do right now.

"Um," I stammer. "One sec." I reach behind him, dragging the curtains closed, cursing myself for purchasing the sheer fabric when there were plenty of other options that were less see through.

When they are closed, I sit down next to Andrew, settling myself into the crook of his arm. He raises his brow, a smirk tugging at the corner of his mouth. "I like the way you think, Josie-girl."

The heat that has been building in my veins bubbles hotter and hotter. I swear, this man is trying to make me combust.

"What can I say?" I mutter. "I think ahead."

"It appears so," he chuckles. Reaching across me, he grabs the remote from the side table, turning the tv on. "What are we watching?"

My eyes widen. He's going to kill me. Seriously. I ooze a little bit of sass into my voice as I reply, "It really doesn't matter."

"Why not?" he asks, his voice thick with humor. "You never know, we could find your new favorite movie tonight."

I choose to ignore the remark. "You can pick something."

Andrew clicks through the streaming service, settling on a movie that was released last summer, but I haven't seen yet. He lifts his legs up onto the ottoman, and I follow suit, entangling my legs with his. I curl into his side, breathing in his scent, cursing the way it makes my pussy flutter. I think my vagina is running the show tonight.

His arm tightens around me, and I decide that I am going to make this night a living hell for him. He wants to watch a movie? *Only* watch? You have another thing coming, Andrew Cunningham. I know he feels the same way I do. I know that he's been fighting the heat between us for weeks. I've felt it in every hurried kiss, every time his hands have ghosted over my breasts, or slid down to the hem of my jeans. I know he wants this. He wants to be a gentleman. I get it. He has proven it time and time again.

Well, fuck it. I want this, he wants this, it's time to push him over the edge.

I let the movie play for the first fifteen minutes, keeping my touches innocent. Andrew seems totally enthralled with the movie, but I'm about to derail him. I need to feel him again. Taste him. I've never craved sex this way before, but I know the minute I get him inside me, I'll be addicted.

I let my leg slide up and down his, hooking my leg around his knee. With the hand I have resting over his heart, I start drawing slow, tantalizing circles with the tip of my finger. He almost immediately reacts, shivering, resting his palm over top of mine. Since my hand is now prevented from moving, I drag my leg up and down, my knee nearly tapping his groin with the movement. Andrew tightens a hand around my splayed palm. He holds it there for a moment, as if pondering how he wants to react, then let's go, leaving my hand free to explore.

I interpret his movements as consent, and slowly drag my fingertip down his chest. I trace every ridge of his body, loving that he's toned, but still soft. He's not pure muscle. He doesn't have a six pack of abs, nor do I want him to. He's perfect, just what I need.

I continue my path, tracing designs over his skin. I didn't get the time to explore him the way I truly wanted last time. We were fueled by lust, passion, and the need to get it out of our system. Now, I want to take my time. Don't get me wrong, I desperately want to pounce him, but that will come later.

"Josie, the movie," Andrew mutters through clenched

teeth. I look up at him, purposefully giving him a look of pure innocence.

"What about it?" I bat my lashes.

"Watch it."

"I am watching," I counter. I turn my face, doing just what I said. I watch the movie... while sliding my fingers underneath the fabric of his tee. His skin is hot, yet goosebumps break out underneath the tips of my fingers. I continue the delicious torture, loving how he's slowly falling apart for me. With a glance up at him, I see that his focus is no longer on the screen, but on my every move. His eyes meet mine, challenging me. If he really wanted me to stop and watch the movie, I would have, but the mischievous glint in his eyes tells me he wants this more.

I drag my hand down, this time to the growing hardness under his jeans. I cup his hard cock through his jeans. The zipper is pressed against it, and I tsk. "Hmm, that must be uncomfortable, should I help?"

I look back at him. His eyes are now pinched shut, forehead creased with tension. He grunts, nodding sharply. "Fuck yes," he groans.

With his consent, I pop the button of his jeans open, sliding the zipper down. The gray fabric of his boxer briefs is tight, pulling against his erection. I cup him through the cotton, giving him a gentle squeeze. The movie plays in the background, and my eye catches Travis.

Yeah, there is no fucking way I can do this knowing that Travis will watch. I give Andrew another soft squeeze, saying, "Hold that thought."

Andrew's eyes fly open, irises burning. "Wha—" he grits out. I climb off him quickly, calling Travis as I sprint down to the guest bedroom. Of course, the good boy that he is, Travis barrels down the hall with me. I feel guilty for all of two seconds when I corral him into the room, pulling the door shut behind me. He gives me those puppy dog eyes again, but he has a queen size bed at his disposal. He'll be fine.

Dashing back down the hall, I'm met with Andrew's heated look again. He's sitting up higher now, one hand wrapped around his erection through his briefs, the other bent at the elbow, holding onto the back of his head. I stop at the edge of the living room, eager to reach him, but also stunned by the sight. I watch as he flexes his arm, squeezing his cock. A drop of wetness appears on the light cotton where the tip is, and wetness pools at my core, surely creating my own wet spot in my underwear.

One hand still on his groin, the other moves to point at me, hooking his finger, beckoning me to him. Hypnotized, I obey. As I move to him, I pull my own basic tee shirt off my body, unbuttoning my jeans.

Andrew reaches out, gripping my wrist and shaking his head as I'm about to push the jeans down my legs. "That's my job," he huskily whispers. I nod, words are not about to come out of my mouth right now. He drops my wrist, using both his hands to slide my jeans off my legs. "C'mere, petals. This is what you need? What you want?" Nodding, I kick off the jeans, and straddle his thighs. His hands slide up my bare thighs, bare stomach, to my old, tattered cotton bra. Not exactly what I would call sexy, but Andrew is looking at it like it's his favorite item on the planet.

"I want it too," he murmurs. His hand continues to tease me, much like I did him, until he cups the nape of my neck, pulling me onto his lips. The taste of him is so familiar now that I almost immediately lose myself in the kiss, tangling my fingers in his hair. I fucking love his hair, the gentle waves and thickness of it.

In between kisses, Andrew mutters, "You're a sneaky girl, you know that?"

I can't help but smile against his lips. "I want what I want."

"And what you want is me?" he guesses.

"Now you're catching on," I murmur.

I grind my hips against his, my panties soaked now. Andrew groans into my mouth, his free hand gripping my hip, hard enough that I will surely have finger shaped bruises in the morning. I untangle my fingers from his hair, reaching down to yank his shirt up and off him.

He takes it from me, and flings it across the room, and then his mouth is on my chest, kissing down to my tits. He flips the cotton cups, letting my breasts fumble out into his waiting palms. They're big enough to fill both his hands, and still have a little overflow. He sucks and marks the skin of one, pinching the nipple of my other until it's hard between his fingertips. I arch into his touch moaning my pleasure. My hands rest on his bare shoulders as he switches to my other breast.

I pull back, needing more. I slide off his lap to the floor, hooking my fingers around the belt loops of his jeans. "Off," I urge. He lifts his hips, and I yank them down, taking his boxers with. I take him in my hand immediately, and start to stroke him. Andrew's head drops to the back of the couch, palms covering his eyes.

"Josie," he groans my name like a prayer. "Fuuuuck."

Licking him from base to tip, I can't help but smile at the shudder that wracks his body. I love that I can completely unravel him. He groans long and low as I take him deep to the back of my throat, holding him there, only releasing when I feel myself start to gag. My fingers are still wrapped around the base, so I use my other hand to cup his balls, rolling them between my fingers.

I bob my head up and down him, sucking hard, flicking the tip with my tongue. The pressure between my thighs grows to the point where I can't handle it anymore. I drag my hand down his leg, to between my thighs.

Pushing my soaked panties out of the way, I slide two of my fingers between my slit, wetting my fingers. My finger-tips find my clit, and I start drawing slow, methodical circles. The ache is instantly relieved, though a different kind starts to stir, low in my belly.

Moaning around his cock, Andrew opens his eyes, trailing them down my body to where my hand disappears between my thighs. Without giving me a second to react, Andrew bunches my hair that was curtaining my face, and pulls me off his cock, directing me with my hair.

"If you need me between your legs that bad, why didn't you say something petals?" Andrew purrs.

He stands, his cock right in my face. I try to take him in my mouth again, but he tuts at me. "No no, you need me now. It's my turn." He tilts my head using my hair, then guides me back until I'm laying on the floor, spread for him.

Andrew's eyes glaze over as he kneels between my legs, devouring my body with one look. He hovers over me, his fingers sliding between my legs to my cunt. The fabric is covering me again, but he touches me over it, groaning when he feels the wetness. Mouth descending, he kisses me deep, rough, claiming my mouth with his. His fingers slip underneath my panties into the hot wetness there.

He searches for a moment, knowing the moment he finds my clit at my ratcheted gasp. He chuckles lowly, then with a measured precision, starts working me like he knows my body inside and out. In minutes, he has me panting, the pressure building with every articulate movement. I'm definitely not the girl who can come on command, or even within a few minutes. Sometimes, it doesn't even happen for me. I desperately want to come, I want *him* to *make me* come, but I don't want him to grow tired of waiting for it to happen. I feel my focus on the moment drifting, but I can't let that happen, so I zero in on his hands on me, his mouth, his touch.

"Andrew, fuck," I moan, bucking my hips into his hand. He uses his thumb, stroking my clit, sliding two thick fingers deep inside me. He slides in easily, rhythmically pumping his fingers.

"That's it. It's your turn." Andrew continues, carrying me higher and higher. I latch onto his words, chasing my orgasm until the embers burn into white hot flames, my entire body pulsing and clenching as he continues to work me over. My cunt squeezes his fingers as I come, yearning for more.

"Fuck me," I nearly shout. "I need you to fuck me, Andrew."

"I think I can manage that, Josie-girl." His thick fingers slide out of me, leaving me aching, needing him to fill me again. Andrew sits up on his knees, reaching for his jeans. He pulls a condom out of his wallet, and if the foil didn't look so crisp, I'd offer to go get one of mine that I keep on hand.

You never know how long guys keep condoms in their wallet.

I sit up, shimmying my underwear down my legs in the process, and sitting up on my knees. I hold my palm out for the condom, and Andrew raises a brow, but drops it into my waiting hand. "Sit down," I direct. He does, sitting so his back rests against the couch, his legs straight out.

I straddle him again, loving this position with him. Tearing open the packet, I take the condom out, pinching the tip and sliding it over the head of his dick, rolling it down his shaft.

He shivers, and I scoot forward, ready for this. So. Fucking. Ready. Andrew grips my hips, scooting slightly so he's in a more comfortable position. "Okay?" he asks, eyes softening.

"Yeah," I reply with a nod, resting my forehead against his. "You okay?"

He nods in reply. "Can't believe this is real life."

I huff a laugh, reaching down to position him at my entrance. "Me either." I press my lips to his. The frenzy from earlier is gone, replaced by this tender moment. My thighs shake as I hold myself over him, his tip just barely inside me.

Andrew drops a hand to my waist, the other cupping my neck. Our foreheads stay pressed together, eyes only on each other as I sink down onto him. Slowly, taking every inch of him until I'm flush with his thighs, I savor the delicious burn of being stretched by him. We both gasp at the feel, my pussy involuntarily clenching around him.

I fight the urge to close my eyes. I want to see every part of his reaction to being inside me for the first time. He must feel the same, because we stay locked like that, unmoving for a long moment, adjusting to this feeling, this connection.

I lift my hips, gently moving up his length. I suck in a hurried breath at the motion, then slide back down. Sweat pools on his brow, dripping down the side of his face to his cheek and onto his neck. I resist an insane urge to lick it off him.

Resting my hands on his shoulders, I find a rhythm. Andrew lifts his knees, changing the angle, giving him a bit more leverage. I drop my hands to his sides, my head to his shoulder, trying to keep the momentum going, but losing it when my legs start to give out.

I really need to do some more lunges or something, because damn, this shit is hard.

Andrew grips my hips, thrusting himself up and into me. He takes over, creating his own pace. "Ahh," I cry out when he hits a spot I didn't know existed.

"God, you feel so fucking good," Andrew grunts, pumping himself inside me.

"You too," I moan. "Holy fuck."

My arms are wrapped around his neck, clinging to him. Sweat beads on the back of my neck, dripping down my spine. My knees are going to be covered in rug burn from the carpet, but honestly, it's going to be so fucking worth it.

I clench my pussy with each thrust of Andrew's length. "Fuck, I'm close," he curses through tight lips. Another rivulet of sweat slides between my breasts.

"Yes," I whimper. The word is barely out of my mouth when Andrew is sliding his fingers between us, playing with my clit, giving me the little boost of pleasure I crave.

"Josie," Andrew roars my name as he comes, his cock twitching as he thrusts into me three final times. When he stills, my cunt tightens around him like the greedy bitch she is, unwilling to let him go quite yet. I didn't come again, but I didn't need to. Having him inside me, hearing him scream my name as he came was euphoria enough.

We pant, coming down from our highs. He starts to soften inside me, and I take that as my cue to slide off him. I do so, flopping onto my back, not caring about the sweat that will be on the carpet. Andrew slides down next to me after a moment. I assume he was taking care of the condom.

He curls into my side. "Okay?" he asks, repeating the question from earlier.

I'm still trying to process everything, my brain a little stunted, zapping with aftershocks. I offer an enthusiastic thumbs up, turning my head to kiss his cheek.

Andrew laughs. "Good."

I nod, letting him hold me for a moment. I can honestly say, I don't think love has ever felt like this before. Because that's what this is.

21

ANDREW

Once I get Josie cleaned up, I let Travis out of the guest room. He ignores me, running down the hall to Josie, who's in the kitchen, getting us a snack.

"Hi puppy dog!" Josie croons. I come around the corner into view of the kitchen to find her sitting down on the floor, wearing only my discarded black tee shirt from earlier, and her panties. Her red hair is a strewn mess from my hands, her lips still swollen and pink from mine. She has her arms around Travis, her head tilted into his furry shoulder. Travis sits perfectly, his tongue hanging out as he pants his excitement. He never sits still for me, but apparently he'll do anything for my Josie-girl.

Before the moment passes, I snatch my phone off the kitchen table where I set it earlier, and snap a picture of the cute moment. Josie doesn't even notice, but I immediately set it as my background. My two favorite people.

Yeah, Travis isn't technically *people*, but still.

I totally tried to play off tonight as wanting to hang out and watch a movie, but that was never my plan. I could tell Josie was getting antsy, and to be honest, I was too. I've craved her taste, her moans, the feel of her warm skin against mine. I wanted to take it slow, especially after I pretty much jumped her that first night, but tonight, things felt right.

Getting to know her, spending every chance I can with her lately, has been like living in a fucking dream. I'm going to ask her to come to Sunday Brunch. My mom won't stop asking me about her. I haven't brought a girlfriend home since I was nineteen.

Isaac and Megan won't stop bugging me about it either, so I know I'm going to have to get us out of our little bubble and start showing her off. Not that I don't want to show her off, *fuck* do I ever want to show her off, but I also want to keep her for myself. It's purely selfish, but she's mine, and I don't want to share.

"I reiterate my earlier point," I say, gesturing to where Travis is still melting into Josie's touch. "He loves you more than me."

She laughs, scruffing the top of Travis's head. "Do you like me more than you like your daddy?"

Travis nuzzles into her. I head over to them, grabbing a glass from the cupboard, and filling it with water. Josie stands from the floor, walking over to where I'm leaning against the counter. I offer her the cup of water, and she finishes it, then fills it again.

"How are you feeling about tomorrow?" I ask. I pull her into my chest when she finishes drinking.

"Okay. I'd be lying if I said I wasn't nervous, but more nervous and excited than anything." She rests her head against my chest, and I run my hand up and down her spine.

"Excited is good. I'll be there for whatever you need, Josie. Feel free to put all your stress on me. I can hold it." I lean down, resting my cheek on the top of her head. Her arms tighten around my torso.

"Thank you."

"What can I say, I make an amazing boyfriend," I boast, totally kidding.

"You do make an amazing boyfriend," she agrees, lifting her head up to search for a kiss.

I peck her on the lips gently. "Should we get to bed? We have a big day tomorrow."

"You're staying, right?" Her voice is eager.

"If you'll have me," I pause. "And Travis of course."

"Hmm." Josie tilts her head as if she's thinking about it. "You can have the couch. I don't think there will be enough room in the bed."

My brow raises. "Why?"

"I think Travis might be a bit of a bed hog."

"You little shit." I slap her ass, loving the way she squeals, then squeeze gently. "For your information, Travis is a bed hog. Tonight though, he's sleeping on the floor."

"Poor baby," Josie says in a baby voice, looking down at Travis. "Good luck getting Velma to sleep on the floor. She's a snuggler."

"It's a challenge I'm willing to take. I need you all to myself tonight." My hands slide under her ass, hauling her into my arms. Her legs wrap around my waist, arms moving to my neck. Her fingers twirl in my hair, gently twisting the loose curls.

"You have me. Now, put me down."

I shake my head. "Nope." I start to head through the kitchen down the hall to her bedroom, listening to her squeal about how I can't carry her and try to get out of my arms with each step. "I can carry you, which has in fact been proven, so enough of that."

I manage to turn the overhead light on when I cross the threshold into her room, lighting up the queen sized bed. The comforter is a pale blush pink, a color that I now associate with Josie, since she seems to love it so much. Velma is curled up into a tiny ball in the center of it, only lifting her head slightly at our entrance.

The little tabby cat seems irritated by our presence, but also doesn't move as I stride closer, dropping Josie onto the bed. Josie laughs as she bounces, and Velma meows at me, scurrying off the bed. "Time for bed," I state.

Josie moves to sit up, but I push her shoulders down. "No, it's bedtime. You need your rest. Big day tomorrow."

"Andrew," she says with a laugh. "I need to get my phone, wash my face, and lock the house. I have to get up." She pushes against me, and I let her get up.

"Fine, but you have five minutes." I point a finger at her, but stand back as she walks out of her room, swaying her hips.

I watch her closely until she's out of sight, and it's then that I realize I am right there with Travis, totally obsessed with this girl. I have puppy dog eyes for her, and I'm not mad about it in the slightest.

22

JOSIE

"Has anyone seen the groom?" I ask the bridal party. I'm met with several searching glances and shaking heads. "Crap," I mutter, spinning on my heels to go in search of him.

This may be the most organized wedding I've ever been to, or worked, but yet, the groom is missing. To top it all off, I asked Andrew to look for him, and now he's missing too. Not that I should be surprised, he seems to become friends with everyone he meets.

I rush down the long hall of the venue, the boutonniere in my hand. I can't even call Andrew because I gave it to him to hold. I didn't think I would need it. My heart pounds, because while it's not my fault that the groom is MIA, it is if he shows up to pictures without his boutonniere.

Andrew's boisterous laughter alerts me to his location as I turn a corner, heading toward the lobby of the hotel venue. Andrew stands side by side with the groom, his hands in his pockets without a care in the world. If he wasn't so dang cute, I'd be a little peeved. Though, he did his job by finding the groom.

"Hey, petals," Andrew greets, holding out his hand for me. I give him a smile, squeezing his hand, and turn my focus to the groom.

"Colin, we need you for pictures," I say.

"Oh shoot, sorry," Colin murmurs. "My mother-in-law to be needed me for a minute. My daughter, Cora, is currently in her 'hate everyone but mom and dad' stage, and she was having a hard time calming her down after she woke up from her nap."

"No worries," I reply. I knew he had a good reason for disappearing. He didn't give me the vibe of a groom on the run. I step forward, showing him the flower I need to place on his lapel. He nods, and I get to work, pinning the boutonniere to his suit. "Now, you're ready. They need you for the first look pictures." I turn him toward the direction he needs to go, and Andrew and I follow him outside to where the photographer is waiting. Colin is a tall guy, but his height is nothing compared to one of the groomsmen. The guy is at least six foot five, maybe more, and is stocky, with wide shoulders and tree trunk legs.

When Colin approaches the group, he's met with jeers and laughter. They tease him about running off, but it's all jest.

I make sure that all the bouquets are ready, and straighten a few boutonnieres before I drag Andrew back inside with me to finish up the reception area.

"You really make friends with everyone, don't you?" I ask as we walk hand in hand.

Andrew shrugs, a coy smile on his lips. "You could say that. Thomas and I are the extroverts of the family. Ironic for me to be the kid that deals with people the least for work."

He hesitates for a moment, seemingly trying to decide his next words.

"You do still need to meet my parents," he says. "Would you like to come to Sunday brunch tomorrow? My mom has been asking to meet you."

"She has?"

"Of course she has." He squeezes my palm. "I kinda talk about you a lot."

Warmth floods my chest. "I'd love to go to brunch."

When we make it back to the reception area, I get to work on the head table floral layout, and have Andrew put the flower filled vases on each table. The clinking of dishes and glasses along with the cacophony of voices fills the room, and I sink into a zone, totally focused on the arrangement in front of me.

I don't know how much has passed when a large shadow looms over me. I tilt my head up, and am graced with Andrew's adorable smile. "Hey," I greet. "All done?"

He nods. "Yeah. What's next?"

"Nothing. I'm almost done here. Could you run around and collect everything? Then we should be able to head out."

"Sure thing, petals." He bends at the waist to kiss my cheek. He takes my phone from his pocket, handing it off to me before strolling off to grab my things. The wedding planner is in charge of collecting all of my vases tomorrow morning during clean up, and I'll pick them up from her tomorrow night.

With a few finishing touches to the head table, I step back, and take my phone out to snap some photos for my social media. Satisfied, I head out to find Andrew again.

Outside, the bride and groom are taking photos with their families. I wave goodbye when the bride spots me but instead of simply waving back, she frantically waves, eager to get my attention. I walk toward them with a smile on my face. She looks absolutely gorgeous. Her brown ringlet curled hair is in a swooping updo, a veil intricately placed in the curls. Her dress is an a-line cut, with thin lace sleeves and lace flowers stitched into the skirt.

"You look incredible, Lainey," I say when I reach her. "This dress was made for you."

Her cheeks redden, and her soon-to-be husband, Colin, wraps an arm around her waist, pulling her in to kiss her temple. "Isn't she perfect?" he murmurs, more for her than for me.

"I wanted to thank you for the flowers. They are absolutely incredible. I couldn't have asked for anything better." Lainey reaches out, squeezing my palm tightly.

"I'm glad you love them," I say. "I hope you have an amazing day," I add before stepping back so they can get back to their day.

A short, blonde woman in a navy blue bridesmaids dress yells from twenty feet away. "Laines, we need you over here! Mom wants to do the sibling pictures!"

Lainey jerks a thumb over her shoulder. "Sorry, Sam can be a bit loud. Thanks again, and I'll call you if we need anything."

I say goodbye, then head down the walkway to where Andrew is waiting in my car. He's in the driver's seat, ready to go. "They are such a cute couple," I say when I climb into the passenger side.

"Yeah they are. Colin seems like a nice guy too. I recognized the bride's mom, though I can't seem to place from where." Andrew pulls out of the parking lot, heading toward home. It's about a forty minute drive from Cinder Valley, the small town where the wedding was being held.

"I'm sure you'll think of it." I look out my window as we drive, admiring the cliffs and jutting rocks that lead to the river. "It's so pretty out here," I comment.

"Isn't it? My parents used to take us out canoeing here a few times a summer. Then we'd go to a nineteen fifties themed drive-in restaurant for lunch or dinner after. I bet it's still here. Are you hungry?" Andrew peers over at me, waiting for my answer.

"I could eat. That sounds really good."

He turns the vehicle down another road, and soon after, the restaurant appears. It's insanely busy, people walking around everywhere. There are people sitting out at the patio tables eating, or in the drive up spots, eating in their cars. Andrew finds a place to park, and we get out and head to the hostess stand. We're greeted immediately and brought to a table.

The spring weather makes for a beautiful Minnesota day. When our food is brought out, we devour the amazing burgers within minutes.

"Hey, are we still meeting everyone at that brewery tonight?" I ask. We mentioned it a few days ago, but Andrew and I weren't sure what time we'd be done with the wedding, so we didn't have the plans set in stone.

"Think so." Andrew wipes his face with a napkin, taking a sip of his water. "I'll shoot out a text, letting everyone know we'll make it. Jason said he's got a local band playing tonight."

"Oh, does Jason work there?"

"He owns it," Andrew says, a goofy grin on his face.

My jaw drops. "Wait, really? So all this time, I've been

gushing about that cider you gave me, and how badly I want to go, and *your brother owns the brewery?*"

Andrew laughs. "Yeah. I probably should have told you, but your reaction was pretty cute. I wanted him to be there when I told you, but I couldn't wait any longer."

"You're acting like it was this huge secret." I laugh.

"Nah, I just like seeing you react to things. Your nose does this thing where it scrunches up, and your eyes squint. It really pops your freckles. You're so damn adorable." He scoots his chair over to me, then boops me on my nose. "See? Scrunched."

Immediately, I unscrunch. "That's embarrassing."

"No it's not. It's one of my favorite things about you."

I feel my nose scrunch again automatically. "Thanks."

When the bill comes, he asks, "Are you ready? I think I could go for a nap before we go out tonight."

"A nap sounds incredible," I agree.

———

23

ANDREW

The brewery is packed. Bodies are crammed together in the golden lit room, while the band plays a surprisingly good cover of *Sugar, We're Going Down* by Fall Out Boy loudly over the chattering voices. Josie is pressed up against my side as we try and make our way through the crowd to find the table Beau and Marley have saved for us. Megan and Isaac aren't able to make it, she's on call at the hospital this weekend, and Isaac is helping his dad with something. From the sounds of it, it will be Beau, Marley, and Thomas, with the occasional pop in from Jason.

I finally spot Beau's man bun at a corner table, and lead Josie in their direction. Mar and Beau have their heads close together, and Marley's brows are furrowed in irritation. "Hey, you two," I say, clapping Beau on the back when we reach the table. He surprisingly changed out of his work clothes, and is wearing a black shirt with the Blue Ox Brewery logo on it, and dark jeans.

Beau looks up first, his face going from stressed to a mask of happiness in two seconds flat. These two need to get their shit together before they ruin their lives. The lives that they should be spending together. "Hey man," Beau greets. Josie rounds the table to give Marley a hug, and sits down next to her.

I sit down next to Beau, thankful we have a small table so I can still touch Josie. Josie lifts a hand to give him an awkward wave. "Hey, Beau. It's nice to meet you." She smiles.

Beau smiles back. "Nice to meet you too, Josie. Sorry it's taken so long to get to meet, but I've heard wonderful things about you from both Mar and Andrew."

Josie does the nose scrunching thing I love. "Thanks. I've heard pretty great things about you from them, too."

Beau chuckles. "I heard you liked the Dry Pear Cider, I think Jase said he has some on tap tonight."

"Oh, yay!" Josie leans over, squeezing my hand. "Honey, can you come with me to get some? I've been dreaming about it for weeks."

"Sure thing, petals." We both stand, and I take her hand, ready to head over to the crowded bar.

Marley stands from her seat as well. "I'll come with you, I need some popcorn."

The three of us make our way to the bar, and Marley veers off, filling a few paper boats with popcorn, adding some salt to it. We haven't even gotten to the bar yet when she returns, handing Josie the second boat of popcorn.

Josie tells her all about how the wedding today went, and of course, Marley is happy for her. I don't know who wouldn't be.

I'm so proud of her for standing up for herself, and following her dreams. Her ex has no idea what he's missing, watching her thrive and grow, doing what she loves.

When we finally make it up to the glossy wood bar, I shout our order to Laila, a girl I went to high school with.

She nods, spinning around to get our brews. She serves us quickly, and when I pull my wallet from my back pocket to pay, she waves me off. "Jase said it's on the house."

I nod, but still pull a twenty from my billfold. I toss it across the counter, making sure she catches it. "That's yours," I say, gesturing to the bill.

She rolls her eyes. "Thanks, but it's not necessary."

"Take it, Laila." I watch to make sure she takes it. With our drinks in hand, we head back to the table. I catch Jason's eye from across the crowded room, and tip my chin to him in thanks. As soon as our table is in view, a feeling of dread simmers in my belly. A girl is sitting in my chair, obviously flirting with Beau.

She's definitely younger than he is, with fake platinum blonde hair, and nails that look like they could claw your eyes out. To be fair, Beau doesn't seem to be paying much attention to her, taking a long pull of the beer he already had when we arrived. Marley doesn't say a word, but I see the way her face pales. If I didn't have my hands full, I'd give her a reassuring tap on the shoulder, or a hug or something, but even if I could, she's moving away from the table faster than I can react.

"Shit," I mutter. Reaching the table, I set our full glasses down. Josie sits in her chair, and I stand behind her, watching the interaction between Beau and the girl. She hasn't even noticed our presence. Her fingers are trailing up and down his arm, tracing circles and patterns. I watch as Beau's hand clenches his cup. Josie leans so that her back is against my chest, tilting her head to look at me.

"I'm going to find Marley," she says, standing up quietly.

I nod, kissing her lips briefly, watching as she strides away in search of our friend.

I sit down on the stool she vacated, since Beau's new friend has taken up occupancy of mine. Clearing my throat, I finally get her attention.

"Oh, hi!" she squeals.

"Hi," I greet.

"I'm Cleo," she says, offering me a hand that's more fingernail than hand. We shake hands, and she starts babbling. "I just saw Beau here sitting all by his lonesome self, and I thought I'd give him some company."

Beau gruffly responds, "And like I told you, I have company, they were just getting drinks."

"I can't help that I'm drawn to such a handsome man," Cleo whines. Her voice grates on my nerves. So whiny.

"I'm not interested, Cleo. I think it's time for you to leave." Beau's irritation grows with each passing second.

"Can I help you?" Marley appears behind Cleo, her voice strong and determined.

"No," Cleo responds, continuing to stroke Beau's arm, even though he's pulled it away a few times. "I'm just spending some time with Ben."

"His name is Beau, and you need to learn how to take a hint." I don't think I've ever heard Marley's voice like this before. She has her hands on her hips, fierceness in her posture. "He's not interested. Get out of my spot."

"I'm waiting for him to tell me he's not interested, then I will leave." Good lord, where does she get this confidence?

"I've said I'm not interested," Beau reiterates, this time, yanking his arm away, and standing. He stands in front of Marley, reaching his hand back, offering it to her. "Please leave."

Finally, Cleo leaves us, and Josie comes back to sit next to me. She takes a long sip of her cider. "That was interesting."

I run my hand down her back. "Yeah. What did Marley say when you found her?"

Josie shrugs. "Not much. I think when I told her that he definitely wasn't interested, her protective best friend instincts kicked in, and she went tunnel visioned in her mission to save him."

"They've always had such a weird relationship," I mutter, glancing over at the two in question. They're huddled close to each other, talking in hushed tones. They don't look mad or irritated with each other, but more concerned. Checking in with each other to make sure the other is okay.

"I can see that," Josie says. Marley and Beau sit back down, all smiles now.

"Andrew, how's your project going?" Marley asks me. Her eyebrows raise.

"Ummm," I try to shut down her question with my eyes, but she doesn't get the hint. I don't want Josie to know what I'm working on for her. It's going to be a surprise. "Well, uh, good."

"What are you working on?" Beau asks, taking a sip of his pale ale.

"Just a commission," I say, again, trying to make them get the fucking hint. They both know exactly what they are doing, since I showed them my sketches for what I want to do for her.

Josie leans into me. "You didn't tell me about a new project. What is it?"

"Nothing special," I answer, kissing her forehead.

"If you're making it, then it's special."

I can't help but kiss her lips, because *she* is the special one.

Thankfully, Thomas arrives at the perfect moment, interrupting the conversation, and taking the heat off me.

"Hey gang," he says. "What'd I miss?"

"Not much," I reply. I stand up, and pull him into a back slapping hug. He gives me a tight hug in return. "Where's Arson?"

Thomas pulls out a chair, sitting down and sliding it in between Beau and me. "Home. I dropped him off after I got off duty. We had a busy day, and he needed a nap."

"Aww, poor baby," Josie says.

Thomas notices her, and breaks out in a huge smile, showing off the small gap in his teeth. His blonde hair is rumpled from the day, slight bags under his eyes, but he still has energy to come out, and be with us.

I squeeze Josie, holding my arm out to gesture at Thomas. "Thomas, this is Josie, Josie, Thomas."

"Hey, Josie," Thomas says. He offers her his hand.

"That's me," she says, shaking it.

"Nice to meet you."

"You too," she answers.

"What kind of crazy day did you have?" I ask, curiosity getting the best of me.

"We got another lead on that drug circle we've been chasing for a while, but it turned out to be a dead end." He runs his hands through his blonde hair. "It's so frustrating."

"Sorry, man." I grip his shoulder, squeezing lightly.

"Just part of the job," he says. "We have a detective from a few towns over coming in a few weeks to do some investigating."

"Shit, it's that serious?" I ask.

He nods. "Yeah. There's been a few OD's, and they're selling laced drugs, as well as we think starting up a trafficking ring."

"Oh my god," Josie gasps. Her hand covers her mouth. "That's horrible."

"Yeah, but we're working on it. If you see anything weird, call it in. Anything helps."

Marley finishes her drink, holding up her empty glass. "Tommy, do you want anything? I'm heading up there."

Thomas shakes his head. "Maybe a water?"

"No problem. Anyone else?" We all shake our heads, and watch her disappear into the crowd.

"Are you still looking for an assistant, Josie?" Beau asks, after he's finished staring where Mar disappeared.

"I'm not sure." She shrugs. "I might need to hire one anyway, because I can't take up all of Andrew's Saturdays."

I turn to look at her, my eyes wide. "You're firing me?" I clutch my chest. "That hurts, petals. I thought I did good today."

She laughs, shoving my shoulder. Her blue eyes sparkle. "You were perfect, but really, do you want to be spending most of your time off working with me?"

"Bold of you to assume that I don't."

Josie shakes her head "Either way, I need to hire someone as a backup, since I have the occasional Friday wedding too. I'm not pulling you away from work."

I guess she has a point. Being my own boss has its perks, like picking my own schedule, but I do occasionally have to schedule drop offs around the client's schedule, not mine. "We will find you someone. If not, I'm happy to help when I can."

"Thanks," Josie replies, grabbing my chin to pull me down for a quick kiss. "I'm sure I can find a college student that's home for the summer, looking for easy work."

"Smart idea."

Marley reappears at the table, this time with Jason in

tow. He's taller than the rest of us brothers, at six foot three. His hair is neatly combed, and short enough that you don't see much of the curls that all three of us have. He's wearing a Blue Ox Brewing shirt, similar to Beau's.

"Hey, look who decided to show up!" Thomas calls. Marley hands him his water, and he takes a gulp.

"I've been here longer than you, jackass," Jason grumbles. He's the definition of a grump for pretty much everyone, except his little girl, Lennie. Though I don't think anyone could be a grump around her with how cute she is.

"Pretty sure that's a lie." Thomas smirks. He's been pushing Jason's buttons since the day he was born.

Jason ignores him. "How's it goin?" Pulling a chair up in between Beau and Marley, he squeezes his large frame into the small area. Our table is officially as fully as it can be. He ruffles Marley's hair, pulling her in for a quick side hug. "How's the little sister doing today?"

Marley groans, fixing her bangs that are now chaotically strewn across her forehead. "I *was* doing good until you messed up my hair." She shoves him off.

Jason glances around the rest of the table, his eyes landing on Josie. "Josie, pleasure to meet you. How are you holding up with Andrew as a boyfriend? Do you need an escape plan?"

Josie snickers. "Not yet, though if I do, I'll be sure to let you know."

Jason nods, smiling. "Good. That's what I'm here for. How are you liking the cider? It's something new we have been playing with."

"Ohmygod, it's SO good." Josie babbles. "I had no idea you owned this place, so when Andrew finally told me today, I got so excited. I was obsessed with the can he gave me a few weeks ago, and it's even better on tap."

"Glad you like it." Jason says with a nod. "We're going to try a few new flavors with that recipe. If you want to try them, let me know."

"I would love that!" Josie smiles back. I gently squeeze her palm. I know how nervous she was to meet my brothers, but hopefully now that it's over and done with, she's feeling alright.

"How's Lennie?" I ask.

"She's been in a mood." Jason groans. "I never knew that a three year old could offer so much sass, but apparently, they can."

"I think three is probably the most sassy age, at least until she's a tween," Marley offers.

"Good to know," Jason sarcastically says. "She gave me the silent treatment for three hours last night."

Marley snorts. "No, she did not. There's no way that girl kept her mouth shut for that long."

"I'm serious," Jason continues. "I even tried offering her ice cream, and she wanted nothing to do with me."

"What the heck did you do?" Thomas asks.

Jason runs a hand over his face. "I told her I couldn't play *princess tea party* with her."

Every single person at the table groans, clearly on the side of our niece.

"Hey now," he tries to defend himself. "I didn't tell her that I *wouldn't*. I needed to finish cleaning up from dinner. I told her to give me ten minutes, but apparently that was too much to ask. I even got dressed up and put the crown on when I was ready, but she walked away, leaving me alone in her toy room."

"Damn dude," I chuckle. "Not surprised though, she gets her attitude from you."

"I am not that bad," he says with aggression.

"Sure," I reply. "Do you not remember the time I accidentally broke your Lego Death Star, and you didn't talk to me for two weeks, even though I fixed it, *and* bought you a new Lego set?"

"Oh shit, here we go," Beau chuckles.

"I have no idea what's going on," Josie says, her voice confused.

"I spent weeks building it, for you to come in and break it in ten seconds!" Jason's voice is exasperated and clearly, he's growing irritated with me.

Thomas leans over, slowly whispering, "Abort mission, abort, abort."

"Whatever." Jason drops it. "She got her attitude from me." He mumbles that last part.

"I'm sorry, I didn't quite hear you. What was that?" I poke.

"I said, she gets her attitude from me," he loudly says. "I've been given a taste of my own medicine, and I don't like it. It helps that she's so damn cute," he grumbles.

"It really does," I say. I offer him my glass, and he clinks his against mine, and we both drink in solidarity. "Josie's coming for brunch tomorrow," I state, figuring I should change the subject.

"Really?" Marley's face lights up with excitement. "It's going to be so nice to have another girl there."

Josie smiles. "Happy to be of assistance."

"Are you ready to meet Mom and Dad?" Beau asks, raising his brow.

"Sure, I mean, I met all of you hooligans, and I'm just fine. I think I can make it." Josie teases.

"Ohhhhh," Thomas jeers. "Yeah, she will fit right in. Just give Dad shit right back, and you'll be just fine."

I pull my girl into my chest tightly. She's a missing puzzle piece, one that fits so perfectly with mine.

An hour later, we're still chatting, everyone getting to know my girl, and overall, we're having a good time. Josie has a light buzz going on, and she won't stop giggling at everything.

My arm is tucked around her shoulder, and she slides me off as she stands, leaning down to whisper in my ear, "I have to pee. I'll be back."

"Do you want me to walk you there?" I ask.

She waves me off. "No, I'm fine."

I watch her walk away, making sure she makes it to the bathroom alright, all while enjoying the view of her ass.

When she's gone for more than a few minutes, I grow concerned. I pull my phone out from my back pocket to see if maybe she texted me before getting up to check on her. I get a message from her right as I pull up her contact. Only, it's not a text, it's a photo. She has her shirt pulled down low in the front, pushing her breasts up to show her ample cleavage. I stifle a groan, biting my tongue and discreetly adjusting myself in my pants.

I quickly type a message to her, thankful we chose to sit against the wall so I don't have to worry about someone walking behind me and seeing.

ME

Petals... are you trying to make me hard in front of my family?

JOSIE

Is it working?

ME

You could say that.

JOSIE

Good

Need any more help?

ME

Josie, you're killing me.

I glance up, checking to make sure none of my siblings are watching me. I'm sure my face is red. Luckily they are all engrossed in other conversations, so I turn my attention back to my phone.

JOSIE

I'm just giving you a little tease of what's to come.

ME

You're definitely going to be coming.

JOSIE

Oh my god Andrew, I think I just had a mini orgasm

picture

Holy fucking shit. Josie just sent me a photo of her blue panties wadded up in a ball in her hands.

JOSIE

Come get them

I'm standing from the stool within a second, thankful the tables are high tops. Four pairs of eyes peer at me, confused by my abrupt movement. "Be right back," I say through gritted teeth.

I discreetly adjust my erection as I rush to the back where the bathrooms are. I have no idea which one Josie is in, so I send her a message.

The door flies open, and Josie peeks out, looking left and right for people. When she finds none, she reaches out, grasping my shirt at my chest, yanking me into the bathroom.

"Fuck," I curse, her lips crashing into mine. She bites at my bottom lip, one hand tangling into my hair. She's ravenous as I kick the door shut with my foot, fumbling with the lock. Once it clicks into place, I'm thrusting one hand into her hair, the other sliding up over her shirt to cup those tits that she teased me with.

"Andrew," she gasps into my mouth, pressing her body as close to mine as she can. My back is up against the cool metal door, and I'm so fucking thankful that the band is so loud, or else everyone and their mother would know what we're doing in here.

I pull back from her lips, breathing heavily. "Give me the panties," I growl.

Her eyes widen, and she drops them into my waiting palm. "That's my girl," I say. Her jaw drops, cheeks flaming red. I tuck them into my back pocket, reminding myself to move them before I leave this bathroom.

I capture her lips again, my hands gripping her hips tightly. I walk her backward so she's against the far wall, and grind my hardness into her. "Mmm," she moans. "I don't want to wait until we get home."

"I have no intention of waiting," I murmur.

I glance around the small, yet very clean, bathroom. To my right is a small wooden bench that I vaguely recall making for Jason when he was opening up the brewery. Why the bench ended up in here, I don't know, but right now, I'm thankful for it. Josie's wearing a skirt, with a pair of black tights, much like she was the night we went to Paint 'N Sip.

"Turn around," I say. She does as I ask, turning around so her chest is up against the wall. "Did you take your tights off just to tease me with your panties?"

"Mhmm," she answers. "I wasn't sure if you would come in here, so I put them back on."

My hand slides under her skirt, smoothing over the globes of her ass. I gently squeeze. "Will you be mad if I rip these?"

"No, definitely not," she breathes.

I rip the tights, revealing her perfect cunt. My fingers slide between her wet slit, loving that she jolts at my touch, then pushes back against it, yearning for more. "There we go, petals," I say. With one hand between her thighs, I flick at her swollen clit, her warmth making my hardness ache with each passing moment.

Josie whimpers. "I need you inside me, Andrew."

My cock twitches with my desire. I quickly unbuckle my belt and pants, undoing the zipper and pulling my cock out of my boxer briefs. Grabbing a condom from my wallet, I open it, sheathing my length in seconds. I sit down on the bench, resting my back against the wall. Pulling Josie's back into my chest, I widen my legs, giving her room to slide down onto my waiting cock.

"Take it," I grunt. I shift her skirt up, giving me a perfect view of her ass as she grips my cock to angle it right, and she sinks onto me. With her ass resting on my thighs, my cock buried in deep, I tug her to lean back. Her head falls onto my shoulder, tilting her head to kiss me. She tastes like pear cider.

She gasps with the slight angle change, and I scoot back so I'm able to thrust into her a bit. I pull my legs in so they're together, and have her rest one leg on each side of my thighs. She's resting on her tiptoes, my hands tightly on her waist as I guide her up and down. Her legs shake with exertion, but I know she's nowhere near close.

"What do you need, Josie-girl?" I murmur in her ear. I nibble at the soft lobe, loving the way she reacts.

"Touch my clit," she says through a gasping breath.

What my girl wants, she gets.

Fingers moving down, I rip her tights further, giving me more access to her. Finding her clit, I circle slowly, building the tension. Josie jumps under the sensation, her pussy tightening around my already aching dick.

Increasing my rhythm, I can feel her getting closer and closer, her body reacting to my every touch, every move. Thrusting my hips, I fuck her hard and rough. Josie meets my movements, her body rising and falling with mine. With one hand between her thighs holding her to me, I slide the other up her chest. My hand clasps around her throat, not squeezing to choke, only holding there, making her aware of its presence.

She moans loudly, and the hand moves, immediately clapping over her mouth to quiet her cries.

"Shhh, you gotta be quiet," I say teasingly. "Can't have anyone knowing what we're doing in here, can we?"

She nods against my hand, an extra gush of wetness covering my cock. She's such a dirty girl, and I fucking love it.

Mine. She's my dirty girl.

Her body tightens, and I can feel her orgasm approaching with the speed of a freight train. "Close!" Her voice is muffled from my hand, but I know what she's saying.

I work her over, keeping pace with my thrusts, until I feel her detonate around me. Clenching around me, her pussy flutters with the shocks of her orgasm. I let myself go, giving into the pleasure of her. I empty myself into the condom with merciless grunts and thrusts into her. "Fuck, fuck, fuck," I chant. I still when the last of my orgasm passes, letting both of us revel in the afterglow of this moment.

The fog starts to clear, and I can hear the band playing loudly in the background again. "I owe you a new pair of tights," I murmur, pulling her into me for a kiss.

"Yes, you do," she laughs. I adjust her so she's able to stand. I slip out of her warmth, watching as her black skirt covers her delectable ass. Thankfully, it's long enough to cover the massive hole I created in her tights, but I think we'll have to excuse ourselves for the night. Don't want her to be uncomfortable.

"That was a new adventure," I chuckle. I tie off the condom, and wrap it in some toilet paper before tossing it into the garbage. We clean ourselves up, and I throw a few extra paper towels over the paper wrapped condom, hoping that it's hidden well. I tuck myself back into my pants, and move her panties from my back pocket to a more discreet location in my front pocket.

"Adventure is one way to describe it," Josie says. She pulls me down for a kiss. "You go first, I'll be out in a minute or two. I have a feeling they will know what we did in here regardless, but maybe for my sanity, we can leave now. Avoid the knowing looks?"

"Of course. I was going to suggest we leave anyway. I'm looking forward to another round at my place."

Josie snickers, her nose scrunching. "Go." She swats my ass as I unlock and open the door. She shuts it behind me quickly, locking it just as fast. There's no one in the hall, so I'd say we successfully got away with it.

24

JOSIE

Nervous jitters run down my arms, and I shake them out for about the thousandth time in the last ten minutes. I know I told everyone last night that I was totally fine, but I was lying. I'm freaking terrified. I spent the night at Andrew's last night, waking up bright and early, excited, yet, panicked. I've never felt so nervous to meet a boyfriend's family before, even though I've already met a majority of his family.

Maybe it's because Sunday brunch is something so sacred to them, there's this extra pressure. After I shake my hands out yet again, Andrew reaches over, clasping both of them in one of his. "Josie, I promise, you'll be okay. We can leave at any time if you're uncomfortable. I totally understand that you're nervous. The family is so excited to meet you."

I love that he's validating my anxiety, while also reassuring me. Zack would have laughed at me, called me stupid for being nervous in the first place. I never realized how unhealthy my relationship with him was, until I found someone that treats me so well.

"Thanks. I know it will be fine, but what happens if they don't like me?" My voice is small, scared.

"Honestly, petals, I really don't see that happening. But on the off chance that they don't like you *-which won't happen-* then we will take it as it comes. The important thing is that *I* like you. That's all that matters."

I nod, giving myself one last shake as we pull into his parents driveway. He points two houses down. "That's the house Marley grew up in. Her parents are still there."

I spare a glance at the house, a two story, with gray siding, crisp white trim, and a dark navy door. There are window boxes below the front windows, bright purple petunias sprawling over the top and sides. It looks like the perfect family home, straight out of an early 2000's sitcom. The driveway has four cars in it, as well as Cunningham's driveway.

Andrew shuts the truck off, and climbs out. I use the extra moment to take another deep breath. The blinds in the front window raise, and I see Earl, holding a young girl in his arms. He points out the window to Andrew's truck, presumably at me. I grab the small bouquets of flowers I whipped together this morning, and tuck them in the crook of my arm. I smile, and climb out. When the little girl begins to wave at me, my heart clenches. "Is that Lennie?" I ask. The smile that breaks out on both Andrew and my face is instantaneous.

"Yeah, that's Lennie-Lou." Andrew waves to his niece, who is now crawling down her great-grandfather's body in an attempt to meet us at the front door. As we walk up the front steps, the door flings open. Lennie is standing there, her long dark brown hair tangled in waves. I can't say I've ever seen such long hair on a toddler before, but it's gorgeous.

She has on the cutest little outfit, and I must say, if Jason is the one who put this outfit together, he has some good style. A mustard yellow long sleeve cotton shirt with flared wrists is paired with a navy blue skirt, and a matching yellow bow in her beautiful hair.

She stands in the doorway, her hands clasped together, swaying slowly back and forth. "Hi, Unca Andwoo," her voice is soft and shy, but she's looking at Andrew like he hung the moon.

"Hi, Lennie-Lou," Andrew greets. He lets go of my hand to crouch down, opening his arms to her. Lennie practically leaps into them, and Andrew holds her close to his chest, groaning. "Jeez, when did you get so strong?" He tips backward so she falls onto his chest.

Lennie lets out peals of high pitched laughter as she tries to climb off him, but his arms are wrapped around her, so she can't move. Earl joins me in the doorway, watching the moment play out.

Lennie is so out of breath from laughter that Andrew has to let her up. Her earlier shyness is gone the minute she's standing on her own two feet, and in her adorable little kid voice, she says, "Hi, Yosie."

"Hi, Lennie," I say, lowering myself to her level. "It's so nice to meet you. Your Uncle Andrew has told me so much about you. I hear you like flowers, is that true?"

She nods enthusiastically, eyeing the flowers in my arm. "Should we go inside and you can pick which one you like best?"

"Yes, pwease," she murmurs, eyes wide at the colorful arrangement. I straighten, and notice Andrew wiping dirt off his ass out of the corner of my eye. I offer him a smirk, and a little hand clasps my palm. I have to literally stop a tear from rolling down my cheek, because *oh my god*, this might be the cutest thing I've ever had happen to me. "Gwammy, look!" Lennie calls as she leads me inside. I barely have time to kick off my shoes or see if Andrew is following. I try to admire the interior of the house, but don't get much of a chance since Lennie is dragging me full speed to the kitchen.

Andrew's mom, Nikki, is standing over the kitchen counter, arranging a small spread of food. I can see her features in every one of her sons. Andrew has her small, curved nose, and the dimple in her cheek. Thomas has the color of her eyes and blonde hair. Beau and Andrew share the curls in her hair, while Jason has the shape of her eyes, and the bridge of her nose.

Andrew's dad, Richard, shuffles around his wife in the kitchen, helping her get organized. He even stops for a moment to wrap his arms around her, kissing her cheek softly.

Nikki lifts her head from the egg bake at her grand-daughter's voice. When she spots me being tugged by the freakishly strong three year old, she smiles. "Josie, it's so nice to finally meet you." She wipes her hands on her floral apron, stepping over to me. Richard follows close behind, a smile resembling Andrew's on his face.

"Hi, Nikki, Richard," I reply. "These are for you."I smile shyly, trying to hide the obvious nervousness I feel.

"They're gorgeous. You didn't have to do that, but wow, am I glad you did." I offer her the bundle of flowers, and she sets them down on the table.

"What kind of florist would I be if I didn't bring flowers to a gathering?" I chuckle anxiously.

"She said we could pick dem, Gwammy," Lennie boasts. She still has her tiny hand squeezed around mine.

"Did she?" Nikki asks. "That's so sweet." Nikki offers

me a side hug since my hand is still being held captive by Lennie. Not that I mind. I shake Richard's hand as well.

Andrew shuffles into the kitchen, Grandpa, Marley, Beau, and Thomas close behind. "Lennie, you stole my girl-friend!" he teasingly accuses.

Lennie shrugs, briefly sticking her tongue out at him. *Ah, so there's that attitude Jason mentioned.*

"Hey, none of that," Jason calls, appearing behind us. "We don't stick our tongues out at people. It's not very nice."

"Sowwy, Unca Andwoo," she murmurs. She drops her chin to her chest bashfully.

I see the spark of mischief in Andrew, and as soon as Jason turns the other way, he whispers her name. Once her head is tilted up to look at him, Andrew crosses his eyes, and sticks his tongue out at her. Of course, Lennie laughs glee-fully. Everyone in the room saw the quick exchange besides Jason, but no one tells him what ensued.

"I wike Yosie," Lennie says. "Andwoo, do you wike Yosie?"

"I like Josie very much," Andrew answers. He slips behind me, trailing his arm around my waist as he does. He steps to his mom, who is still standing next to me. "Mom," he greets, kissing her on the cheek. "Sorry I missed the intro-duction. I was wiping dirt off myself, then Tommy tackled me into the grass."

"You would think that I raised monkeys," Nikki says with a sigh. "I'm so glad you were able to make it today, Josie. I heard you had a wedding yesterday?"

"Yeah," I answer. Lennie tugs me over to the large dining room table, pulling me down onto the bench seat. Marley sits down next to us, greeting me with a smile. The rest of the boys, Richard included, follow Jason out onto the back deck. Looking at the table, I can tell that it was made by Andrew, or his grandpa. Very clearly handcrafted. Gorgeous wood stained a dark mahogany, sanded down to smooth perfection. "Andrew was a lot of help."

Nikki waves her hand flippantly. "I don't care about Andrew, I want you to tell me all about the flowers you picked. Did you do a flower arch? Oh, I just love those arches you see on Facebook. So beautiful."

Her interest in me and my craft is unexpected, but also welcomed. "We didn't do a flower arch for this one, but I've done one before. Tough to construct, but the end product makes it worth it." I pull my phone out of my pocket, sliding the screen open.

As I do, the screen glitches as an incoming call rolls in. *Tessa.*

Irritated, I decline it, then before I can think twice of it, I send her a message.

ME

I'm busy, I'll call you later.

TESSA

Please. I miss you, Josie.

I read the message, and turn on do not disturb and swipe to my photos app. I don't need her bothering me today. Nikki comes over, sitting next to Lennie and me in one of the chairs.

I hold out my phone to show her some photos of my arrangements. She lifts a pair of reading glasses from her shirt, resting them on her nose. She holds the phone out, tilting her head back to get a better look. "My my my," she murmurs. "You have talent my darling."

Her words fill me with so much pride, I might burst.

Sure, I've received plenty of compliments, but she's so forward with her praise that it gives me a giddy sense of achievement.

"Thank you, that really means a lot," I say. She passes my phone back, and I slide it into my back pocket. I hear the front door open, and footsteps heading in our direction.

"Nikki, did you need butter?" a feminine voice calls.

Nikki stands from the chair next to me, heading toward the entryway of the kitchen. Before she can reply, an older woman appears, her dark brown hair twisted into a chignon on the back of her head. She's wearing clothes that could only be described as her "Sunday Best." Navy slacks with a pastel pink shirt on top, and a white floral cardigan over that.

"No, I had enough, Jane," Nikki says. She takes the platter in Jane's hands, and Jane spots me sitting next to Marley. "You must be Josie."

"That's me," I say, awkwardly raising my hand to wave.

"I'm Jane, Marley's mom."

"Oh, it's so nice to meet you." I stand from my chair to offer her my hand. Instead of the handshake, she pulls me into a hug. She smells of warm chocolate chip cookies, and for some reason, I feel so much comfort in her embrace.

When she pulls away, she steps to the side, revealing a tall bald man behind her. "This is my husband, Gabriel." Gabriel shakes my hand firmly, smiling softly at me.

"Pleasure to meet you, Josie."

"You too," I reply. I sit back down on the bench where Lennie takes my hand back in hers. The little show of her feeling comfortable enough with me to do so makes my heart do a little pitter-patter. It's a simple thing, but a kid liking you makes you feel like a thousand bucks.

Marley stands to greet her parents with hugs, and

directs her dad out onto the porch where the rest of the guys are. Jane starts helping Nikki get brunch organized, and when I ask if I can help, they shoot me down immediately, saying that today I'm a guest, and next week, I can help. I already feel so included, and welcomed into their family, and I haven't even been here fifteen minutes.

"Marley, you have siblings, right?" I ask.

Marley pushes her bangs out of her eyes. "Yeah, Prescott and Kenny. Kenny works overnights in the ER as a PA, so he usually can't come. Prescott doesn't grace us with his presence unless it's Christmas or Easter." She doesn't sound bitter at all over her brother's lack of attendance, only a hint of sadness.

"I see," I answer. "I'm sorry they can't make it."

Marley shrugs. "I'm used to it, and honestly they were never as close with the Cunningham's as I am. The Cunningham boys were more protective of me, treated me more like their sister than Prescott and Kenny did. I have no malice toward them, we just aren't close."

I nod thoughtfully. "My sister, Jess, and I are the same way. No hatred, just not as close as some families."

Lennie drops my hand to tap my arm. "Yosie?"

"Yes, Lennie?"

"Can I pick my fwower now?"

I smile down at the little brown eyed girl. "Of course you can."

AN HOUR LATER, we're huddled in the living room, waiting for the baseball game to start. Lennie is settled in my lap, her eyes drooping shut every few minutes, only for her to jerk herself awake. She has a small, light pink carnation in her hair, replacing the headband she whipped off the moment I suggested putting a flower in her hair. She insisted that I have one too, so I have a matching flower tucked behind my ear.

Andrew is next to me on the couch, his arm around my shoulder. His fingers twirl around a piece of my hair so casually, that I don't even notice it until Marley sneakily snaps a photo.

There isn't enough seating in the living room, so Beau is sitting on the floor next to Marley, and Thomas is sitting on the other side of her. I offered to sit on the floor, but they wouldn't let me. Earl is sound asleep in the faded green recliner, his mouth hanging open.

"Should we get going soon?" Andrew asks. He leans down, pushing my hair away to whisper in my ear.

I lift my shoulder, tilting my head back to whisper to him, "It's up to you. I don't want to disturb Lennie though."

Andrew shifts to glance down at Lennie. I can't really catch a glimpse of her at this angle. When he leans back, he whispers, "I think if we left now, before she fully falls asleep, it might be better. That way she doesn't get upset when she wakes to find you gone."

I nod, agreeing. Andrew stands from the couch, stretching his arms above his head. "We're going to head out I think."

I rub up and down Lennie's arm softly before adjusting her. I turn her to face me, and she snuggles right into my chest. Of course, I now want to snuggle in with her, but Andrew is staring me down with a weird expression on his face.

I slowly stand from the couch, talking to Lennie as I do.

"I have to go, but I promise we will get to see each other again soon, okay?"

"Otay," Lennie whimpers. "Can I come wif you?"

I glance up at Andrew, giving him my best earnest glance. I don't think it does me any good, since he chuckles, and shakes his head.

"I wish, but not today. You can come over soon, okay? I will show you all of the pretty flowers I have."

She perks up slightly, lifting her head off my chest, those big brown eyes holding me captive. "Do you have owange ones?"

"I do," I whisper. She gasps softly, then squeezes me tightly.

"I wike owange."

"Me too," I say. I whisper goodbye, then hand her off to her dad. He's sitting on another couch next to Richard, and she snuggles up into his large chest immediately. He's so big compared to her, it's slightly comical seeing such a large man holding such a small child.

After final goodbyes to Jane and Nikki, Andrew and I make our way to the front door. Earl has woken up, and is following us to the door. He's moving a little slower than he was the last time I saw him, his overall appearance slightly more harried.

His gravelly voice spurns me from my thoughts. "Andrew, how's the project coming along?"

Andrew's eyes widen, and I think he's silently trying to tell his grandpa to shut up. I chuckle softly, though I really have no idea what is going on. I wonder if it's the same project Beau mentioned last night. He clammed up just like this last night too. Is he hiding something?

"Good, it's going good, Gramps. Come by and see it this week, 'kay?" Andrew gives him a quick hug, and I open my arms as well. I've learned that this family loves their hugs, which is certainly fine by me.

He hugs me close, the husky scent of his aftershave wafting my senses, whispering in my ear, "He got lucky with you Cindy. You're too good for him."

I laugh. "I think it's the other way around, Earl. I'm very thankful our paths crossed when they did."

Earl squeezes my shoulder. "Call me Gramps, Cindy. Everyone does."

"Okay... Gramps." I smile, and let Andrew take my hand. He leads me out the front door, and into his truck.

25

ANDREW

"Are you going to tell me what you're working on?" Josie asks from the passenger seat.

"What do you mean?"

"Everyone keeps asking you how the project is going. What project?" She looks over at me inquisitively.

Shit. I knew she noticed last night, and then Gramps asking about it just added fuel to the fire. Is it considered lying if my project is a surprise for her?

I laugh to try and hide my panic. "It's really nothing. I got a commission a few weeks ago to make a puzzle table for someone, and it's not something I've ever made. I asked Gramps for advice at brunch last week, and apparently it really interested everyone." There. That's believable. *Right?*

"Huh, that's cool," Josie murmurs thoughtfully. "Is it one that opens up on top? Or does the puzzle portion slide out?"

What the hell kind of fancy table is she talking about?

"Um, it slides out."

"You'll have to show me when it's done. I've always wanted a puzzle table."

"You like to puzzle?" I ask. *Nicely done, Andrew. Change the subject.*

"I mean, I don't *not* like to puzzle." She shrugs. "It was something we did as a family every so often, but we had to finish them in one sitting, because we didn't have a good spot to keep it away from our dog."

"Why did you have to keep it from the dog?" I ask, because that's kind of odd.

"She used to eat the puzzle pieces." She says it so nonchalantly that I'm taken aback.

"She *what?*"

"Yeah, she'd sneak up when we weren't looking, or when we'd take a break. She would swipe a few off the table and chew them up. We realized when she threw them up a few hours later." Again, Josie speaks as if this is no big deal. Meanwhile, I'm slightly petrified.

"Was she okay?" I dare to ask.

"Oh yeah, she was fine!" Josie waves me off. "We just had to watch her closely when we did puzzles."

"Oh, good." I swing my truck into the driveway. Travis sits perched in one of the front windows, patiently awaiting our arrival. "Looks like someone missed us for the four hours we were gone."

I lead Josie inside, knowing that we definitely are in need of a relaxing day. Between the wedding yesterday, the brewery last night, and brunch today, we are both running on fumes. We are barely in the front door, and Josie is bolting for the couch.

"I didn't realize how tired I was until we got into the truck," she whines.

"I feel the same. I'll let Travis out, then we can take a nap, or watch a movie or something."

"Mhmm," Josie mumbles, her eyes already shutting.

I chuckle to myself, heading to the sliding door where Travis is doing his tippy-tappy potty dance.

He takes care of business in record speed, rushing up the porch steps to come back inside. I let him in, and he bolts to Josie's side. He climbs up next to her on the couch, where she opens up the blanket she's curled up in. Travis slides right under the blanket, nuzzling into her side.

"Wow," I say with a laugh. "Nice to know where I stand on the cuddle pyramid."

Josie flails her arm around, eyes squeezed shut. "C'mere, honey," she murmurs. "You need cuddles too."

"Travis is taking up all the space," I say in a whiny voice. I'm intentionally being dramatic, but really, I just don't want to nap on the couch. I'll wake up with a crick in my neck. I'm not the young kid I used to be. I used to sleep on the cold ground after a late night bonfire party.

"You can push him down?" Josie says as a question. Almost like she's saying, "*Duh?*" She cracks open an eye, pursing her lips to stop her laughter.

"Sure, like that's an option." I stand in front of her, offering her my hand. She takes my outstretched hand, and I slowly pull her up.

When she's standing, she taps Travis on the head, and he slides down off the couch, grumbling as he does so. Josie adjusts the blanket, wrapping it around herself like she's a burrito.

"Look at my little Josie-girl burrito," I tease.

She has to tilt her head to glare up at me. "You wish you were as comfortable as I am right now."

"Good thing we're about to get into bed." I swing her into my arms, letting the blanket trail behind us. After we reach the side of the bed, I set her down on her own two feet. I pull down the comforter and sheets, opening up the bed for her. She bends down, sliding off her socks, then her tight jeans. She's left in just her purple lace thong, and t-shirt. I have to physically hold myself back from groaning, because holy fuck, I don't think I'll get enough of her anytime soon.

I curse the way my dick hardens, because now is not the time. Josie does some fancy maneuver, yanking her bra out from underneath her shirt. She heaves a sigh of relief, and I pause for a moment, a question popping into my brain out of nowhere.

"What does it feel like?" I ask.

Josie sits on the edge of the bed, then lays down. "What does what feel like?' she asks through a yawn.

"Taking your bra off. You made the happiest sound when you took yours off just now."

Josie snickers, rolling onto her side. She reaches out her hand for me, beckoning me into the bed. I kick off my jeans, throwing my shirt onto the floor so I'm in only my boxer briefs.

"I don't know how to describe it, Andrew." I slide into bed next to her, covering us both with the blankets. She curls herself into my side, burrowing her head in my chest. I wrap my arms around her, holding her close. "Imagine your balls being over five pounds each. Next, imagine having to put something on to lift them up, making your back hurt and your shoulders ache. Then, try to picture what it might feel like to take them out of their cotton prison at the end of a long, exhausting day. Pure relief, that's all I have to say."

A shudder wracks through my body at the horrible mental image. That must be a form of torture, and Josie, and all other women experience it everyday? Fuck, that sucks. Josie yawns again, her eyes falling shut. Travis is circling at the foot of the bed, before finally plopping down on my feet.

"Huh," I answer. "I've never thought of it like that. I'm sorry, petals. That sounds horrible."

She sleepily laughs. "Can't say I've ever had someone apologize to me for having to wear a bra, but thank you, honey. I appreciate it."

With a kiss to her forehead, she slips into a fast sleep, while I'm left thinking about how much I like this girl. Things with her have been so easy, so natural, I feel like I'm waiting for the other shoe to drop, or for things to go south.

26

JOSIE

Andrew's hand palms my breast underneath my shirt, squeezing gently. The hand relaxes after a long moment, but holds there, cupping my full breast in his large hands. I'm on my side, facing away from him now, the opposite of where I was when I fell asleep. My ass is tucked into his groin, and I can feel how hard he is, just by shifting my hips ever so slightly.

Is he awake? Or is he just holding me like this in his sleep? I try to angle my head to peer back at him, but I'm not successful. I listen to his breathing, and decide that he's still sleeping. I snuggle in, not willing to leave his warmth just yet. I doze off and on for a while, not sure of how much time has passed, when his hand slides down my stomach.

He trails his fingers up and down the softness there, then up to pinch my nipple between two fingers. Andrew groans into my neck, the vibration tickling my skin. Gasping, I reach my hand back to hook around his hip, pulling him as close to me as possible.

"Hello, sleepyhead," he murmurs, kissing up and down my neck.

"You're the sleepyhead," I reply. I try to shift myself to face him, but he doesn't let me move. "I've been awake for a while."

"Why didn't you wake me?"

"You needed to sleep. We've been busy."

"Hmm. Maybe next time, I'll have to make sure I'm awake first," he murmurs thoughtfully.

"Why?" I gasp when he nips my collarbone.

"So I can wake you up using my tongue on that pretty little clit of yours." He squeezes my breast one last time, then moves his hand down my stomach, under the hem of my lace thong. "Would you like that?"

"Yes," I breathe, his fingers delving into my wetness.

"Good." His voice is husky, gravely from sleep and lust. Fingers find my swollen, ready clit, and begin to circle, teasing me with a deliciously slow rhythm. It's not enough though. I need more if I have any hope of coming.

"More," I mumble through bated breaths.

"You need more, petals?"

"So much more," I whimper. Andrew takes his fingers away, sliding his warm body away from mine. He rolls me onto my back as he rises to his knees on the bed. He grips his cock through his briefs, squeezing it tightly.

Andrew practically dives head first into my body, his messy hair tickling my chin. His nose slides down my shirt covered chest, his lips finding my nipple through the thin fabric. He bites my peaked nipple gently, licking it after to ease the soft ache. With a hand, he pulls my shirt up, revealing the other breast to the cool air.

"You're so stunning, Josie." His voice is tight, almost emotional. My hands thread in his hair, yanking him up to my mouth. Our lips connect, my tongue thrusting into his mouth. He kisses me harshly, desperately. "How did I get so lucky?" he murmurs against my lips.

He doesn't give me a second to say that I'm the lucky one, when he pulls away, stepping off the bed. I sit up, glancing around the room. Travis is nowhere to be found, which is a good thing.

Andrew stands in front of me, eyes glazed and heady. He reaches forward, grabbing my ankles in his large hands, yanking me to the edge of the bed. My ass just barely hangs off the side, my feet landing on the floor so I'm resting on tiptoes. I squeal at the abrupt movement, but Andrew barely gives me a moment to think. His hands are on me, pulling me up to take my shirt off, then dropping me back onto the bed with a soft bounce.

Hands slide down my waist, hooking around my panties. He drags them down my legs and off. Andrew stares down at my bare cunt, which is probably dripping in anticipation. "Fuck, petals. I love this pretty pussy," he mutters.

Where the hell is this dirty talk coming from? Wherever it came from, he can keep it up, because I'm obsessed. His words distract me momentarily, but I'm brought right back to the present when his tongue slides between my slit, lips latching on to my clit and sucking. He flicks his tongue, and the burn low in my belly turns into a blaze as he touches me.

I cup my breasts, playing with my nipples, pinching them until they tingle, sending flutters between my thighs where Andrew's head is currently taking up occupancy. He ups his pace, one of his fingers collecting some of the wetness from my pussy, then sliding in deep. I cry out in ecstasy, my hips moving at their own accord, seeking out his touch.

Andrew chuckles against my clit, and the vibration is too much. I reach down, yanking his mouth off me. I know that right now, if he keeps going, I will never come. My clit is throbbing, needing the release, but fighting against the sensations. "I need you inside me."

"You- but you didn't come?" His eyes narrow.

"I know, but right now," I pause to catch my breath. "It's too much, too oversensitive."

He thoughtfully nods. "You're sure? I want you to come first."

"I'm sure. I need you to fuck me, Andrew. Please."

My words seem to unhinge him, and he nods, reaching over to yank open his nightstand drawer. Retrieving the little foil packet, he shoves his boxers down and kicks them away. I scoot up so I'm sitting, my wetness getting all over the sheets, but I don't think either of us care. I reach out, taking his cock in my hand. I spit on his length, stroking my hand up and down his shaft.

"Josie," he warns.

"What?" I bat my eyelashes, glancing up at him innocently. "I'm just having fun," I explain.

"You're going to end the fun before it really starts."

I shrug, licking my tongue on the underside of his erection, base to tip. "I love your cock," I whisper, kissing the tip gently. Andrew shudders, eyes rolling to the back of his head. I take the condom packet from his fingers, and open it, sheathing him. I lay back down, letting my hair fan out behind me.

Andrew's eyes widen as he takes in my naked body. His tongue darts out, wetting his lips before he bites down on his bottom lip. I shove down the momentary anxiety over the stretch marks on my boobs, thick thighs, and cellulite, not letting my insecurities ruin this moment.

"Can't fucking believe you're mine," he murmurs. He folds over to kiss me, cock prodding at my pussy.

27

———

ANDREW

I'm throbbing, literally aching to get inside her. "I need you, Josie-girl," I say. Her irises are burning blue flames, waiting for me to do anything.

She nods. "Yes."

I grip her hips, sliding her closer to the edge of the bed. Her thighs hook around my hips, pulling me close to her. I grip the base of my cock in my fist, sliding it up and down her wet heat, coating my condom covered dick.

In one hard thrust, I'm sinking deep inside her. Guttural moans escape our mouths at the same time, and I hold there, letting her adjust to the feeling of me inside. Bending over, I nibble at her neck, tangling my fingers in her red hair at the root. I use my grip to angle her head back, giving me better access to her neck.

"You feel so fucking good," I mutter into her skin. "So tight, so perfect. You're so perfect, Josie."

She whimpers in my ear as I slide my cock out slowly, thrusting back in till I'm flush with her body. "Andrew," she moans my name, hands grasping at my skin, scratching me with her nails. I couldn't care less if she marks me, makes me bleed.

My hips pick up tempo, her cunt clenching around me, squeezing the literal life out of me. She's going to drain me dry, and fuck if I want anything less than that. "Need more?" I'm fully aware of the fact that she hasn't come yet, and I'll do anything to make that happen.

"Yes," she gasps.

My fingers find their spot, and I move, making her writhe under my touch. "More, please," she begs.

"Say less, petals." I give her clit a little pinch as I roll my hips. She hitches under my touch, and I can feel her cunt fluttering with pulses. "Tell me what you need," I grit out through clenched teeth. There are so many words that I want to say to her right now, but I bite them back. I'm doing my best to hold on, to make sure she gets what she needs. I will not come until she does.

"Don't stop," she breathlessly says. "Just like that."

I do as she asks, not changing a thing about my movements. Her eyes squeeze tightly shut, lines forming on her forehead. A slick of sweat slides down into her hair, and her hands tease her tits. Josie bites her plump bottom lip, and I curse that I'm not the one doing that right now, but if I stop, she might lose her orgasm, and I never want that to happen.

"Close," she stutters out. "So close."

"As soon as you come, I'm going to come, petals," I groan. My hips snap into hers, our skin hot and sweaty as we connect. I feel the moment her orgasm explodes. It sends me into a spiral, but I do my best to keep my pace.

Her mouth opens in a soundless scream, thighs shaking around my hips. Once I'm sure she's starting to come down, I let myself go. I thrust into her with everything I have, letting my own peak rise and rise, until I'm spilling into the condom, wishing I could be filling her with my cum.

When my hips stop jerking, and her thighs stop shaking, she drops her legs, letting her feet fall to the floor.

I slide out of her, already missing the feel of her, and dispose of the condom in the bedside trash before I collapse onto the bed next to her. I pull her into my chest, letting myself hold her while we learn how to breathe normally again.

"That was..." Josie murmurs. "I don't think I've ever had an orgasm like that before."

"Really?" I brush away some of the hair that is stuck to her damp forehead. She does the same, pushing back my sweat soaked curls.

"Yeah. Then again, I've never communicated what I need during sex, until you. I feel comfortable enough to do that with you."

My heart thumps in an unsteady beat. She's mentioned this before, but hearing it again makes it that much sweeter. Josie licks her lips, her eyes darting down to mine. I know she needs a connection from me right now, so I pull her into me, taking her lips in a sweet and sensual kiss.

"Thank you for telling me what you need, Josie-girl," I mutter into her mouth.

"Hmm," she replies, "Thank you for making me confident enough to do it."

"That's all you. I'm just the guy here to make you feel good."

"You succeed," she says with a small laugh. "Shower?"

"Oh most definitely," I reply. I sit up, pulling her with me. She stands, looking back at me with a mischievous glint in her eye before sauntering out of the bedroom, still completely naked.

Against my better judgment, I decided to place an ad in the local paper for an assistant. Very part time, only for events that are still TBD. Andrew was supportive, while also making me agree that I have his help anytime I want it.

Marley agreed to sit in on interviews with me, because even though Andrew's support is appreciated, I also fear he would scare any of the people applying. Megan offered to help too, but she has patients this morning. I'm mainly looking for college aged kids in need of a few extra hours of work this summer. Nothing too extravagant, and paying in cash, so I don't have to do too much accountant work. I'll have to hire an accountant someday, but for now, I manage fine.

I decided to host the interviews at a coffee shop in town. I don't want random people knowing where I live. If things continue the way they're going now, I might have to ask Beau about leasing options for a store front. I'm still working at the diner, only once a week now though, giving myself more time, as I've had more orders to fulfill.

It's pretty incredible what word of mouth can do for a business.

Marley walks through the door to the coffee shop, a notebook clutched to her chest in one hand, a canvas bag in the other. She glances around the shop, her eyes searching for me. She spots me waving to her, and rushes over to our table. I ordered myself a hot tea, and Marley, black coffee, per her request.

"Hi, I'm so sorry," she rapidly spews the words. "Am I late? Crap, I'm late, aren't I? I haven't been sleeping well lately, and my alarm didn't go off, and ugh, Josie, I am the worst friend in the world."

"Woah," I stop her, holding my hand out, standing up to rest my hands on her shoulders. "Marley, you're not late. In fact, you're still thirty minutes early. Sit down, I just got your coffee. Do you want any cream or sugar?" Marley sits down, a little dazed.

For how out of it she seems, her appearance is still very well put together. She has on a red floral patterned skirt that falls to her ankles, a white top that's tucked into the hem of the skirt and fluffed out a bit, with a jean jacket over top. Her hair is pulled back into a tight ponytail, bangs neatly over her forehead. She sets down her notebook on the table, her bag on the floor. "No, black is perfect."

She inhales deeply, seemingly grounding herself. She takes a sip out of the steaming mug, closing her eyes and taking another breath. She relaxes, most of the tension leaving her body after she gives herself time to reset. "Marley, I can do this alone if you need to go home, get some rest."

Her eyes widen. "No, no, I'm fine, really. Just life."

I settle into my seat, knowing that if she needs to, she'll

talk to me. My phone buzzes on the table between us, and I pick it up to read the message.

ANDREW

Good luck today, petals. I'm so proud of you. Your dreams are coming true, and I couldn't be happier to be the one by your side, cheering you on.

P.S. last chance to take me on as your assistant. I'd make it worth your while, rewarding you with lots of orgasms.

A small laugh bubbles from my lips. A smile finally appears on Marley's face. "Let me guess, Andrew?"

I nod, taking a sip of my tea. "Yeah. He wished me luck today, and said he was proud of me." I try to hide my emotion, but to be honest, I'm close to tearing up. I've never had this kind of support before from a partner, and him showing up like this means more to me than he will ever know.

"He should be proud of you. I mean, hell, I'm proud of you. You've been here just under a year, and you're already hiring an assistant? That's huge, Josie." Marley reaches out, clasping my hand on top of the table. "You're killing it."

I push down the urge to minimize the accomplishment. I mean whoever I hire will only be for events, not a full time employee, so it's not all that great, but I still am doing it. It's still a step forward in my business, and I need to acknowledge that.

"Thanks. I don't think I could have done it without you," I say.

She waves me off. "Bullshit. You're incredible. I just gave people the nudge to see it. It would have happened eventually, regardless of anything I did."

I send off a reply to Andrew, telling him just how

grateful I am for him, itching to say those three words that mean the most. We aren't there yet, or maybe we are, but we've been together nearly four months now, and I'm biting the words back more often than not.

Interrupting my happy moment, is of course, the one person I don't want to hear from. I groan, shoving the phone away as it rings.

"What's wrong?" Marley asks, her forehead scrunching in concern.

"Have I told you about my ex?" I ask.

"I don't think so."

I nod. "Long story short, he was a bit of a controlling, insecure guy. For instance, with my business, he was pretty vocal about the fact that he didn't want me to follow my dreams of becoming a florist. I asked him if he wanted to come with me when I moved, and he said no, so I broke up with him."

"Hell yes, girl. We don't need that negativity in our lives."

"Exactly. But now, he's dating my best friend. Or the girl I thought was my best friend. I don't know. I have sort of been avoiding talking to her, because I don't know what to say to her. She knows how he treated me, and I don't know. It just makes me feel gross that she'd jump into a relationship with him right after I moved. " I let out a breath.

"Fuck that. Want me to talk to her for you next time she calls?"

"No," I say with a chuckle. "I can't ask you to do that."

"Why not? That's what I'm here for. I'm not afraid to tell her how shitty her actions were."

"Thanks, but I think I can handle her. I appreciate you, though." I reach across, squeezing her palm.

My phone buzzes yet again, but instead it's my Dad's name on the screen.

DAD

Hey, kiddo. Checking in. Still on for dinner tomorrow?

ME

Yep! You guys still planning on coming?

DAD

Wouldn't miss it for the world.

I put my phone into my bag, and get my notebook with the questions I plan to ask out.

"Ready for interviews?" I ask Marley.

"You know it," she says with a proud smile.

29

———————

ANDREW

I've got about a week of work left on my project for Josie. I have a few more drawers and little details to add, but otherwise, it's almost ready. I have it all planned out. She has that wedding scheduled next Saturday, and while she's there, I've enlisted Beau and Jason to help me load it and get it set up in her garage.

There's a knock on the shop door, and Gramps strides in. Travis darts over to him, wiggling his body in excitement. "Hey, Gramps," I call, writing down a measurement before I forget it.

"How's the work bench?" he asks, slowly walking in. He's moving a little slow this week, and I wonder if he's feeling alright.

"Coming along nicely." I gesture to it, my heartbeat picking up as he looks it over. Over the years, I've received endless amounts of constructive criticism from him over the years, but I've never been so anxious before, never been so hopeful that he will be proud of my work.

He smooths his hand over the sanded top, then the

curved edges. "Gorgeous," he mutters. "I think you're better at this than I ever was."

I shrug off his praise. "No way. I learned everything from you, and I will never live up to your work."

Gramps chuckles. "We could go back and forth on this for hours."

"True." I laugh. Gramps heads over to the couch in the back, sitting down with a huff. Travis curls up at his feet. "You alright, Gramps?" Anxiety nips at the back of my brain.

"Oh sure, just tired. You know how it is. Getting old is for the birds." Gramps waves me off, adjusting on the couch.

"Alright. Well you know if anything changes, we can help, right?"

"You shut your trap," he teases. "I'm old but I ain't that old. I'm just fine. Having an off day."

"Whatever you say, Gramps." I sit down next to him.

"Where's Cindy?" he asks.

"Out with Marley. They are interviewing a few candidates for a part-time assistant for Josie. Mainly weddings over the summer, and events."

"Well that's awesome. Good for Cindy."

"I can't believe you still call her Cindy," I say.

"She's your Cinderella, of course I call her Cindy," his voice is filled with mirth. "You're going to marry her, aren't you?" This is one quality I love about Gramps. If he has a question, he's going to come right out and ask it.

"She is my Cinderella," I concur, nodding. I haven't even told her I loved her, but something within me knows that Josie is the woman I'm going to marry.

"HOW DID INTERVIEWS GO?" I ask. Josie is curled up in my arms on the couch in her living room. Travis is laying on his belly, his paws out in front of him as he tries to get Velma to play with him. She's staring at him like he's an alien. It's pretty fucking funny.

"Good," Josie answers. "I'm trying to narrow it down between two. One of them was really great, local, and sweet, but it sounds like she wants more hours than I can offer her, with limited availability."

"What about the other?"

"She was good too, she didn't seem as interested in the position, but she had really good availability. It's going to be hard to decide, especially with the event I need them for a week away."

"Is your gut telling you to pick one over the other?"

"No, and that's what's irritating. Normally I have a gut feeling with these types of things, but I can't get a read on what it's telling me," her voice is frustrated, and I can see the furrowed lines of her forehead from where she rests on my chest.

"You'll figure it out," I murmur. Leaning down, I press a kiss to her forehead, smoothing out the frown lines with my thumb.

"Hey now, what are the tears for?" I murmur. "You're okay. Don't cry, petals." I swipe away her wet tears.

Josie nods, hugging me tightly. "I'm sorry, I'm extra emotional today. I don't even know why I'm crying? My period is coming, and I always cry at the stupidest stuff."

"Josie, this isn't stupid. It's stressful, but you don't have to do it alone. I'm here for you, and I've got your back. Okay?"

"Okay," she whimpers. I can tell she's trying to stop her flowing tears. Her bottom lip quivers and she bites down on it, hard. With a few deep breaths, she stops crying. "I think I'm better now."

"Good." I tug her bottom lip free from her teeth, kissing it softly. "Now, what are we making your parents for dinner tomorrow?"

"Hello?" Tessa's voice answers the phone after one ring, like she's been sitting by the phone waiting for it to ring.

"Tessa?"

"Yeah, hi, Josie."

"How are things?"

"Things are good. I'm glad you finally called. I've been sick over this, and us not talking."

I sink into the couch next to Andrew. He finally convinced me to call her, promising not to leave my side.

"Me too. I'm sorry I reacted the way I did, but really, I needed some space to think, Tessa. Can you blame me for feeling a little blindsided?"

"No, I guess not. It just hurts that you're shutting me out like this."

"I'll be fine, but I needed the time." It does feel good to talk to her again. "How's everything going?"

She understands what I'm really asking. *How's Zack?*

"It's really good, actually. I moved in last week, and we've been talking about getting engaged."

"Wow, really?" I say. *That's fast.*

"Yeah, we went and picked out rings the other day, so it's only a matter of time. He wants me to lose a little weight before the engagement and wedding though, so I need to get on that."

My throat squeezes. "He wants you to lose weight?"

She answers, her voice ever so nonchalant. "Yeah, but he's right. I should be looking my best for photos."

"Tessa, you don't need to lose weight, you're a perfect, healthy weight." He's doing the same thing to her that he did to me, and she doesn't see it.

"We'll see. There's a dress I'd really love to get, but I need to lose fifteen pounds to get it."

I swallow the lump in my throat. "Tessa, you know that's the kind of stuff he would say to me, right?"

I can hear her scoffing. "Yeah, but he's right. I need to lose the weight."

I pinch my nose. There's nothing I say that will change her thoughts on this.

"Also, if I have a summer wedding next year, is that enough time for you to lose some weight, too?"

"You want me to lose weight?"

"Well, I don't really care, but Zack said if I want you in the wedding, and I do, that you should lose some weight. I want the photos to turn out good."

"Okay, Tessa. I— I don't know what to say right now, but I'm not sure I can do this anymore." My voice shakes as tears threaten to escape. She's never made comments before about my weight.

"Do what, be my friend?"

"Yeah. If you're going to treat me like this, I can't."

"Oh my god, you're being so dramatic. Think about it and call me back. I'll send you some dress options."

The line clicks off, and I drop my phone, shifting into Andrew's chest.

"Did what I think just happened, happen?" he asks.

I nod, not trusting my voice.

"Don't fucking believe her, petals. You're perfect, just how you are. I don't want you to change a thing."

I nod again, knowing he's telling the truth. I've never felt the way I do for Andrew, nor have I ever felt so safe with someone.

ANDREW'S ARMS wrap around me from behind as my parents pull into my driveway. I haven't seen them in a few months, and the nervous excitement I'm feeling sends my heart rate to a new high.

My mom flies out of the car, her thin, graying hair styled in loose waves on her shoulders. Dressed in a pair of casual jean shorts, and a tank top to battle the mid summer heat. She practically runs to where we stand at the garage door, engulfing me in her arms, just as Andrew steps to the side, letting go of his grip on my waist.

"Oh, I've missed you so much," Mom whispers in my ear.

"I'm sorry, I know it's been a while since I've visited." I squeeze her tightly.

"Stop that," Mom scolds. "You are living your best life, and I couldn't be more happy for you." I chuckle into her shoulder, not realizing how much I needed a hug from my mom until one was offered. "And, your boyfriend is so. Hot."

"Mom!" I pull back, smacking her shoulder.

"Am I wrong?" She raises her brows, eyes peering over to glance at him from the corner of her eye.

"Oh my god, please stop right now," I groan. She laughs, and thankfully, Dad comes to rescue me. He looks the same as always, the red hair I got from him slowly turning white, his blue eyes still bright and happy. He's wearing a Brooks Hill Sheriff's Department polo, tucked into his jeans, and the classic white dad sneakers.

"It's so good to see you, Josie." Dad squeezes me tightly, and the familiarity of it all has my heart pounding with joy.

"You too, Dad."

When he releases me, I turn to start introductions with Andrew, but find that my mom has already done that. She greeted and hugged him in the short period of time I was hugging Dad.

"Dad, this is Andrew, Andrew this is my dad, Kevin," I introduce Andrew to my dad, and they shake each other's hands. "And well, clearly my mom has made her own introduction."

"Nice to meet you, Kevin, Lori," Andrew greets. He pulls me back into his side, arm wrapping around my waist.

"Why don't we go inside, Travis is in there, and then you can see my setup," I say, opening the rickety garage door to lead them in.

"Who is Travis? Is he another boyfriend of yours? Are you part of a throuple?" Mom asks.

I shake my head, laughing. "Mom! How do you even know what a throuple is? But to answer your question, no Travis is not another boyfriend, he is Andrew's golden retriever."

"Ah." She bursts into laughter. "That makes more sense. I remember you saying that now."

After I show them my work setup, and we introduce them to Travis, we settle in the dining room to eat. I arrange the toppings while Andrew finishes up the fajita meat. We dish up, then sit together at my small dining room table. Andrew sits next to me, while my parents are across from us.

"Have you talked with Jess at all lately?" Mom asks as we begin to eat.

I shake my head, chewing my bite of delicious fajita. "I called her a few weeks ago, but she didn't answer. I meant to call again, but forgot."

Mom nods thoughtfully. "I spoke to her for some time yesterday. She mentioned that she and Brandon might be moving home soon."

"Where would they move?" I ask.

Dad interjects. "There's a base about an hour north of us. It's all very tentative though." He glances sideways at Mom. "I told Lori not to get her hopes up, because they could be transferred somewhere else."

"I can't help that the thought of having both my girls in the same state again gives me an excitement I can't contain. Jess always said that once they were permanently transferred home, they would start trying for kids. You can't blame me for getting excited, Kevin."

Dad sighs heavily. "I never said you couldn't be excited. I just don't want you to be devastated if they don't end up here. I'm trying to protect you, dear." Dad pulls Mom into his embrace, kissing the top of her head. Andrew drops a hand from the table, sliding under to squeeze my thigh reassuringly.

"I'll try getting in contact with her soon, it seems like we have a lot to catch up on. Anyway...." I start, hoping someone hops in to change the subject.

Mom moves on to the next item of business. "Tell me, how did the two of you meet?"

I furrow my brows. "I told you how we met, Mom? Remember?"

"Hush," she says, waving me off. "Andrew? I'd love to hear how you met and swept my daughter off her feet."

Andrew nearly chokes on his bite of fajita. He takes his hand off my thigh as he coughs, then takes a sip of his water to wash it all down. "Sorry about that," he grits out. "I met Josie the day of my best friend's wedding. I was tasked to be her right hand man, and she put me to work."

He clears his throat, leaning back in his chair to wrap his arm around my shoulders. "I kept finding reasons to talk to her the rest of the day, and after the ceremony, I planned on asking for her number."

Mom dreamily sighs. She's such a romantic.

"Unfortunately for me, she was already packed up and gone. Thankfully, my friend, Marley, was the photographer for the wedding, and had a plan up her sleeve."

Mom leans forward, setting her elbow on the table, resting her chin in her palm.

"Marley set up a blind date photoshoot for us, and I knew I wouldn't let her get away from me that time. I asked her out after we got dunked into freezing pond water, and she still agreed. The rest is history."

Dad eats his food like he's heard the story a million times, and Mom clutches a hand to her heart. "It's so sweet, like a fairytale. Meant to be," she sings.

Andrew leans over, kissing my temple. He winks quickly. "My Gramps, he actually calls her Cindy because of how we met."

"Cindy?" Dad perks up. "Why Cindy?"

Andrew clears his throat, his cheeks flaming red. I lean

into his chest, resting my hand on his thigh. "I found a... crap, what is it called, petals? A crocodile clip?"

"Claw clip," I correct.

He snaps his fingers. "Right, claw clip. I found the claw clip she left behind. I had planned on finding her somehow, and when I found her again, I'd give it back to her. Both Marley and my Gramps compared it to Cinderella, and when he met her, he started calling her Cindy right away."

Mom sighs. She hasn't even taken more than a bite of her food at this point. "That's precious."

"Mom, you need to eat your dinner before it gets cold." I point out. "There's plenty of time for talking after."

ONCE DINNER WAS CLEANED UP, we moved into the living room, where Mom and I had a glass of white wine, while Dad and Andrew had an IPA from Jason's brewery. We talked for a few hours, discussing my business and its future, Andrew's business, and everything in between.

It's about nine, and Dad is currently doing his *I'm ready to leave, but need to start showing Mom signs so she gets the hint and wraps it up* act. He stretches his arms above his head, groaning loudly. "Lor, I think it's about time we head out, don't you think?"

"Just a minute," Mom says, waving him off. Andrew and I share a humorous look when we watch him deflate into the armchair at her ignoring his signs. She pointedly asks, "Can you show me your workstation again?"

Eyeing Dad, because this is totally his chance to slowly lead her out the door, I jump at the opportunity. "Let's go," I say. We stand and head toward the garage. Travis follows us dutifully, running through the door and sniffing under every bench and table for a sign of something out of the ordinary. It's something I've noticed in the last few weeks, that he's very protective, but not in an aggressive way. He just wants to make sure both Andrew and I are safe.

Mom runs her hands up and down one of the plastic tables I have set up. "Are you happy, dear?"

I had a feeling she was pulling me out here to get me alone, and I was right. "Yeah, I really am." I can't help but smile when I think about all the reasons I have to be happy. I have a home that I'm happy in, a business that is growing, and a boyfriend who treats me better than I've been treated in my entire life.

She thoughtfully nods. "I wanted to apologize for my behavior when you moved. It was uncalled for. I was being selfish, and I understand that now. Zack was never good for you, and I was too blind to see it."

I nod, letting her say her piece.

"I'm so proud of you, Josie Rae. You've always been my little ray of sunshine, and you've proved that you always will be."

Tears sting the back of my eyes, and I didn't know how badly I needed her to say those words. I reach out, taking her in a hug. "Thank you, Mom. It means a lot. Really. I'm glad you understand that I was doing what was best for me, not out of spite."

"I'm so sorry I made you feel less than your worth." She pauses for a moment. "You're in love, aren't you?"

I nod. "We haven't said it yet, but yeah. I'm in love with him."

We collide into a hug that lasts minutes, tears sliding

down both our cheeks. A throat clears behind us, signaling Dad's arrival.

"Lori, I think it's about time for us to head out, don't you think?" he asks.

Mom and I part, and I spot Andrew standing behind my dad, his brow furrowed in concern. *Okay?* He mouths. I nod.

I hug Dad goodbye, and walk them out, watching until they pull out of my driveway, and their taillights disappear into the distance. Andrew stands behind me the whole time, arms around my chest, tucking his chin into the crook of my neck. My hands reach up to hold his arms, appreciating his embrace.

31

ANDREW

"I'm not going to go all 'macho man' dad on you, but I will ask you this. Do you love her?" Kevin asks. He's currently staring me down from where he sits across from me. His elbows rest on his knees, hands clasped in front of him.

I mimic his stance, nodding.

"And you have good intentions?" he asks.

"I do, I promise. I haven't told her yet, so respectfully, sir, I'm going to wait to tell her first, but the answer is yes, to both. I think I knew the minute I laid eyes on her. I was never one to believe in love at first sight, but that changed the moment I met your daughter."

Kevin thoughtfully nods, then offers his hand to me. We shake, then Kevin laughs, pulling me into a tight hug. "Welcome to the family, kid. Never liked anyone she's dated, except you. Don't make me regret that." He pulls back, clapping me on the shoulder.

"I won't, you can count on that." Without thinking it over too much, I speak again. "Can you keep a secret?"

Kevin leans back, growing wary. "Depends on what kind of secret."

I chuckle. "Nothing crazy. The night of our first date, when I picked her up, she showed me her work space, and since then, I've been working on something for her." I pull my phone out of my back pocket, opening it and finding the photos I'm looking for.

I swipe through the photos, explaining each little nook and crannies special purpose. When I've shown him all of them, Kevin smiles. "Good work, kid. She's been waiting for someone like you."

He starts walking toward the door into the garage. "Now, if it's all the same to you, I'm going to see if I can get my wife to leave. I'm beat."

I chuckle, following him out to the garage. Standing in the open doorway, I catch just a glimpse of their conversation.

"In love with him," Josie's quiet voice murmurs. It doesn't take a genius to figure out what they're talking about. My heart thumps hard in my chest, overflowing with love for this beautiful girl.

Kevin and I stand by and watch as they hug, shoulders shaking with quiet cries. It's a beautiful moment, one that I don't want to break, but Kevin is ready to go, so he clears his throat. I have to choke back a laugh, because this man really does not care, he does whatever he wants.

We say our goodbyes, and Josie and I watch as they drive away. "Did you have a good night, petals?"

Josie sighs, spinning in my arms to look up at me. "I did. I didn't know how badly I needed to hear my mom apologize, but when she did, it felt like this weight was lifted off my chest, like it was the final piece holding me back."

I lean down, kissing her gently. "It makes sense that you needed that. I'm so proud of you."

She kisses me back, arms wrapping around my neck. She hops up, wrapping her legs around my waist, and I catch her, my hands gripping her ass. "Take me to bed, Andrew," she whispers.

"You don't have to tell me twice, petals."

32

JOSIE

Against my better judgment, I hired the girl who seemed less intrigued by the position, but had better availability. Andrew tried to talk me out of it, and at this moment, I really should have listened to him.

I shouldn't have hired Brooklyn. That fact is currently being proven to me for the third time today. The first was when she was thirty minutes late for the time I told her to be here. The second, when she asked me if I thought she should take a selfie with one of the groomsmen to make her on and off again boyfriend jealous.

The third is right now. We're at Meadow Grove Winery for the wedding, and I asked her to run and find an extra pair of scissors for me since mine broke. It doesn't help that my period started this morning, ruining my sheets and favorite pajamas set. Andrew willingly helped me clean up, but it didn't ease the embarrassment I felt. I'm crabby as all get out, and feeling ready to burst into tears at any possible moment, because seriously, it shouldn't take twenty five minutes to find a pair of scissors.

Ignoring the cramps low in my stomach and my

bubbling irritation for this nineteen year old girl, I continue to arrange the vases in the reception area. The bouquets are ready and prepped, as well as the corsages and boutonnieres. I'm waiting to hear from the photographer about when they want them brought over. It should be any minute, and I could really use Brooklyn's hands so I don't have to take as many trips out to the gazebo they're taking pictures in.

Finally, she walks through the double doors, spinning the scissors around her pointer finger. "There you are," I say, trying to keep my voice level. "What took so long?"

Brooklyn runs a hand through her stick straight blonde hair. "I was hiding."

"You were *hiding*?"

"Yeah. One of the busboys is a guy I hooked up with a few weeks ago, and it was so bad, like *gag in your mouth* bad, so I hid in one of the utility closets till he went away." She nonchalantly drops this factoid on me, as if I'm supposed to just accept it, and move on.

"Brooklyn, I needed these like twenty minutes ago. You could have hid by grabbing the scissors and coming back in here. You didn't have to hide in a closet."

She tilts her head to the side. "Um, I'm pretty sure I did. You have no idea how bad it was. I mean, his dick was like two inches too short, and there was no motion in the ocean, if you know what I mean." She winks, then heads over to the table where I have the extra vases waiting.

I hold back the mini temper tantrum I want to throw, taking a minute to collect myself. My phone buzzes in my pocket at the perfect moment. The photographer is ready for us.

"Brooklyn, I need your help with bringing the bouquets and everything to the gazebo," I call, waving her over. She surprisingly does this without complaint, the first time all day.

Reaching the gazebo, I organize the arrangements on the wood benches, thankful it's an enclosed gazebo so the wind doesn't take any of the flowers for a ride. Brooklyn flops down onto one of the benches, leaning back and crossing her legs.

I inwardly sigh. The photographer shows up a moment later with the bride and the bridal party. I greet them, then pass out bouquets, internally cursing Brooklyn for sitting there, not helping at all.

The bride can't stop hugging and thanking me for how perfect the flowers are, and how I helped make her vision come to life. When the girls are all taken care of, it's time for the boys. Of course, this is when Brooklyn perks up and starts helping. She pins boutonnieres on as many men as she can, flirting with each and every one of them. Never mind the fact that all of these men are at least ten to fifteen years older than her, but who am I to judge? Maybe she's got a thing for older men.

Once the groom and groomsmen are on their merry way, I corral Brooklyn, and we head back into the venue to finish up. As soon as we walk in the doors, Brooklyn stops me.

"Hey, listen, I'm really sorry, but I don't think this is working out," she says. She pats my forearm as if she's the one firing me. "I thought there would be more of an opportunity to flirt with guys, and maybe hook up with some hot groomsmen, but it's not worth it."

I'm stunned speechless, my eyes wide, brows raising all the way up to my hairline. "You're quitting?" I ask.

"Yeah. I'll take my hundred bucks now." She holds out her palm, waiting for me to drop cash into it.

I scoff. "You aren't getting the full payment, seeing as you only worked for maybe an hour total. In fact, you made my job about ten times harder than it needed to be today." I stalk over to where my bag sits against a wall, and dig through it for a bit of cash. "Here's thirty bucks. That's all I'm offering. Take it or leave it."

She swipes the crumpled cash from my palm, and stomps out the door. When the door shuts behind her, I let out a sigh. To be honest, I feel better now that she's not here. I feel like I can actually accomplish my job, instead of having to babysit her. I pull my phone out to text Andrew before I get back to work.

ME

You win. She lasted two hours before demanding her payment and walking out. I'm texting the other gal tomorrow, begging for forgiveness.

ANDREW

Crap, do you need help? I can be there ASAP.

ME

No, I'll be fine. You enjoy your day with your brothers!

ANDREW

Well, I'll still be there to pick you up at four thirty. If you change your mind, call me. I'll be there.

ME

I'll be fine, but thanks. See you soon!

Andrew drove me to the venue this morning since there's more room in his truck. I didn't think about it earlier, but in the long run, it probably would have been easier to take my own car, regardless of space.

A tap on my shoulder pulls me out of my mind. I whirl around, not sure who I'm expecting to see. I'm surprised to see Isaac, dressed in a nice button up shirt and tie.

"Hey, Josie?" he greets. "I know we haven't officially met outside of when Megan and I married, and you're dating my best friend, but I just wanted to stop and say hi," he says. He offers his palm to me.

"Yeah, hey Isaac," I say. "It's good to see you again. Sorry we haven't gotten together, I know Andrew's been wanting to set something up."

He waves me off. "No worries. Life is busy. Megan's told me a lot about you, sounds like you two get along really well."

I nod. "Yeah, she's a great friend."

Isaac glances around the room. "How's the wedding going? Looks gorgeous."

"Oh, thanks," I say. He's still looking around the reception area. "Yeah it's going well. Had to work out a few kinks with the assistant I brought today, but otherwise, it's good."

"Good." He nods, shoving his hands into the front pocket of his dress pants. "Say, before you leave, would you have time for a quick meeting? I want to run something by you."

My gut churns with anxiety. He must sense it, because he reaches out, resting a hand on my shoulder in a friendly way. "Nothing bad, I promise. If anything, it's a good thing."

"Um, sure I guess?" I'm a little nervous. What could he want to talk with me about? "I only have about an hour of work left here." I gesture to the room around me.

"Perfect. You can meet me in my office when you're done, but no rush. I'll be here all afternoon." He spins on his heel, leaving the large reception area to head down the hall to his office.

I watch him leave, a little confused, but no longer worried. *Maybe he wants to plan a surprise for Andrew?*

"I'LL TRY to keep this short and sweet so you can get back to it," Isaac says. After I finished setting up, I collected my things, putting them in one of the side rooms until later. I have to do a final sweep through, but I wanted to chat with Isaac before my anxiety got the best of me.

"Okay? You're making me nervous," I say with an anxious laugh.

"I'm taking on more of a leadership role here at the winery, specifically with event planning. We've already been offering your information to clients, but I was wondering if you'd like to be our exclusive florist." Isaac pulls out a manilla folder, opening it to a bunch of paperwork.

My throat squeezes shut, and I do my best to hide the tears burning in my eyes. Is this really happening? There's no way this is happening.

Isaac explains the logistics of it. I'd be contracted with them for all their events, from retirement parties, weddings, you name it. It doesn't prevent me from being my own entity, but gives me consistent work, enough to where I could be one step closer to owning a storefront.

"Now, you don't have to answer right away, I want you to think about it. I'll give you all the paperwork, and my number in case you have any questions."

I'm sitting in his crisp, clean, office, completely at a loss for words. "You're serious?"

He laughs. "Yeah. I'm serious. I'm looking to change

things up a bit here, make things more streamlined. This was one of those things, and you were the first person that came to mind when thinking of a potential florist."

"Wow, I mean, thank you, Isaac. You have no idea how much this means to me."

"Of course. Now, take some time, think about it. If it's not something that interests you, let me know. Otherwise, we'd be lucky to have you."

I leave his office in a daze, taking the manilla folder of paperwork to the small room where my stuff is. I shoot Andrew a quick text message when I note the time, figuring that he should be on his way soon.

I do a final sweep of the venue, then I collect my things, and head outside, sitting down on a wooden bench, trying to process. I see Isaac climbing into his car across the lot, pulling out to head back to town.

Andrew still hasn't replied, but if anything, he's probably driving, and I'd rather he not text and drive anyway.

33

ANDREW

Putting the finishing touches on the work station for Josie has me giddy. I smooth my hands up and down every angle, searching for any imperfections or mistakes. I cannot wait to see her reaction. The shop door opens, and Beau is the one who steps through. His shoulder length hair is tied up in his signature man bun, and he's dressed casually in a faded U of M shirt and basketball shorts.

"Hey," he greets. He smiles when he sees the finished product. "Shit, man. That looks fucking awesome." He eyes it up and down taking in every angle and ridge.

I went all out with this. I knew that I wanted to make her something that she could someday bring when she's able to have a storefront. The top is maple hardwood, sanded and shined to perfection. There are two extenders, one on each side that make the table longer in length in case she needs more room.

Underneath, there's a thin drawer that slides out, which can hold her wire cutters, scissors, ribbon, and any other small thing she might want. Then, there is another plank of wood as a base, where she can rest her feet, or use for boxes, vases, and storage.

I had an idea pop into my head a few weeks ago that I quickly added to the design. Attached to the back side of the table, there is vertical shelving of sorts. Round dowels cross to the opposite side, where she can hang a bucket for petals, or scraps. I threw a few hooks on it in case she wanted to hang something else.

To finish it off, I made a stool for her. Maple wood, to match the rest of the project, and a cushion on top that my mom made. She found a perfect floral pattern, and made sure to make the cushion extra soft so she doesn't get uncomfortable.

"Thanks," I answer Beau. "I'm pretty proud of it."

"You should be. She's going to love it." Beau continues to admire it, when Thomas and Jason walk in.

Thomas brought Arson, so he darts through the shop, looking for Travis. "Where's Travis?" Thomas wonders when Arson can't seem to find him.

"Inside. I figured we wouldn't want him circling our feet as we try to load this up," I explain. "Though, he's probably whining because he now knows that Arson is here. I'll go get him. We have some time." I decide to ask the question that's been niggling at my mind for a week or so. "Have you guys noticed anything off about Gramps lately?"

The room falls deathly silent. Eyes flicker to each other as we have a near silent conversation with our eyes, almost unwilling to put the words out into the universe.

Beau is the first to speak. "Yeah. Seems like he's been moving a little slower."

Thomas nods in agreement. "Agreed. I saw him on Wednesday, I think? I don't know. He was a little out of it."

"Remember last week at brunch? He barely wanted to

get off the couch, let alone move around the house," Jason adds.

"I asked him about it last week. He basically shut me down. Said he was tired, just having an off day. Maybe he's fine, but something feels off." I shove my hands into my pockets, willing my anxiety away. I know that he's going to die eventually. I mean, he's in his eighties. He's always been in remarkably good health, so for us to notice this, it's a bit scary.

"I'll mention something to Dad," Jason says. "But we can't force Gramps into anything. He does what he wants."

We all nod in agreement. Feeling a little better that I'm not the only one who noticed the change, I direct the conversation to something less serious.

"You guys want some lunch or something?"

Jason raises a brow. "I could go for lunch. Lennie and I made French Toast this morning, but it was more goo than toast. I gave her the good pieces."

Thomas cringes. "Is it bad that I would have given her the gooey pieces? She probably wouldn't notice."

Jason incredulously looks at our brother. "Seriously?"

He shrugs. "Yeah, why not?"

"That's probably the quickest way to create a food aversion for her. It's hard enough finding things she wants to eat." Jason pinches the bridge of his nose. "I cannot wait until you have kids."

Oblivious, Thomas asks, "Why? Cause they'll be awesome?"

Jason chortles. "No, cause they're going to be insane, and you'll understand why I couldn't give Len the gooey pieces."

"As enlightening as this conversation is, I'm hungry as

fuck," Beau interjects. "Let's get some food, then we can load this thing up."

Jason leads the way out of the shop, clearly hungrier than he's willing to say.

AFTER LUNCH at one of the local bar and grills, we head back to my place. It's just about one, which gives us plenty of time to load everything, and get it set up at Josie's place. My phone buzzes in my back pocket as we pull into my driveway. Just seeing her name on my screen brings me happiness I can't even comprehend.

JOSIE

You win. She lasted two hours before demanding her payment and walking out. I'm texting the other gal tomorrow, begging for forgiveness.

Shit. I had a feeling the girl she picked wouldn't work out. Mind whirring, I try to come up with a plan to help her, while also getting her workstation set up as a surprise.

ME

Crap, do you need help? I can be there ASAP.

If we load it now, I can tell the guys where her spare key is so they can get in and get it unloaded, then I can hit the road and get to Josie within an hour. I'm about ready to tell the guys about the change of plans, when another text comes through.

JOSIE

No, I'll be fine. You enjoy your day with
your brothers!

Stubborn girl. I never should have told her I had plans with them, otherwise, I guarantee she'd take me up on my offer.

ME

Well, I'll still be there to pick you up at four
thirty. If you change your mind, call me. I'll
be there.

JOSIE

I'll be fine, but thanks. See you soon!

I do my best to ignore my desire to change plans and show up anyway, but I know how desperately she wants to prove that this is something she can do on her own. She can, I know she can.

I know I need to let her do this on her own.

Letting out a sigh, I run my hand through my hair, pushing it off my forehead. Beau notices, eyes catching mine. "You alright?" he asks.

I nod. "Yeah. Josie's having a rough day. The girl she hired quit halfway through the day, and it was a rough morning for her in general."

"Damn. Hopefully this will cheer her up," he says.

Determination runs through my veins. "It will. I'm going to make sure it does." I've been waiting for the perfect moment to tell her that I'm in love with her, and I think tonight is the night.

We all climb out of the car and head to the shop. We put Arson inside with Travis before we left, so the two of them are perched in the front window, tracking our movements.

I made the workstation in a way that parts of it can be disassembled for easy moving, so we get to work taking it apart. The back part with the hooks comes off, and Thomas and I carry it to the back of Jason's truck.

We chose to use his, since it has a topper, and even though it's a short drive to her place, I want it to be as safe as possible. And, my truck has all sorts of wood scraps and tools back there, and I may or may not have forgotten to clean it out in preparation.

"Ready for the big piece?" I ask my brothers. "It's going to be heavy."

"No shit, Sherlock," Beau says with snark.

"Hey, I'm just warning you," I say. "If you throw your back out, that's your own fault."

"Dude, you know my back sucks," Beau groans.

"Yeah, cause you're old," I refute.

"Fuck you, you're only a year and a half younger than I am."

"I'm just telling it like I see it, old man."

Beau doesn't say anything else, only steps up to the table. I take my phone out of my front pocket, throwing it onto the couch behind me. I don't want it to be digging into my leg if the table hits up against it.

We lift on three, each of us groaning at the weight. "Why the fuck did you make this so heavy?" Thomas grunts as we shuffle out the doorway of the shop.

"Cause, I wanted it to last," I grit out through my clenched jaw.

"Pretty sure this thing will outlive us all with how much this weighs," Jason says.

"That's the point," I groan.

We make it to the truck, lifting it in with lots of grunts and groans, but thankfully no problems. The boys are acting like they've never helped me move any of my commissions before. I've had projects way heavier, and more cumbersome than this one, but I get the feeling they are just being dramatic.

With the workstation loaded, we all pile in. I take shotgun next to Jason, and Beau and Thomas bicker about who has to sit in the middle, since Lennie's car seat takes up one of the window spots.

"You two are worse than toddlers, just fucking pick a spot and sit in it," Jason barks.

"Hey now," Thomas tries to defend himself with no luck. Beau shoves him in the truck, claiming the window seat for himself. As soon as the door closes, Jason is backing out of the driveway.

The closer we get to Josie's house, the more anxiety claws up my throat. What if she hates it? What if she thinks it's stupid, or too fast? We've only been together a handful of months. Am I assuming things about our relationship?

"Wait," I say. "Is this too much?"

Jason stops at a stop sign. He heaves a sigh, clearly irritated. "Don't."

"Don't what?" I ask. Because I'm going to need more than one word to stop the panic in my mind.

"Don't second guess this, man," Beau calls from the back. "You've been head over heels for this girl since day one. Not sure why this is making you panic, but stop it. Anyone can see that she's just as in love with you as you are with her."

His words calm me slightly.

Jason chimes in again. "You've spent the last month

working on this beautiful thing for her. Don't negate your feelings, or downplay your relationship with her now. This is a stepping stone, and you can either jump to the next rock, or turn around and move backwards."

I pause for a moment, letting his words simmer. He's right, I know he is, I just need to get over this momentary panic, and move forward. I'm ready for my future with Josie, I just hope she is too.

"Damn, when did you get all insightful?" Thomas asks. "That was so poetic, I think you gave me a little chub."

"Jesus," I groan, rubbing my hand down my face. "You just had to say that, didn't you Thomas?"

"Hey, it's not my fault I'm a hopeless romantic!" he yells.

"Fucking hell, Thomas," Jason groans. He looks over at me. "You good?"

I nod. "Yeah. I'm good. Thanks."

He nods back, leaving the stop sign behind us. "How did you keep her out of the workshop the whole time anyway?"

I shake my head. "It was tough. I was able to hide it the first week or two, then I think she started getting suspicious, especially when Gramps asked about the project I was working on. I told her I was making a puzzle table, and that helped for a bit, then she kept asking to see it. Eventually I had to sketch something up to show her, and now I actually want to make this puzzle table too," I say with a resigned huff.

"A puzzle table?" Beau quirks his brows.

"Yeah it's a thing."

"Good thing you led her astray," Thomas adds.

We're pulling into the driveway when Jason's phone

rings. Mom's caller ID pops up on the navigation screen on his dashboard, and he clicks the button on his steering wheel to answer the call.

"Hey, Mom," he says. "How's Lennie?"

"Jason, where are you?" Her voice is tight, shaky, and immediately puts me on edge. Something is wrong. One glance at my brothers, and I know they feel the same. Thomas leans forward in his seat, and Beau stares at the screen.

"I'm in my truck. Beau, Andrew and Thomas are with me," he answers. "We just got to Josie's house to unload her work station."

The line is silent. "Mom?" I ask, my own voice shaking. There's a lump in my throat the size of an apple, and my gut churns as we wait on bated breath for her to say something.

"I need you boys to get to the hospital." Her voice cracks on the last word. "Something happened to Gramps. We don't know what yet, but he passed out, and was unresponsive."

She's not even finished talking when Jason's pulling out of the driveway, skidding onto the street. "Which hospital?" he asks.

"They're transporting him to Twin Lakes General Hospital in St. Paul." I can hear the sound of the sirens through the phone.

"Where's Lennie?" Jason asks.

"Jane is watching her," Mom replies. *Thank god for Jane.*

"Okay."

"Your father is with me. We will meet you there. I'll let them know you're coming, and go from there." Mom's voice breaks, and that's my final straw. A tear slides down my cheek, the pain of the unknown wracking through my body. I lean forward in my seat, dropping my head into my hands. I do my best to take slow, deep breaths, but it's no use. The panic is too great, too strong.

"We'll be there as soon as we can," Jason says. He's speeding through town as fast as possible.

I stop paying attention to the conversation until Jason ends the call. I sit up, trying to breathe, noticing that Jason is immediately dialing Jane's number.

She doesn't even greet him as she answers the phone. "Lennie is just fine, Jason. Don't worry. I've got her. She can spend the night, and we will work things out tomorrow."

A small amount of tension leaves Jason's body. "Thank you, Jane. I know she's not at an easy age, but I appreciate this more than you know."

"You know this girl is like a granddaughter to me. I don't mind one bit. That's what family is for. We help each other. We went back to your parents house, and got all the things we need for a slumber party."

Jane's voice is soft and soothing, and it brings me back to the time I fell off my bike in front of their house when I was nine. I tried to shake it off, because if my brothers saw me crying over my scraped knee, they would've made fun of me the rest of the day. Jane saw me fall, and came out to help. She soothed me, let me know it was okay to cry, okay to feel the pain.

"Do you know what happened, Jane?" Jason asks.

"I know as much as you do," she replies. "I saw the ambulance pull up, and ran over to see what was happening. Your mother asked me to take Lennie so she wouldn't see any more of what was happening, and I did."

"Is Lennie okay? What did she see?"

"I think she saw them trying to wake him. She's okay now, but I think she's pretty confused, and a little shook up. We've been snuggling. Do you want to talk to her?" Jane asks.

"Yes," Jason answers immediately. "Put her on, please."

We hear the phone switch to speakerphone, and Lennie's scared little voice. "Daddy?"

"Hi, sweetpea," he responds. "Are you okay with spending the night at Grandma Jane's?"

"Yeah," she murmurs. "I was weally scawed. Is Gwamps okay?"

"I'm going to the hospital with Grammy and Grandpa, and your uncles to check on him, baby. The doctors are taking really good care of him though. I'll come get you in the morning, okay?"

"Otay. Can Mawey come over?" she asks.

Jane is the one to respond. "How about we call her when we are done talking to your Daddy?"

"Otay," Lennie says.

"Lennie, I'll call you in a little bit, okay? I love you, and I want you to have a fun night with Grandma Jane and Auntie Marley."

"Otay. I wuv you, Daddy."

"Love you too, Lennie-Lou."

Jason says goodbye to Jane, and the phone disconnects. None of us say a word for a long moment, my only thought being, *"get to the hospital, get to the hospital."*

"I knew something wasn't right with him," Beau mutters. I turn back in my seat to look at him.

"What the fuck are we going to do?" I ask.

"We're going to go to the hospital, and take it one step at a time," Jason responds. He's always been the most level head. The most calm of us brothers.

Thomas nods, his eyes empty, tears streaming down them. I probably have a similar look on my face. I don't know how to process this pain, this fear, so I shut down. I make my mind go blank, and I slowly breathe in and out, letting that be the only thing I focus on.

34

———

JOSIE

Something is wrong.

Andrew is over an hour late to pick me up, and I haven't heard from him since we last messaged shortly after one, even after my texts letting him know I had news. Usually he's texting me all the time, whether it be an emoji, a picture of Travis, or actual conversation, I hear from him often. I don't mind the frequent messaging, but the fact that there's been radio silence for the last two hours worries me. He knew he was supposed to pick me up at four-thirty, but ever since I told him I didn't need him to come help, he's been absent.

Did I upset him? I worry for a moment that he's doing this out of malice, that he's angry that I didn't accept his offer for help, but I shut it down instantly. Andrew would never do that. No matter how angry he might be, he'd never do something like this to spite me.

Something has to be wrong.

I put my phone to my ear, calling him for the fifth time. It rings and rings, then goes to voicemail. I leave him yet another message.

"Hey honey, it's me. Can you call me back? I'm starting to worry." I hang up, shoving my phone in the pocket of my black leggings. I bounce up and down on the balls of my feet as my nerves tingle with anxiety.

I pull my phone back out of my pocket, checking it again to see if there's been any change in the two seconds since I last checked it.

I wish I had any of his family's numbers so I could call them and see if they've heard from him, but then again, I wouldn't want to unnecessarily worry them. He was with his brothers for most of the day. Maybe they got drunk and are asleep? That idea gets shoved away immediately. It's five thirty in the afternoon. I don't think he'd get drunk that early, especially knowing he had to come get me.

My eyes burn with tears, because god, I'm so fucking scared. I try not to let my mind stray to the possibility of him getting in an accident, but the thought is there. How could it not be?

Think, Josie. What are your options here? I could ask an event staff member to hold my things in a room, call a ride share to get me home, and go from there? Or, I could sit here, and keep waiting, because he'll show up. He has to.

Or I could call Marley and ask her for a ride. Maybe she'd know where he is. She could ask Beau what they've been up to.

My finger is sliding across my screen to unlock it without a second thought. I have to get some sort of infor-mation, and if she doesn't know where he might be, then at least she can help me find him.

The line rings and rings, and I worry it will go to voice-mail when Marley answers on the last ring.

"Josie, thank god," she breathes. "How are you? How's

Andrew?" The anxiety in her voice cracks my already breaking heart.

A tear slides down my face. I don't even know what is happening, but yet I'm crying. "Marley, what is going on? Why are you asking me how Andrew is?"

"Aren't you with him?" she asks.

"No!" I nearly shout. The tears are streaming freely now, and I'm almost sobbing. "He was supposed to pick me up after I finished this wedding, and he didn't show. Now he's not answering his phone, and I have this feeling that something is *wrong*."

"Fuck," Marley swears. I can hear her mom in the background and the jangle of keys. "Where are you? I'm coming to get you."

"Meadow Grove Winery, but Marley, *what is happening?*"

"Earl passed out, and they couldn't wake him. He was being transported to a hospital in St. Paul last I heard." The sound of a car door slamming and a car starting is the only thing I hear.

I slide to the ground, the words sinking in. "Oh my god," I whisper.

"Andrew and the boys are at the hospital with their parents." Marley continues to speak, but I don't have any other thoughts besides getting to him. "I'll be there in thirty minutes to get you. Don't move."

"I won't," I murmur. The call disconnects. I lean back against the siding of the winery, trying to collect myself. I need to be strong for him now.

Time passes, and soon, Marley is whipping into the parking lot in her crossover SUV. She throws it in park, getting out while leaving it running. I collapse into her arms as soon as she reaches me, letting her squeeze me. "I'm a horrible person," I murmur into her neck.

"What? No, you aren't," she replies as she pulls me back.

"I thought he was mad at me, or that he got drunk and forgot to come get me."

"Josie, I would have done the same thing. That doesn't make you horrible. Come on, let's get you to the hospital." We load my things into her trunk, and then we're off. I continue checking my phone, waiting for any sort of information from him.

"I'm so worried about him," I say. "He's so close to Gramps. If he passes, this will destroy Andrew."

Marley looks over at me, her eyes sad. "I know. All those boys are so close with him. But they'll get through this, whatever happens."

I nod. "Do you think he wants me there? I mean, maybe I should just go home and wait."

"Fuck that," Marley snips. "You're his girlfriend, and you want to be there, right?"

"Well, yeah."

"Then I'll bring you. I know he wants you there. He's probably not in his mind right now. I've known Andrew for a long time," she says. We're on the freeway now, and the GPS on her phone says we will arrive in thirty five minutes. "When bad things happen, he shuts down. When Grandma Irene died, he barely talked for a week. It's not healthy, but it's how he processes."

My heart breaks at the thought of Andrew suffering in silence. I ache to be there for him, yet still worry that he might not want me there.

Marley and I make most of the drive in silence. With around five minutes left, her phone rings. It's Beau.

She answers immediately, putting it on speakerphone. Beau's voice is panicked as it fills the car. "Marley, we forgot Josie, you need to go get her," his voice is laced with panic. "I don't have her phone number to tell her what's happening"

"I've got her," Marley says. "She called me. Where are you? I'm dropping her off in five minutes."

"Fifth floor, neurosurgery. I'll let them know you're coming. There's a parking garage connected, so you can park there."

"I'm just dropping Josie off," Marley says.

"Marley, I need you," Beau's voice breaks.

Marley's eyes turn glassy, and she subtly swipes away a tear. "Okay. We'll be there soon."

"Okay," Beau replies, and hangs up.

I reach over, squeezing Marley's hand. She squeezes back, and I try to hold back my tears.

35

JOSIE

The hospital is cold, a sterile smell infiltrating my nose. Marley walks by my side as we step onto the elevator to ride up to the Neuro ICU. We still don't have any additional information, other than he was unresponsive, but the fact that he's in the Neuro ICU worries me further.

The elevator dings with each level we pass, until we reach the fifth floor. The doors open to a brightly lit waiting room. My eyes search for him in the chairs, coming up empty. The TV in the far corner plays an old sitcom, though no one is there to watch it.

Marley and I walk around the small waiting area, searching for any sort of clue as to where they are. "I'm going to text Beau," Marley says. As she pulls out her phone, a set of double doors to our left swing open.

"Marley and Josie?" the nurse who walks through asks. She's a petite woman, probably in her late twenties, so close to my age. Dark, almost raven colored hair is pulled back into a curly ponytail on the crown of her head. She's wearing a pair of mint green scrubs, a deep plum colored stethoscope hanging from her neck.

Marley drags me over to the door where the nurse stands. "Yes, that's us."

"Wonderful. My name's Zoey. I'll bring you back to wait with the rest of the family." She guides us through the doors, letting them shut behind us.

"Can you tell us any information?" Marley asks.

Zoey somberly shakes her head. "I'm really sorry, but I can't."

"No, it's okay," Marley says. "I figured it wouldn't hurt to ask."

"Absolutely. We have them settled in a family room down the hall, and I'm sure they'll be able to give you more info."

I nod, feeling a little numb. If I'm feeling like this, I can't even imagine how Andrew, and the rest of the family is feeling. Our shoes slap against the shiny flooring as we follow Zoey down the hall. Patient rooms flock us on either side. Some with patients, signified by a door being closed. Others empty, the doors open, showing the pristinely cleaned rooms with untouched bedding. "Do you guys need anything? Water? Juice?"

Marley and I share a look, checking in with each other. We both shake our heads. "No, but thank you."

"If that changes, there's a button on the wall you can press." We nod, and reach a room at the end of the hall. The placard hanging from the ceiling reads *Family Room*. Zoey stops in front of the closed door, gesturing to the room. "Here we are. Like I said, if you need anything, let me know." She steps around us, heading back toward the nurses station that we passed along the way.

I take a long, deep breath as Marley opens the door. Heads swivel to see who's entering, every face tearstained and tired. Beau is the first to react, rising from the brown leather couch against the far wall.

This room is much more welcoming than the other, with warm colors, and comfortable looking furniture, rather than the plastic waiting room chairs.

Beau strides over to Marley, his arms wrapping around her waist, head tucking into her shoulder. He softly sobs, and the sound is like a knife to my breaking heart. I hear Marley quietly shushing him, softly soothing his pain.

Nikki is enveloped in Richards arms, holding a tissue to her eyes. Jason and Thomas sit side by side on the couch, nodding softly at me, both their eyes red and hollow. Jason jerks his head in the direction I need to be.

Andrew is in a recliner against the farthest wall, tucked into the corner of the room. His head is in his hands, and he's unmoving. He's completely unaware of my presence, but my legs automatically go to him. I'm pulled to him, aching to comfort him, however I can.

When I reach him, I run my fingers through his curly hair, sinking to my knees at his feet. Cupping his face, I lift it so he can see me. "Andrew," I whisper.

His eyes are squeezed shut, puffy and red. When he opens them, his beautiful brown eyes are haunted. "Josie," he rasps. I nod, sliding my hand from his face to the back of his neck. "You're— how—" he whispers, voice breaking. "I'm so sorry, oh god, I forgot my phone, I— I forgot about you," he cries.

"Hey, hey," I soothe, letting him wrap his arms around me, pulling me up to sit in his lap. "It's okay, I'm okay. Shhh," I whisper. His cries shatter me to pieces, and all the strength I'd tried to muster up crumbles at our feet.

His pain is so raw, and trying to carry that pain is impossible. I hold him, letting him cry into my shirt. Andrew tries to speak, to tell me what's happening, but the only words I can pick up are *Gramps, fall,* and *surgery.*

Moments later, I hear the door open, and hushed voices begin to fill the room. Andrew lifts his head off my shoulder, and we turn to see who it is. A man in a white coat and pale blue-gray scrubs stands in front of Richard and Nikki. I slide off Andrew's lap, letting him stand from the recliner. I use my thumbs to wipe away his tears, and take his hand, walking us over to the rest of the family.

The doctor begins to update us on Earl's condition. "Earl had something called a subdural hematoma, or more commonly known as a brain bleed. In his case, it was minor, but a brain bleed is still extremely serious."

We all listen carefully, soaking up every word. He continues, "Typically people get brain bleeds after a fall, or injury to the head. From other bruising to his elbows and lower back, we can make an educated guess that he fell sometime, possibly earlier today, and hit his head on a wall, or the floor. What we did to fix the issue, is we performed a craniectomy. Essentially, this is a procedure to help relieve swelling to the brain. Once the swelling goes down, we'll replace the portion of the skill we removed. The bleed has been controlled, and will resolve on its own. We will keep him intubated and sedated for a few days to help restrict his movement and aid healing. He should make close to a full recovery if he remains stable, and follows the treatment and therapy plan. All in all, he's a lucky guy."

A collective sigh of relief escapes from all of us. Richard asks a few follow up questions, but I'm not paying much attention anymore. Andrew is stepping backwards to the recliner. I follow, well, more so I am dragged with him.

He sinks into the leather, pulling me down with him. I land in his lap, and let him pull me in close. He holds me like that, not speaking, not crying, just holding me, for a long time. The doctor leaves, and shortly after, Zoey stops by to let us know he's in recovery, and we can see him shortly. I listen to everyone's hushed conversations, making sure to stay on top of potential information that Andrew might need to be aware of.

Out of the corner of my eye, I notice Marley and Beau sitting next to each other on the couch. Beau is leaning into her, his arms wrapped around her waist, head resting in the crook of her neck. Her cheek rests on the top of his head, and she strokes his hair softly. I think he's asleep, with the way his eyes are shut, face so deeply relaxed, but I can't tell for sure.

Andrew, on the other hand, is completely knocked out. His head is resting back against the cushion of the recliner. Our feet are kicked up now, the recliner pushed back so we're almost flat. He's sound asleep, but still has his arms around me, holding on to me tightly. I wouldn't move, even if I wanted to.

36

ANDREW

A soft hand shaking my shoulder wakes me.

"Andrew, honey, we can go see Gramps now."

Josie.

The events of the day, *or is it night now?* Flood back into my memory. My eyes flutter open. Josie is still resting on my chest, but sitting up, shaking me awake. "Hey you," she murmurs. Pressing a gentle kiss to my cheek, I sink into the feel of her touch. She's grounding me more than anyone ever has.

She sits us up in the chair, kicking the footrest down. She scoots off me, standing and stretching. "I have to go to the bathroom, but I'll be right back, okay?" I nod, still a little dazed. My eyes are crusty and swollen, burning from dryness.

A look across the room reveals Jason and Thomas sitting on one of the couches, Marley and Beau on the other. Beau is completely wrapped up in Marley, seeking out her comfort the way I did Josie's.

I stand from the creaking recliner, stretching my arms

over my head. Jason jerks his head, beckoning me over. I head over, sitting on the couch next to him.

"How are you holding up?" he asks.

I nod. "As good as I can be," I say. "This day has been a fucking trip."

He scoffs. "You could say that again."

"I can't believe I forgot about Josie." I rub my hand up my face, pushing my hair back. "I'm the worst person ever."

Thomas shakes his head. "No you aren't. You're human. You forgot your phone, and the unthinkable happened. It was a perfect storm. The rest of us forgot too. Beau's the one who realized, and called Marley. Luckily, they were already on their way. I guess Josie called Mar in a panic."

Guilt eats me alive. "Fuck."

"We really need to get her number," Thomas says with a chuckle. "Not to make light of the situation, but if she had our numbers, she might not have waited as long as she did to get ahold of someone."

Josie reenters the room, her face red and splotchy from the tears shed over the last few hours. God, it feels like weeks ago that she texted me letting me know that she fired Brooklyn, or she quit, whatever happened. Josie walks over, sitting down on the armrest of the couch. She pushes some of my hair back. "You ready?"

I nod, turning to my brothers. "Are you coming?"

They both shake their heads. "We already saw him. We have to go in turns, since it's the ICU. When you get back, we'll send Beau, then I think we should get home. It's getting late."

A look at the clock says that it's past one in the morning. Shit.

"Fuck, the dogs," I curse. "Travis is prob—"

"Already taken care of," Thomas interrupts. "Gabriel stopped by the house after work and picked them up."

"Thank god," I breathe.

"Ready?" Josie asks, squeezing my shoulder.

I nod, standing up. I take her hand in mine, and head out the door, catching Marley's eye as we head out. I give her a grateful nod, hoping she can sense my appreciation for her in the small gesture.

She nods back, and I take that as my confirmation that she does. Josie leads us down the dimly lit hall, past the nurses station. She waves at one of the nurses sitting there, who gives us a sweet smile.

Outside of the room, my blood runs cold. Josie squeezes my hand three times, and I do the same. "I have to stay out here, but I'll be right here when you're ready," Josie says, and a pang of anxiety hits my chest.

"Right," I say. I drop her hand, but not before kissing her quickly. I cup her cheek, resting my forehead on hers. "I'm scared."

She nods. "I know. You can do this. He's still Gramps, just with a few tubes and cords."

Josie kisses me one more time, patting my chest over my heart, and sending me on my way. I open the door and step through. The air is stuffy, the only sound is the hushed whispers of my parents talking to each other, and the steady sound of a ventilator and heart monitor.

I feel small as I walk toward them. Like a child, walking down this seemingly endless hall to darkness. The curtain is pulled, so I don't see him at first. When I reach it, I push the curtain aside, and my heart clenches at the sight of my grandfather, my Gramps, in the bed.

His skin is gaunt and pale. He looks weaker than I've ever seen him. His head is wrapped in gauze, and there's a tube coming out of his throat. A choked noise escapes me, and I clasp the foot of the bed to stabilize me.

My dad stands from his chair in the corner, coming to wrap his arms around me. I fall into the hug, needing this. I begin to cry again for what feels like the hundredth time today. Dad whispers words of reassurance into my ear, reminding me that they're keeping him sedated as a precaution and that his outlook is good, but I don't focus on that. I focus on a new emotion I'm feeling.

Anger. Anger at my grandfather, because he was injured, somehow, someway, whether it be a fall, or something else, and he was too damn stubborn to tell us. So stubborn, that it nearly killed him. I break away from the hug, and step to the side of the bed, sitting in the chair there. I clasp Gramps' hand, avoiding the wires and tubing. Anger at the world for being so cruel, for making us feel this type of pain.

I squeeze his hand, and begin to speak, knowing full well that he more than likely cannot hear me. "You're a stubborn man, Gramps." I chuckle halfheartedly. Maybe delusion is taking over, who knows. "Fuck, you scared us today. You know that?"

Mom laughs softly from the corner.

"You're lucky you're gonna live, or I woulda been even more mad at you then I already am for not telling us you fell." I suck in a deep breath. "Don't do that shit. We need you here. At least for a while. You've got lots left to see. I'm gonna marry Josie someday, and I want you to be there, sitting in the front row. You've got future great-grandkids to see, and all sorts of other stuff to tell Grandma about when you get there, but that's not now. Not yet."

I squeeze his hand again, setting it down on the bed. When I turn to face my parents, they're both tearing up.

"Sorry," I mutter through my clenched teeth, trying not to cry again. "Just had to get it off my chest."

Dad pulls me into another hug. "We're proud of you, son. We're so happy you've found the woman you want to marry."

I nod, now choked up for a whole other reason. I hug my mom, then give a final look to Gramps. He still looks frail, and small, but I don't feel as anxious as I was before. I feel more hopeful now, despite the fact that nothing about his condition changed in the last five minutes.

Walking out of the room, I shut the door behind me softly. Josie is leaning against the nurses station, talking with the other nurses there. I come up behind her, resting my hand on the small of her back. "Home?" I ask. I need a bed, and fast. The fact that we have a near forty minute drive before we get there is painful.

Josie nods. "See you later," she says to the nurses. They all smile and wave, offering us goodbyes. My arm lands around her shoulder, pulling her into my side as we walk. Taking a deep breath, I lean down, kissing the top of her head.

"Thank you," I say.

"For what?" she asks.

"Being here, not being mad at me for forgetting you, just... thank you."

"Thank you for allowing me to be here," Josie responds. "You could have told me to leave. I'm not family. But I'm grateful you didn't."

"I'd never. You're family. Whether it's legal or not, you're my family." I stop, turning so that we are facing each other, I need to see her reactions.

Josie peers into my eyes, those blue-gray eyes that I love so much shining with tears. "I'm not going to lie, I totally was mad at you for like two minutes when I thought you ditched me, or were mad at me for not hiring the other girl. But then I thought to myself and knew that you would never do something like that. Something had to have happened." I nod, letting her say her piece. "I was so worried you were hurt. That you'd been in an accident of some kind." She drops her head to rest on my chest.

"No, baby, I'm okay." I run my hand over her hair, now taking my turn to soothe her.

"I know, and I'm so glad Gramps is going to be okay. I went from panicking about you, to panicking about him. I owe Marley big time for coming to get me."

"You and me both," I whisper. I kiss the top of her head again. "Come on, let's go wake Beau, then get home."

37

———

JOSIE

The two car caravan pulls into Andrew's driveway, just after three in the morning. Andrew, Beau, and I rode in Marley's car, while Thomas and Jason followed in his truck. The boys still have their vehicles here, as they were all in Jason's truck heading to get lunch or something when they got the call.

It was pretty lucky that they were all in the same place at the same time.

We slowly climb out of the vehicles, and when I notice everyone following us inside, I pause. "Are you guys coming in?"

Thomas is the first to speak. "Yep. I don't care if I sleep on the floor, but there's no way I could drive home right now."

Marley and Beau both agree. Jason, too. Andrew opens his front door, flicking on the light to the living room. The room glows with warm light, I head into the kitchen to grab water for everyone. We've all been crying for hours, so we definitely need to rehydrate. Come to think of it, I don't think any of us ate.

I'm not hungry in the slightest, but offer anyway. "Does anyone need anything to eat?"

A chorus of no's comes from the living room, so I head back in with the water bottles. Everyone takes one, chugging until their bottle is empty. Andrew reappears from down the hall, blankets in tow.

"Guest bedroom is open, and I have an air mattress. Someone is either going to have to share a bed, or sleep on the couch." I toss Andrew a water as he drops the pile of blankets to the floor.

He drinks his bottle as fast as everyone else. "Marley can have the guest room," Beau offers. "Is there still a trundle bed in there? We could share the room like old times."

Andrew rubs his forehead. "No idea, man. I don't even know what the fuck that is."

Beau chuckles softly. "I'll check. Come on, Mar." He offers her a hand, helping her to stand, and leads her down the hall.

"Marley, I'll grab you some clothes," I call to her back. She offers me a thumbs up. "Andrew, do you have clothes for your brothers?"

"Yeah I think so. You guys can fight over who sleeps where," Andrew says, looking at his other two brothers.

Jason is already laying flat on the couch, his arm over his eyes. "Yep," he groans.

Thomas rolls out the full size air mattress, plugging it in to inflate it. Andrew heads down the hall to his bedroom, and I follow, grabbing an extra pair of sweats and t-shirt I have tucked in a bag of clothes I keep here for Marley. Andrew tosses me a pair of shorts and a shirt for Beau. I head back down the hall to the guest bedroom, knocking on the door.

"Come in," Beau's low voice calls.

I open the door, finding him on his knees, pulling out the trundle bed. "I'm not surprised Andrew didn't know this existed," he says with a laugh.

I chuckle. "I had no idea either."

"He always slept in the basement when we were kids, so it makes sense," Beau explains. "Marley's in the bathroom washing up. I can take those for her if you'd like."

I nod, handing him the folded up clothes. "There's some in there for you too."

"Great, thanks," Beau mumbles. He stands, stepping over to me. "Thank you for coming today. Your support means a lot."

"Of course," I reply. "I weirdly get the feeling that your family would have done the same for me, and I'm just one person."

"You're a special person, Josie."

"Thanks," I reply awkwardly.

"I look forward to having you as a sister someday." His words catch me off guard. He winks, like he didn't just shake me to my core. "I think we both know you two are getting married."

I coyly shrug, not really ready to admit to anyone but myself that I can see myself marrying Andrew, sooner rather than later.

Beau holds his arms out, and I hug him tightly. "Thanks, Josie." I nod into his chest. For as grumpy as he can be, Beau also has a bit of a soft side.

"Goodnight," I say, stepping back from the hug and out the door. I walk down the hall to Andrew's room, finding him in bed.

"Did you bring the other two some clothes?" I ask.

He nods, his eyes already closed.

"Do you need anything else?" I ask, stepping over to him, pushing his hair off his forehead.

He shakes his head. "Just you."

"Okay. Let me turn the light off and change."

I change quickly, and turn off the light. I plug my phone in, making sure the sound is on before I set it on the nightstand. I got all the numbers of everyone in the family tonight, and Nikki promised me that she would call if there were any urgent updates. With the craziness of today, I realize that I'd completely forgotten to tell Andrew about the potential contract with Meadow Grove Winery. Tonight isn't the time though, we both need sleep, and there are other things that are a priority.

I pull down the sheets, crawling into bed next to Andrew. His arms and legs tangle around my body. "You're like my little octopus," I murmur.

Andrew sleepily snickers into my ear. "Goodnight, petals. Thank you for everything."

I press a kiss to his cheek. "Goodnight, Andrew."

I love you.

38

ANDREW

"This goddamn spoon won't cooperate," Gramps grumbles, watching the spoon that was once full of pudding shake as he attempts to bring it to his mouth. He's been awake and extubated for just over a week and has not stopped complaining since.

The physical therapist in the room offers him reassuring words, while aiding his movements so the spoon makes its way to his mouth.

The last few weeks have been the definition of chaos. Gramps is no longer in the Neuro ICU, but moved down a floor to the regular Neuro unit. From what we can tell, he's healing well. He's struggling a lot with weakness, and can't walk or stand without assistance for now. It's hard to see, since he's always been able bodied and healthy, but the doctor has assured us that this is normal, and to be expected after what he went through.

We've been on a rotating schedule as to who is here with him so he's not alone during the day. Today is my turn, though I've stopped by everyday, whether he was awake or not. Josie's been with me a few times. She plans to stop by later this afternoon once she finishes up this weekend's wedding. She hired the other gal, Kenzy, as her new assistant, and they met a few times this week already to prep for this event. Josie hasn't stopped talking about her and how incredible she is.

I haven't had the chance to surprise her with her work-station. It's still safely in the back of Jason's truck, waiting for the right time. I also haven't told her I love her either. I want the moment to be right, when I show her what I made. Though it's almost becoming painful not telling her how I feel.

I'm so fucking proud of her. The day everything happened with Gramps, Isaac met with her, and offered her a contract with the Winery. All her dreams are coming true, and I get to be the one by her side to watch it all. She seemed almost nervous to tell me, especially since she waited a few days until things had calmed down. She had nothing to be nervous about. If anything I was a little bummed she hadn't told me right away, so we could've celebrated. But, she had a point, things were a little crazy with Gramps in the hospital, so it was probably best to wait, especially since she wanted some time to read over the paper-work and details of the contract first.

The physical therapist helps clean up the splattered chocolate pudding, still using words of encouragement. I can visibly see Gramps getting irritated with her, but it's not her fault, or his.

He's frustrated because something he could do with ease a week ago now feels impossible. He slowly lowers his head to the bed, shutting his eyes. "Sorry I'm such a sour-puss, Ava, " he apologizes to the physical therapist.

"Nothing to be sorry for, Earl," she says, patting the top of his arm. His hands are still full of tubing and medical tape after getting his blood drawn multiple times a day. "I know this feels impossible, but you're already improving. Day by day, you'll get stronger."

Gramps opens his eyes, softly smiling at Ava. I can tell she's his favorite, and I can see why. She's good at her job, and has a natural ability for it.

After she finishes up the therapy session, she helps get Gramps settled in for an afternoon nap. He's tired all the time nowadays as his body tries to heal. Gramps reaches with a shaky hand for the remote on his rolling table. His movements are slow, and the furrow between his brows shows me just how focused he is on the task. They told us to let him be as independent as possible, so I sit in the crappy hospital recliner, watching his progress.

What feels like five minutes later, he has the remote gripped in his hand, and is able to press the button to turn the TV on. The hand that holds the remote drops to his lap, and he uses his pointer finger to scroll the channels. He's sort of cheating, but I'll give it to him.

He settles on an episode of M.A.S.H., and I sit back to watch the show with him.

"Did you finish the workstation?" Gramps surprises me by asking. His voice is still hoarse from the tube.

I clear my throat, sitting up in the chair. "Yeah, I did."

"What does she think of it?" he asks.

"I haven't given it to her yet."

"Why the heck not?"

I clasp my hands together in my lap, cracking a few of my knuckles. "Haven't had a chance, since you've been in the hospital. I want it to be a surprise, but haven't been able to get over to her house when she's not there."

He nods thoughtfully. "Where is she now?"

My eyes narrow, because I know where he's going with this. "Working a wedding."

"So why the heck aren't you doing it now?"

"Because I'm here with you?"

Gramps glares at me like I'm the stupidest person alive. "Here's a thought," he mutters sarcastically. "Leave, and go set it up."

"I can't leave," I say with a slight hint of exasperation.

"Why not?" he asks. He's testing me, getting me to say the words.

"Because, we all agreed we wouldn't leave you here by yourself," I explain. I know exactly what he's going to say before he says it, but I indulge him anyway.

"That's just plain stupid. I'm not a toddler. There are doctors and nurses here. And I can't sleep for shit when you kids are sitting there, staring at me. It's like you're waiting for me to croak, and I'm sick of it."

Annnnd there it is.

"Gramps—" I start. But he interrupts me.

"Now don't you 'Gramps' me. All of you need to get back to your regular lives. I'm heading to that rehabilitation center soon, and there's no reason for any of you to be sitting at my bedside day after day. In fact, hand me your phone." He slowly lifts his hand from the remote.

"Why?" I ask. I slowly clutch my phone in my palm, hesitant to hand it over.

"I'm going to call your dad, tell him I'm not a toddler."

I sigh, knowing this is a battle I won't win. "I'll call him, and put it on speaker."

"Thank you," he says.

I stand from the recliner and walk over to the bed. I pull up Dad's contact, tapping the call button, and putting it on speakerphone. I set the phone on the rolling table in front of Gramps, letting it ring.

Dad answers fairly quickly. "Hey, Andrew. How's it going today?"

"Richard, you listen to me," Gramps sternly says.

Dad sighs, sounding similar to my resigned sigh from just a moment ago. "I'm listening."

"I don't need a damn babysitter everyday. I am more than fine to be here alone with these lovely doctors and nurses. If you want to visit everyday to check in, that's just fine. But only a visit. You need to get back to your lives and jobs. I'm fine." Gramps nods his head, clearly pleased with his little speech.

The air is thick with silence for a long moment, then finally, "Alright. One of us will come by every day though, and if you change your mind and want someone here, you *will* let us know. Deal?"

"You got a deal, son," Gramps agrees. "Now, tell your kid to get outta here so he can surprise Cinderella with that beautiful piece he made."

Dad chuckles. "Andrew, you're good to go. Dad, I will stop by this evening."

They say goodbye, and I end the call. Shoving my hands in my pockets, I rock on my heels. "Need anything before I go?"

"Nope. Get out. I'm going to watch M.A.S.H. and take a nap."

I nod. "Thanks, Gramps. Josie and I will be by later today or tomorrow to visit."

He waves me off. "Go."

I give him a smile. Walking out of the small hospital room, I'm already texting my brothers, forming a plan.

39

JOSIE

"Josie, the bride is wondering if you have any extra pins?" Kenzy, my new, *amazing*, assistant asks. She's carrying a bucket that previously had loose flowers and greenery in it, but has since been arranged on tables in vases.

I direct Kenzy to the table where I have my extra supplies, and she grabs a few pins and heads off in search of the bride. I slip my phone out of the back pocket of my jeans, and walk around the small venue, taking pictures of the flower arch, and other things to post on my social media.

The venue is just outside of Ivy Ridge, about five miles. A small barn that has been specifically renovated for weddings and events. It's one floor, everything all in one place. It's rustic and chic, everything brides seem to be wanting these days.

I upload the photos, tagging the location, and adding a cute caption. I've been trying to be better about posting more consistently on social media, and it has seemed to help. People like the videos I've posted of me putting together wedding bouquets and other arrangements.

Kenzy reenters the reception area, tugging her blonde hair into a ponytail as she does. "Everything okay?" I ask her.

"Totally fine," she answers. "One of the groomsmen was trying to adjust his boutonniere, and dropped the pin in the tall grass." She shrugs.

"Ah, that will happen," I reply. "Are you ready to do the second arch?"

"Sure am," Kenzy says, already striding over to where the flowers are in buckets waiting for us.

All in all, the second arch takes us just over an hour to complete, but I anticipated it. Yet another reason I'm so thankful for Kenzy, and the fact that she gave me a second chance. Had I not had her help, I never would have been able to complete both arches. The bride was pretty insistent on having two separate arches. One that she could use for the ceremony, and pictures at the reception, and one behind the head table. I didn't question it. If that's what she wanted, then that's what she was going to get.

Kenzy and I had to drive separately, as there were *so many flowers*. Between the bouquets, boutonniere, corsages, and table settings, that alone filled my car. Throw in the two flower arches, and you've got two vehicles filled to the brim. Luckily, Andrew was able to let me borrow his work truck this week to get the flowers from the wholesale market. I definitely need to look into getting a van of some sort, but I'll add it to the list of all the things I need to do.

I officially signed the contract with Meadow Grove Winery yesterday, which is an incredible step for me. Isaac and I are going to be meeting a few times this week to discuss the different package levels we want to do, and what they would all offer. I suggested we go to the brewery, and have Megan and Andrew join us, since we haven't been able to spend time with just the four of us.

At the end of the job, we bring load after load of buckets, boxes, and other supplies back to the vehicles. Thankfully, with fewer flowers and boxes, we can fit everything in my car for the trip home, so Kenzy doesn't have to stop by my house.

Kenzy shuts the trunk of my vehicle with a loud *thunk*. I turn around, putting the last of my things into the backseat. I grab the cash I'd set aside for Kenzy, and shove it into my back pocket. Shutting the door, I round the back of my car to meet her.

I pull out the cash, handing it to her. "Kenzy, I really don't think you know how much of a help you were today. I wanted to apologize again-"

"Don't, really." She stops me. "I get it, my availability sucks. I'm just excited you saw the light," she says teasingly.

I laugh, pulling her in for a quick hug. "Thank you. You're amazing, and I'm lucky to have you. Can we leave it at that?"

She nods. "There's an engagement dinner next week, right? Do you need me?"

"If you're around, then yes, please," I answer. "But if not, I can probably convince my boyfriend to help me."

Kenzy softly laughs. "I'll check my calendar when I get home, but I think I can. I'll let you know, okay?"

"Perfect. Otherwise, I'll see you for the Scott/ Langston wedding at the end of the month, right?"

"Yep, I have that one marked down."

"Awesome." We say our goodbyes, and head to climb into our vehicles. Kenzy's car starts, and I watch her drive away. I pull my phone out to send Andrew a quick message, letting him know I'm on my way home. He's with Gramps today, so I won't see him for a few more hours.

ME

Leaving the venue as soon as I get my audiobook queued up. Want anything specific for dinner? I can swing by the grocery store. Oh, I'll also stop by your house and grab Travis.

ANDREW

Travis is good, I'll grab him on the way home.

And to answer your question, I would like to eat you for dinner, please and thank you.

Specifically with chocolate syrup dripped all over you.

Leave it to Andrew to make me all flustered, then have to wait for hours before I can get any relief.

ME

Isn't that considered dessert then? You're mean, I'm all… hot now, and I have to wait till you get home. Unless…

ANDREW

Don't. You. Dare.

I take it back, but please for the love of god, do not do anything without me.

ME

Guess you better get home as soon as you can.

ME

See you soon, petals. I've got a surprise for you tonight.

A nervous flutter tickles my belly. A surprise? What could he possibly have as a surprise? Unless it's him, wrapped up in a bow with chocolate syrup drizzled over his dick, with whipped cream and cherry on the tip, I'm not so sure I want it.

Rapping knuckles on my window pulls me out of my daydream. I gasp in surprise, and shriek when I see the face staring through my window. Dark eyes, greasy hair hanging over his brows, and unkempt scruff covering his face.

Zack.

40

ANDREW

Did I have to tease Josie about a surprise tonight? Not really, but she teased me about taking care of herself without me, and that's a no go in my department. Not that she can't take care of business herself, but at least let me hang out and watch.

Great. Now I'm hard. My brain does nothing to stop me from thinking about Josie, covered in chocolate syrup, sliding her finger up her chest, licking the chocolate that she collected off her fingertip.

A smack to the back of my head pulls me out of the wonderful fantasy. I whip around to berate the culprit.

Jason.

Beau and Isaac stand behind him, both smirking.

"Dude, really?" I ask Jason, lifting my arms in question.

"Stop daydreaming about Josie, you have shit to do. She's on her way home, is she not?" Jason raises his brow, then turns, heading out of the open garage door to the bed of his truck.

We were able to get everything unloaded and set up fairly easily, and in decent time too. Thomas is on patrol right now, and thankfully Isaac was able to pop over and help Jason, Beau and I. Jason closes up the back of his pickup, and latches the topper.

"You need any help, or can I go get Lennie?" he asks.

"Go get Lennie-Lou," I say, waving him off.

He offers us a final wave, climbing into his truck and starting it, heading down the road in the direction of our parents house.

I look around the small workspace Josie has created, insanely proud of my girl, and how far she's come in such a short time. Shortly over a year ago now, she moved into this house, with no clients, no professional connections, and no way to know if she would succeed. And now? Now she has a steady clientele, thanks to word of mouth, Marley's recommendations, and the contract with Meadow Grove Winery, thanks to Isaac's recommendation to his parents. She's booking weddings and events left and right, and has become a reputable business in our small town.

I couldn't be prouder to call her mine. And tonight, she will know just how much I love her, and just how much I can't wait for our life together.

"I found a studio for Mar," Beau says, interrupting my thoughts. I glance over at Isaac, noticing his intrigue to the conversation as well. He's been around just as long as Marley has, and has watched right along with us as the two of them fight their feelings for the other.

"She's looking for a new space?" I ask.

Beau shrugs. "She mentioned the other day that she wanted to casually start looking at a bigger space. Have separate areas for different types of shoots. She specifically asked for a place with a sort of rustic look, brick walls, that sort of thing."

"Did you find something?"

"Yeah." He clears his throat. "Would you do something for me?"

"Anything," I answer. Obviously I would do anything for him.

"If I give you dimensions, would you be willing to make a desk for her? And not like a normal desk. I want something huge. Something she can spread stuff out on, something dark, and eclectic like her."

"Of course. Just send me some inspo photos, and I'll get to work on it."

Beau steps to my side, slapping a hand between my shoulder blades. "Thanks."

"Should I ask?" I wonder out loud. Isaac snickers behind me.

"If you want to live to see Josie's reaction, I'm going to have to say no." Beau stares me down, the brown eyes that are so similar to mine filled with an emotion that I can't name.

I raise my hands in surrender. "Alright, dropping the subject. Got it."

Beau nods in resignation.

Isaac pipes in, "Just saying, as someone who married his best friend, fighting this is more painful than the potential reward."

"When did we get married?" I tease Isaac. He smacks me between my shoulder blades as he laughs.

Beau grimaces, tugging at his hair. "Thanks."

I grab a broom from the corner, and start sweeping the garage floor. She was running a few minutes behind this morning so she didn't have time to clean up the random leaves and petals that fell to the floor.

Beau follows suit, swiping the stray petals off one of the

metal tables she uses. My phone starts to ring, and I pull it from my back pocket, expecting it to be Josie.

When it's Thomas' name on the screen, I have to tamper down the smallest hint of irritation, all because it's him, and not my girl.

I answer the call, putting it to my ear. "What's up, chicken butt?" I expect a laugh or an irritated groan in reply, but get nothing.

"Thomas?" I ask. "Everything okay?"

"Yeah... I don't get you."

"What's up?" I ask again.

"What are you doing tonight?" he asks. "I'm on duty till seven. I was going to see if everyone wanted to go out for a drink tonight."

I ponder for a moment, but then think about all the plans that I have for Josie tonight. "No can do, big bro. I've got plans with my girl."

A low chuckle passes through the line. "Ah, I see how it is. Ditching everyone else just for her."

"Can you blame me?" I laugh.

"Honestly? No."

"Exactly."

Beau chuckles from behind me, and I know he's listening into the conversation.

"I'm kicking Beau out anyway. Josie should be home soon."

"Loud and clear, little bro. I'll catch up later," Thomas hangs up the phone after saying goodbye.

"I take it, that's my cue?" Beau asks with a laugh.

"You got that right."

41

JOSIE

My throat tightens when I spot Tessa hooked on Zack's arm. She's wearing a beautiful baby blue dress, blonde hair in long, loose curls framing her face. She looks like the same Tessa I've known since I was a kid, though it's weird to see her on the arm of the man I once loved. The love that I felt for him is so different from the all consuming love I feel for Andrew.

Tessa's waving at me through my car window, and I don't really know what to do in this situation. They must be attending the wedding, based on their attire. Zack taps the window again, saying something over the blaring music that automatically plays when I connect my phone to the stereo, instead of the audiobook that I want. I disconnect my phone, turning off my vehicle. They step back as I open the door, climbing out. "Hey..." I greet, awkwardly waving.

"Hey!" Tessa squeals excitedly. She drops her arm from Zack's elbow, reaching to tug me into a tight hug. "Ahhh," she croons. "I've missed you sooo much! We can't go this long without talking again."

I chuckle, not quite knowing how to respond. I give her

a squeeze in return. "What are you guys doing here? Do you know the couple?"

Zack nods. "Yeah, the groom is a family friend."

"Ah."

"The flowers are gorgeous," Tessa remarks. "It gave me some ideas for our wedding."

"Oh, good," I say, I'm about to change the subject, not really wanting to discuss their potential nuptials, when Tessa holds out her hand, displaying the very large, very gaudy looking ring.

"He proposed last night," she giggles.

"Wow," I say, taking her hand in mine to take a look at the ring. It's definitely not something I would choose for myself, but for Tessa? It suits her. "It's beautiful, congratulations."

"Thank you," Tessa says. She pulls back her hand, wrapping herself into Zack again. "We are just so happy. I suppose we have you to thank."

"Me?" I ask.

"Yes!" Tessa says. "If you two hadn't dated, then we never would have met. And if you hadn't broken up..." she drifts off.

"Happy to be of service," I reply with a tight laugh.

"You'll find someone who loves you the way Zack loves me," she says. "Just the way you are." Her eyes pointedly glance at my midsection. *Love that for me.*

I choke out a strangled cough. "Right. Um, I'm actually with someone."

"You are?" Zack asks incredulously, as though he just can't believe it.

"Yeah. We met a few months ago at a wedding, and then we got set up on a blind date together, and have been together ever since." I wring my hands in front of me. I shouldn't feel awkward right now, but I do. Why is it so hard to believe that I've found someone to love me?

"Is that the groomsman you were telling me about?" Tessa asks.

"Yes," I say. "Andrew. He's a woodworker."

"Well, that's great, Josie."

"Thanks," I reply.

This is so fucking awkward. What do you say to the person who you once considered your best friend after she gets engaged to your ex?

"We'll have to hang out soon," Tessa says half-heartedly. "Discuss wedding plans."

Zack narrows his eyes, looking up and down my body as if gauging my size.

"Oh, for sure," I say. I almost know she won't be calling me, and to be honest, I don't know that I want her to. I'm completely fine to close that chapter of my life, and move forward, with Andrew at my side.

We say goodbye, an awkward hug with empty promises from Tessa, and a pat on the shoulder from Zack. They walk away, hand in hand, and I feel a weird sense of finality. Those two might just be perfect for each other, and I'm glad I'm not in the middle of it.

I climb back into my car, fixing the music and queuing my audiobook, and head for home. To Andrew. He should be getting home from the hospital with Gramps, and I'm so excited to see him.

I pull into my driveway, and spot Travis in my front window. He's perched right next to Velma, both of them looking at us. My brain has one of those record scratch moments as I realize something. Travis wasn't here when I left this morning. He was with Andrew, who dropped him off at his house before going to sit with Gramps.

Is Andrew already here? I don't see his car anywhere. He must be, if Travis is here. I get out of the car, and my suspicion is answered when the garage door opens, and Andrew strides out, a sly grin on his face. He's in a pair of dark wash jeans, and a deep blue flannel, his curls mussed, hanging over his eyes. He definitely is in need of a haircut.

It's then that I remember the surprise he mentioned. Seeing Tessa and Zack kind of threw my brain for a loop.

42

———————

ANDREW

Josie steps out of her car, smiling when she sees the smile on my own face. It's impossible to hide my excitement from her, and I did tell her that I had a surprise for her. She walks to me, and I reach out my hand for her.

I bend down, kissing her quickly. "How was the wedding?" When I pull back, I notice that she seems a little off.

She shrugs. "The wedding was great. Kenzy was incredible." Josie takes a deep breath. "Apparently, the groom was friends with Zack in college, so I unexpectedly saw him and Tessa."

My brows pinch together. "Did you talk to them?"

"Unfortunately. They're engaged."

"No fucking way," I say. I search her eyes for any sort of hint as to how she feels about it.

"Yep. In itself it was fine, just very awkward. She wants to meet up and discuss the wedding, but I get the feeling she won't call. Not that I really want her to."

"Did they say anything else about..." I start to ask. I don't want to say the words, because the thought of her feeling pressured to lose weight makes me sick. My girl is fucking gorgeous, and I wouldn't change a thing about her.

"It was insinuated, but not said."

I nod. Pulling her in close to me, I kiss her cheek. "I'm proud of you for standing up for yourself, petals."

"Thanks," she murmurs. "It sucks losing your best friend, but to be honest, I'm better off without them."

"You are. You've got new people to stand by you."

She softly squeezes my hand. "So, what's this about a surprise?" The light starts to burn back in her beautiful eyes, and I chuckle.

"I thought you hated surprises?" I joke.

"I do, but I need a distraction," she says. "Unless you want to distract me another way?"

I press a soft kiss to her plump lips. "Should we go in?"

"Now," I say, anxiety rising within my chest. "If you hate it, I can get rid of it, or I can change anything you want different." I rest my hand on the doorknob, waiting for her to give me some glimpse of a reaction.

She finally smiles. "Andrew, whatever it is, I'm going to love it. I'll love it because it's from *you*."

I nod, opening the rickety door. The lights are off, so I reach over, flicking the knob on the light switch. With the room now bathed in light, I watch Josie's reaction. Her eyes adjust to the brightness, widening as she takes in the new addition to her workshop.

"Andrew..." She gasps. "You made that?"

I nod. She steps forward, reaching the edge of the piece. Her hand trails up and down the smooth wood surface. "I— I don't know what to say."

"Do you like it?" I ask, the nerves creeping in again. Her hand reaches up to cover her mouth.

She doesn't speak at first, only nodding, her eyes filling

with tears. "I love it," she finally says. "I've never had anything like this before."

"I started making it the day after our first date. I knew that even if for some reason things didn't work out, I wanted you to have something for you to work on." I gesture to it. "There is a drawer here," I pull out the drawer to show her. "That you can use for scissors, wire cutters, ribbon, tape, or something else, and hooks here," I point. "To hang things from."

"This is incredible," Josie swipes a tear from under her eye. "I'll never be able to thank you enough for this, Andrew."

"There's something else," I say. I grab her hips, lifting her to sit on the edge of the table. Her legs open, creating a spot for me to stand between. I rest my forehead against hers. "I was supposed to do this the day Gramps went to the hospital. Obviously, things didn't go according to plan that day."

She nods, her eyes still filled with tears.

"Josie, I love you. I love you more than I've ever loved anyone in my life. I think I knew it from the first moment I saw you, that you were meant to be mine."

Josie sniffles, letting out a soft chuckle. "I love you too," she says. "I love you so much, it's crazy. I don't think I've ever felt the way I do for anyone else in my life." She sniffs again, and wipes her eyes.

"I still haven't given you back your crocodile clip," I murmur as I press my lips to hers.

Josie snorts. "Claw clip, honey. It's a claw clip. You can keep it, just as long as I get to keep you."

"Good luck keeping me away." I kiss her again, this time, threading one hand into her hair, wrapping the other arm around her waist. Her legs tighten around my waist as she moans into my mouth. "What do you think, petals? Should we christen your new workstation?"

"Yes, please," Josie breathlessly replies.

I kiss my way down her neck, untangling my hand from her hair to cup her breast. I lightly squeeze, loving the way she feels under my palm. She arches her back, letting a palm slap against the wood, holding her up.

Josie rocks her hips into my growing erection, moaning as she does. My lips are on her neck, tasting her skin, loving that this girl is mine, and nothing will change that.

"Andrew," she gasps. "Take these off." She yanks at my pants, and I oblige, kicking off my jeans, and throwing my shirt off across the room.

"Your turn," I mutter between kisses. Her shirt is on the floor in an instant, and she leans back, lifting her hips for me to pull down her pants. Her light pink cotton underwear come with her pants, leaving her bare and ready for me. "Goddamn, babygirl."

I drop to my knees, desperate to have her taste on my tongue. My tongue finds her clit, and I soak up the whimper my girl lets out. I glance up at her. She's leaning back, her arms holding her up against the wood, legs wide open, giving me access to the feast that is her.

I groan into her cunt as I press two fingers into her tightness. She squeezes herself around my fingers, and my cock leaks, aching to be inside her. "Harder," Josie says, her eyes falling closed, mouth open in a silent cry.

I do as she asks, fucking her with my fingers, harder, harder, harder. I curl my fingers upward, hitting a new angle. Josie screams, her body jerking. She tries to scoot away from the pleasure, but I don't let her. My arm lays across her soft stomach, holding her down. "Andrew, I'm going to—" she cries out, her words cut off. I don't stop, my tongue on her clit while my fingers fuck in and out of her pussy.

A warm wetness gushes out of her, soaking my chin and chest. Holy fucking hell, did I make her squirt? I keep going, not stopping until she wiggles herself away from me. She's gasping, sucking in huge gulps of air as her body comes down from the orgasm.

"Holy—" she mutters. "I've never done that before."

"Glad I could be the first, petals." I stand from the concrete, ignoring the pain in my knee from the floor. "Not even kidding, my ego is pretty high right now," I tease. I hold up my hand above my head, showing her the level it's at.

"Andrew," Josie says with a laugh. She smacks at my chest, her fingers hitting the wetness still dripping there. "Get over here and fuck me, please." Her eyes soften, legs opening up to me once more. I step back between her thighs, scooting her ass to the edge of the table.

"Condom," I mutter.

"No, I want you bare," Josie says. She reaches down, gripping my shaft in her hand, stroking me softly. "If you aren't comfortable, you can get one. But I'm okay to forgo it. I have us covered."

I nod, my mind going blank, because the thought of fucking her without a condom? No, scratch that. The thought of coming inside her, without a condom? Hottest fucking thing I've ever imagined. I can't stop thinking about my cum dripping out of her, sliding down her legs.

"Did I break your brain, honey?" Josie pulls me out of my daydream.

Why the hell am I daydreaming about this when she's offering me the real thing? Yeah no, my brain is broken, because holy shit.

I angle my cock at her entrance, filling her in one deep thrust. I'm not playing around anymore. I need her full of my cock, full of my come, full of me. "You want my cum, baby?" I ask her between thrusts. Sweat drips down my spine, heat building inside me.

"I need it," she moans. "I need your cum, Andrew. Please."

I rock into her again and again, until that familiar tingling in my balls starts, the ache growing and growing until I'm exploding inside her. Wetness coats my cock from her and my orgasms combined.

My head falls to her chest, using her tits as my own personal pillow. I muster up the energy to reach up and caress one. "Sorry, I neglected you," I say to them.

"Did you just apologize to my boobs?" Josie asks through heavy breaths.

"Is it a problem if I did?"

"No, just not what I expected to be the first thing out of your mouth."

I slowly rise from my boob pillow, tracing my finger across her cheekbone. "I love you," I say.

"I love you, too."

I slide myself from her warmth, and together we watch my come drip out of her pink, swollen cunt. I bite my finger, letting out a feral moan. Unable to stop myself, I slide my fingers between her folds, scooping up my cum and pushing it back inside her. "That was hot as shit."

Josie shivers, looking down where my fingers are inside her precious cunt.

"This thing is waterproof, right?" Josie asks.

I lift my eyes to hers. "Oh yeah it is." I know exactly where her mind is going. "Next time, I'm laying you over the edge, and I'll fuck you from behind."

Josie shivers in anticipation.

I lay a palm on the table, attempting to push it, see if it moves at all. "Damn, I'm good at my job," I say.

"What?" Josie asks with a laugh.

"I mean, we just fucked like animals on this thing, and it didn't move. I'd say I'm pretty good at my job."

"Whatever you say, honey. Let's go get cleaned up, then we need to bring your ego down a bit."

I help her down, and follow her inside, teasing about all the reasons as to why we definitely don't need to bring my ego down.

43

JOSIE

In the weeks after Andrew gave me the workstation he so beautifully made for me, things have been a little hectic.

Gramps was released from the hospital, and now resides in a short stay rehab center while he builds up his strength. Andrew and I are on our way to pick him up for Sunday Brunch. He hasn't been able to attend since his surgery, and I think everyone is a little antsy to have him at brunch. I'd only been to a few before he fell, but even I can feel the shift without him there.

When we arrive at the rehab center that's about twenty minutes from Ivy Ridge, Andrew heads inside, leaving me in my car. We drove my car so Gramps wouldn't have to try and climb up into Andrew's truck. A few minutes later, Andrew pushes Gramps in his wheelchair out the set of automatic double doors.

Gramps has a scowl on his face, but he looks good. There's a small divot on the top of his head where they removed the piece of his skull. Thankfully, he's slowly starting to gain back the weight he lost while in the hospital.

He's part of a rigorous physical therapy program, and it seems to be working.

He'll go back to the hospital in a few weeks for an outpatient procedure to replace the piece of skull, and then from there, it's back to the rehab facility. He's already ready to go back to his small apartment, but it's going to take some time for him to be strong enough to do so.

It's still hard on Andrew, seeing his grandpa like this, but he's adjusting to it as well.

I get out of the car when they get closer, leaving my door open for Gramps to sit in the passenger seat. "Hey, Gramps," I say. I lean forward, giving him a quick hug.

He gives me a shaky armed squeeze in return, his gruff voice in my ear. "Hi there Cindy. How's life?"

"Life's good, Gramps." Andrew and I assist him into the car. It's not too difficult, though he is still moving pretty slow.

Andrew starts folding his wheelchair to put in the trunk, but he stops, leaning down to kiss me softly.

"What was that for?" I ask.

He shrugs. "'Cause I love you."

I can't help but smile. "I love you, too."

AS ALWAYS, the Cunningham's and Bell's driveways are both packed full of cars.They left a spot open for us, so we could get Gramps in and out easier. Andrew and I get him out and up to the front door, and it flies open before we can even think about knocking.

Lennie stands in front of the door, her long brown hair in a pony on top of her head. She's breathing heavily, as if she sprinted to get to the door. In a pair of jean shorts and a Disney Princess tee, she looks cute as a button.

"Gwamps!" she yells. He doesn't even have time to say anything when she's climbing in his lap, throwing her arms around his neck in a big hug.

"Hey, sunshine," Gramps says, squeezing her tightly. She starts babbling nonsense, talking so fast none of us can quite understand her. Marley comes to the door next.

"Lennie, let's let Gramps get in the door, huh?" She gently pulls her off Gramps, and Andrew adjusts the wheelchair to make it over the lip of the door. We kick off our shoes, and head into the dining room, wheeling Gramps with us. Marley sets Lennie down, so she's walking beside the wheelchair, talking. Gramps listens intently, nodding and humming in all the right places.

The dining room smells of cinnamon, a small glimpse of what might be for brunch today. Nikki's in the kitchen, her canary yellow apron dusted with flour. "Hey guys, the rolls will be ready in five minutes," she calls.

"You better have bacon, Nicole," Gramps says.

"What kind of daughter-in-law would I be if I didn't have bacon for you?" Nikki teases. She sidesteps the kitchen counter, holding her flour covered hands up. She leans down, kissing him on the cheek. "Good to have you back."

"Good to be back," he replies, his voice thick with emotion.

We settle him in at the table, then Andrew, Marley and I go off in search of the rest of the siblings. Beau, Jason and Thomas are settled around the patio table on the back deck. Beau is the first to speak. "Josie, I'm not pressuring you, but do you have a timeline on when you might open up a storefront?"

I shrug. "To be honest, I haven't thought of it all that

much. It's probably going to be another year though. If I have a storefront, I'd have to hire at least one or two full time employees, and that's not in my budget quite yet. Why do you ask?"

Beau nods thoughtfully along with my words. He pushes some hair off his face, displaying the array of tattoos on his forearm. "Nothing concrete, but I think there's a really awesome listing coming on the market soon, and it could be perfect for you."

I try my hardest not to get too excited, but the thought of having my own location, not just the garage of my house, makes my heart pound. I could have employees running the front, while I'm in the back, making arrangements, having client meetings for events, and a dedicated office. It's tempting, but I'm not there yet. I only left the diner and became a full time florist a month ago, so this feels like a pretty steep jump.

"Did I mention it's next door to Mar's new studio?" Beau adds, and that's it. I'm about ready to hand him my checkbook, and sell a kidney to make this happen. Marley catches my eye, a wide grin on her face as she too, thinks of the possibilities.

Andrew chuckles. "I think you might have gotten her there, Beau."

"You kinda did. Do you have any photos?" I ask.

Beau grabs his phone from the table. He opens it, swiping a few times before landing on a website, filled with photos of the location. He morphs into realtor mode, telling me all the specs and information I need to know. As I swipe through pictures of the beautiful brick building, ideas start to bud in the back of my mind. I shove the phone back at Beau.

"It's perfect, but I can't do it, not yet. And there's no

way a property like that will stay on the market for long." I mentally try to think it over, but there's no way. I can't afford a mortgage, a property payment, and continue to pay Kenzy, whom I desperately need. My excitement deflates, and Marley gives me a sad shrug.

"I get it," Marley says. "Who knows, maybe there's a chance it stays on the market, and we can be neighbors."

It's hard to believe that the property will still be there in a year, or who knows, maybe longer, but I so desperately want it to happen.

Nikki opens the sliding door, calling us in to eat.

The homemade cinnamon rolls are so incredible that I ask for the recipe. Do I bake often? Not at all, but you never know when you might want a cinnamon roll. Nikki freely shares the recipe with me, as well as Marley, who decided she wanted it too.

"I need to head out." Beau stands, the chair squeaking loudly as it's shoved back.

"Have a few showings today?" Richard asks through a mouthful of roll.

"No." He hesitates, his next words coming out quiet, and slow. "I—uh—, I have a date."

The room falls deathly silent. I risk a glance at Marley, whose face is pale, eyes unseeing as she moves a piece of her cinnamon roll around her plate.

"Well," Nikki says. "Have a fun time."

"Thanks," Beau replies. He waves to everyone, stopping to rest a hand on Marley's shoulder. We see her tense, but not for long, as Beau is leaning down to hug Lennie. Then, he's gone.

No one brings it up, and no one talks about the giant elephant in the room.

44

ANDREW

The rest of brunch was awkward as fuck. I can't believe Beau would do that to Marley. He could have easily lied, and said he was off to do a few showings. But no, he had to be a fuckwad. I mean, we all knew there was a possibility of them not ending up together, but no one actually thought it would happen. If anything, I thought we were closer to getting them to crack, and breaking the tension between the two of them, but I guess not.

Josie and I dropped Gramps off about an hour ago, and now we're camped out on my couch, her laying between my legs. I twist a piece of her hair around my finger, and spit out the thought that has been living in my head for the last few hours.

"Can I ask you something?"

"Of course," she says. She tilts her head back to look at me, her blue gray eyes confused.

"When you told Beau you couldn't afford that space, I thought of a solution."

"And what might that be?" Josie raises a brow, begging me to give her an answer. "Any way that I've looked at it, I can't afford it. Between the rent, supplies, my mortgage, and paying Kenzy, it just isn't possible."

"What if you didn't have a mortgage?" I ask.

She opens and closes her mouth a few times, like she's trying to find a reason, and is coming up with nothing.

"If I didn't have a mortgage, then yeah, maybe it would be possible. But what am I going to do, sell my house and move into the office of the store? That's not exactly logical," she laughs.

I stay silent, waiting to see if she catches on. I watch as her eyes widen, a small smile appearing on her lips. She scoots forward, turning so she's sitting cross legged and facing me. "Wait." She holds a hand up. "I need you to tell me if I'm thinking what you're thinking, or if I'm being totally crazy."

I lift my brow. "Are you thinking that you should sell your house and move in with me?"

Josie gasps, clasping a hand over her mouth. "Oh my god, you're serious?"

"Of course I'm serious."

"Andrew. I mean, we've been together, what, five months?" She shakes her head. "There's no way we could live together."

"Why not?" I clasp her hand. "Velma and Travis get along, and I'm sure Velma would love all the extra windows in here."

"Oh my god," she repeats. "I—I don't."

"You don't?" I chuckle. "You don't have to agree right now, but think about it. If you didn't have a mortgage, then you could pay the monthly payment for the shop."

"What about rent here?" she asks.

"If you're insistent on paying something, you can take over utilities and wifi, but things are mostly paid off here.

Gramps paid off the house, and when I took over the business, he wrote the house into the agreement."

"Is this happening?" she asks incredulously.

"Text Beau," I say. "He's probably waiting for you to text him about the property anyway."

"He's on a date." She tries to defer it until later.

"A date he shouldn't be on. Text him, Josie. For me."

She hesitates for another long moment, then pulls out her phone. I watch her type up the message and hit send.

"Should we start packing?"

Josie playfully smacks my chest. "No, we have a lot to do before then."

I catch her hand, pulling her into me. "I'll just grab something every time I leave your house, and bring it here. We'll have you moved in no time."

She laughs. "I'm trying not to get my hopes up about the property..." She pauses. "We haven't even seen it in person yet."

"No, but I have a good feeling about it," I say.

Josie nods into my chest. "I do too."

"OH MY GOSH," Josie says. "It's perfect." Her eyes are wide as she takes in the space. It's small, but not crowded. It's perfect.

The walls in the front of the shop are all exposed brick, with shelving already installed. My mind is whirring with all the potential things we can do to the space to turn it into her dream shop. In the far corner, built into a wall, there is an L shaped desk, and Josie smooths her hand over the textured surface. I don't say anything, but I'm already thinking about ripping it out and replacing it with something I create for her.

However, if she likes this desk, I'm more than happy to fix it up for her.

Josie doesn't say anything else as we explore the property. Her mouth is slightly agape the whole time, and I can practically see the ideas rolling around in her brain.

The back is neatly updated, with gray walls and metal counters. It looks like the previous owners might have used this as a restaurant, or attempted to at least. Tucked into a corner is a small empty office, the bathrooms on the opposite wall.

I catch Josie's eye as she glances around the office. I raise my brows, and waggle them at her. Of course, she catches on to what I'm insinuating immediately. Her mouth drops open in shock. "Andrew, no," she gasps. "We couldn't do that here."

"You also said that about my shop last week, but you weren't complaining when I fu—"

"Andrew!" Josie stands on her tiptoes, covering my mouth with her hand. I laugh into her palm. Beau is standing on the other side of the room, biting his knuckle to hold back his laughter.

She glares at me, though it isn't much of a glare with how cute she is, and takes her palm from my mouth. Her eyes narrow as she silently dares me to say something else. I won't, but it's fun to mess with her.

Beau pipes in from across the room. "Anyway, they even have a commercial fridge back here. From the sounds of it, the owners were going to open a coffee shop, but the husband began to have some health issues, so they decided to put it on the market."

Josie sighs. "That's too bad. I can't imagine how hard it must have been for them to shelve their dream."

Beau nods. "What are you thinking? Do you want to put an offer in?"

Josie bites that plump bottom lip of hers in contemplation. She looks up at me as if searching for the answer on my face. I step back, leaning against the wall and holding my hands up. "Don't look at me, petals. This is all your decision. I'm your cheerleader, that's all."

She nods as I remind her of what I've been saying for the last week ever since I suggested she sell her house. I didn't pressure her. I let her take the lead, and while she didn't give me an official answer about selling her place and moving in, I don't need one to know that she's who I'm supposed to be with. I need her to know that while I would love her to sell her place, buy this, and move in with me, it's not something that she has to do. This is all her choice, her future. Sure, I'm a part of her future, but it's her dreams that have given us the opportunity to meet and start new, so who am I to tell her what to do?

"Yeah, let's put an offer in," Josie says. She steps over to my side, taking my hand in hers. She squeezes my hand, and even though this is the first step to having her wake up next to me every morning for the rest of our lives, I can't help but feel content and sure.

"Great," Beau says. He starts typing up the offer on his phone, asking her a few more questions before submitting it. Josie and Beau met a few times in the last week, going over her budget, plans for potentially selling her house, and everything in between, so they have a plan in place. "I'll let you know what they say."

45

———

JOSIE

ANDREW

Can't believe I don't get to come with.

ME

Next time

ANDREW

There's going to be a next time???

ME

Possibly ;) I asked Marley if we could do a couples shoot sometime. She needs practice with this type of shoot.

ANDREW

Fine. But only if I get a little sneak peek.

ME

Just as long as you don't take care of things by yourself.

ANDREW

I'll be waiting for you, petals.

ME

Love you.

Love you too. Have fun with Mar.

"Andrew is still pouting," I say with a chuckle. I'm standing in Marley's new studio while she sets up her camera for my boudoir shoot. Since she moved into the location, she's been bugging me to do this. I was hesitant, only because I have never found lingerie I feel comfortable with, and my insecurities are screaming at me that I'll look like a potato.

That is, until Andrew found out why I was hesitating. He made sure to tell, and *show* me in many different ways how beautiful he thinks I am. Now, I'm excited, albeit still a little nervous, not because of the shoot, or lingerie, just because it's something new. I'm not used to being so on display, and purposefully sexy.

"I'm not surprised." Marley swipes her brown hair into a ponytail, fixing her bangs with her fingers. "He's always been like that."

"I told him that maybe someday we would do a couples session." I shrug, sliding my fingers over the lace on a deep purple bodysuit that Mar set out for me to try on.

"Anytime," Marley replies. "It might be weird to see Andrew nearly fucking you, but hey, it's art."

I snicker. "Yeah, that might be weird, but what's life without a little weirdness?"

"Speaking of," Marley says. "I've seen that some photographers wear lingerie during the boudoir sessions too, to help the client feel more comfortable. Is that something you'd like me to do?"

"Oh my god, I think I've seen videos with that!" I say. "I would love that. As much as I love you, and no matter how much I love Andrew and how he lifts me up, I'm still feeling a little insecure."

"Say no more." Marley steps over to the makeshift wardrobe station. There's an abundance of options to choose from on the garment rack, and I watch as she plucks through, clearly looking for a specific item.

She pulls an army green lace set down, holding it up over her curves. She smiles, and raises her brow in question.

"Um, yes, one hundred percent," I say.

"Perfect," she says. "The purple is going to look so good with your red hair. Go change in the dressing room, I'll change in the bathroom, and we will get started."

I head into the dressing room, changing into the purple lace. The bodysuit is sheer on the sides, with lace patterns trailing up the bodice. The cups are also sheer, showing off my nipples, but have wires underneath to give a little boost. Garter straps hang down over my thighs, attaching to the thin stockings I slide up my legs.

I adjust a few straps and check myself in the mirror. I try not to look at the way my skin rolls underneath the lace, and instead focus on how great my boobs look, and how sensual I feel. Running my fingers through my curled, yet tousled hair, I give myself one final pep talk, before I step out of the small room. Marley sits on the black velvet chaise lounge, fiddling with her camera. She lifts her head when she sees me, and the smile that appears is instantaneous.

"Hell fucking yes, Josie." She stands, striding over to me. She looks sexy as hell in her own lingerie, the deep green accentuating her skin tone and hair color perfectly. The bottoms are high waisted lace, the top pushing her tits together and up, with crisscross straps going over top of her bust.

"Marley, you look hot," I say. On second glance, I notice bars running through her nipples. "Oh my god, you have pierced nipples?!" I screech.

"Not as hot as you, girl!" she spins her finger at me, motioning for me to twirl. I do, albeit awkwardly, holding out my palms. "And yes, I do have pierced nipples. Spur of the moment thing when I was twenty, but I love them." She shrugs. "This is going to be so amazing," she says. "Your ass looks phenomenal."

My face heats at her praise as I stop my turn. "Where do you want me?" I ask, looking around the room.

She's set it up perfectly. The lighting is perfect, accentuating the brick walls surrounding us. There's one wall of sheetrock that she's painted a deep royal green. The floor is hardwood, with a queen size bed in the corner. The comforter is fluffy, a crisp white, with feather pillows resting against the headboard. A gold standing mirror sits against the green wall, giving it that pop of color it needs. There are various gold accents around the whole room as well.

"I think we can start on the chaise," Marley says. She directs me into a pose on the couch, vaguely reminding me of that scene in Titanic where Jack draws Rose. My arm rests above my head, while the other slides down my stomach, looking as if it were to be heading between my thighs.

Marley adjusts my face to the angle she needs, and then she's snapping photos, one after the other, coaching me on my facial expressions, down to the poutyness of my lips. We do a few different poses on the chaise before moving to the bed.

With every pose and click of the camera, my confidence grows until I'm no longer nervous, but suggesting poses and ideas. Marley eats up every bit of it until we are giggling, having the time of our lives.

"Okay, I have one more idea," Marley says as we start wrapping things up. "If you're comfortable with it, I'd love to take some of you in the sheet. Only the sheet."

I hesitate for only a moment. "Yes."

"Hell. Yes." She rips the plain white sheet off the bed, handing it over to me. "Go take off the bodysuit, and wrap that around you."

I do as she says, coming back out of the dressing room a moment later, wrapped tightly in the thin sheet. It's almost sheer, not really leaving much to the imagination, but I suppose that's sort of the point. Marley positions me in front of the brick wall, and has me drape the sheet so it's covering my breasts, and slides between my thighs. She angles me so that the camera doesn't get a full view of my ass, but enough to tease.

Once she's happy with the photos, I sit down next to her on the velvet chaise, still dressed in only the sheet. Marley pulls up the screen of her camera, flicking through the photos.

The photos are stunning, and I can only imagine what they might look like after she edits them. Not to toot my own horn, but I look fucking good. I don't look like the Pillsbury Doughboy like I'd feared, but instead, a sexual, confident woman. I barely even recognize myself.

"You should totally fuck with Andrew," Marley says. "Take a picture of this, but only show your leg or something."

"That's so smart," I say. "I was going to send him a little something earlier, but forgot." I stand, grabbing my phone from the makeup table we had set up earlier.

Marley picks out a photo that's perfect. I'm kneeling on the chaise, my palms flat on my thighs. My hips are popped so that my back arches slightly, and my head is tilted toward the camera, but my gaze is down. I snap a photo of it, then crop it down so he can only see a corner of the lace, and the skin of my thigh.

I send it off, and await his response. "He's going to flip," I say.

Within seconds, the bubbles appear.

ANDREW

Josie.

half the photo is missing. Something must've happened to it. You need to send the rest before I spontaneously combust.

ME

I meant to send it like that.

ANDREW

You cruel, beautiful woman. Please tell me you're almost done. I'm aching over here.

ME

Soon. Going to help clean up, then I'll be home.

ANDREW

Fuck, I can't wait.

"It's a little weird, knowing I more than likely helped my best friend get laid, but hey, what kind of friend would I be if I didn't?" Marley teases.

I'm about to respond, but I hear the sound of the front door of the studio opening. I squeak, wrapping the sheet tighter around my body, running to the dressing room. I pull the curtain shut, breathing a sigh of relief when I'm behind a barrier.

"Mar?" Beau's voice calls.

"What are you doing here?" Marley asks. Beau's footsteps carry down the hall until he arrives in the open area of the studio.

"I was in the area, so I figured I would stop by, see if you needed help with anyth—" His voice cuts off with an audible gulp. I can't see their faces, but if I had to guess, Beau just saw Marley in her hot as fuck lingerie.

The silence is deafening. God, what I'd give to see this standoff, but I don't want to break the moment.

Beau's voice is husky when words finally come to him. "Wha—" He clears his throat. "Why are you in lingerie?"

"I read up on it. Clients can feel more comfortable when they're not alone in being half naked." Marley's voice is strong, unafraid. I never thought she'd cower in front of Beau, but if I were her, I would be.

"You did a session today?"

"Yes. The client is still here actually, so can we make this quick?" Marley's voice grows more and more irritated. "Why are you really here, Beau?"

The room falls silent. "You've been ignoring me," Beau finally says.

Marley scoffs. "I haven't been ignoring you. I'm busy."

"You sure? Because the minute you found out I was dating someone, you shut me out. Why is that, Marley? You're my best friend. I don't want to live without you. We're in our thirties, it's normal to date."

Marley doesn't say a word. I can feel the tension radiating between them through the dressing room curtain. "I don't want guys to see you wearing that," Beau mutters.

An irritated laugh comes from Marley. "Oh that's *real* fucking rich, Beau. Why, might I ask, don't you want guys to see me wearing lingerie? I'm going to go out on a limb and say it's *not* because you think I don't look good in it."

Beau starts to speak, but Marley interrupts him. "No.

Just go. I don't want to do this with you. You have a girl-friend, and I'm *just* your best friend. The one there to hold you while you cry, the one to make sure you're okay after she inevitably breaks up with you."

There's another long silence. "I'm sorry," Beau quietly says. "I'll go."

Marley doesn't say anything.

His footsteps are heavy as he walks to the door. "I'll talk to you later, Mar. I hope you'll forgive me for being an ass."

"We'll see." Marley's voice is fed up.

When the door opens and closes, I finish dressing, then give Marley a minute to herself. Opening the curtain, I find her in the same spot I left her, only this time, her head is resting in her open palms.

"Hey, sweetie," I say, sitting down next to her, rubbing her back.

"Guessing you heard that?" she asks.

I wince, then slowly nod.

"Why does he have to be like this?" she asks. "I know, I'm part of the problem too, but it's getting too hard to fight whatever is between us, and I'm so scared to lose him."

"I know," I murmur. "I know you are. You'll get through this. You love him, and he loves you."

"He doesn't love me," she says.

I pinch her arm.

"What the fuck?" she screeches.

"Of course he loves you!" I nearly shout. "He loves you so much, just the way you love him, but like you said, you're both so scared to lose each other, that you won't get your heads out of your asses long enough to see it."

Marley shrugs. "Guess I'm a glutton for pain."

"Good thing you've got a best friend to bring you all the chocolate."

"I knew I liked you," Marley says.

"You're kinda stuck with me," I say. "Especially since you helped me become the happiest I have ever been."

I pull her in close, hugging her tightly, giving her the time she needs to get her emotions out.

46

JOSIE

FOUR MONTHS LATER

"Honey, can you come here?" I'm in the back office of my store front, Ivy Ridge Floral. After I put the offer in, things moved pretty quickly. They accepted my offer within an hour, and a closing date was set for a month later. We put my house on the market, and after a few weeks, it sold. Andrew promptly started packing up my stuff the night I accepted the offer, and I've been totally moved in for about two months.

Gramps is doing well. He opted to move into assisted living, as he still has good and bad days, but overall, he is strong and healthy. One of us picks him up every Sunday for brunch, and sometimes, Andrew will pick him up to spend the day at the shop with him.

Kenzy has also turned into one of my greatest assets. Once the store opens, she plans on working at the store front during the week, and helping with events on weekends. All of her classes are online this semester, and when I brought up the possibility of her coming on full time, she was eager and willing.

Andrew steps into the back, looking hot as fuck in his

tight, sweat soaked shirt, dusty jeans, and tool belt around his waist. He even has a pencil tucked behind his ear, which is sexy as fuck. The store is set to open in two weeks, and we've been hard at work getting things set up between weddings and other events.

"What's up, petals?" Andrew asks. He rests his hands on his hips, waiting for me to say something. My mouth has gone dry just looking at him, and yet again, I'm reminded of just how hot this man is.

I clear my throat, trying to rid myself of the lump of cotton lodged there. "I—" Shit. What did I call him for? I shake my head, looking away from him to try and gather my thoughts.

"Forget what you were going to ask?" Andrew teases. He saunters closer, a devilish grin on his face. "Or did you just want to ogle your sexy boyfriend?" He crouches so he's eye level, and rests his warm palms on my legs. His heat melts through my leggings, making me shiver.

"I needed something," I murmur. His chocolate brown eyes are alight with humor, since he knows how much he threw me off. "Now, I can't remember."

"I remember what I wanted when you asked me back here," Andrew says. He leans forward brushing a kiss to my lips. I move to deepen it, but he pulls back. I whimper with need as he kisses up my jaw to behind my ear. "I think it's about time we christen the office."

I shake my head. "This is a business, Andrew," I mutter, but my resolve is slipping with every passing moment. "We can't."

"Why not? The door is locked. Kenzy's not coming in today. It's just you and me, petals."

I lean back into the swiveling chair, my body going pliant under his touch. When he puts it that way... "Yes, okay, but this is the *only* time. I won't be doing this once the store opens."

"Wouldn't dream of it, petals." Andrew moves from crouching to his knees, fitting himself between my thighs. "You know how much I've been imagining this moment, so we're going to make it last." He unbuckles the tool belt, shoving it off and over to the corner of the small room.

"The door," I say, pointing to the open door. Andrew chuckles softly, but closes the door.

He takes the pencil from behind his ear, tossing it to the desk. For a moment, I contemplate asking him to put it back, because it's so fucking hot, but then I think better of it. No one wants to be stabbed by a pencil during an orgasm.

Andrew touches me soft and slow, fingers deftly removing my clothes one item at a time. "I love you," he whispers between skillful touches. He gets me so wet, so ready for him, giving me a heart stopping orgasm before he's even removed one article of clothing.

I repeat the sentiment, knowing I will love this man for the rest of my life.

I rid him of his clothes, and then we're both naked. Andrew lifts me easily, again reminding me again of how much I love when he does that. Despite my many protests about my weight and size compared to him, he reminds me to never doubt him. This man can go from treating me like I'm precious glass, delicate and soft, to throwing me around like a rag-doll and ravaging me.

With one swift movement, Andrew lays me over the desk, thrusting himself into my soaked cunt. I love that first moment that he takes me, that first feeling of being connected again as one. Andrew covers my body with his, thrusting into me in perfect time.

"I love you, so much," he grits out against my neck. He

nips and bites at my skin, sending trickling heat through every one of my extremities.

His thrusts turn feral and rough as he chases his orgasm with hurried gasps. With one final pump, he's filling me with every drop of him. He holds there, then slides out, letting his cum drip out of me. He loves watching it, and I love watching him watch it. He turns into a caveman, viewing it as a sort of claiming. What can I say, I'm a slut for my boyfriend's cum. I'll take it any way I can get it.

Andrew helps clean me up, gathering my strewn clothes to help me dress. I spot a knocked over frame in the corner of my desk. Smiling, I set it upright. It's a photo of Andrew and I, the day we did the stranger photoshoot.

It's the photo of us on the dock, moments before disaster. Our mouths are locked together, my hands tangled in his hair. He has a strong grip on my ass, my legs wrapped around him tightly. All of the photos from that shoot are incredible, and are displayed around our home, but this will always be my favorite.

We have a copy of it in our bedroom on a canvas. Every morning, I roll over, and I'm greeted with three things. One, being the canvas photo of us on the wall behind Andrew. The next being Andrew himself. I typically wake up before him, except for the rare occasion that he wakes up first, waking me with his tongue on my clit. Definitely one of my favorite ways to wake up.

The last thing I usually see is Travis. He sleeps between us most of the time, as if he's a child. The dog even has his own pillow. Velma is usually cuddled in there too, but she gets irritated with Travis easily, so she ends up at my head, or on the couch in the living room.

Andrew also has some of the photos from my boudoir shoot printed. I didn't let him make canvases out of any of the photos, but I did print him some wallet versions, as well as made him a photo book so he can look through them anytime he wants. When I gave it to him, he promptly declared that he would never be reading another book in his lifetime.

Not that there are any words in the book, but he wouldn't let me try and dispute it.

I'll never be able to thank Marley enough for her scheming ways to get us together. I wish there was something I could do to make Beau see how perfect they could be, but he's insistent on putting on his blinders and looking the other way. He's been dating the same girl for a few months now, but no one has met her, and he doesn't talk about her much. I get the feeling that she's just someone to fill the void that he insists on having since he won't pursue Marley.

I follow Andrew out into the front part of the shop, taking in all our hard work. We moved the custom workstation that Andrew built me into the back of the shop so I can use it back there.

Things are coming together, and soon, we will be decorating and opening the doors. I can't believe this is my life. I get to live out my dreams, with the most incredible man, and friends and family at my side.

My parents come and visit every few weeks, and Jess and her husband are moving to the Brooks Hill area next month. Mom is excited to have both her girls close by, and even more excited about the fact that Jess is pregnant with the first grandchild.

Thomas is busier than ever, working more often than not. He's still working on the drug ring case, and it sounds like they are bringing in an investigator from another town to assist in the search.

Lennie loves to come spend time with me, helping arrange bouquets and picking flowers to add to stock. Nikki will usually bring her over one or two days a week, and then I get to spend time with both of them.

Marley, Megan and I also hang out often. We have movie nights, go out to the brewery, or just spend time with each other. Marley is my best friend, and I don't think I'd survive without her anymore. I don't know how I made it twenty nine years without her, to be honest.

"Are you done for the day?" Andrew asks. He's sweeping up some of the sawdust from his work on the desk.

"Yeah, I can be. I got everything in the back done that I wanted today. What are you thinking?"

"Brewery night with everyone?" he asks.

"Perfect." Andrew finishes up a few last minute things, and takes my hand to head home. Once there, we snuggle up on the couch, and I can't even describe how good it feels, knowing that I get to be with this incredible man.

ANDREW

FIVE MONTHS LATER

"Andrew, calm down." Marley adjusts my tie for the tenth time. I notice yet another new tattoo on her forearm. A butterfly, with one wing in perfect condition, the other fading into flowers. It's beautiful, and I know I need to ask about it, but my mind is a bit preoccupied.

"I can't," I mutter. Bouncing on the balls of my feet, I check that the box is still in the pocket of my dress pants.

"I'm having flashbacks," Marley laughs. "You were just like this the day of that photoshoot."

"Can you blame me? I'm asking Josie to marry me, Mar. It's not like I'm asking her to have a cup of coffee. This is a big deal." My heart pounds, making my point.

"Do you really think she will say no?"

I shake my head. "Of course not, but it's the delivery that matters. We're going to think about this for the rest of our lives, and if I do something stupid, I'll never live it down."

"That's true," Marley agrees. "You do have an audience." She gestures to the trees behind me, where our families lie in wait.

I groan, rubbing my face. "C'mon Mar. Why'd you have to say that? I just forgot they were there."

"Well you better forget again quick. Jason just texted that they're pulling up." She steps back, hiding herself behind a tree, getting her camera ready.

I lured Josie here under the guise of taking Lennie for a playdate. Jason dropped her off at our house an hour ago, and I told her we needed to run a few errands, when really we were coming here to set up. Jason made plans to pick Lennie up here, and a lot of this operation runs on Lennie. She knows that she has to be very careful so she doesn't blow the secret, and that she can't play at the playground until after. Fingers crossed she doesn't forget her mission as soon as she sees the curly slide.

I can vaguely hear Lennie's voice in the distance, pulling my girl to where I stand. I can't see them yet, but I know they are coming. I take a glance around me, checking to make sure the flowers are all in the perfect spot. Kenzy was a big help. I enlisted her to place an order for me, and she even drove down to the wholesale market to pick them up. I made the small arrangement in my hand myself, and used the rest in the small vases that surround me on the wooden planks of the newly-constructed dock. I covered the rickety dock with a blanket, spreading petals over top.

"Lennie, don't you want to go to the playground?" I hear Josie ask.

"No, Auntie Yosie, I want to go this way," Lennie sounds determined, and they come into view. Lennie is dragging Josie by her hand in our direction. Lennie started calling her Auntie Yosie about five months into our relationship, and Josie cried the first time she did. It makes me excited about our future, with our own kids, and hopefully lots more nieces and nephews.

The moment Josie sees me standing on the dock, she halts in her tracks. Lennie however doesn't stand for it. "Yosie, c'mon, Andwoo is waiting for you," she says.

Josie covers her mouth with her free hand, and I can see the tears running down her face from here. Her red hair is curled and pulled back into a half-ponytail. Her makeup is soft, subtle, and just the way I like it. Dressed in a beautiful olive green sweater dress, tights, and brown boots, she's so fucking adorable. I'm glad to see that Lennie's other task of getting her dressed up worked. Lennie, too, is dressed up, her hair curled and half of it pinned in a pale pink bow on her head. Lennie wears a sweater dress too, but hers is navy blue.

When they get closer, Josie slows her steps, eyes scanning the area around me. I see her reaction as she takes in the flowers surrounding me. Lennie drops Josie's hand, turning and running toward where her dad is hiding in the tree line.

Josie tries to call for her, but then she sees the group of people. "Oh my god," she whispers. "Is this what I think it is?" she softly asks.

I reach out, taking her palm in my hand. "Hey petals," I say.

"Hi," she answers, her voice soft. "Andrew..."

I interrupt her. "I need to tell you something," I begin. "The day I met you, I didn't know it was going to be the day my life changed. I knew I was ready to find someone to spend my life with, but I never imagined it would be the florist at my best friend's wedding."

Josie chuckles softly. I hand her the flowers in my hand, and swipe a few tears from her cheek with my thumb.

"Then, you disappeared. I couldn't find you, and only

had one thing to remember you by." I reach into my pocket, pulling out the other item in there. I hold out the very claw clip that I've had for a year and a half now. Josie chuckles, her cheeks flaming red as she takes the claw clip, holding it in her right hand with the small bouquet. "I had this. Then, fate, *aka Marley*, intervened, and I got to see you again. Right here," I point to the dock. "Is where we had our first kiss. I wanted to bring it full circle today."

Sinking down onto one knee, I reach into my pocket to grab the small velvet box. Josie's left hand is covering her mouth, eyes widening.

"Josie Rae Carter, I love you. I want to spend the rest of my life making you happy, and supporting your dreams, and the dreams we have together. Loving you is the easiest thing I've ever done. Would you do the honor of marrying me, and becoming my wife?" My voice wobbles and breaks on the last words, my emotions showing. Tears sting my eyes as I wait for her response.

She silently nods, her hand still over her mouth. Tears stream down her cheeks, but I can see the smile on her face. Finally, she speaks. "Yes, oh my gosh, Andrew. Yes, I'll marry you. I love you so much," she cries.

I quickly realize that I forgot to open the ring box. "Oh, shit," I mutter. "You probably want to see the ring before you agree," I nervously chuckle.

Josie drops her hand, waving me off. "I don't care about the ring right now, I get to marry you," she says.

I open the box anyway, gauging her reaction when she sees the ring. It's simple. Nothing over the top, but so her. The center diamond is oval shaped, with smaller leaf shaped diamonds on either side. The band is soft gold, thin and delicate. Josie gasps.

"It's gorgeous," she says. I take the ring from the box with shaking hands, and slide it onto her finger. I stand from my knee, and we both stare down at the ring I bought her on her finger, where it will be for the rest of our lives.

Josie pulls me into her, the hand with the ring on it cupping the back of my head as our lips meet in the middle. I fist bump the sky, because hell fucking yes.

Cheers and laughter surround us, and our families race to the end of the dock to congratulate us. Gramps meanders over with his arm looped in my mom's. We receive hugs from each member of the family, and of course, Lennie is asking if she can wear a pretty dress to the wedding.

Gramps reaches me, slapping me on the back. He pulls me into a tight hug, and my throat thickens with emotion. "Congratulations, kid," he says. "Cindy is perfect." I chuckle at the nickname he still uses for her, and hug him tightly back.

Josie hugs him, laughing when he calls her Cindy. I don't think he'll ever call her by her real name, not that I mind. Nor does Josie. If anything, it makes it even more special.

I'm thanking my lucky stars as I hold Josie in my arms on the solid ground, that not only did we not fall into the water this time, but that she just agreed to be mine for the rest of our lives.

The End.

IF YOU HAVEN'T ALREADY GUESSED... Marley and Beau are up next! Can't wait to get your hands on them? Turn the page to get a glimpse into the start of their love story.

** Please note this is not the finalized prologue, and is subject to change, and edits**

The needle of the tattoo gun pierces my skin repetitively, but it doesn't hurt. If anything, it feels good. Sort of like relieving an itch that you just can't quite reach. The leather chair underneath me is starting to become uncomfortable, but there's only so much I can do about the position I'm in.

"How's the pain, Mar?" my best friend, Beau, asks. He has a devilish grin on his face, like he's anticipating me to whine about how bad it is. He's sitting on a stool next to me, watching the tattoo artist work.

"Not bad," I answer truthfully. My right arm is laying out on a padded armrest, while the artist, Nina, does her job. It's my eighteenth birthday, and Beau and I have been planning this for months. His birthday is a month to the day before mine. Beau's already done with his tattoo. He was in the chair just before me. It's on his right bicep, the same spot as mine. The tattoo is covered in a thin film wrap, the skin underneath red and raised from the repeated needling.

Nina was kind enough to draw up a sketch for us, and it's everything I could have wanted. Two hands clasped together, one in the water, one out. It symbolizes a lyric from the song Dead Sea, by our favorite band, The Lumineers.

Beau has been my best friend since the age of eleven. My family moved into the house next door to him, and we became fast friends, despite my initial hesitancy. When I found out the next door neighbors had four boys, I was devastated. I was convinced that they would only be friends with my older brothers, Kenny and Prescott. Beau proved me wrong. Kenny and Prescott are four and five years older than I am, they wanted nothing to do with hanging out with their eleven year old sister.

Shortly after we moved into the new house, I was reading a book on the front lawn when Beau and his younger brother, Andrew rode by on their bikes. Beau noticed me first. He stopped, calling out to Andrew who had zoomed by, not even realizing that his brother had stopped. Andrew kept going, saying something out meeting him at the baseball fields, but Beau waved him off. He dropped his bike onto the lawn, and strode over to me.

His brown curly hair flopped over his eyes and he pushed it back off his forehead. Wearing an Ivy Ridge Base-ball tee and basketball shorts, he looked ready to head to practice. I wore a bright yellow sundress that mom always said made my brown eyes pop.

He introduced himself, asked what book I was reading, and promptly declared us friends. Ever since that summer day, Beau has been my rock, my one person I know will always be there for me. He's helped me through some of my darkest days, and I'll never be able to thank him enough for it.

Nina swipes the towel across my aching skin, clicking her tongue. "Done," she sang. I look down at my arm, at the artwork that was now permanently on my skin. A smile grows on my face, and I look up, meeting Beau's eyes. His smile mirrors mine. "What do you think?" Nina asks.

"I love it," I say. It's perfect.

She finishes cleaning my skin, covering the tattoo with a thin layer of ointment and wrapping it in gauze and tape. I meet Beau over by the counter at the front of the shop, pulling out my money from my back pocket.

"I got it," Beau says, pushing my hand with the money out of the way. "My birthday present to you."

I scoff, trying to slide in and pay. "Then I should pay for your tattoo," I say.

"Nope," Beau says with a sly smile. "I already paid for both of ours while you were getting cleaned up."

"Beau, seriously?"

"What, am I not allowed to treat my best friend on her birthday?"

"Not when it's a tattoo, and you paid for your own, too! You should have saved that for your college fund."

He shrugs. "It's done now. Besides, you can just buy our next tattoos."

"Ugh," I grumble. "Fine. Thank you," I begrudgingly say.

"You're welcome." Beau catches my eye, winking quickly. My heart flutters, not for the first time today. Things with Beau have been... different lately. To the point where I think something more might be evolving between us.

I'm off to one of the local community colleges in a few weeks, where I plan to study all things photography. Beau's heading off to business school in the city. Sure, we will only be an hour from each other, but I can't help but worry that things will be different.

I climb into Beau's truck, a hand-me-down from his Gramps. It's a '97 Chevy Silverado that used to be used as the company truck for his woodworking business, but has since been retired to each of his grandsons. Beau starts the forty minute drive home, but instead of taking a right into town, he turns left, heading toward Cinder Valley. "What are you doing?" I ask.

Beau shrugs. There's a sort of scheming glint in his eye, but I don't question it. He drives us through the small town, heading to the river landing. He parks, then jerks his head toward the river. "C'mon."

I get out, following him. The rocky gravel crunches beneath my sandals, and the landing is surprisingly calm, despite the late summer day. There are groups of canoers heading down the river, but I don't really pay them any mind. Beau sits down on a log, patting the spot next to him.

I sit down, and he wraps his arm around my shoulders, pulling me into his warm chest. He smells of his cologne, clean, and sharp. I chuckle when I think about the phase he went through with AXE body spray. He sprayed that shit everywhere, seemingly coating his skin in a layer of the potent stuff.

"What's funny?" he asks.

I tilt my head to glance up at him, admiring his chocolate brown eyes and mussed hair. "Just thinking about your AXE body spray phase."

He groans, squeezing me tighter. "That wasn't nearly as bad as your Warm Vanilla Sugar phase from Bath and Body Works."

I gasp, pulling away from him. "Hey, I smelled like a cookie, which is much better than... whatever you smelled like."

"Alright," he chuckles. "You've got me there. You did

smell like a cookie." He pulls me back into his side and I relax into his touch. A lot of the time, people assume we're dating, because of the way he holds me, or hugs me sometimes, but we're both quick to correct them. Beau's just a physical touch kind of guy, and he's a great hugger, so it's a win-win, in my opinion.

"I feel like things are going to change," I murmur. I gaze off into the distance as I speak, too afraid to meet his eye. I know he's going to tell me that it won't, but I can't help but feel like he's just saying that to appease me.

"They will," he says. I whip my head off his shoulder to look at him. He's grinning maniacally.

"Beau," I squeal. "You're supposed to tell me that things aren't going to change!" I smack his chest lightly.

"They are, though!" He tries to defend himself. "Just because things in our lives are changing, doesn't mean that *we* have to change."

I nod, hearing what he's saying. "I guess. I'm just so scared I'm going to lose you. You're the best thing in my life, Beau." I squeeze him tightly.

"Marley, you could never lose me." He grips my chin, tilting my face upwards. "Eventually, we're going to get married to someone, have kids, grow old, but I will *always* be there for you. You're my best friend."

I don't know why, but his words feel like a knife straight through my heart. Leaving me aching and bleeding for everyone to see. I nod, words failing me.

His eyes stray from mine down to my lips. They dart back up when he realizes what he's done, but it's too late. I saw, and I know what he's thinking. He pulls away from me, shifting slightly. I straighten so I'm no longer tucked under his arm, trying to shake off the embarrassment that is currently forcing its way through my body.

When I'm confident I have my breathing under control, I turn back to Beau. "You're my best friend too, Beau. You're right, we'll always hav-"

I'm cut off by lips crashing onto mine. *Beau's* lips.

Holy shit, is Beau kissing me?

I pull away, gasping for air, trying to process this new feeling. "Beau, wha-"

He stops me, tucking a hair behind my ear. His eyes are wild, breathing ragged. "I just couldn't go another moment without knowing what your lips feel like."

My eyes flick down to his lips, where his tongue is darting out to wet them. He notices, and his hand slides down my jaw to cup my cheek. "What do they feel like?" I ask.

"Otherworldly."

I nod. "And that's good?" I ask.

"So flippin good." He presses a softer kiss to my lips, lingering there for a long moment. I've been kissed before by one other guy, but he had braces. When I tried to make out with him, my tongue got caught on one of the wires. Talk about embarrassing.

Beau's tongue slides between my lips, tasting me, teasing me. I wrap my arms around his neck, holding him to me. He skilfully moves our tongues together, the hand not on my cheek sliding around my neck. I begin to lose myself in the kiss, the alarm bells screaming at me that this is *Beau*, and we shouldn't be doing this, starting to quiet in my head.

Someone wolf-whistles from the river, and we spring apart like someone shocked us with a live wire. I hold my breath for a moment, scooting away from him. I release it, trying to calm my pounding heart. "So..." I start to say. Does this change literally everything I thought I knew?

Beau stops me. "I... I don't know how to say this."

Was my heart pounding before? Because now it's not even beating. Blood drains from my face, because I know what's coming. I'm not girlfriend material. At least not for Beau. I'm just the best friend.

I resign myself to this fact, taking a deep breath before I interrupt him. Saying what I know he's going to say. "We can't do that again. Not if we want to keep our friendship."

Beau nods, blowing out a breath, running his hands through his hair. "Yeah."

"Good." He doesn't say anything, but he doesn't need to. I just single-handedly saved myself from the inevitable heartbreak of hearing him say the words that I dreaded hearing him say. I mean, sure, there's been tension leading up to this moment, but that's all it was. We are teenagers, after all. And you know what they say about hormones.

Beau pulls me in close again, and I let myself pretend for just a moment that things could be different, that I could be his, and he could be mine. But I know it's just a silly dream. If I want to keep him, I'll never get to have him in the way I really want.

ACKNOWLEDGMENTS

I don't know where to begin. Honestly, my mind is a little blown. The last year of publishing has been such a whirlwind, but in the best way. I have so many incredible people to thank, and this is going to be a long acknowledgment section, but I'll start here.

Aria, my fellow Swiftie, you've been with me since day one, and I'm so thankful you messaged me one day. You've become such a close friend, and I love how much we connect and all you've helped me with. You've listened to me vent, hyped me up, and been a pillar of strength for me. I know that I can rely on your friendship and guidance.

Emily J, This book would not be what it is without you. You helped me rework so many scenes and plots, and I'm so thankful for that. Thank you for being a listening ear, and letting me bounce ideas off you.

Abbey H, Girl. You know I love you. Thank you for your endless support, encouragement, and friendship. I love you.

Brittany... or should I be thanking Matthew? I'm not really sure. We can't give him all the credit. Either way, I'm so freaking thankful that he introduced you to my books, coordinated the meeting, and spent half of Christmas Day in my sister's living room so we could spend hours talking. You're stuck with me now, and I couldn't be happier about it. Welcome to our insane family. I hope you like White Elephant.

HBC: For talking me off ledges, and convincing me to shelve the project that wasn't working, even when I wanted to push through. It's the reason why this book exists.

Victoria, I feel like I can't write a book without mentioning you. I love you, and I'll never thank you enough for cornering me in the kitchen of our college dorm/apartment. I'm lucky you chose me to be your friend.

Holly Rose, I know this book aligned with the craziest time of our lives, but as always, I'm thankful for your editing and encouragement. I love you so so much.

Sami, I will never be able to thank you enough for your friendship. You became one of my best friends when I needed it most. I love you.

Lastly, I'd like to thank my parents, and my siblings. The last few months have been insane, and I promise to never release a book and sell a house at the same time ever again. I love you, and I'm so grateful you support me and my books. -Pie

Cinder Valley Series

Tip Of My Tongue- Lainey & Colin

How Do I Tell You?- Mallory & Tyler

Give Me A Minute- Theo & Peyton

Ivy Ridge Series

Flowers in Your Hair- Josie & Andrew

Never Really Mine- Marley & Beau

Can't Let You Go- Jason & Fallon

In Plain Sight- Thomas & Hannah

Minnesota Blue Herons Hockey Series

TBA

ABOUT THE AUTHOR

Alice Daniels is a born and raised Minnesotan who loves to write books based on the small town she grew up in. Her books are sweet, heartfelt, and sexy, with relatable characters.

As a child, she was an avid fiction reader, which evolved into a deep love for romance novels and the community surrounding them. She recently discovered a passion for putting her ideas into writing and decided to pursue her childhood dream of becoming an author.

She spends time with her family and friends when she's not writing, especially on the lakes or outdoors in the summer.

Follow Alice on Facebook, Instagram, and Goodreads for book updates, teasers, and future releases!

Join her Facebook Group, Alice Daniels Reader Group to get all the insider info, sneak peeks, and more!

https://alicedaniels.com/

amazon.com/author/alicedaniels

facebook.com/authoralicedaniels

instagram.com/authoralicedaniels

goodreads.com/authoralicedaniels

bookbub.com/authors/saylor-ann